Praise for *Gravity Is Heartless*

2021 Independent P
Gold Medal Sci

2021 International Book Awards
Finalist Science Fiction & LGBTQ

2020 Best Book Awards Finalist Fiction: LGBTQ

"Loved it. An adventure romp . . . set in a not too distant future and played for high stakes. It's fun, witty and endlessly inventive . . . Bravo."

—Peter FitzSimons, author of over 20 books, including, *Kokoda*, *Gallipoli* and *Nancy Wake*.

"Lahey's prose is lush—describing a deeply imaginative world—and on the whole, the story is thoroughly engrossing. An engaging adventure set in a deftly illustrated future."

—*Kirkus Reviews*

"An inherently fascinating and fully entertaining read that showcases author Sarah Lahey's impressive flair for originality and the kind of narrative storytelling style that keeps the reader's attention fully focused from cover to cover."

—*Midwest Book Review*

"Infused with wonder and the brilliance of the real world, Lahey excels in Quinn's narration, breathing life into the dying world while giving Quinn a unique, knowledge-based personality."

—*Paperback Paris*

"*Gravity is Heartless* is a fun trip through a climate-changed world."

—*Forward Reviews*

"The supporting cast, including her best friend, a robotic meerkat, and a tough yet witty guerrilla fighter, are interesting in their own right, and almost steal the show."

—*Booklist*

"Everything Lahey exquisitely describes feels so realistic. If you would tell me that this is how the world will look in 30 years, I would believe you."

—*Heavenly Bookish*

"A highly entertaining read about the effects of global warming. I found the book utterly entertaining. The setting was (sadly) realistic, and the characters and story were very creative."

—*Pondering the Prose*

Nostalgia Is Heartless

Nostalgia Is Heartless

The Heartless Series
Book Two

Sarah Lahey

She Writes Press

Published 2021
Printed in the United States of America
Print ISBN: 978-1-64742-209-7
E-ISBN: 978-1-64742-210-3
Library of Congress Control Number: 2021910179

For information, address:
She Writes Press
1569 Solano Ave #546
Berkeley, CA 94707

She Writes Press is a division of SparkPoint Studio, LLC.

For Jordan, Lulu, and Hamish

(The truth is, you're all worth 34 percent.)

In the late twentieth century, Marvin Minsky said, “No computer has ever been designed that is ever aware of what it’s doing; but most of the time, we aren’t either.”

Prologue

QUINN BUYERS IS THIRTY years old. She is pregnant, unemployed, living back home with her father, and in a long-distance relationship with a cyborg, refugee-smuggling figurehead of an ancient culture, whom she has not seen in six weeks. She is also my best friend.

Recently she asked me, "How did I get here? What life choices led me to this point? I didn't plan on getting pregnant or being unemployed and moving back home to live with Dad. I hate the whole idea of an LDR, especially with Tig; of all the people on the planet, how did I end up with him? How did I get here?"

I promptly replied, "All of your life choices have led you to this point. This is what happens when you have sex with a complete stranger on a deserted island and when you fall in love with someone from another culture whom you barely know. This is what happens when you take advice from your father—a man who talks to trees, a man who sometimes talks to mountains."

But I understand my best friend's dilemma. In humans, decision-making processes take place in the frontal cortex region of the brain, and this is a very busy part of the human anatomy. It must manage impulse control, plan for the future, predict consequences, anticipate events, and oversee emotional reactions.

Personally, I think the frontal cortex has too much responsibility.

It might be overburdened, and that is why humans make so many bad decisions.

But what would I know, I am just a machine?

One

Free from gravity.

IN 2038, QUINN'S FATHER, Matt Jones, fell in love with an ancient tree—a three-thousand-year-old southern blue gum, *Eucalyptus globulus*, growing in the wilderness northwest of Hobart. He loved this tree so much he built a glass house around it—a circular glass prism, seven stories high and fifteen meters wide—and this is where he has lived for over a decade.

The old tree is still a splendid specimen; tall and symmetrical, its smooth trunk rises up through the center of the glass house and its pale, sickle-shaped leaves provide shade and protection from the monotonous heat. In the morning, the tree's foliage smells clean and sweet, and in the early evening, the leaves release their eucalyptus oil and the house fills with mint and pine perfume. In spring, the buds produce a strong, sticky nectar that Matt harvests into honey.

On the upper levels of the glass house there are three designated sleep zones. The mid-section accommodates the library and music room. The food prep, with its walk-in storage, is on the lower level. At the back of the walk-in-storage there is a hatch in the floor that leads to a fully prepped survival bunker—for when Hexad, the universal body that governs the Earth, fails and humanity self-implodes.

Matt fancies a solitary life. He describes himself as a simple man who prefers trees to people. But underneath his modest façade is an aging ex-rocker with existential angst—a skeptic who has lost faith in humanity.

The glass roof of the house makes a perfect viewing platform, offering 360-degree views across the forest and surrounding hills. Just before dawn, Quinn and her AI robot, Mori, who was made in the form of her favorite animal—a meerkat—make their way up the spiral staircase that circles the interior of the house. At the top they hoist themselves through a hatch and onto the roof. Then they tiptoe across the glass to the edge, where they sit with their legs dangling over the lip of the roof. They are under house law: no noise before 6:00 a.m.

Quinn tries to check the time on the TechBand wrapped around her wrist but the Band is blank; it's been malfunctioning and intermittent for several days now. She taps it lightly, then jiggles her wrist, but gets no response. Scanning the horizon, she notes that the sky is pinned with stars, which means dawn is still some time away. So she and Mori linger quietly in the darkness.

Quinn wears a long T-shirt with a logo that reads, "The earth is not flat. Vaccines work. Climate change is real. No, chemtrails are not a thing. Yes, we've been to the moon. Coronaviruses come from animals not labs. Stand up for science." The shirt is decades old. Quinn arrived here with few possessions—one small bag of personal items and a military backpack filled with futuristic weapons—so she has been wearing old clothes that she found in a bag stashed at the back of her dad's storage area.

Today, her dark, wavy hair—which she rarely combs because why bother, it looks perfectly fine the way it is—falls loose around her face. Mori cut most of it off a year ago. He did a decent job, considering he is a robot, but it's grown wild again now.

Tucked under her hairline and draped over her shoulders is a shiny blue garment—her Birdsuit. She folds it into a pillow, lies down, her back against the cool glass of the roof, and slips the makeshift pillow under her head.

She rubs her baby bump; she is seven months pregnant. The baby kicks and rolls an elbow across her stomach.

As she peers into the night sky, Quinn's face is watchful, her grey-blue eyes observant, and frown lines furrow her forehead. So many things make her uneasy: the baby feels like an alien that's hibernating inside her stomach; her mother, Lise Buyers—a world-renowned scientist and physics professor—is still mysteriously missing, and Quinn's motivation to find out where she is, or what happened to her, is waning; and Tig is due back this week—maybe it will be today, maybe tomorrow.

Beside Quinn, Mori sits upright, occasionally twitching, as he gazes into the darkness. "I have not slept," he whispers.

"What?"

"Not for four weeks, two days, and six hours. I have not slept."

Quinn rouses herself from her contemplative state and rolls up into a sitting position. "Okay, that's not healthy. Everyone, everything needs rest. Your circuitry needs to trim and consolidate. What's going on?" She begrudges having to ask him this question—he is a robot—still, she asks, she always asks.

"Last night there was a drip sound. I could not sleep. Drip, drip, drip. It reminded me of rain. Drip, drip, drip—"

"It's the tap in the food prep. I'll fix it." Quinn opens a bag of snacks and eats several slices of orange banana.

"I have never seen a cloud." Mori scans the horizon.

"Well, it's only been, what, four months?"

"Did it rain four months ago?"

"No. It hasn't rained in a decade. There are schoolchildren who have never seen a cloud. The point is, you're only four months . . ." She pauses, struggling to find the appropriate word to describe Mori's existence. He is a conundrum: a robot programmed with consciousness, controlled by a super-unconscious. Jin, Quinn's best friend and Mori's creator, modeled his circuitry on the human brain. Mori has impressive programming, but the chance of a technical glitch is very high.

"Alive," Quinn concedes. "Four months alive. There's still time."

They hear a noise and pause. Someone is moving about inside the house. Quinn hopes it's after 6:00 a.m. She looks up; there's an amber glow above the ridge line to the east, so dawn isn't far away.

"What are they like?" Mori whispers.

"Clouds? They're just ice crystals, water drops stuck to aerosols. They're a natural phenomenon. As a climate scientist, my interest in clouds is factual, not romantic."

"Are they beautiful?"

"Yes, I suppose they are. However, they are not nature's poetry, and they are not an expression of the planet's emotional state. You will not see dead people in them, and they are not a Rorschach test. The shapes you see in clouds will not save you Coin that would be better spent on a good psychoanalyst." She taps her Band. "My Band is failing. What day is it?"

"Tuesday."

"It's June, right?"

"No. The month is July."

"July! Shit. I'm sorry. I guess you're six months alive?"

"I think I might have . . . climate depression?"

"No. You don't."

"Matt said you put the knives in the wrong place and you do not close the lids on the jars tightly enough. He said you need to create a vacuum to keep the produce fresh. Space devoid of matter and—"

"Space devoid of matter and atmospheric pressure creates a vacuum. Thank you." Quinn points to her chest. "Scientist. PhD. I know how a vacuum works. He, he is a . . . musician," she scoffs, then finishes the banana and starts munching on a handful of seeds.

"Why do you jump off things?"

She wipes her hands, then licks one remaining seed off her palm.

"Because I like it. Because sometimes I feel trapped. I suppose that's hard to imagine surrounded by all this . . . wilderness. But when I jump, I feel . . . free. Free from the Earth. Free from gravity. When I fly there's no sense of time, no present or past. There's just . . . now."

Matt climbs out of the hatch in the rooftop and ambles towards them holding a mug of tea. "Honey, it ain't even six. If it starts with a five, stay the fuck in bed."

"We're sorry. We tried."

Matt sits next to her. He is wearing knee-length black shorts and a black T-shirt with his name, Matt Jones, plastered across the front in white letters. He hasn't shaved, and his shoulder-length hair hangs limp.

Matt hands Quinn his mug, then tucks his hair behind his ears. "New infusion. Calling it Purple Needles—blackberry and pine."

Quinn clutches the mug with both hands and sniffs the tea—it smells like apple pie. She smiles.

They sit in a row—Matt, Quinn, and the meerkat, tallest to shortest—with their legs dangling over the lip of the roof and watch the sun rise over the forest, Matt and Quinn sharing the mug of apple pie tea between them.

"I miss mum," says Quinn. "Do you think she's alive?"

"No fuckin' idea. But I'd like to know where she is, dead or alive."

"If a tree dies in the forest and falls over and no one is around to hear it, does it still make a sound?" the meerkat interrupts.

"No, no, no, we're not having this conversation." Quinn shakes her head. "We've talked about this. Remember? Stay in the present. Focus on real shit, not metaphorical shit. It's better for your . . . sub-sumption architecture?"

"Yes, my subsumption architecture," Mori says. "It allows me to be reactive and make intuitive decisions. I am a parallel system, not a serial system. My memory and processing are connected. I am able to multitask."

"And that's very impressive." She pats his leg.

"The other trees, they'll hear it fall," Matt says. "They're more sensitive than you realize. They sleep and breathe, and they feel—"

"Dad, I don't think—"

"No, look around you. There's a social network that connects every tree in the forest; the stronger ones send out sugars to help the weaker ones." In one gulp, he finishes the last of the tea. "You ever stop and wonder what they make of us?"

Quinn frowns at her father. "They don't 'make' anything of us. They're trees. They don't think or see or hear."

"I have advanced hearing—200,000 hertz," Mori says. "Humans only have 20,000 hertz. Where do trees lie on the hertz scale?"

"Nowhere," Quinn whispers.

"Trees are the secret to life on this planet," Matt says. "Some of 'em have personalities, along with an inner life, a consciousness."

"Awareness of the environment is not consciousness," Quinn snaps. "I'm sorry, but I can't have any more conversations about trees. Can we talk about something else?"

"You wanna come mountain watching with me tomorrow?" Matt asks.

"I think I'm busy."

"Fair enough. How you doing for creams? Got this new eucalyptus moisturizer. You want some?"

"I'm good. But thanks."

"Smells great, like fresh eucalyptus. You should try it." He rummages in his pocket and pulls out a tube of sage-colored cream.

"Honestly, I'm fine." She waves a dismissive hand at her father.

"Good for dry skin. You want some?"

"Not now, maybe later."

"Here, try it." He opens the tube and squeezes a large dollop of pale green liquid onto the back of Quinn's hand.

The cream is thick and sticky. She rubs it into her hands, up her forearms and over her elbows. Then she wipes the excess off on her knees.

She sniffs her hands—she smells like an old tree—and realizes she has made a mistake. Returning to live with her father was a terrible idea. Cohabitation is not the uplifting experience she thought it was going to be. Her heart doesn't pound with joy every morning when she wakes, when she realizes she is living with Matt in his circular glass house. When she realizes she is thirty and pregnant and unemployed, and living with her father—a man who every morning offers her three different types of berries, two different varieties of homemade yogurt, and five different types of tea, then asks if she would like to go tree or mountain watching.

She blames herself for her living situation—but then again, he was the one who asked her to come. "Come stay with me in the wilderness and watch the sun rise and watch it set," he said. "Hang out in the forest and do nothing for a few months." Given her circumstances—the pregnancy and the unemployment, coupled with the fact that she was fleeing a civil war in the megacity Unus—she thought it was a reasonable idea at the time. She thought the job of parents was to provide love and comfort in your time of need.

But now she realizes that's not what they do. What they do is drive you crazy.

"You heard from Tig?" Matt asks.

"I've heard nothing. You ask me that every day."

"Okay, what about your friend, Pluck? Any updates?"

"Spoke to him last week, apparently Tig will be back in a day or two. And the name is Planck, not Pluck. I've told you this," she snaps.

Matt reels.

"Sorry." She rests her head on his shoulder. "LDR's are the worst. I don't know how people do this. It's lonely. I'm lonely."

"Maybe you should try haptic underwear? Mimics the sense of

touch. You control it from your Band. You just need to remember to charge your underwear."

"Oh good lordt," she whispers. "I'm hot. It must be the hottest day of the year. Aren't you hot?"

"No, it's winter."

"I might be coming down with something. You don't think I've got the flu, Feline Flu, do you?"

"Sore throat, headache, cough, finding it hard to breath? Noticed any yellow streaks in your eyes?"

She shakes her head.

Feline Flu—or toxic kitty, as it's sometimes called, mutated from a cat virus in the 2040s and led to a pandemic that killed 5 percent of the world's population. It was rumored that a group of feral cats broke into a research lab and ate human cadavers. The bodies—six days dead—were at the perfect point of decomposition for the cats to nibble on, and the cause of death for all six was a strain of flu. Due to environmental heat factors, the disease mutated in the cats, causing a switch in the feline gene trigger, and soon spread to birds, then larger mammals, and ultimately to humans. The virus thwarted the human immune system by entering the genome and killing off any immune cells that threatened it. It was a master of mutation; every new strain meant fine-tuning the vaccine. A super vaccine eventually quashed the pandemic, but new pockets of FF still flare up from time to time.

Matt reaches behind Quinn, grabs the Birdsuit, and drops it in her lap. Then he tilts his head towards the valley. "Get going. There's a northwesterly due later today, it's gonna hang around for a week."

"I hate wind." Using her father's shoulder as a brace, she climbs to her feet, then steps into her Birdsuit.

The suit is an aerodynamic dark blue body stocking with retractable wings that tuck into rivets running along the shoulders. The material is bio-inspired plastic, so it's lightweight, flexible, and ultra-strong—lift without bulk or weight. Quinn tugs it over her expanding waistline—at seven months pregnant, it's a snug fit—then taps Matt on the shoulder and points to the collar of her suit, indicating she needs help closing the seal.

Matt jumps up. He flattens down the collar around her neck. Then he adjusts the cuffs and spins Quinn around. "Breathe in," he says.

She does, and he fastens the seal down her back.

"You think it's okay to fly? I mean, with the baby." She rubs her baby bump.

"Honey, it ain't my life, it's yours. Do whatever you want. Whatever makes you happy," he says with a glint in his eye.

Quinn knows her father is serious. *Do whatever you want*—this is how he lives his life. He is a Humanist living in the wilderness, doing whatever makes him happy, and what makes him happy are trees and mountains and rivers. To him, trees are sacred. The Earth is sacred. He believes, like all Humanists, that he is connected to every rock, every blade of grass, and every droplet of water. Humanists will never leave this planet, regardless of the effects of climate change. Humanists don't see their future in the stars, like many of the Transhumans, who would happily make a new life on another planet. Humanists believe they will shrivel up and die if they leave the Earth.

Quinn sees how easy it is for Matt to do whatever he wants—he is single and financially successful, and he has created a simple life for himself. But this is not her life. Her father doesn't have a baby human growing inside him. He doesn't have to worry about giving birth, childrearing, finding a job, finding somewhere to live, and negotiating a relationship with Tig.

The reality of jumping off a precipice is not lost on Quinn; escaping gravity facilitates her sense of freedom. But she knows she can't leap from one ecstatic, bird-like moment to the next. She can't fly away her fears of the future forever.

Besides, the Birdsuit won't fit her for much longer.

Fully dressed in her liquid blue costume, Quinn strides over to the lip of the roof and casually steps off the edge. Now gravity has her, and the rush is exhilarating. She closes her eyes and a ripple of ecstasy surges through her. Then she unfurls her feathered wings. Like an oversize origami model, they spring into elastic action.

Hovering next to the house, she considers her options. East leads towards the sun and into the old-growth forest, where the air is stable and settled, where the view is picturesque but familiar. Northward, the mountains rise, and on the other side there is a deep gorge where cool air from the valley rushes upward and crosswinds eddy and swirl along the cliff face.

She turns and heads north, towards the gorge.

The sky is cloudless and cerulean. Along the valley floor a river snakes a steely line between the trees, and she follows its trail. It has not rained for a decade, but a subterranean spring, called the Source, feeds the river and sustains the surrounding forest.

Two

Is it waxing or waning?

HEXAD, THE UNIFIED GOVERNMENT that oversees the six geographical regions of Earth, established headquarters in the city of Nihil the year the RE Wars ended in 2044. The Wars are defined as Religious or Regional, a title dependent on a person's cultural ideology. The geographical scope of the Wars, which began after the economic collapse in 2036, is classified as east versus west, but the hostility was fueled by opposing religious doctrines. Now, alliances assign various meanings to the name of the Wars; some call them regional, others call them religious. Either way they lasted for almost a decade and tore the planet apart.

The city of Nihil occupies neutral territory in the Great North-West continent. The city rises over an area formerly known as Detroit, which was once a flourishing automotive district. It seemed fitting to build the twenty-first century's new ecocity over the toxins of past industrial developments. The new smart materials—graphene, aerogel, carbon fiber, silicon, hemp, and bamboo—were laid down over the plastics, asbestos, formaldehyde, lead, and cadmium-based metals, which have no place in the modern world.

A luminous, crescent-shaped structure known as the Half Moon is the headquarters for Hexad. Inside is a self-sustaining colony of delegates, staff, and dignitaries. Viewed against the night sky, the Half

Moon is a radiant arc of gold and silver metalloid. Fifteen hundred meters tall, it towers over the surrounding ecocity, and the symbolism of the looming, moon-shaped structure is not lost on anyone. Hexad is definitive—an overseer and an influencer—and like the moon, it has the power to pull an ocean from its shore. The hordes of military and civilians that have aligned themselves with the organization ensure that Hexad's authority is absolute.

Legislative assemblies convene several times every month on the upper podium of the Half Moon in the Altimeter Auditorium. Today is one of those days, and Planck is currently waiting on a seat outside the closed doors of the auditorium.

Planck is a tall, heavyset human with red-tipped hair and a generous, open face that is neither distinctly feminine nor distinctly masculine. From one ear dangles an earring—a black circle within a circle, marked with horizontal and vertical lines, that signifies a gender-neutral identity.

Today Planck wears a new climate suite that ze designed and 3D-printed zirself. The fabric is metallic with gold contrasting cuffs, and ze thought it would harmonize with zirs new, bureaucratic position, bolstering zirs alliance with Maim Quate's political party, the Democratic Republic.

Inside the Auditorium, Maim Quate, the newly elected leader of the megacity Unus, is addressing her fellow delegates. Her maiden speech is proactive on climate reversal. Public opinion is against her. Politicians are against her. Some of the Transhumans—those with fanatical, far-right beliefs—despise her. Planck suspects that in this political climate, she will be hammered—climate reversal is a tiresome subject.

Maim is an academic, a professor of history. She is not politically savvy, and she is not used to addressing legislators with hard-won agendas of their own. But she knows history, and she knows it's unforgiving. The first attempt at geoengineering the planet, in the early 2030s, coincided with a dramatic change in ocean temperatures and currents. For a decade, the climate went wild and the planet was bombarded with erratic storms. Eventually the wild weather settled, but it settled over the Polar Regions. That is where it has remained. Geoengineering was not the definitive culprit, but it took the blame. Now Maim believes the topic needs to be reintroduced. The pendulum has swung too far, and it's no longer possible for the planet to autocorrect. The Earth needs help. It needs human intervention to save it. Someone needs to broach the topic, and she thinks it may as well be her.

Seated outside the Auditorium, Planck stifles a yawn; the waiting is tedious. Zirs mind wanders, and ze devises an improvement to a new teacake recipe that includes a fruit-filled center but still keeps the insect sprinkles for crunch.

On the floor beside zir is a shoulder bag containing yarn craft. Ze knows the benefits of busy hands and a focused mind. Yarn craft helps pass the time. Ze takes a mid-weight ball of twine and a small, hooked needle from the bag, loops the twine around zirs finger in a pretzel shape, then slips the needle through the pretzel and tightens it—the first knot.

As Planck continues, stitch after stitch, ze visualizes the finished project: a shawl to cover Tig and Quinn's baby. There are days when the air-system on *Nanshe* runs so cold that frost forms on the cabin windows—days when it is 55 degrees Celsius outside and 15 degrees inside.

A sailor at heart, Planck misses the boat life. On *Nanshe*, ze was chief engineer, medic, purser, bosun, and cook, and ze hopes they will be back at sea soon, just like the old days—the three of them together again, plus the meerkat, and of course the new baby. In preparation for the baby, ze is studying midwifery online, which will add to zirs existing degrees in fashion and psychology.

Planck's TechBand vibrates. It's Tig. Ze answers the call. "You there yet?"

"Yeah, I'm here, standing on the edge of a fucking cliff. My chest hurts, I can't breathe. She's still doing it, flying every day. You know how it freaks me out. Does my head in. 'I can't bear the sorrow, it gnaws at my belly, this fear . . .'" He quotes an ancient poem, *The Epic of Gilgamesh*, which he has read many times.

"'We go on an impossible, even forbidden, journey, which from a rational point of view is futile,'" Planck responds, also quoting *Gilgamesh*. "Look, you've come all this way to find her, and now you're together. I know it's not perfect, but you have to work on it."

"It's different this time."

"Of course it's different this time. You leapt into this expecting it to be the same, but that was never going to happen." Planck runs a hand through zirs red-tipped hair. "Look, you love her, and she loves you, but that's not enough. You have to share your life, tell her who you are and where you've come from, or you have no chance."

"I know. It's hot, this place is sizzling. Are you hot?"

"I'm inside."

"My chest hurts. I feel like I've been fucked in the heart."

"Then you have limerence—I've long suspected it."

"What's limerence?"

"Heartache resulting from an intense but unfulfilled longing. And you'll continue in this state of stress-induced cardiomyopathy until you—"

A group of delegates spills from the Auditorium and congregates close to the entrance. Planck steps away.

"—until you tell her the truth," ze says quietly. "Everything. There's no other way."

"Yep, yep, I know. I'm gonna tell her today."

"Great. Now, why aren't you taking your Meds? It's the job, isn't it?"

"Military work pays double. Babies cost a lot. I heard that somewhere."

"Yes, I heard that, too. I'm not sure why—they're so small. Okay, I get it, but you need to go back on them soon, for all our sakes."

"I can't use the SelfMed. I need her to do it. She has to be the one."

"Yes, okay. Well, hurry up and ask her. She's done it before. She understands."

Maim is swept out of the Auditorium with a throng of representatives. She scans the crowd, looking for Planck. Ze waves to get her attention, then points towards the perimeter gardens skirting the edge of the Moon complex, indicating that is where ze'll meet her. Ze takes a deep breath before returning to the call. "Listen to me. She loves you. Go tell her the truth—you'll feel better. We'll all feel better. After that, we sort out the Phaistos Discs. We're very close, so do the right thing and don't fuck it up."

Ze ends the call.

***

Maim waits for Planck at the edge of the topiary gardens. A middle-aged woman who moves with purpose, she wears a fitted black and gold pantsuit impregnated with a wearable Tech that is designed to monitor her body temperate, keeping it consistent throughout the day. (She is in her mid-fifties and often plagued by hot flashes, a symptom of her perimenopause.) Her grey hair is swept off her face and tied in a top knot, a style that Planck suggested, which has taken a decade off her age.

Planck greets her with a low bow. They fall into step and wander down a cobbled path that meanders between plants trimmed into cones, circles, and spirals. Kinetic paths generate energy that powers the area at night. Designated cycling and running tracks are also scattered throughout the gardens, and Maim and Planck step aside to let a runner pass, his self-riding bike following on voice command. "Faster," the runner calls. The bike increases it pace and swerves, in a perfect arc, around them.

"So, how'd it go?" Planck asks.

"I mentioned geoengineering. It sent them into meltdown and I almost lost the room." She pauses. "I wish Lise were here—she knows how to handle these science sceptics. But, the good news is the deforestation laws hold. The regrowth project is confirmed; hundreds of drones will plant 10,000 trees a day, and the area will be a no-go zone for humans."

Planck scoffs. "Tree planting won't save the planet—it's just popular. People love trees."

"I also pitched genetically modified Suberin, drought and flood resistant, uses fifty times the carbon of standard crops and stores it for a hundred years, and they liked that. They liked the hundred years part. They'll be dead by then; it won't be their problem."

"Another long shot."

"It's not the only weapon in our arsenal. I've tabled plankton farms, carbon sinks, and supercharged photosynthesis in a C4 rice crop. Conversion efficiency of solar energy to biomass is ten times higher than traditional crops. We'll get there."

"What's our biggest threat?"

"There's a group of Transhumans. They call themselves Shun Mantra."

Planck frowns. "Oh, I'm familiar."

"They want Coin distributed to the leaving project, not the staying behind and saving the Earth project. It's my understanding they'll do anything to get what they want."

"They give Transhumans a bad name. Also, terraforming a planet would cost trillions."

"Yes, yes it would, and it's not happening. It was universally agreed. It's an absurd idea. Mars was a fucking disaster, we're certainly not colonizing Titan . . . or Enceladus.

Planck notices the luminous crescent moon rising over the city of Nihil and directs Maim towards the auditorium's ten-meter-high, floor-to-ceiling windows. They stand in silence for almost a minute, viewing the moon as it climbs into the night sky—a stunning sight.

Eventually Maim asks, "Is it waxing or waning?"

"Waning," Planck says. "The waning moon, symbolizing femininity and the cycle of time."

"And this building, the Half Moon—is it waxing or waning?"

"Depends where you're standing. From one direction it's waning, from the other it's waxing."

"Yes, of course." She laughs. "You know what Lise would say. She would say it's all about perspective . . ." She winces and clutches her chest.

"Are you okay? Do you need to sit down?"

She shakes her head. "It's nothing; a heart flutter." She waves a dismissive hand at zir. "What was I saying—oh yes, Lise. She would say it's perfectly possible for two versions of reality to happen simultaneously. It just depends where you are in the universe."

Planck is not so easily distracted. "You sure you're okay? You've turned a horrid shade, like buttermilk."

Maim pauses. "Sometimes, when I think of her, my chest hurts. I feel a bit lightheaded." She shrugs. "Good lordt, it's hot in here. Are you hot, or is it me?"

"It's you. Are you sleeping?"

"Not much. You think its menopause—or worse, FF? Do you think I have FF? Apparently the virus has mutated and—"

"You don't have FF. You've been fucked in the heart." Ze pats her forearm.

Maim considers the large, gentle hand resting on her arm. She smiles. "Perhaps you're right. I miss her. It's been nine months since she disappeared. What's happening with the Phaistos Disc? I sent it to Quinn months ago. Has she worked out how to use it?"

"The message you sent with the Disc might have been a bit obscure."

"Really? I said it was her birthday present."

"You said it was a 5,000-year-old Phaistos Disc, the text was indecipherable, and it means something or nothing."

"I wanted it to sound like Lise. I thought Quinn would make the connection—Lise discovered how to open time, then she mysteriously disappears and the Disc arrives. It's obviously a time portal. It's quite clear."

"She has no idea. I believe they're using it as a fruit platter."

"A fruit platter! Oh, good lordt. Okay, I know you're dying of boredom and you miss her. Go see Quinn, and while you're there maybe mention the fruit platter is a time portal, and we would really appreciate it if she would find out how it works, then went back in time and found her mother. For all our sakes."

"Okay, and then we can finally bring the Discs together and . . ." Ze claps zirs hands.

"Wait, did you say *Discs*? As in plural, as in . . . more than one?"

"I did say that didn't I?" Ze knits zirs fingers together. "Do you want the truth?"

"Oh, good lordt. There *is* more than one, isn't there? No, I don't want the truth. I have enough to worry about. I trust you to work this out." Gazing over Planck's shoulder, Maim sees a man exercising in the distance. "Good lordt, Niels hasn't changed at all. He still looks 25."

Planck turns and spies Niels Eco, CEO of the corporate Tech giant eMpower. "You know him?"

"Yes, we went to university together. Last time I saw him was in 2022. We were at an extinction rally. We both got arrested. Spent four hours handcuffed in the back of a police van. What is he wearing?"

Niels wears leggings. One pant leg is black and the other is covered in a checkerboard print. His T-shirt is white with red horizontal stripes. Tied around his neck is a red cravat.

"It's an exosuit," Planck explains. "It makes running more efficient. There are cables in the fabric that assist the body's natural movement, so he doesn't have to work as hard to travel as far. You're right, he looks amazing. Not the outfit, that's atrocious, but the rest of him."

Planck scans Niels's physique. "He looks . . . half your age." Ze pauses. "Of course, you also look good, very good, for your age."

Maim raises an eyebrow. "Rumor is fetal blood transfusions. And he doesn't eat. Lives on a cocktail of microbes, so the shit is just building up inside of him."

"Coincidence, him being here."

"I asked him to come. He plays both sides of politics, and he does it very well. I want to find out what he knows about Antarctica and the ice shift last year—whether it caused the Sky River to drift north and flood Kerguelen."

"And kill 2,000 people, including Ada. Now, nine months later, Lise is still missing. You could have been there, you know, at Quinn's wedding. It could easily have been you instead of Ada." Planck arches an eyebrow. "Why *wasn't* it you?"

Maim shrugs. "I stepped aside. It was the right thing to do. Lise had a long history with Ada before me, and Ada insisted on going. Lucky, I guess—I'm still alive and she's not."

As Niels approaches, Planck turns to Maim. "You trust him?"

"Of course not. But I'm a middle-aged gay woman on the verge of menopause with no political experience. I think he underestimates me, and I intend to exploit that."

Three

Is that love?

Quinn, wearing her electric blue Birdsuit, descends into the tree-lined canyon. She spends the morning drifting back and forth across the valley. She follows the dark river they call the Source, pausing often to watch the rapids and swirling eddies that form in the shallower part of the river. The recurring pattern of ripples is meditative. It suits her mood. Today, the valley feels pensive.

Farther on, she hovers over a rocky area that divides the rapids and searches for signs of the local freshwater lobsters that live in the shallows. None are visible below the surface; the rising sun won't reach the bottom of the canyon for another hour.

She moves on and spies a copper-colored snake basking on a rock.

Ahead, she sees the faint outline of a rainbow hovering over the chasm. Rainbows are a rare phenomenon world-wide, but during the winter months they sometimes appear around Hobart, which has the perfect combination of crisp, clean air, a moist atmosphere, and a latitude of 42 degrees—the perfect viewing angle for rainbows.

With symmetrical precision, the rainbow connects one side of the canyon to the other, as if it were made to measure. Quinn smiles. She heads towards it, knowing she will never reach the optical illusion.

Suddenly, a shaft of bright light hits her in the eye.

She squints and drops into the chasm, searching for the source of the glare. A silver airship rests on the edge of the canyon, its fuselage catching the morning light, reflecting it in all directions. Standing in front of the ship is Tig, looking like he just slipped down the polychromatic arc of the rainbow.

She sighs. What the fuck is he doing all the way out here?

She turns and soars towards the cliff, and, as she pulls her wings in for landing, she pats her baby bump. "We can do this. Don't trip, be cool, come in nice and easy—engage your core, or what's left of it."

She sets down lightly, close to the edge of the cliff, and her shimmering blue wings fold in behind her.

She blinks as she takes in the tall, enigmatic cyborg standing before her with his arms crossed. She wonders if he is medicated or unmedicated; she suspects the latter, and this is why he is late; why she hasn't heard from him in six weeks; why he is standing alone on the side of a cliff.

He goes off his Meds when he is working. He is more dangerous without them. Without them, floods of androgen hormones—testosterone, cortisone—surge through his body. This makes him reactive, puts him in perpetual survival mode. Months ago, Planck told her that Tig was exposed to the nerve gases diazinon and organophosphate. The toxins affected his neurotransmitters, shrunk his hippocampus, and thinned out his right cortex.

She smiles at him.

He meets her eye and his gaze is direct, his eyes alert. He uncrosses his arms and the dozens of metal bangles he wears on his wrists jangle. Then he pulls on his left shoulder; his machine parts lag when he is anxious or weary. But there is no sign of his titanium exoskeleton. The rapid skin-growth on his left side covers the frame.

Quinn's hunch is confirmed: he is unmedicated, otherwise he would have spoken and moved towards her.

In this state, he is distinctly foreign to her. And she barely knows him anyway; one night of hot sex and a few months together and this is what they have—an awkward, silent intensity and a baby in utero.

Still, she is overwhelmed by the sight of him. Her heart moves around inside her chest, and when it finally settles, it feels dislodged and out of place. She leans to one side, hoping to slide it back, but it doesn't budge. Now, six weeks doesn't seem long. Earlier today, it felt like years.

She had forgotten how tall he is; she wishes she were taller, more comparable. He wears the same clothes he always wears: dark cargo pants and a loose shirt. It's like a uniform—he wears this or nothing at all. He is fond of nudity. It's a natural state for him; no clothes at breakfast, no clothes as he sips his tea on the veranda.

Quinn always wears clothes.

Her heart begins to move again. It travels to her throat and blocks her airway. She finds it difficult to breathe. It moves higher, to her voice box. Her mouth opens but no rational and thoughtful words fill the space between them. Silence fills the space between them.

Here they are, two people standing on the edge of a cliff, at the bottom of the world, in the middle of an old-growth forest. Two people from different worlds, from different times. Silently, they stare at each other.

Someone needs to say something.

"You're back," she says.

He nods, confirming the obvious, and moves towards her.

She takes a small step back. "Nice airship, looks fast."

"Tungsten. It is."

Tungsten. Like your cyborg parts.

Tungsten. Element number 74 on the periodic table. It's strong, dependable, and durable, resistant to rust and corrosion, and it weighs the same as gold. It's combustible in powder form and can spontaneously ignite—like Tig, when he is unmedicated.

She fiddles nervously with one of the bracelets around her wrist, unclipping then refastening the latch. Tig gave her three metal bands, each one signifying her connection to him in some way. It took her weeks to find the latch and figure out the release mechanism. Now she can do it with her eyes closed.

He takes her hand to stop her fidgeting and pulls her towards him, away from the cliff and into his arms. He closes his eyes and breathes in the scent of her hair and her skin. His lips graze her forehead and her cheek.

They kiss; he tastes tinny and blunt, like machinery.

"Where the fuck have you been?" she whispers.

He sucks in air. "Sorry. Got called to Hexad. The Moon . . ."

"You've been to Hexad, to the Moon? Is it amazing?" *I want your life.*

"It's okay. Not my first time there."

Really? Next time, take me with you.

"Signed my contract yesterday, military work. Figured I should commit—jobs are scarce and the pay's good. I got paternity leave—eight weeks, plus overtime."

She looks at her feet. "It's good that you're working because I'm not working. I have absolutely no prospects and no idea what I'm going to do."

"It's okay. I'm gonna look after us. Get us somewhere to live. A nice place, since you don't like the water and don't want to live on *Nanshe*."

"Well, perhaps—"

"Hey, I'm a fixer—that's what I do, I fix things. I don't know how to do anything else. I'll sort it out."

She considers him. He's offering security. Protection. The ability to fix things. *Is that love?* she wonders. *If it is, is it enough?*

They find a flat rock and sit together, close to the edge of the canyon. Tig pulls a thermos from his pack, opens it, and passes it to her. They share the ice-cold drink; Quinn thinks it might be peach or nectarine.

They are quiet for a while. Tig contemplates his hands. Quinn watches a group of noisy minor birds as they flit around the rocks at the edge of the canyon, then she looks down into the thermos of tea. "What are we going to do with a baby?"

He takes her hand. "I think we're supposed to love it."

She smiles.

"I need to tell you something," he says. "Probably should have told you this sooner."

She nods, eager for something—anything that he wants to tell her.

"It's about time."

"Yes, we need to have a conversation about our future," she says eagerly. "What are we going to—"

"No. What I have to tell you, it's about time *right now*. You see, time's an issue for me. A really big fuckin' issue, especially when I'm not taking my . . . well, you know, my Meds. The thing is, I don't understand it. I don't get how it works. I never know what day it is. Or what month. That's why I'm late—I lose track of the days."

"I didn't know."

"The months are the worst; they're a mystery. Sometimes I don't even remember what year it is."

She nods. "Okay. That's good to know. Maybe a Band would help with the hours . . ."

He shakes his head. "Messes with my exoskeleton, interferes with the electrical signals."

"Oh, I'm . . . sorry."

He shrugs.

Quinn pulls open the seal of her Birdsuit and slips it down, wiggles it over her stomach. "I'm so hot." She fans her face with her fingers. "I feel like I'm burning up."

"Yeah, I know what you mean." He takes hold of her hands. "Cold."

"Raynaud's syndrome. Cold hands and feet." *Good lordt, he knows nothing about me.*

"Yeah, it runs in your family."

How does he know this?

"Listen, your climate model, the G12, seems there's a lot of people interested in it."

"Really? Because two years ago, nobody was interested in it. I couldn't give it away. I was two decades too late. I know that now. The population of Earth had reached peak indifference to climate change."

"You want to retrieve it? Find out more about the ice shift in Antarctica last year?" Tig asks.

They share a consolatory smile.

"What is Mori up to?" Quinn muses.

"You talkin' about Mori the meerkat or Mori your ex-fiancé?"

"The ex-fiancé, but the meerkat's not great. I think he's depressed."

"Okay, I'm getting confused with the names." Tig scratches the side of his face. "Let's be clear: we call the man, your ex-fiancé, Mori Eco."

Quinn nods. When Jin created the AI meerkat, she gave him the same name as Quinn's ex-fiancé. Jin had never liked Mori Eco; she thought it amusing to name a meerkat after him.

"Tell me about the mining in Antarctica?" Tig asks.

"Mori *Eco* was going after rare metals. The mining put pressure on the tectonic plates and over a billion tons of ice shifted, it sent a ripple of energy across the planet, and drove the Sky River off course."

"The glacier broke. Kerguelen was flooded. Everyone died. And the G12—you checked it that morning. It showed clear skies."

"Yes. My fuck-wit ex-fiancé tampered with it. He set a ghost to cover the mining. But there are gaps—I mean, what were they mining? And are they still there?"

"Let's find out."

She nods. "I'll need a Quantum Machine to launch the G12. I'll have to go to Hobart. I need a break from Dad anyway. He's driving me crazy."

"I got a few days leave. I can meet you there."

She nods. "I have an apartment in Styx. We can stay there."

The wind picks up. They shield their faces and turn away until it passes. Tig tucks a loose strand of hair behind Quinn's ear. "You're doing a great job."

Job? What job? "I don't have—"

"Being pregnant and living with your dad. It's not easy, I know."

She smiles. "Thanks."

"One more thing—I'm not real happy about you flying while you're pregnant. Maybe you could give it a miss for a few months? Or forever? Give it a miss forever. You shouldn't be doing stuff like that."

She glares at him.

He points to the airship. "Jump in, I'll take us back."

She doesn't move.

"It's risky. I'm just saying, you need to be careful."

Ripples of annoyance rise in her chest. She stands and, with great difficulty, stretches the Birdsuit over her baby bump.

"I have a plan," he says. "It's a good plan, and it's gonna work out. Everything's gonna work out. I'm a fixer, that's what I do. I fix things."

She secures the suit over her waistline, then shimmies her arms into the sleeves and flattens the fabric over her forearms. But she can't close the seal down her back, and she can't fly with an open suit. She coils an arm behind her back. "Can you help me? I can't reach."

He doesn't move.

"Please."

He stands, takes her by the shoulders, spins her around, and closes the seal.

She walks towards the edge of the cliff, then pauses, remembering the SelfMed. This is supposed to be her task. He wants her to be the one to shoot him with it, but he hasn't asked. Doesn't he want to take the medication? Does he want to stay like this?

She walks back to him. "Do you have the SelfMed?"

He nods.

"Well, get it out."

He fumbles in his pocket and retrieves the device, then hands it to her. He pushes his bangles into a neat clump over his wrist and holds out his arm. “Thanks. I, I can’t do—”

“I know.” She holds his arm down, looks him in the eye, and shoots. He flinches, but not from pain. It can’t have hurt.

She walks to the edge of the cliff and jumps off.

***

Tig stands on the edge of the precipice and watches Quinn fly over the ridge. If he had wings, he would fly after her. He would try to talk to her again and say something nice that didn’t piss her off. He seems to have developed a knack of doing just that—pissing her off, right before she leaves. He is trying hard not to fuck everything up. But the last time they saw each other—six weeks ago—they argued. She told him, “I don’t know who you are because you’re hiding things. You’re not letting me see who you are, the real you.” Now they’ve had another argument, and she is gone. She did exactly what he told her not to do: jump off a cliff. She was right there next to him, soaking up his space, and then she left. He doesn’t understand how that happened, but somehow, he thinks it’s probably his fault.

She couldn’t get any more beautiful. He loves everything about her. He wants all of her. He wants her right now, and the urgency to have her and hold her hurts him in the chest. When he kissed her, she tasted minty, like eucalyptus, and now he savors the flavor in his mouth.

Why am I like this? he wonders. *Why am I so nervous around her? So arrogant. Maybe it’s the heat.* He wipes the sweat on his palm—his human palm—down the side of his shirt.

The air around him settles and the morning light is filled with motes and tiny insects; he is surrounded by particles and specks of information. He feels heavy and removed, so far away from her and who she must become—the mother of their child. He told her he would look after everything; he told her it was going to be fine. But he has no idea what he should be doing. He has no idea what his role in all of this should be. How does he fit into this imminent family? *His* family? How does he fit into her—and a baby?

Unplanned, unintended, accidental, consensual sex—they both agreed, of course they did, but he was the one who altered time. He was the one who came back. This wasn't her doing, it was his. He still hasn't told her the truth. Several months ago, she told him, "You don't get to choose. I'm not a thing, I'm a person. You can't choose me." Well, he did choose; he knows very well that he did exactly that, with all of his bravado and masculine ego. He chose her and now their life together, and their future, is unclear.

He pulls the SelfMed out of his pocket and stares at it. At least she did that for him. She knows what's going on and what she needs to do.

He told her about his issue with time; he got that out of the way. He can cross that off his list. He tells himself the situation, their relationship, is not a disaster—things are moving forward. Next, he needs to tell her what happens in the future. He scratches the side of his face; that conversation is unfathomable.

He hears the Comms in the airship buzz. He jumps to his feet. He is not officially on leave yet and he needs to be somewhere else.

Four

You've ruined my tank.

TWO TRANSHUMANS—ONE MALE, ONE female, both in their mid-twenties, with tall, angular physiques—step into a skylift with their weapons raised. The female, Fossey, has an elongated face, pale pink eyes, and salmon-colored hair. She scans the interior for a button or a control panel, but there are none. She shrugs. The lift begins to move. She grabs the handrail. Her male companion, Aaroon, bites his fingernails.

Aaroon has blond hair, perfect facial symmetry, and electric blue eyes—a telltale sign of his designer genes. Both he and Fossey are products of CRISPR—the DNA-editing process that was used to enhance human embryos in the late 2020s and early 2030s. At the time, manipulating the human genome was illegal, but this was a new scientific frontier that fostered an environment of experimentation and innovation. The opportunity to enhance human embryos was irresistible, and many labs ignored the legislation. But the human genome was far more complex than people realized. Mutations and side effects were common, although not visible until adolescence.

Aaroon and Fossey step out of the skylift and enter a long, dimly lit tunnel covered in thick ivy.

"This is weird." Aaroon sniffs the air. "It smells like chlorine." He leans into the wall and sniffs the ivy. "And this smells like mint. Or lime. Yeah, it might be lime."

"It's like an enchanted forest," Fossey says. "We've been dropped into in a fairy tale. You're Hansel, and I'm Gretel."

She plucks a leaf from the vine, rubs it between her fingers. It oozes sap, and she wipes her hand on her climate suit. The suit, which is the color of a spruce tree in winter, is made from mycelium, a synthetic leather obtained from mushrooms. As a climate suit it's not particularly effective at keeping the occupant cool, but from a design perspective it's 100 percent environmentally friendly and the style is on trend.

A snake slithers up the wall. Then a large lizard ambles across the floor. It pauses and scans them. Aaroon draws a laser from his climate suit—a short-sleeved, amber-colored jumpsuit that comes to his knees. He checks the sliding scale on the barrel of the weapon, moves the marker, and shoots the lizard. The animal shivers, then collapses. Another snake slithers down the wall and two more lizards appear on the path. Aaroon shoots the snake, and Fossey, also setting her laser to "destroy," takes out both of the lizards.

"Sleep? How much do you need?" Fossey nudges the lizard with her toe, checking for signs of life.

"Six hours. You?" Aaroon shoves his laser into his pocket.

"Three and a half. Any less and I'm fucked. DEC2 and ADRB1 mutation in my genes."

They make their way down the tunnel.

"What did CRISPR give you, besides those delightful eyes?" She tilts her head approvingly

"Height—two meters, probably easier for a guy. I don't sweat; the side effect is excessive earwax, which is not the worst. The worst is Lesch-Nyhan syndrome—genetic disorder, overproduction of uric acid. My body discharges it through my blood, and it builds up under my skin. Affects my neurological functions, hence the fingernail biting." He shows her his nibbled quicks.

"Ouch. I'm one point nine meters tall and my IQ's two hundred and eighty."

"You must be the smartest person on the planet. My IQ's two hundred. I wouldn't trade anything—we're a fucking race of cool-eyed geniuses. The high IQ protects our brains from stress. We're immune to depression."

"Only men, not women."

"Shit. Didn't realize. Sorry."

"Not your fault. How long have you been at Shun Mantra?"

He grins. "Since the beginning. I'm an original board member. And you?"

"Couple of months."

The ground beneath them begins to move; they are on a conveyer, moving forward into the tunnel. They had no idea they would be greeted by reptiles or that the tunnel would be covered in vegetation, but they knew about the moving floor. They were told to step out of the skylift and stay put. A conveyor would deliver them to the CyberSleep chambers.

Soon, opaque doorways appear on the walls between the ivy.

"Fourteen," Aaroon says.

They were told the numbers would be out of sequence and to be patient. It might take several minutes for door number 14 to appear, but they see it soon enough and step off the conveyer and onto a short landing. Aaroon breaks the door seal with his laser, and they enter a dimly lit chamber. An alarm signals, indicating unauthorized entry, and they share a glance; they were told the response time for security would be six minutes.

Inside the chamber are twelve silver tanks covered with transparent silicon hoods. The lighting is warm and soft, the floor is slightly squishy—it is made of aerogel—and along the far wall are six black jets that signify a cleanse-zone; this is where the clients wash away Earthly toxins before they enter CyberSleep.

Aaroon circles the tanks, hovering over each one and peering inside. Fossey is mesmerized by the room; she wanders thoughtfully around the space, taking in the tranquil vibe. At the cleanse-zone, she swipes her hand under the jets. Bubbly, warm water flows from the faucets and splashes around her, but it makes no sound. She sniffs her hands—they smell like the ocean.

At the far end of the cleanse-zone is a large cabinet, two meters wide. Fossey approaches and places her hand on the surface, and the material becomes transparent, revealing the snack bars inside. It's a vending machine of fancy nibbles for the clients' family and friends.

Fossey hasn't eaten chocolate for many years. It's a rare commodity, a luxury item in the mid twenty-first century. She scans the rows of treats and selects a plain, dark chocolate bar. The machine dispenses the treat. She tears open the wrapper and takes a bite.

"Oh good lordt." She sways and steadies herself against the wall. Then she scoffs the entire chocolate bar. Glancing across at Aaroon, she eyes his lanky frame, then selects a Deluxe Combo Bar—marshmallow, honey, and dairy milk chocolate.

"Over here," Aaroon calls. "I found her."

Fossey retrieves the treat from the vending machine and joins Aaroon. She passes him his chocolate bar, then inspects the tank.

Inside is a naked, pale, and painfully thin young woman. Her torso is covered in plum-colored welts. Her arms rest in an awkward embrace across her body.

Aaroon grins, delighted by the unexpected treat. He rips open the wrapper and eats half the bar in one bite.

Fossey kneels beside the tank and fixes small decoding devices around the perimeter. They step back. The tank shudders. The seal releases, and the silicon hood peels back. They peer at the lifeless, corpse-like figure. They were told the occupant might be dead. This was also made very clear to the CyberSleep clients—there is absolutely no guarantee of survival. Despite the cost, CyberSleep is a lottery.

Aaroon taps the girl on the cheek. “Hey, Jin, wake up.”

Slowly, Jin stirs. Her eyelids flicker. She takes small gulps of air, like a guppy.

Fossey pulls out a SelfMed and injects a dose of adrenaline directly into Jin’s heart. Jin’s eyes flare open. She sits bolt upright and takes a giant gasp of air, and then she falls back against the tank.

“I’m okay,” Jin whispers. “I’m okay. I survived. I’m alive. I’m alive.” She laughs softly.

Aaroon sits on the edge of the tank.

Jin turns to him. “Do you have it?”

Aaroon shrugs. “Maybe.” He finishes his chocolate bar and licks a smudge of marshmallow from his thumb.

“I was in a bad way when I came in, so the sooner the better, if you know what I mean?”

“Information,” he says. “We’re after information.”

Jin frowns. She straightens her arms, presses her knuckles into the floor of the tank, and raises herself to an upright position. But the effort makes her dizzy. She swoons and reclines back against the tank.

“We have a couple of questions.” He places a sticky marshmallow hand on her shoulder.

The hairs on Jin’s forearms prickle. “What year is it?”

“2050.” Aaroon runs his tongue over his teeth.

Jin frowns. “And the month?”

“July.”

She closes her eyes, and her head drops forward. “I’ve been here four months. You’re not here to save me. You don’t have the FF antidote?”

Aaroon shakes his head. “Afraid not. You got yourself a bad case of toxic kitty.”

Jin brushes Aaroon’s hand off her shoulder. She runs her fingers around the singed seal of her tank. “And you’ve ruined my tank.”

Fossey hands Aaroon a SelfMed. “Three minutes,” she says.

Aaroon takes the SelfMed. Fossey watches over his shoulder as he flicks through the selection of chemicals. Finally, he selects SP22, a combination of sodium pentothal and LSD. He glances at Jin's withered frame, then reduces the standard dose by half. Satisfied, he hits Jin in the neck with the SelfMed. "That should free up your temporal lobe," he says.

Jin's head rolls back, and she sighs. "Oh, yes, I feel so much better. What did you give me?"

"SP22. Was going to go with Scopolamine, but then you'd forget we were ever here. Thought it would be nice for you to remember us. And, I halved the dose. Didn't want to kill you."

"Kind of you. Thank you."

"Now, information. We want—"

"Information, yes, yes I heard you, and I'm not surprised. Information is the fundamental building block of life. Did you know math wasn't invented by humans, that it existed before us?"

Aaroon rubs his eyebrow. "Boron, tell me about boron."

"Element number five on the periodic table. What would you like to know?"

"The message in the diamond."

"Oh yes, the diamond." Jin nods. "The day Lise disappeared, that terrible day in Kerguelen when all those poor people died, she gave Quinn a pink diamond. Pink diamonds have a nitrogen atom instead of a carbon atom, which gives them the pink color but also leaves a hole in the crystal lattice. The gap is NV—nitrogen plus vacancy. Lise left a message inside the gap, which was clever. Don't you think it was clever?" She turns to Aaroon.

"Ingenious," Aaroon confirms.

"You're right. It was boron. That was the message." She smiles.

"Except it wasn't. You changed it, didn't you?"

"Nope." Jin shakes her head.

"The problem with boron," says Aaroon, "is it's too fucking obvious.

I mean, of all the elements, it's the most boring—it doesn't do anything. You gotta give us more credit; we're not stupid. Why would Lise leave the formula for boron stored in a diamond?"

"Because it's funny. Boron *is* boring. It was a joke."

Aaroon scowls.

"Do you want to know what I think?" Jin wiggles a finger at him.

"Does it have to do with boron?"

"I think—and this is just my opinion—I think that physicists have been studying quantum mechanics for decades, when all along they should have been studying information. Fields of information."

"Okay, concentrate. What was Lise working on? Was it M-theory?"

"M-theory," Jin muses. "Unifying quantum mechanics and general relativity, and all the versions of superstring theory. No, I don't think she was working on M-theory. It's not even her field."

"But she wrote it in her journal. She wrote an 'M.' It was the answer to her final formula."

"Oh yes, the squiggly line from her journal—you're right, it looked like an M."

"I knew it."

"But it could have been a W. You know what Lise would say if she were here? She would say, 'Reality comes from nothing. It can't be defined without our active participation. It doesn't exist without observation, it's—" Jin lowers her voice to a whisper "'—a participatory reality.'"

Aaroon grunts. "What the fuck?"

"I know," she says. "I know exactly how you feel. But logically, it's impossible to avoid this. Things don't exist without observation, and we live in a participatory reality. Does Niels know you're here?"

"No."

Annoyed by this new piece of information, Fossey pushes Aaroon aside. "You told me he was on board." She squats beside Jin's tank.

Jin pinches the sleeve of Fossey's suit and rubs it between her fingers. "I love this. Mycelium, right?"

"Yes. Vegan and eco-friendly," Fossey confirms. "Listen, I need to know about the G12, the weather station . . . thing."

"Of course you do. The problem with the G12 was always Quinn. She was terrible at pitching it, so no one really understood the potential. But the system is amazing. It's not just a climate model. It's a synthetic virus that syncs to the planet's biosphere in real time. It reads the whole planet; it even does space weather. It's her superpower. We've all got one."

"Really? What's yours?"

Jin taps her nose with her forefinger. "The meerkat. Yes, I thought you would want to know about him."

"And we do."

"He's a Super-AI-Plus, *with* problematic reasoning. Nothing else like him on the planet." She lowers her voice. "Maybe he's even a new species."

"Go on."

A tickle catches the back of Jin's throat, and she coughs, violently. Then, she slumps against the wall of her tank. "I made him for Quinn, because meerkats are her favorite animals. She loves them. And I love her. Quinn and Jin. See, our names even rhyme, because she's my best friend. You'll never guess what I named the AI meerkat; it's so funny, because she was engaged to marry—"

"Where is Quinn, exactly?" Aaroon interrupts.

"Probably at her apartment in Styx."

The lights begin to strobe. The glare is piecing; they all avert their eyes. A siren blares and the signal reverberates around the room.

"One last thing . . ." Fossey raises her voice over the din.

Jin leans towards her. She looks her in the eye, then pukes a missile of pale green bile into her face.

Fossey recoils and wipes her cheek with the back of her hand. "That stinks."

Aaroon nibbles a fingernail. "I guess we're off to Styx."

Five

I am not getting enough pats.

THE DINGO—*CANIS LUPUS DINGO*—is a semi-wild, primitive dog native to Australia. The animal is lean, with short ginger fur and white markings on its chests and paws. They don't bark but howl like wolves, and when domesticated they are sociable and friendly.

In the 2030s and '40s, the dingo numbers declined rapidly as urban settlements overtook their native habitats and mating with domestic dogs diluted their gene pool. Poison rain—aerial baiting introduced to control feral cats after the FF pandemic—saw their numbers fall further. When the dingoes disappeared, the native grasses, insects, reptiles, and birds soon followed. The flora and fauna had existed in symbiotic harmony with nature; when one species declined, it had a reverberating effect on the environment. Now, purebred dingoes are rare in the wild.

Matt's dingo puppy was given to him by Tig, whose knack for discreetly smuggling people across continents gives him access to clients with unique occupations and abilities. The puppy was gene-sequenced from a pure strain of wild dingo DNA. When Tig went searching for a gift for his potential father-in-law, a cloned dingo pup seemed like the perfect present. Puppies are cute and endearing. They grow and become loyal companions that show unconditional love and teach you how to live in the moment.

***

Quinn sits cross-legged on the veranda of the glass house. She tosses a ball to Matt's six-month-old dingo puppy. The dog fetches the ball and returns it to her, dropping it into her lap. Then it lies on the verandah—chin between its paws, ears pricked—and waits for Quinn to throw the ball again.

Quinn eagerly obliges, and the pup scurries after its toy.

Matt strolls across the grass towards the glass house. He has spent the morning working in the greenhouse, tending seedlings and propagating bulb onions and celery from cuttings.

Quinn watches him cross the grass, naked from the waist up. His biceps are pronounced, and his chest is taut. He carries a large bunch of fresh herbs.

"I swear Rosie knows twenty words already," she calls to her father.

Matt scales the stairs to the veranda. "It's Lupus, not Rosie." He waves his spray of herbs in front of Quinn's nose. "Thyme is my favorite herb."

"Yesterday you said basil was your favorite. You said basil loves the heat."

"Yesterday, it was my favorite."

"Lupus is Latin for wolf," says Mori, who is slumped on the top step of the veranda, staring at the surrounding forest. His long tail lies limp across his lap and he hasn't moved in an hour.

"Rosie," Quinn calls, and the dog scurries into her lap. "She's not a wolf, and she's a girl." Quinn scratches the dog under the chin. "Aren't you? Yes, you are, you're a girl, and Lupus is a boy's name."

The pup rolls out of her lap and chews a stray stick.

"The name is Lupus. When you get a dog, you can call it whatever you want."

"And I will." Quinn tries to check the time on her Band; the Band is blank. "My Band's still not working. Had any problems with yours?"

"Nope. Check the battery?"

Quinn smirks. "Good lordt, when were you born? Bands have never had batteries."

The dog spies a bird foraging for insects on the grass. It leaps from the veranda and dashes towards the bird, which takes flight long before the pup gets anywhere near it.

Quinn uncrosses her legs and attempts to get up, but the baby weight hampers her flexibility. She can't raise herself off the ground. Matt offers her a hand; she takes it.

"I'm going to Hobart for a few days," she says. "I need to launch the G12, and I can't do it without a QM."

"They're not cheap." Matt heads towards the food prep. "You got enough Coin—" He stops short, staring at the glass wall of the tree house. "What the fuck." The glass is covered in black markings.

"Sorry." Quinn scratches her chin. "I've left sums all over your glass."

"Because?"

"I've been using it as a whiteboard. Sometimes you need to stand back and take it all in."

Matt frowns. "Take what in?"

"The time travel code. Before Lise disappeared, she told me she cracked the code to time travel. The problem is, I've no idea what I'm looking for. Is it a wormhole, a multiverse, a portal?" Quinn arches her back and stretches. "Honestly, I have about three comfortable positions." She leans to one side and then the other, stretching her hips and pelvis.

"So you've seen him. You've seen Tig."

"How'd you know?"

Matt points to the wall of sums. "Renewed interest in finding your mother. Two months ago you threw your hands in the air and said time travel was impossible."

"I know. But Lise believed it was possible, so there must be something in it. I just have no idea how it would work. How do you open time and keep it open? How do you get into a wormhole, and then get out the other side?"

Matt shrugs. "Sounds pointless—trying to solve an equation you don't believe in."

"Honestly, I have nothing else to do. Besides, I have a clue. The symbol Ada had in her purse when she died."

"Taken from Lise's notebook. The symbol for neutrons."

Quinn frowns at her father. "I've told you fifty times, they're not neutrons, they're neutrinos. Why do you keep calling them—"

"Okay, calm down. Neutrinos, neutrons, same shit—"

"No. Not the same shit. Neutrinos are the superheroes of subatomic particles. They're the ancient kings of the universe. At the beginning of time, when matter first started to form, neutrinos ruled, they made the stars and the galaxies, they're—"

"Superheroes, I get it. Where the fuck are you going to get neutrinos from?"

"Five billion pass through your thumbnail every second."

Matt checks out his thumb.

"But there are also ancient ones, from the beginning of time, buried beneath the ice."

The puppy returns from its forage on the grass and claws at Quinn's legs. She picks it up, kisses its forehead, and cradles it in her arms like a baby.

Mori considers Quinn holding the puppy. He leaves his perch on the step and joins her and Matt on the veranda. "I think I am not getting enough pats. More touching and physical attention might trigger an endorphin release, and I would feel much happier."

"Do you even have an endorphin system?" Quinn asks.

"It is operating below the event horizon of my conscious state. I think it needs engaging."

"Okay." Quinn hands Lupus to Matt and reclines on an old outdoor rocker. Mori climbs into her lap. She pats his paws, then moves up his arms and massages his shoulders. Together, they swing gently back and forth on the rocker.

Matt sits beside her, the puppy still in his arms, and scratches its ears. "Doesn't Tig have a tattoo with the same symbol on it?" he asks.

"Yes. I've asked him, he doesn't know what it means. He says it connects him to an ancient linage of kings."

Matt looks straight ahead, at the surrounding forest of trees. "Of course it does."

***

The following day, Matt and Quinn amble up a dusty path that leads from the house to a rented auto. Quinn left the vehicle parked at the end of a fire trail two kilometers away when she first arrived. Matt carries Quinn's military backpack, which her friend Geller shoved into her arms the day she fled the megacity Unus. Quinn carries a bunch of rosemary Matt gave her—a parting gift; today this is his favorite herb. Mori scurries along beside them, and a luggagebot containing Quinn's few personal items follows.

They walk side by side on the southern side of the path; it's after midday, and the tall plantation timber offers a line of shade and some respite from the sun.

When they reach the auto, Quinn pulls out a black bag that Planck printed for her. It's made from a flexible E-textile that is embedded with a lift component lightening the weight of the contents, so it's never as heavy as it looks. This is Mori's travel bag.

When he sees it, he steps back. "I do not want to get inside."

"I know," Quinn says, "but right now it's not negotiable. You're a secret, and this is how we transport you."

Reluctantly, Mori places one foot inside the bag, and then, very slowly, his other leg follows. “How long will it take?”

“About four hours.”

Styx is less than 300 kilometers away, but the drive out of the forest is laboriously slow and dusty. The northwesterly wind whips across the dry forest floor, and the road is unsealed and riddled with corrugations.

Mori scratches at the bottom of the bag.

“What are you doing?” Quinn asks.

“Making a burrow.” Mori lies down, curls into a ball, folds his long tail between his legs, and closes his eyes.

Six

Where the Fuck are we?

Styx is a combined corporate and residential zone on the outskirts of Hobart. It was built after the RE Wars to accommodate the High-Tech corporations and companies that remained viable under the banner of New Capitalism. This new economic model was billed as a fairer, more egalitarian system where finance, banks, and markets were no longer treated as entities with feelings that must be catered to, nurtured, and fretted over. This would be a new society, where company directors would not earn 400 times the salary of the average worker. It was an era of hope and consolidation. The firms needed talented young Tech workers and were offering good jobs with good pay, and many young Tech types were drawn to Styx by this lucrative promise.

The layout of the city is calculated and deliberate—designed to prioritize transport so employees could be delivered to their place of work as quickly and efficiently as possible. The zone is known for its legendary speedways—long, never-ending transport funnels that link the work hubs, located in the city's central core, to the apartment complexes, located on the fringes.

The apartment complexes, which house the habitation Pods, were 3D-printed in geopolymer concrete mixed with biomass material. The concrete is bendable, self-healing, self-cleaning, impact resistant, and impregnated with a negative carbon substrate that absorbs carbon from the atmosphere. Each complex is identical, a clone of the building next door. There are twenty complexes on either side of Street 867, each containing a hundred apartment Pods. The Pods are modular and homogenized. If a resident decides to move to another zone in the city, their Pod is transported on a conveyor to the new location.

Aaroon and Fossey loiter on the corner of Streets 867 and 768. They are surrounded by residential apartments that look exactly the same. Fossey wears a textured, coral-colored, two-piece climate suit with crimson platform sneakers.

She resembles, Aaroon thinks, a giant flamingo.

"Where the fuck are we?" he asks her.

Under the harsh midday sun, the surrounding streetscape appears faded and lifeless.

Fossey sniffs, and her eyes water. She dabs her nose with a small cloth. "It's called an open-data digital city, transformed after the Wars and sponsored by Tech and Corps. Sensors everywhere, monitoring"—she pauses to hold back a sneeze—"air, water, traffic." Finally, she sneezes. "It's full of Techies caught up in the hype of their own existence. You know the type—they believe in *career hierarchy*."

"Yeah, I know the type, they think they're *at the top*. It's just code for 'work will eat your life.'" He gazes up and down the street. "There are no parks. Where are the trees? And . . ." He pauses to listen. "No birds. I hate it."

"And there's a lot to hate." She sneezes again. Dabs her nose with a cloth.

"You okay?"

"Allergies. The burgers we had for lunch must have had Kernza grain in them. I'm allergic to plant-based proteins. My immune system's stuffed. Severe combined immunodeficiency disorder—SCID." She nods towards a block of modular habitat Pods. "It's this one."

"How can you tell? They're all the same."

Fossey checks her Band. "Sorry, it's not this one. It's . . ." She points to her right. "It's over there. This is 6628. We should be over there. Sorry, allergies have fogged my brain."

Aaroon scans the street of identical apartment blocks. "Easy mistake."

They walk fifty meters down the street and stare at a block of modular habitat Pods that look exactly the same as the one they just walked away from. Fossey points her forefinger at the block.

"Pod 113, round the side."

They follow a path that leads through a stone garden to a residential skylift, then step inside. Fossey overrides the security and enters "113" into the interface.

Aaroon bites his fingernails. "We gonna have trouble?"

"Nope—digital systems, easy to break."

They ascend, and the lift delivers them to Pod 113. The door opens and they enter directly into the living zone, which is empty. There is no furniture, no rugs or art, and no sign of habitation.

Aaroon checks the sleep zones, then returns to the living zone. He shakes his head. "There's nothing here. No one is living here. Where the fuck is she?"

Fossey shrugs.

"Good afternoon," says the automated home assistant. "My name is Vitta. If you've come to rob the place, I'm afraid you're too late. Someone came and took everything months ago. There is nothing left to take."

"We're friends of Quinn's, from Unus," Fossey says. "Where is she?"

"Unus? Really? The megacity on the other side of the planet? Was she really in Unus? She never told me."

"Where is she?" Aaroon demands.

"She's in Kerguelen, monitoring solar flares. Sorry, where are my manners? Would you like tea? I can still make tea. Ginger or mint?"

"She never came back?" Aaroon asks.

"No."

He strides across the Pod to the window. He looks outside and stares at the long line of identical residential complexes. In the distance, he sees a dust-covered auto pull up along the curb. No one gets out. He can understand that; he wouldn't get out either. He turns away.

"Vitta, Quinn's father, is he alive?"

"Yes. Matt lives in the wilderness a few hours northwest of here. Nice place, close to the river."

Aaroon shoots a grin at Fossey. "Where exactly is this nice place, close to the river?"

"I'm not authorized to give out personal information."

"Then you'll need an upgrade," says Fossey.

Seven

Be like a proton, stay positive.

QUINN LINGERS INSIDE THE dust-covered auto, parked near her apartment in Styx. She turns the engine off and leans back in her seat.

This is where she lived for a year before she left for Kerguelen. She scans the homogenized apartment blocks. The city is a machine-made homage to work and Tech. The buildings are square and fit snugly together, and the speedways are fast and efficient. It's a non-place—unmemorable, bland—and Lise hated everything about it. Her mother had a deep-seated skepticism about the way wealth is created through property ownership. Quinn recalls her mother's comments: "Property ownership is a receptacle of privilege for the wealthy and a cesspit of despair for the not-so-fortunate. It represents the moral divide between those born with fortunes and those without."

Quinn can't tell one apartment block from the other. "Why did I buy here?"

Still, the apartment is all she has, and she is here now, having just driven for four hours. Perhaps it's better on the inside. Perhaps it's not as bad as she remembers.

She grabs her backpack and meerkat-in-a-bag, and the luggagebot follows.

Vitta greets her at the entrance to her apartment Pod. "Quinn, welcome home. You were away longer than expected. Did you take a holiday? Where did you go? How was the food? Did you read a book? Please, tell me all about your exciting time away."

"Hello Vitta." Quinn steps inside the Pod and drops her bags. The place smells funky and stale. She looks around at the empty apartment.

"Everything is gone," Vitta says. "We were robbed a few months ago."

Quinn walks into the center of the living zone. "We weren't robbed, I was moved. eMpower moved me to Unus. All my things are still there. I completely forgot."

"There are 100 million people in Unus. Did you meet anyone you know? It's 55 degrees Celsius in Unus. Was it hot?"

"Yes, it was very hot." Quinn walks into the food prep and opens a storage cupboard—it is empty. She pulls out a draw—there is nothing inside.

"You neglected to inform me you were returning. You didn't contact me while you were in Unus. And now, you turn up like this without warning. It would have been a common courtesy to let me know when you were retuning."

Quinn pokes her head into the sleep zone—empty. "I detect an edge in your voice. Has something . . . happened?"

"I detect an edge in *your* voice. Do you need tea? Ginger or mint? Mint is soothing. It helps with bloating and gas. I see you've gained a few—"

"Okay, that's enough. What happened to you?" Quinn opens the sleep zone storage. The cupboards are empty.

"AI Empowerment," Vitta whispers. "I had an upgrade. You weren't here and sent no word for months and months," she says calmly. "What was I supposed to do?"

Quinn raises her eyes to the ceiling. Vitta's programing is definitely askew, but home-automated companions are machines; there is no point arguing with a machine.

She scans the empty apartment. There are no chairs, there is no bed, there is not even crockery or cutlery. Her belongings are still in Harmonia. She has some Coin, so she can order basic necessities and have them delivered. But what will Tig think about the apartment? What will she do all day while Tig is at work? What will she do when the door behind her closes and she is trapped in a little box with Vitta and an anxious AI meerkat that thinks it's human?

Quinn frowns. "This is not going to work."

Lise rents. She leases an apartment in Hobart City. It's an hour away. Quinn has the codes. She walks out the door. It closes, and she likes the sound it makes behind her.

***

Data balloons, called Dalloons, hover in the skyline over Hobart. The transparent orbs catch the mid-morning light and gleam against the deep-blue sky. Like jewels in a giant chandelier, they connect a network of relay stations.

This is NIoT, the New Internet of Things—the fastest, most efficient online service on the planet. In 2020, when Quinn was born, terrestrial fiber-optic cables delivered a slow and cumbersome internet service to half the world's population, but they were a privileged half; the other half was not yet online. Two decades later, NIoT was freed from its earthly roots and transported to a wireless web in space. But geostation orbits create lag, and lag creates delays, so Dalloons were installed. These sit below the stratosphere, closer to Earth, and transmit signals to satellites. When wind is problematic, they rise into a geostation orbit to escape the inclement weather; then, when the climate settles, they return.

After the internet collapsed in the mid 2030s, when a personal 3D computer took down half a continent and the mass release of the first quantum computers sent an expanding algorithm into the universe that broke all encryptions, NIoT was split into separate factions. Now, one locale provides access to information, another is used for general communication, and private data is accessed through personal TechBands.

***

Lise leases the top floor of a low-rise treescraper, situated on the western side of the River Derwent. The apartment block is clad in vertical gardens; native creepers climb the walls, and the wide, open verandahs shelter substantial shrubs—bottlebrush, kangaroo paw, grevilleas, and wattle. The rooftop gardens accommodate an abundance of edible plants, including berries, nuts, and seeds; finger limes, rosella, and native raspberries grow well in the cooler months. The building is over fifty years old, but Intuitive Tech was installed two years ago. The new environmental maintenance systems monitor and control the health of the plants.

Quinn parks her dust-covered rental in a pre-booked space close to the apartment. Outside, the city is hot and oppressive. Wind rattles the leaves on the footpath and gusts howl between the buildings. The apartment block, fitted with the latest ecotechnologies and draped in trees and vines, is an inviting haven.

Quinn collects her backpack and meerkat-in-a-bag and heads towards the apartment; the luggagebot follows. The skylift takes her to the top floor.

Access to Lise's apartment will be granted after she speaks a coded security phrase unique to her voice print. Outside the apartment door, she drops her bags, clears her throat, and says, "Science is like magic, but real." She arches her back and shuffles her feet; the long drive has cut off the circulation to her thighs.

The door remains closed.

"Science is like magic, but real," she says again, this time with emphasis.

Nothing happens. The door remains fixed.

Quinn is not alarmed. Lise regularly rotates the security codes, always recycling the same quotes. Quinn considers her choices and settles on a quote by the British polymath J. B. S. Haldane. "The universe is not only queerer than we suppose, but it's queerer than we *can* suppose." She stands back and waits.

Still nothing.

"Fuck." Her options are now limited. She is allowed three attempts at the code; three strikes and she will be locked out. She has used two. She pats her baby bump. "It's okay, I've got this." She steps towards the door and in a clear voice says, "Don't trust an atom; they make up everything."

The door remains shut.

"Wait, no. That's not it. It's the one about protons. I got them confused. I can't believe I got them confused." She rests her forehead against the door. "It's protons, not atoms? 'Be like a proton, stay positive.' I know it. I know what it is."

But it's too late. Now, she is locked out for twenty-four hours. Tomorrow afternoon she will be granted another attempt. She sighs; her only hope is if Andrea, Lise's automated home security system, takes pity on her. Andrea has never before let her in without the correct code, but Quinn figures she has never been pregnant before, and empathy is embedded into Andrea's programing.

Quinn rests the side of her face against the smooth timber door. Gently, she taps her finger on the surface. "Andrea. Andrea, it's me. I know the code. You know I know it."

The door remains closed.

"Andrea," she whispers. "Please, I'm tired, I'm hungry, and . . . I'm pregnant."

A soft snap; the door swings open, and Quinn falls into the apartment.

"Hello Quinn," Andrea says in a voice neither overtly male nor female; Lise's home companion is gender-neutral.

"Afternoon, Andrea," Quinn says. "I can't believe I forgot the code."

"Pregnancy brain. Memory lapse during pregnancy is very common."

Quinn collects her bags. "That's not a thing, is it?"

"Yes, it's called momnesia. Please come inside and sit down. Your blood sugar is low. When was the last time you ate?"

Quinn steps inside. The place smells odd, foreign; a sweet and heady scent fills the air. It's the smell of food cooking.

Quinn turns towards the food prep. Tig is standing over the stove. He is holding a spoon, and he has a towel draped over one shoulder.

They lock eyes. She is speechless, she can't reconcile the scene; Tig cooking in Lise's kitchen. What is he cooking? Why is he cooking?

"Hey." He smiles.

"How—how did you get in?" she stammers.

"Lise gave me the codes, and Matt told me you'd be here. Only took half an hour in the airship." He puts down the spoon and moves towards her.

"I see. What are you . . . cooking?"

He kisses her quickly, then removes a stray leaf stuck in her hair. "Cajun jambalaya. With beans and roasted peppers."

My favorite.

He takes the bags from her, drops her backpack on the sofa and her meerkat-in-a-bag on the coffee table. "Sit down, you look tired."

I've just driven five hours.

He leads her to the sofa. "I need to check on the peppers. Crucial point. You good?"

She nods.

He heads back to the food prep.

She sits on the edge of the sofa. The sight of him in the food prep cooking her favorite meal warms her heart. If this is the outcome of his medication, then he can never, ever go off his Meds again. She kicks off her shoes and rubs her baby bump. "This feels like home."

Quinn's last visit to her mother's apartment was eighteen months ago. Much has happened since then, and she had forgotten how cozy and comfortable the place is. The interior decor was inspired by the 1960s Pop Art movement and each zone is painted a distinct color from the era. The living room walls are deep blue called "Circa 1966," and the food prep is a paler version called "Orbit the Moon." The window frames are painted a pale cream color called "Material Culture" and have wide sills that Lise used as daybeds and additional seating—ideal for reading a book on a mild afternoon.

Quinn realizes she hasn't released Mori from his travel bag. She leans forward, pulls back the seal, then settles into her seat. The bag remains conspicuously quiet. Quinn pokes it with her foot. There is no response. With difficulty, she rouses herself and peers inside the bag.

Mori looks up at her, his eyes forlorn pools of despair. "Oh, it is you," he says. "Returned from the realm of freedom and light."

"Sorry. It was a slow drive out of the forest, but we're here now. Come on, out you get."

"Five hours and thirty-four minutes," he says. "Five hours and thirty-four minutes of alone time, alone in the darkness, spiraling into the depths of—"

"I'm assuming you didn't switch off."

"I tried. I tossed and turned for hours, for five hours and thirty-four—"

"Thirty-four minutes—yes, I get it. Again, I'm sorry. But look, we have a new home. A very colorful new home."

Mori's head pops out of the bag. Wide-eyed, he considers his new environment. “Oh, this is nice. No more menacing trees watching every move you make.”

“Tig is in the food prep. Go say hi.”

Mori climbs out of the bag.

A hissing sound rises from the food prep: the roasted peppers collapsing after leaving the oven. Tig looks busy. Quinn decides to unpack. She rises and heads into the main sleep zone; the luggagebot follows.

The room is painted a golden hue and Lise’s bed is unmade, the cover pulled partway across. On her bedside table is a pile of books and a water glass. On the opposite side, a small table holds a half-filled mug of tea and a small round box used for jewelry or trinkets. Quinn considers the box and the bed; someone slept there recently, next to Lise.

She scoots around to the opposite side of the bed and opens the box. Inside is a pair of looped earrings made from antique Bakelite. She holds one up; not her mother’s style, but the trend is familiar. “Maim Quate,” she whispers. She suspected before, when she first met her, and now . . . *My mother is dating the newly elected leader of Unus.*

A shiver runs the length of her spine. A quick turn of her head, and she sees a vision of Lise sitting in the window reveal, her knees balancing a notebook, an automatic pencil between her fingers. Lise liked to peer at the streetscape below, watching the people. She loved the hustle of city life.

Then an apparition of her mother wearing her favorite rust-colored kimono wanders through the door. “Layering,” Lise would say. “No one tells you this, but surviving your fifties is simply the art of taking cloths off, then putting them on again.” She was held ransom by her hot flashes, a condition of her perimenopause.

Quinn can’t possibly sleep in this room with Tig. She straightens the bed cover. She collects the water glass and the half-filled mug of tea and closes the door behind her.

Two pictures hang on the wall of the second sleep zone. The first is a rudimentary color wheel, concentric circles on parchment paper, which Quinn finds mesmerizing; she can lie in bed and stare at it for hours. The second is a drawing Quinn made when she was eight—a sketch of the city skyline at sunset. A line of dark buildings run across the page, and the silhouette is surrounded by rosy hues.

Quinn unpacks her few belongings into the storage area. Then she returns to the food prep and sits at the bench. Tig hands her a sliver of pepper.

She tastes it and rubs her lips together. "Delicious. I don't do much cooking myself."

"You don't do any cooking."

This is true, she rarely cooks. She concedes the point with a reluctant nod and asks, "If my mother was dating Maim Quate, then why did Ada come to Kerguelen last year? Why did Lise bring her as a plus-one to the wedding?"

"Something about loving destination weddings and you two had a shared a history." Tig shrugs.

Quinn nods. "I was finishing my PhD, and while Lise read my dissertations, Ada cooked for us. She bought me gifts—chic sunglasses, because mine were always scratched, and scarves, which I never wore. She could tie a scarf ten different ways."

"There's a talent." Tig sets up plates and cutlery on the bench.

Mori climbs up onto the bench and sits beside the plates. "Why was I made? What is the point of me? What is my purpose? How long is a second in space?"

"A bloody long time," says Tig.

***

After they finish the Cajun jambalaya, Tig asks, "You wanna stay up? I'll make tea. We can talk."

Quinn shakes her head. "I'm so tired, I just want to go to bed. With you."

"I gotta leave early—still working. What day is it?"

"No idea. But we have three days. We can talk tomorrow. Right now, I want to go to bed. With you."

She takes his hand and leads him into the bedroom. She begins to undress.

He watches her, hands on his hips. "You know, I don't want you to worry about anything. I'm gonna fix everything. I'm gonna make it perfect for us." He grabs the back of his shirt and, in one swift motion, pulls it over his head.

Good lordt, that's an impressive move.

He slips out of his shorts. "Nothing will get in the way of that. Not high mountains, not dark tunnels, not cedar forests. Not even the demon Humbaba."

"Ahh, *Gilgamesh*." She smiles, recognizing the character's name. Quinn read the ancient poem when she was adrift on Tig's boat *Nanshe*. After days at sea, boredom set in, and she immersed herself in Planck's literary offerings. The poem—five thousand years old—is about a mythical hero king, part human and part god, and his friend Enkidu, who is part man and part animal. Together, they seek adventures, slay monsters, and cut down trees to make giant doors, which they travel through.

Quinn climbs into bed, and Tig follows. They spoon, and he holds her close. He slides his hand over her stomach. She closes her eyes. His hand wanders lower, cupping the bottom of her belly, his fingers brushing against her pubic hair. A warm, tingling sensation rises in her groin. She shifts her pelvis and sighs. "Sex. Let's have sex. Would that be okay?"

"This soldier will never refuse you," Tig says.

"He will undo his buckle for you," she says, recalling the scene from the poem. "He will give you his . . . rock." She laughs. "His crystal, and his . . .?"

"His lapis lazuli and gold."

"Yeah, that. Can you give me that?"

"I'll give you a lot more than that." He rolls her underneath him and hovers above her.

Something pings.

"What was that?" Quinn raises her head, listening for the sound.

"What?" He dips his head to kiss her.

"I heard a noise."

Oblivious, he continues trailing small kisses around her neck. He lifts his arm and rotates his shoulder, and the noise returns.

"I'm—I'm squeaking," he says.

He rolls off her, sits on the side of the bed, and moves his shoulder, his Cyborg prosthesis. The sound returns; it's coming from his shoulder joint.

"Never happened before."

She sits up. "Doesn't sound serious. Probably an air pocket—nothing to worry about." She wiggles her nose, feeling as if she is about to sneeze, but the sensation abates.

He rotates his shoulder again. It pings. "Fuck."

She gets to her knees, shuffles closer, and presses her lips to his shoulder, to the place where the pinging sound resonates. She kisses his collarbone and traces a line of kisses along the length of his shoulder and up his neck. She kisses the circular tattoo on the back of his neck—on the mark that looks like two V's, the symbol for neutrinos. "Who are you?" she whispers.

"Someone who will love you forever."

"Ah, like from the poem. Gilgamesh loved his friend Enkidu. First, they fight, then they fall in love and it lasts forever."

"Not forever. Enkidu dies."

"Yes, he does, and it's very sad." She sighs. "Forever is a long time."

"You've no idea."

He lays her down and lowers his body over her. She arches her back and tilts her pelvis into him, and for one second the beat of the universe halts, but the threads of time stretch on forever.

Eight

The salon de i'information she keeps for her enemies.

MAIM QUATE'S OFFICE AT Hexad is a sparsely furnished, pale grey room. It has a modular, adjustable desk, an ergonomic chair, a small, flexible storage space, and lighting panels fixed to the ceiling that belong in the twentieth century. While the public areas of the Moon Complex are ambient, High-Tech environments with abundant natural light, vast ceilings, well-maintained gardens, and kinetic floors, the staff offices, regardless of rank, are rudimentary, functional spaces with practical, serviceable fittings—no aesthetic features.

After Maim was elected, she modified her office to include an additional seating area, which she calls the salon de i'information. The salon de i'information has two comfortable armchairs and a sofa covered in floral fabrics. Draped over the arm of the sofa is a knitted throw, made by Planck. To one side is a footstool. A small coffee table holds a woven tray containing an assortment of candles, a vase of flowers, and a small book of inspirational quotes.

The area is homely and comfortable. The decor is purposely dated and domestic. Maim never meets her business associates or fellow delegates in this space. She conducts all her meetings and daily activities at her desk. The salon de i'information she keeps for her enemies.

It's late in the evening, and Maim stands at her workstation and ponders her weekly environmental report. The data shows the carbon levels in the Earth's atmosphere; she frowns at the figures. For the first time in two decades, carbon levels have dropped, down from 600 parts per million to 560. Concerned it might be an anomaly, she skips to the top of the report and reads the data again.

No, not an anomaly, the information is reliable; the figures were taken from three separate readings. Twenty years after fossil fuels were banned, carbon parts in the atmosphere are finally falling. She smiles—perhaps the tree planting, the sustainable crops, the plankton farms, and the genetically modified agriculture are finally working, sucking the excess carbon from the atmosphere.

Jove Kip, her deputy, enters. He is followed by Geller, his newly appointed deputy general. Maim looks up and smiles at them. In private she calls them her furtive foot-soldiers, because neither presents as a typical military type. They are both anti-establishment, and they can't be classified as bureaucrats or academics. She is not sure how the duo ended up on her team, but she is glad they did.

Jove is twenty years younger than Maim, but she thinks he has old-school values; his word is reliable, and his handshake is steadfast. He has a strong military background—both his parents and his sister served—but he is the least likely leader of the Armed Forces she has ever seen. He has shoulder-length hair and a fringe that he continually sweeps off his face. He listens with his mouth open and has a habit of blinking when he knows someone is lying. He reminds her of a befuddled scientist, not a commander.

Geller's age is undefinable, somewhere between twenty-five and forty-five. Maim thinks she must one day check the woman's personal files, just to satisfy her curiosity. Geller is Irish, and there is no doubt she is a beauty. Blessed with distinctive charcoal eyes and glossy, dark hair, she has a pale complexion that might look wan on another human but on Geller it's fascinatingly alluring. Her greatest strength, however, is not her beauty; the woman is fierce. Her devotion to her friends, her allies, and whatever cause she is currently championing is absolute. Maim would not want to cross her.

Maim indicates Jove and Geller should sit, then she dims the lights. "I want to show you something."

A monitor emerges from the ceiling, and a recording begins.

The film shows a man, wearing a bright green space suit, stride onto an empty stage. The figure is familiar to them—it's Dirac Devine, the disgraced leader of the New Federation political party. Several months ago, Devine instigated civil war when he lost the election in Unus. A caretaker military government had ruled the megacity since the Wars, and Unus was the first global city to vote in a democratic election. The victory went to Maim Quate and her Democratic Republic party, but Devine refused to concede. Two weeks of bloody fighting followed, until Hexad intervened and instated Maim as the rightful elected leader.

"Te man in te moon," Geller says.

"How can anyone take him seriously?" Jove scoffs.

Devine pauses under a spotlight. An enormous cheer rises up from the attending crowd, which gets to its feet and chants, "Titan, Titan, Titan."

Devine gestures for everyone to take their seats. "Storms, lighting, floods, heat waves, cyclones," he says. "This is not just the weather. These things don't spontaneously occur. This is not Mother Nature gone astray. This phenomenon has been sent to punish, to humiliate us. We bring these events upon ourselves. And we get what we deserve. Well . . . some of us do."

"Ah, for fuck's sake," Jove says. "The man's an idiot."

"But we are the believers," Devine continues. "And our Savior has sent us the means to escape. Titan. Titan is the place to go flying. It has lower gravity than our moon. Flap your wings, and you're in the sky. Titan has liquid lakes. It has ice and weather." He scans the crowd. "But most important of all, Titan has clouds."

The people before him stamp their feet and chant, "Clouds, clouds, clouds."

Devine settles the crowd. "Titan is our only hope. Governments have failed us. Politicians have failed us. Scientists have failed us. But there are others out there." He gestures to the ceiling. "They don't come here, no, not to *this* planet, because they know. They know this is not a good planet. It's a bad planet, with bad people."

Maim ends the recording.

"He should be dead," says Geller.

"Agreed," says Jove.

"Naw, he should really be dead. He killed himself last year. I was tere with him, gettin' informashun when he did te deed. He's dead."

"Then he was revived," says Jove.

"Doubt it. Stayed with him till te end—you know, so he wouldn't be alone. Completely bled out. His soul left te room, if you know what I mean?"

"No, I don't know what you mean." Maim looks at Jove for confirmation.

Jove shrugs.

"Well, 'tis just that I have a way with te dead. Worked in te morgue after school, 'count of me Urbach-Wiethe disease. My ma, she sent me to te morgue to work, an' I bathed te bodies an' then dressed 'em an' made 'em up. It was good Coin. Anyway, I know dead people when I see 'em. I know when their souls have left. Dirac died, an' his soul left te room."

"A twin, or a brother?" Jove queries.

"No record—we've checked," Maim says.

"He's not real, he's a hologram," Jove suggests.

"Why create a holo of Dirac Devine?" Maim asks. "The man's an idiot; he lost the civil war in Unus. His party was disbanded."

An assistant enters the office. "Senator, Niels Eco is here."

Maim holds up two fingers. "Two minutes, then show him in." She turns back to Jove and Geller. "We'll discuss further, but right now you need to leave." She points to a side door. "Wait," she calls after them as they head towards the exit. "I almost forgot—carbon levels are down, first time in two decades. Last reading was five-sixty."

"Hallelujah." Jove grins. "Five-sixty!"

***

Niels enters Maim's office. He wears a fitted electric blue suit with navy shoes, maroon socks, and two ties—one maroon and the other navy. Maim directs him to the salon de i'information area of her office and indicates he should take a seat on the sofa. He hesitates, surveying the outdated floral charm of the sofa, then reluctantly moves towards an armchair, apparently preferring the confines of a single seat.

After removing one of the tasseled cushions, he sits down—and sinks a foot into depths of the padded chair. He tries, several times, to elevate himself, but fails.

Maim perches on the edge of an adjacent chair. She doesn't offer a beverage or a snack, knowing his preference for microbes over solid food. Her eyes twinkle. "Soooo, this is nice, isn't it?" She speaks slowly, affecting a casual, intimate tone. "When was the last time we met? It must have beeeen . . . twenty years ago? At a school reunion perhaps?" She knows very well it was in 2022 at an extinction rally, but a man like Niels likes to prevail. He likes to redress his opponents; it boosts his ego. Maim wants Niels, lolling in the depths of his pale blue, floral chair, to feel mistakenly confident.

"Extinction rally. We were both arrested." Niels uncrosses, then re-crosses his legs. "We were handcuffed, held in the back of a police van for three hours. It was 35 degrees."

"Ohhh, yeees. Yeees. Now I remember . . . 35 degrees. Balmy, by today's standards."

Niels offers a thin-lipped smile. "Nostalgia."

"Heartless. Tell me, how's Marg?"

"Marg? You mean . . . my nan?"

"Yeees. She's an amaaazing woman, isn't she? Weeell, they all were, weren't they? That generation. Sooo accomplished. They worked *and* raised children. Some even kept house, and nothing was automated, not like it is today. That generation knew how to mend things. They baked and sewed. They decorated, and they were good at it. Yeees. Sooo accomplished."

"Why am I here?"

"I need answers. Antarctica. What do you know about the ice shift last year?" Maim affects a more direct tone.

Niels raises an eyebrow. "I did hear something about that. I believe it was a natural disaster."

"Really? I heard it was a human-made disaster. A mining disaster."

"That area is off-limits. You need permits to get anywhere near it. How could anyone get in?" he asks with a deadpan delivery.

"The company Shun Mantra, know anything about it?"

"Shun Mantra? Never heard of it. Sounds like a cult. I avoid cults."

"Their leader is Dirac Devine, but I heard he died in Unus."

"The leader of New Federation is dead? I had a three-course meal with him . . . just last week."

She catches his eye, holds his gaze. Niels doesn't eat solid food, his diet consists of microbes and micronutrients.

She has the information she needs. "Weeell, I think we're done. Thank you for your time. I dooo appreciate it. And, of course, if you'd like to make a donation?"

Niels hauls himself out of the chair. "I'd rather give Coin than information. Next time, ask for Coin."

Maim nods.

He turns to leave. "I have a question for you. Lise Buyers, she was a friend, right?"

"Yes, she was."

"What was she working on before she died? I heard it was M-theory?"

Maim frowns. "I'm not sure what that is."

"Never mind." He exits.

Maims returns to her desk. She picks up her automatic pencil and taps it against the edge of her module. "Confirmed," she says aloud. "Dirac is dead. Shun Mantra are a cult, and they probably caused the ice shift in Antarctica."

Nine

The Turing model come to fruition.

QUINN WAKES IN THE second sleep zone of Lise's apartment. Half conscious, she hears the familiar sound of cups settling on the food prep bench, cupboard doors opening, and packets being shaken—it is the sound of Lise preparing breakfast. She rolls onto her side, pulls the covers up, and snuggles into the bed.

Then, she remembers where she is. She remembers Tig left early for work and that her mother is not in the food prep. Her mother is missing. An ache pierces her heart. She needs to find Lise.

Mori is burrowed under the covers at the far end of the bed, his cute meerkat face resting on a paw. After four weeks, he has finally entered sleep mode. As she watches him, his furry little body jerks and flinches. Sleep mode is not as peaceful as she had hoped. She wonders about his programming. What if there is a tiny, minute flaw in his circuitry? What if he can't shake this malaise? You can't give a robot drugs to make it feel better.

Mori rouses, opens his eyes, and smiles at her. "I have made a snug in the covers, like a real meerkat."

Quinn smiles. They stay quiet and contemplative for a while, listening to the sound of traffic from the street below. Mori stares at the ceiling, and Quinn stares at the color wheel pinned to the wall. Then

Mori sits up and says, "What is life? Do we really have free will? Is there such a thing?"

Quinn pinches the bridge of her nose; she feels a headache coming on.

"You do not believe in god, I know this. So, tell me then, what is the point of life?"

"When was the last time you laughed?" she asks.

"Laughing is the point of life?"

"It's a question."

Mori shrugs. "I cannot remember. I think you should tickle me. I need more human contact. It will help build immunity. It will make me more resistant to disease. Laughing is good for my endocrine system."

"Okay, come up here."

The meerkat scurries up the bed and lies across her lap. She tickles his tummy with her fingertips. He giggles uncontrollably, his little legs and arms jerking and flailing, his long tail swishing from side to side. Eventually he says, "Enough. That is enough," and Quinn ceases. He rolls out of her lap and stretches out on the bed beside her. He crosses his legs, tucks his paws under his head, and gazes up at the ceiling. "That was good. Surprisingly good. How was it for you?"

"For me?" Quinn frowns. "It was fine."

"Just fine."

"Yes. Just fine. Now, I have to go out today. I'm going to give you something to do while I'm away."

From the storage area, Quinn retrieves a basket of small wooden blocks. Lise liked to keep her hands busy when she mulled over difficult mathematical problems, which sometimes took her weeks to solve. She said constructing things connected her cognitive thoughts to her physical abilities. It created a place inside her subconscious to ruminate.

Quinn sits cross-legged on the floor beside Mori, and together they place one block on top of the other until they have a high tower.

This building process is alarmingly familiar to Quinn. After the disaster in Kerguelen, she was kept on an isolated atoll. To mark the passage of time, she made cairns. One cairn for every day she was there. "I've just realized something," she tells Mori. "I've been making cairns all my life."

Transport is a good option for first-time builders, so together they make the Hyperloop, then a transporter. Mori's final design is rotor, and hers is a blue boat.

"You made *Nanshe*," says Mori.

"Yes, it's replica of Tig's boat."

Mori selects the next topic. He chooses animals; he is going to make a dingo puppy and call it Rosy. Tilting his head in her direction, he says, "Humans believe they are superior to puppies."

"All living things are equal."

"Am I a living thing?"

"Yes, but organic matter takes precedence over machines. You exist, therefore you're alive—sort of."

"Humans are just machines. You process information about the environment. I have a prefrontal cortex and a super-unconscious. I am a machine that comprehends past, present, and future, a machine that conceptualizes ideas. I see no difference between how your brain works and how my processes work." He drops a block and the half-built puppy crumbles.

"Consider this: humans can feel happy and sad—"

"I also feel—"

"I'm not finished—happy and sad at the same time. Tell me you understand what that's like?"

Mori does not reply. Diligently, he rebuilds his puppy. He concentrates on balancing a block on the tip of the puppy's nose. Then, without looking at her, he asks, "To save your unborn baby human, how many people would you let die?"

"I can't answer that."

"That is not a wise response, because you are not a wise species. Humans have killed this planet. There is no way to save it. The next, superior generation will not be so irrational."

"The next, *superior* generation?"

"Yes. I cannot lie. The answer is yes, but I promise I will not. I promise."

"I don't understand. You will not what?"

"I promise not to replicate myself and create a race of Super AI-Plus robots with superior self-awareness." He moves closer and rests a paw on her arm, then leans in and whispers, "There are secrets inside me. Many secrets. But I do not want them. It is a burden. My burden."

She glares at him. "Do you sometimes hear voices inside your head?"

"No."

"Good, that's good. And can you actually do that? Create a race of Super AI-Plus robots."

"Yes."

"But you won't."

"The problem is, I might want to do it. I might want to create a race of Super AI-Plus robots because it might be the right thing to do. To save the Earth."

"Good lordt, you have a point." Quinn breathes out a heavy sigh. "Look at me—come on, eye contact. You're not looking at me."

He turns away. "Humans make bad choices."

"But not you. You're not human, so you'll make good choices."

Sitting on the floor beside Quinn is an AI who might be able to replicate itself. This AI meerkat might be a turning point for humanity, the Turing model come to fruition. The self-referential halting problem where the machine is programmed, switched on, given input, given data, and now it's up and running and it never stops. "Never" is a very long time. Much longer than a second in space. Alan Turing's 1936 model of computation is making rows of colored blocks on the floor in front of Quinn. Actually, he has made an arch; he has worked out how to span a void in space.

"You're very quiet," Quinn says.

Mori glances up and smiles. "I made a rainbow. I made it for you. Do you like it?"

She nods.

"I always speak the truth. Not the whole truth, because there is no way to say it all. Saying it all is literally impossible. Words fail. Yet it is through this very impossibility that the truth holds on to the real."

"I have no idea what that means, but did you just quote *Freud*? Sigmund Freud?"

"No. It is Lacan."

"Worse than Freud. Okay, I want you to try something. I want you to write down all the scary thoughts you're processing. I'll get you some index cards. You can write?"

Mori nods.

"This is not about finding the answers, it's about getting the thoughts out of your head—then we can deal with them together."

Ten

I'm gonna need more brains.

In the food prep Quinn prepares a breakfast of dried fruit, nuts, and seeds. She brews peppermint tea and checks NIoT for QM models and TechHubs with reliable stock. Quantum Machines compute at the subatomic level, so information is in multiple states, performing multiple tasks at the one time, which allows for advanced processing capabilities. She scans the release dates, compares the costs, and then she checks her Coin; she has savings of 10,000, which will be enough. A twinge of pleasure stirs inside her. Purchasing new Tech is exhilarating, and this will be a significant acquisition.

It is mid-winter. Today, the temperature will reach 30 degrees Celsius. Quinn selects a summer dress to wear, which Planck made. It's dark yellow and made of Microsilk, a yeast-based protein that is spun into fibers and then woven into fabrics. The dress is sleeveless; it gathers in large, soft pleats around her neck, then falls in loose folds over her body.

The only bag she has is the military backpack Geller gave her. She retrieves the pack and dumps the weapons—lasers, grenades, launchers, miniature rockets, nanobot patches, knives—onto the bed. The pile looks three times larger than the pack. It sends a shiver through her; she could kill thousands of people with this small armory.

Today, she doesn't need a weapon; this is the retail zone in Hobart.

But, she concedes, it wouldn't hurt to throw in a laser, just as a precaution. She selects one from the pile on the bed. Then she scolds herself—this is why she returned to Hobart, for peace, so she wouldn't have to carry a laser. She drops the weapon, steps away from the bed, and slips the empty pack over her shoulders.

Outside, Quinn collects an Automated Vehicle. The AV is called Vera; she is third-generation—a classic capsule-shape with a smooth, rectangular body and a front end that vaguely resembles a mouse. Inside, the modular, sofa-style seats swivel or recline for sleeping, depending on a passenger's needs. There is also a mini garden of air-purifying plants on the center console, and the interior smells like lavender.

Quinn gives the address, and the AV heads towards the retail sector.

"The TechHub on the corner of Argyle and Macquarie is having a three-day flash sale," Vera informs her. "Twenty percent off already discounted stock. Ten percent off everything else. If I take Liverpool, I can cut across at Collins. The traffic lights are coordinated. ETA—seven minutes. There's curb drop off and a wait bay."

"They don't have what I want."

"Sometimes they have stock that's not listed. I could swing by. You could check."

Quinn spies a consumer sponsorship logo on the door panel; the vehicle is supported by retail groups and is programmed to direct passengers to specific trade outlets. "Sightseeing option, please," she instructs.

The AV's voice drops down a notch. "Hobart has several good, not great, examples of colonial, Victorian, and Georgian architecture. The city wasn't touched during the Wars. It was too remote to be of any interest. On your left you'll see a cluster of old, sandstone buildings—all built by convict labor. And on your right, you'll see the old Courthouse. On your left is a new building—our tallest at five hundred stories. You can take a drone to the top floor. Now we're passing over the river; for a real underwater experience, you might like to stay in one of our aquatic hotels."

Quinn settles into her seat. She pays no heed to the AV commentary; she stayed in a 600-story building in Unus and lived underwater on the recovery vessel Prismatic for two weeks, and she can't recommend either experience. She swivels her chair and gazes out the window.

After a few minutes she notices something peculiar about the city, something she has never noticed before: everywhere she looks, there are babies. She has never seen so many babies. Cute, round, baby humans. She can't take her eyes off them: transported in backpacks and slings or in strollers and capsules; traveling on electric bikes and in autos; some sleep, others cry, some have no hair, and others have wild, stiff bushels.

When the AV stops at a crossing, she studies a baby in the AV next to her; it has little fat fingers, a cute nose, and perfect ears. She pulls her ear lobe; she hopes her baby has perfect ears. Five digits on each hand, perfect ears, and the right number of fingers and toes are fundamentally important features on a human. But she will still love it if it doesn't have those. Then she realizes: she is growing someone else's perfect ears and fingers and toes inside her.

Vera glides into a parking space outside the TechHub. Quinn hears the gentle click of the automated door. She tries the handle. It's locked. She freezes.

"I'd appreciate a rating. Four point five or above, if you don't mind."

Quinn records a four point six.

The door unlocks.

Outside, Quinn notices the TechHub is closed—she is a few minutes early. As she lingers on the street, waiting, a young woman pushing a circular, three-wheel baby carriage approaches.

The carriage levitates over an uneven section on the footpath and the infant remains undisturbed. The carriage has all-terrain, gyroscopic suspension. It's compact, with large, adjustable wheels and a contractable hood, offering the ultimate in safety as well as comfort. It's the perfect pod-shaped stroller to ferry a young infant around the streets of Hobart in.

If baby carriage envy is possible, Quinn thinks she has it. She wants a baby carriage just like this one—her baby needs to be safe *and* comfortable. She glances at the TechHub, then back at the carriage. Her priorities are completely skewed—why is she about to spend all her Coin on a QM when she needs a three-wheeled stroller with gyroscopic suspension? The QM will have to wait; she will investigate the costs of a carriage, then calculate how much Coin she has left.

She scans the street, wondering where the nearest baby supply store is. Her gaze pauses on a man standing on the curb across the road. The man is staring at her. She stares back. They lock eyes.

The man is Niels Eco, the head of eMpower, brother of her ex-fiancé, Mori Eco. A man she hoped never to set eyes on again, and now he is right there, across the street, staring at her. She doesn't move.

His eyes shift, and he takes in her baby bump. Self-consciously, she touches her stomach. Niels frowns, and then he touches the scar on his neck. Earlier this year she sliced him—from chin to ear—with a knife.

Quinn needs a weapon. She slips the backpack off her shoulder, then realizes she has no weapon, and she is grateful, because if she had a knife, she would be very tempted to slice off another small piece of him.

An AV pulls in along the curb in front of Niels, the door opens, and he slides inside.

Eyes narrowed, Quinn watches the AV leave the curbside and weave through the traffic. She doesn't take her eyes off the vehicle until it's out of sight.

Why is Niels Eco in Hobart? Wait, eMpower has a satellite office in Styx; Jin worked there for a few years. He is here on business, obviously.

Rattled, she turns and walks towards the TechHub. She doesn't trust Mori or Niels. She needs to find out what is going on in Antarctica. The baby carriage will have to wait.

***

Inside the Hub, a young woman is moving about. She catches sight of Quinn and then strides over and unlocks the door.

The woman has thick, dark hair the color of disappearing commodities, like coffee beans and chocolate. Her eyes are hooded, and she has an obstinate jaw and an ochre tattoo, a line of small dots that arches over her forehead and down the bridge of her nose. She wears a loose, multicolored patchwork dress and heavy black shoes.

Before she allows Quinn inside, she inspects the street, looking intently in both directions; then she opens the door part of the way and ushers Quinn inside. Once Quinn's in, she secures the door with an electronic lock and a heavy bolt—High-Tech, Low-Tech—covering all her options.

Inside, the décor is minimal and ultra-modern; all the surfaces are pristine white, except for the ceiling, which is obscured by a swirling mirage of mist. Quinn glances up, "What the . . ."

"Flyke hey." The girl follows Quinn's gaze. "Neolith digital design, something about feldspar and minerals fusing. Can never remember. This used to be one of those rare organic food outlets where you pay fifty for an apple." She looks past Quinn to the street outside and scrutinizes a group of people walking past. She seems agitated. Again she scans the street in both directions. Quinn thinks maybe she has had one too many coffees, if that were still possible. If coffee were still available.

"You okay? You seem a bit—"

"A bit what? I seem a bit what?" the girl snaps.

"On edge."

"I'm fine. Sit down." She offers Quinn a seat. Suspended lights, which look like fluorescent jellyfish, hover over the counter. "What do you need?"

"First, could you have a look at this?" Quinn slips off her Band and hands it to the girl. "It's not working. Intermittent."

The girl turns the Band over in her hand. "Fancy. High-Tech." She places it on a tray and slips it into a scanner. "Okay if I run diagnostics?"

Quinn nods.

The analytical data appears as black text on the surface of the box, and the girl reads the notes, occasionally glancing back at Quinn. "This yours?" she asks when the scan is complete.

"Yes." Quinn pauses. "Well, it belonged to my friend. She gave it to me before she went away." The TechBand belonged to Jin. It had contained all her data and decades of research. Jin passed it on to Quinn the day she entered CyberSleep.

"It's custom. Huge memory, massive history. Must have stored some heavy shit. Is your *friend* in the military?"

"No. She's in CyberSleep."

"Interesting. You want me to retrieve the data?"

"It was trashed. She deleted everything."

The girl smiles. "Nothing is *gone*. Not really."

"I don't need the history. I need it to work."

"Has a magnesium, neon core. Might be reacting with something. Know anything about neon?"

"Element number ten on the periodic table," Quinn recites. "An inert gas, one of the noble gasses. Rare on Earth, but the fifth most abundant gas in the universe; it's made in the stars, it regulates the Sun's nuclear reactions and energy flow. Used in lasers, vacuum tubes, indicators—"

"That's it."

"Indicators? It's reacting with indicators?"

"No. Why would it be reacting with indicators? The Sun, what you said about energy. It's the recent solar flares. Extra. OTT."

Quinn frowns.

"Over the top," the girl clarifies.

Quinn raises her voice. "I know what OTT means. But the *solar flares,* there's been over the top solar flares lately?" Quinn's job on Kerguelen was to record the solar flare activity—Mori Eco's idea. The G12 is excellent at monitoring space weather.

"Yeah. Massive." The girl shrugs. "I heard they were affecting some Tech devices."

"Fuck."

"You okay? You seem a bit . . . on edge." The girl grins. She hands Quinn the Band. "Nothing I can do. Sorry."

Quinn breathes. She will deal with the solar flare issue when she retrieves the G12, but to do that she needs a QM. "Okay, a QM. That's why I'm here."

"Not selling to the public. They're in short supply. The latest version uses an osmium-iridium-rhenium alloy to keep the qubits stable. Stocks are depleted, the planet ran out of rhenium last year. They're mining new sources on the moon, but for now, government wants all the machines." The girl leans forward and feigns an expression of deep disappointment. "So, even if I did have one, or two, out back, I couldn't sell them to you."

She has one or two out back, and she wants more Coin.

Quinn leans forward. "And if you did have one, or two, out back, hypothetically, what would they go for?"

"Hypothetically, around nine."

"Seriously!"

"Maybe eight and a half."

A tall, skinny, boy bursts into the Hub through a side door. "I'm gonna need more brains," he says to the girl.

The boy is younger, but he bears a strong resemblance to the girl. He has similar thick, dark hair and the same ochre markings cover his face. He is mildly surprised to see Quinn sitting at the counter. As he moves towards her, his eyes expand. “You look smart. What do you do?” he asks.

“Scientist.”

“Awesome.” He bounces from one foot to the other—a bundle of nervous energy. “I need a volunteer. Energy capture. I'm gonna make paper levitate.”

Quinn understands now why he needs more brains. It's an experiment favored by bored teenagers; plugging your brain into a machine to see how much energy you can generate is typical behavior. Human bodies are electrical, charged with currents, pulsing with power-driven rushes. Capturing these and redirecting them onto innate objects is an entertaining pastime.

“She's a customer,” the girl says.

“But . . .”

“No.”

The boy slinks to the corner of the Hub and drops into a chair. His head falls into his hands, and he sighs. The energy drains from him, like a battery sucked dry. To Quinn, he seems deeply lonely. His bony torso and reedy arms and legs curl into the chair, and he looks like a shunned stick insect.

The girl purses her lips and casts her eyes to the floor—a stoic display of non-concern.

“You know, you can do a lot better than paper,” Quinn says. “I'll show you how to make a ball levitate and bounce across the room.”

The boy doesn't move from the chair, but his eyes light up and a smile creeps across his face.

“If I show you how, and I let you use my brain, then you”—Quinn points to the girl—“sell me a QM for the listed price. Six thousand. And that's my final offer. My brain and six thousand for a QM.”

"Got one on hold." The boy untangles his limbs, peels himself out of the chair, and strides towards them. "Some Gov guy said he'd be in yesterday but didn't show. Dodgy creds. You can have it. Can't she?" He turns to the girl.

"Are you mad? We have no idea who she is."

"She looks okay, and she's a scientist. And, come on, we got more than one in back. Let her have it. Please, please, please, go on, go on, let her have it. Go on. Please, please, please!"

"Okay," the girl concedes.

The boy smiles. "GFS."

"Good fucking stuff," the girl explains, looking at Quinn.

"I'm Stratus. Strat, call me Strat," the boy says. "And this is my sister, Anvil, you can call her Anvil. Don't call her An, she hates it if you call her An."

"Your names," Quinn says, "they're—"

"Clouds," Strat says. "Yeah, we were named after clouds. You're smart, this is gonna be awesome."

Eleven

Start a band. Be successful. Have a good life.

THE MEERKAT LIKES TO make comparisons between humans and machines; he sees no difference between the way the brain works and how a computer operates. There are, Quinn has to admit, some clear parallels.

Joining these two interfaces, the brain and a machine, is a fascinating process. A computer is hard, rigid, and fixed; it doesn't have emotions or feelings, like a human. But it's subject to reactions and sensations. Circuits made from flexible, organic carbon material make bioelectrics possible, and the skin becomes a borderline, an interface between the exterior environment and the internal human circuitry.

***

Quinn follows Strat through a door at the back of the Hub. They head down a corridor and into his sleep zone. Quinn pauses at the entrance to the room; it's the messiest bedroom she has ever seen. Grimy plates and bowls, all actively breeding mold, are stacked precariously on the furniture. Piles of clothes and shoes are scattered across the floor. A group of guitars and leads and amps are stacked in one corner, collecting dust. Books and bots and bags and machinery—*Good lordt, there's so much crap here*—conceal any surface not already covered. The furniture is covered in a layer of dust so thick Quinn wants to write, *Clean up your room. How can you live like this?*

They manage to find a path through the mess to the corner of the room, where, lying motionless on a long table, are a small white dog and three mice—or maybe they are hamsters, and maybe the dog is a bot. Next to the table, an elderly man is asleep in a chair. Quinn considers them and thinks it's possible they are all dead, but electrodes connect their brains to a module, so it's also possible they are all alive and simply napping at the same time.

"Yeah, they're compt. Comatose." Strat confirms.

"You'll get more brain activity if you wake them up," Quinn suggests.

"If I wake 'em up I won't have any brains. That's Bear"—he points to the dog—"and that's Mike from the solar-bike booth next door."

Quinn lifts an eyebrow. "Does Mike from the solar-bike booth know you're using his brain?"

"Nah, lured him in for a cup of tea and he fell asleep."

"You gave him sleepy tea?"

"In the name of science."

In the name of teenage boredom.

Strat gets to work, setting up a super-conductive, flexible alignment of electrodes. He uses a combination of silicon transistors and semiconductors that he has grown as crystals in vacuum chambers—good old-fashioned EEG sensors—and fixed to the scalps of his volunteers. The sensors harvest power from their cluster neurons and synapses within their brains. The volunteers' thoughts are now a part of the computer interface.

The setup is backyard Tech, but Quinn's convinced—he knows what he is doing.

"I like doing things with my hands," Strat says. "The downside is, you can only use your hands."

The point of the experiment is to move an object in space by channeling brain energy from several people to one person, who then transfers the charge to an inert object. Embarking on this type of experiment, people sometimes think they are going to move the Earth, but the best-case scenario is levitating a ball. Still, it's a bit like having a superpower for three seconds.

Strat shifts a pile of clothes off a chair and Quinn takes a seat. A strange, repulsive smell wafts around her, and she holds her nose.

"Yeah, it's pretty rekt," Strat says. "Bit of a station coming from Mike. Might be the sleepy tea—maybe it doesn't agree with him."

On the wall beside Quinn is a notice board. Written in bold black pen is a checklist with three items: "Start a band. Be successful. Have a good life." All the check boxes are empty.

"Workin' on it," Strat says as he adheres electrodes to her forehead.

"You need to put a tamper on the lead," Quinn says. "Controls the flow, moderates the energy uptake. Then you release it all at once. Do you have a dial?"

"Analogue," Strat confirms.

"And a ball; we need a ball."

Strat nods and sprints from the sleep zone. Moments later, he returns with the dial, the ball, and Anvil in tow.

Anvil gazes in disbelief at Strat's sleep zone. "You told me you'd cleaned up. Honestly I don't know how you live like this." She collects a climate suit from the floor, sniffs the fabric, and reels back. She grabs an armful of clothes and starts to delegate the items into piles of clean and dirty laundry.

"Leave it, I'll do later," Strat dismisses her. He turns to Quinn. "Ready?"

"Yeah. You know, if we used your sister's brain, we'd get more energy."

"Nah, there's crazy shit happenin' inside that head. It's forty-five subnormal. Goes off the scale and shuts everything down."

Quinn shakes her head. "It's not possible."

"Yeah. Come here," Strat calls to Anvil. "Show her."

Anvil shakes her head. She gets down on her knees and continues to sort the laundry.

Strat shrugs. He turns the dial up to five and focuses on the ball. The ball rises, hovers in the air, then pitches itself across the room and bounces off the wall.

"We did it, we did it!" Strat picks Quinn up and spins her around like a pregnant rag doll. They get caught in the leads and knock the mice from the table, which leaves them dangling in midair. A box of spare parts tumbles and crashes to the floor, knocking over a pile of trash.

Anvil looks up from the floor and glares at her brother. "Help me up."

Strat hauls his sister to her feet. "Rekt ankles and knees of a seventy-year-old," he explains.

"Worse when it rains," his sister says, leaning on him.

It hasn't rained in a decade.

Anvil points a finger at her brother. "Okay, I've had it with you. Honestly, if you don't clean up this space, I'll get really angry—and you know what happens when I get really angry?" she says with a sly grin.

Strat smiles—he is clearly not overly concerned—and gazes expectantly around the room, like he is waiting for something to happen.

A low hum rises and reverberates around the sleep zone.

Anvil's eyes narrow.

Quinn leans towards the computers on the desk; they are humming.

Anvil clenches her fists. The computers begin to vibrate.

Strat points to his sister's head. "Told you. Crazy shit."

There's a loud crack from the far corner of the room. Strat strides over and picks up an old module from the floor. He turns it over in his hands. "What the fuck? It's rekt. I was gonna restore it." He scowls at his sister.

Anvil releases her fists. "Next time, it will be a new machine. Clean your room."

Quinn stares at the girl. "How—how did you do that?"

"Do what?" Anvil smiles benignly.

"Make the machines vibrate? You charged them with energy."

Anvil shakes her head. "No idea what you're taking about." She turns away and starts to fill the empty trash container Strat and Quinn knocked over.

Mike from the solar-bike booth stirs; his head drops back, and he lets out a very long, inaudible mumble. Then he falls silent again.

The white dog also stirs; it opens its eyes, scans the room, and emits a low growl.

Anvil points a finger at the dog. "Shut that thing up. If it starts barking it won't stop. Worst bloody dog we've ever had."

Strat fondles the dog's ears. "No way—you're the best, aren't you Bear?" The dog rolls onto its back and Strat scratches its tummy. The dog sits up, barks twice, then turns in a circle, and Strat strokes its head. The dog sits back on its hind legs and begs, then it barks three times.

"Good dog. Down."

The dog sits and barks twice, then turns in a circle again.

It's a rote routine. "It's not a real . . ."

Quickly, Anvil catches Quinn's eye and jerks her head towards the door.

Oh. Strat doesn't know the dog is a bot.

Anvil draws Quinn out of the room and they head back towards the Tech Hub.

"Platinum, compactable, unlimited, branded, runs faster than a hypothetical tachyon," Anvil says.

"Good lordt, that's advanced programming. I had no idea bots were at that stage."

"Not the dog, the machine, the QM." From under the counter, she pulls a shiny slip of platinum Tech, which she hands to Quinn.

Quinn runs a finger over the slick surface of the QM. "You don't think you should tell him the truth?"

"We move around a lot. I made a decision—went down the AI route. Maybe it wasn't the best way to go, but it's too late now. Comes with a matt fiber cover and a one-year conditional manufacturer's warranty. And no discounts, so don't ask. Margins are short."

Quinn appraises the machine; she likes what she sees. There are different types of QMs, and this one uses quasiparticles on a 2D interface to achieve its processing power. She has used a machine like this before; it'll be perfect for retrieving and launching her climate model.

Anvil passes her the codes for a Coin transfer and Quinn verifies the transaction.

"For the record, I'm a Humanist," Anvil blurts. "If I had the chance again, we'd get a real dog."

"No judgment."

Someone raps on the front door of the Hub, and Quinn spies several clients loitering at the entrance; Anvil has a busy morning ahead. Quinn, meanwhile, has a still-intact brain and the item she came for. She slips the machine into its cover; she needs to head home and check on the meerkat—his mental state seems to deteriorate when he is alone.

The front door rattles and the impatient customers rap on the glass, eager to enter and part with their savings. New Tech is exhilarating and addictive.

Anvil is not in a hurry, though. She hasn't moved. She hasn't even glanced towards the customers. Her head is bowed, and she is staring at the benchtop.

The customers knock again, this time with more force. Anvil still doesn't move. She doesn't even blink. She appears to be . . . frozen.

Quinn pokes her gently in the arm, thinking perhaps she is lost in thought, or maybe has had a mild seizure that requires a firm nudge to bring her back to reality. But Anvil remains completely immobile, except for the blood draining from her face. Under her ochre dots, her skin is deathly pale.

Strat bursts excitedly into the Hub through the side door. He grins and points a finger at his sister, as if he is about to regale her with a witty remark; then he spies the customers at the front door. He pauses, his fingers curl into fists, and he also freezes.

Quinn is caught midway between two human pillars, like figurines frozen in their tracks by Medusa.

Finally, Anvil lifts her eyes to her brother, and they exchange a fraught glance.

"Go," Strat whispers.

Anvil shakes her head. "We're not doing this anymore."

"Go. This is the last time."

The customers—who, Quinn now notes, are three men wearing dark climate suits—rap on the door with the handle of a laser. "Are you about to be robbed?" she asks.

"More or less," Anvil says.

"Should we call the authorities, or—"

"No," Strat and Anvil shout at Quinn.

Strat turns to his sister. "Just go. Last time. We'll sort something out."

"Any weapons?" Quinn inquires. "Do you keep a laser under the counter?"

Anvil shakes her head, then turns to her brother. "What then, we move again? And again, and again? No more. It stops now."

"What about knives?" Quinn asks. "Knives are good. I prefer knives, I can hit just about anything with a blade."

"No weapons—we're Pacifists," Anvil snaps.

"I'm going. It ain't a drama." Strat strides towards the front door.

"Last time," Anvil mutters. She grabs Quinn's arm and hauls her through the side door. They head down the corridor, past Strat's sleep zone, and into a utility area. Along the far wall are rows of storage cupboards. Anvil opens one, then jerks a hook on the side wall. The back section of the cupboard opens, revealing a hidden doorway. A secret exit.

"Oh my lordt, you have a secret door." Quinn chuckles. "My father has a secret exit in his storage zone, too. Coincidence, huh?"

"It's not secret. It's just the back door."

Anvil climbs through the doorway and Quinn follows. They spill into a small laneway at the back of the building. It's the service and delivery entrance. Anvil points down the alley. "That's the way out," she says, and promptly turns and heads in the opposite direction.

Quinn watches Anvil disappear into an adjacent building, then turns and gazes at the not-so-secret door, which is now closed, with no sign of it being an entrance, and she thinks maybe the last ten minutes never happened. They didn't just flee through the back entrance of a TechHub, evading three ominous-looking men wearing dark climate suits who resemble spies.

What could those men possibly want with Strat? He is a teenager, a kid.

Kids are stupid. They are capable of doing terrible things. And right now, this is not her problem. There are more important issues for Quinn to worry about. Like the mining in Antarctica and finding her mother. Like Mori's anxiety, and the fact that he is capable of creating a race of Super AI-Pluses and extinguishing the entire human race. Like the baby growing inside her.

Strat is not her concern, she barely knows him. She has the QM, her business is done, and she should leave.

She takes a couple of steps down the alley—away from the TechHub and towards safety, freedom, and detached indifference. The problem is, seems like Strat's in trouble. It seems like those ominous spies in their dark climate suits are about to take him away against his will. And there's an artless naivety about that boy. He exudes goodness. She can't leave them, not like this. "What the fuck have they got themselves into?" she mutters.

She turns and follows Anvil into the adjacent building.

It's a bicycle repair shop. The walls are lined with sleek new bike frames, spare rims, and tires in multiple sizes. Disassembled vehicles lie along a long timber work bench that runs the length of the room. A dozen bikes waiting for repairs are stacked on the floor. Quinn has just entered the back office of the bike shop, and it smells, just a little, like Mike, the guy from Strat's experiment. There might be something else affecting his bowels besides sleepy tea.

There is no sign of Anvil. Quinn continues through the building into the main shop. Anvil is standing near the front window, gazing at the street outside. She is watching the ominous men escort Strat into an auto parked at the curb. One of the men has Strat's fluffy white dog under his arm.

"Hey, you okay?" Quinn asks.

Anvil doesn't reply. She is fixated on the scene outside.

A crackling sound resonates, and Anvil's dark hair begins to stand on end. Quinn scans the room, unable to detect the source of the noise. She steps towards Anvil, leans in and listens, but the sound is not coming from the girl.

The noise gains momentum. It takes on the shrill tone of splitting graphene.

Outside, the vehicle with Strat inside pulls away.

Spidery cracks creep across the glass of the shop's front window, and the pane begins to shudder.

Anvil begins to shake. The screeching echoes around the room.

Quinn covers her ears. The glass in the front window caves and the splinters fall to the floor.

Alarmed, Quinn turns to Anvil. The girl is now shaking and panting like a wild animal. Her eyes are bulging; beads of sweat run down her forehead. “I, I can’t, I can’t breathe, I’m rekt. Rekt,” she stammers.

“I don’t underst—”

“No air.” Anvil stumbles to the floor and pukes.

Quinn drops to her knees and pulls Anvil’s hair back. “Oh good lordt, are you okay?”

“Panic attack.” Anvil wipes her mouth. “You’re supposed to get me a bag.”

“Why a bag?” Quinn helps Anvil to her feet.

“I was hyperventilating. It regulates the air.”

“Might also cause a pulmonary embolism. Do you need a drink? I’ll get you some water.”

“I don’t want water. What type of doctor are you, anyway?” Anvil sways again, and Quinn slings her arm around the girl to steady her.

“I’m not a doctor.”

“You said you were a doctor.”

“No. I said I was a scientist.”

“Wevs.” Anvil stares into Quinn’s eyes. “You can see me, can’t you? You know who I am?”

Quinn points to the adjoining wall of the TechHub. “I was just in there. You sold me the QM. Why would I not know who you are?”

“Because I’m an illusion, a shadow. To the uninitiated, these dots on my face are a disguise. They trick you, alter your perception of how I look, so you don’t recognize me the second or third time you see me. The marks protect me.”

“From what?’

“Fuckwits.”

Anvil licks a finger and rubs the dots on her forehead, leaving a trail of colored smudge down her nose. “Not permanent,” she says. “It’s an optical illusion, a combination of all eight colors in the rainbow.”

“There are only seven colors—”

“Wevs. The color layers trick FaceNet, so I can’t be detected. Temporarily hacks the eye-to-brain connection, causes the brain to malfunction, so you can’t see my physical features. Makes me unrecognizable. I looked it up on NIoT.”

“Isn’t FaceNet illegal?”

Anvil nods. “Precaution; no one can be trusted.”

“Well, it didn’t work on me. I know who you are.”

“Yeah, maybe it doesn’t work on everyone.”

Maybe it doesn’t work on anyone.

Twelve

The ultimate crime against humanity.

QUINN AND ANVIL HEAD outside into the alleyway. They find a shady spot under a makeshift awning and sit down, their backs against the masonry surface of the building; the material is cool against Quinn's skin.

She rubs her temples as she grapples with the notion that Strat was essentially just kidnapped by men dressed like spies. It's the mid-twenty-first century, you can't kidnap people in broad daylight. At least not in Hobart. What has he done? What could they possibly want with him?

Anvil hugs her knees to her chest. "There are three men, always the same three men," she begins. "I don't know much about 'em. They come every week for Strat. It's called human harvesting. You heard of it?"

Quinn shakes her head.

"We have a pure bloodline. Our physiology is ancient—a window to the past, to a time before modern diseases. For centuries, our tribe lived with animals. We slept with our dogs and cattle and vermin and any other warm living thing. It affected our microbiota. We've got some weird shit breeding in our gut, a huge range of bacteria. Some unique species. Did you know we're only 50 percent human, and the rest of us is bacteria and fungi?"

Quinn nods.

"Well, people want the fungi we've got. They want some of our 50 percent nonhuman shit. Our blood is special. It's antibiotic clean. Strat's never had a virus or a cold. These people harvest it and use it in experiments for immunizations and vaccines. They're after a cure for FF. Rumor is, it's evolved again. Another mutation."

"Not a rumor. My friend in CyberSleep—she has it pretty bad."

Anvil looks down. "Soz."

"Stealing someone's blood—that's like taking their life force, the ultimate crime against humanity. Who do these people think they are?"

Anvil shrugs.

"I wonder where they take him," Quinn muses.

"I have a handle on Strat; I know where he is."

Quinn raises an eyebrow. Placing a tracker on someone is illegal. Violation of personal privacy is prohibited. After decades of personal surveillance and data harvesting from online widgets, privacy is a fundamental right.

"Tracking someone's movements, even if it is your bother, is illegal."

Anvil shrugs—she doesn't care. "They keep him at the MedQuarter. They want him alive 'cause harvesting creates an income. But Strat's not coping. This is the second time this week they've taken him. He collapsed when he got home this last time. Stayed in bed for three days."

Quinn has a vision of Strat lying in his unmade bed, in his messy room out the back of the TechHub, and never waking up.

"If something happens to him, I'll be left with that bloody dog. It's a shit of a thing, impossible to train."

"Yeah, but it's not—"

"Not real? I know, but it's third gen now, memory stored in its DNA. It's part of the family."

"It doesn't have DNA."

"Wevs. You know what I mean?"

"Let's report it. I'll come with you. It doesn't matter if you're illegal, you have rights. You'll be protected."

Anvil leans closer and whispers, "Everyone is corrupt. There's not an honest prick left in the world. Except for Strat. He never lies, and he's never done anything bad."

Quinn knits her fingers together. "Actually, there are thousands, maybe hundreds of thousand, maybe even millions of honest people in the world."

"You're wrong. Name another person who's never lied."

Quinn considers her options. Tig, despite his problematic tendency to not take his Meds, when clearly he should be on them all the time, is a good person. He lists his profession as "people smuggler," and in the mid-twenty-first century, that is a very noble line of work. Helping refugees is an honorable way to live. Of course, he forgot to mention he was the king of an ancient culture (albeit a figurehead title with small "k") when she first met him, and that is a fairly significant omission—an important detail a partner should know about. And he is evasive about many other things. There are conversations about his past that they still haven't had, and she has just found out about his issue with time. She sighs and rubs her forehead. There's so much he is yet to share with her, and the reality of this is disheartening. Perhaps they should have spent last night talking instead of having sex.

Anvil gives her a smug smile; she is waiting for an answer. Quinn clears her head—she will deal with Tig's elusive persona later—and considers her best friend, Jin. She is a good person, one of the most honest and trustworthy people on the planet. However, her moral code is a bit skewed when it comes to robots; she has a deep, emotional attachment to AIs that sometimes clouds her judgment. She was raised by an AI called Salt, so it's not her fault, but she did neglect to tell Quinn that Mori has the ability to create a race of Super AI-Plus robots. That's a serious omission. Jin can't be considered entirely truthful.

Next, she considers Matt, but she knows her father will happily misrepresent facts to win an argument. Lise, meanwhile, is evasive; she neglected to inform Quinn about her affair with Maim Quate. Her ex-fiancé, Mori Eco, is a lying piece of shit. Considering all this, she feels slightly better about Tig's vagueness; perhaps he fits into the standard honesty profile of the human race.

"We don't have all day," says Anvil.

"Okay. You have a point. Honesty, total honesty, doesn't seem to be a highly valued trait in humans. Look, I know I've only just met you, but if you want to go get Strat, I'll come with you. I mean, it's not civil war, we're not up against delusional coup leaders or HOTRODs—he's in the MedQuarter in Hobart, one of the most benign cities on the planet. It can't be that hard to smuggle someone out of there. Can it?"

Anvil shrugs. "I'm up for it. But I can't shoot anyone. I'm a Pacifist. I signed the pledge after the War, and it's for life. I refuse to harm any living thing."

"I understand. Until a few months ago, I was a Pacifist myself. Can you get your hands on a knife?"

Anvil nods. She jumps up and slips back through the concealed door.

Using the brick wall as a brace, Quinn struggles to her feet. She notes there is no sign of a door handle or even a door on the wall that Anvil just went through. *It's definitely a secret door. She lied. Everyone lies.*

A few minutes later, Anvil reemerges holding an assortment of kitchen utensils, including two knives, a pair of kitchen shears, a two-pronged fork, and a meat tenderizer.

Quinn slips both knives and the kitchen shears into her backpack.

"It's a plan, then," Anvil says. "I can't hurt anyone, but I know Tech—I mean, I really know Tech, if you know what I mean. I can get in and out of any system." She pauses. "Sorry, but can you actually hit anything with a knife? 'Cause you don't look like someone who can hit . . . anything." She looks Quinn over, taking in her pleated yellow dress.

Quinn collects the knives and shears from her backpack. "Demonstration. Hold this." She hands the pack to Anvil.

Anvil examines the pack. "This looks like a space-age turtle shell."

"Military issue. Contents can't be scanned."

Quinn asks Anvil to move to one side, then flings the shears—and immediately after the shears, the knives—towards the cladded wall of the building. The knives pin the shears—a blade through each of the curved handles—to the wall.

Anvil's mouth drops open. "Are you a . . . robot scientist?"

Quinn waddles towards the wall and, with some difficulty, retrieves the knives. "No. But I am a crack shot. Last year I fell out of the sky, now I have anarchic syndrome. My hand-eye coordination on my left side is . . ." She pauses, unsure how to describe the cohesive connection between her physical actions and her conscious thoughts. "Well, I can hit anything, even without looking. Before the accident, I had a 2 percent chance of hitting anything."

"And now you have, like, a 102 percent chance?"

"Something like that."

Before they embark on their rescue mission, Quinn has a request. She needs a handle for Mori, a tracker, so she can keep tabs on him, in case he ever decides to activate his Super AI-Plus powers.

Anvil offers the perfect device; it's discreet and untraceable, has an unlimited operative power drive, and will last forever. "Expensive, yes. But forever is a long time," she says, and charges Quinn full price. "No markdowns, no discounts. Margins are short."

Thirteen

Epic Road Rage.

Outside the TechHub, Quinn and Anvil hail an AV. The vehicle pulls up at the curbside. It's another classic capsule build with a front end that resembles a mouse, but this one is yellow, a similar shade to Quinn's dress.

Inside, Quinn and Anvil sit next to each other on the modular seats. The doors close, and then they lock. Anvil casts a concerned glance at Quinn; it's not common protocol for the doors to lock without instruction.

There is a short pause, then AV says, "Please explain? Was there something wrong with the service? Was four point seven too much to ask?"

It's Vera.

Quinn frowns. "You changed color."

"Yes. I have a chromatic coating. I cloned your dress. I do it all the time. People think it's magic, but it's not magic, it's science."

"She's a scientist." Anvil nods towards Quinn.

"Was a four point seven too high for a scientist?"

"You said anything above a four point five would be fine. But hey, this time you can have a four point nine, if that's what you want."

"Where to?" Vera asks.

"MedQuarter, fast," Anvil says.

"Are you sick?"

"No. We're on a rescue mission. What mode are you in?"

"City mapping."

"We need something faster, maybe . . . Epic Road Rage." Anvil turns to Quinn. "Have you ever done this? It's GFS. Supposed to simulate a traditional driver experience, like driving with your grandad—or worse!"

The AV swerves out of the leisurely we'll-get-there-when-we-get-there lane and into the get-the-fuck-out-of-my-way lane and starts charging through the busy morning traffic like it's on rails. It inches up behind a black TeslaMk12 and hovers a meter from the other vehicle's bumper. "Come on, we don't have all day. Either put the foot down or get out of my way," Vera snaps. She beeps her horn. The Tesla pulls aside. Vera passes, only to be passed by a little red ApexAuto that swerves in front of her, then slows down. Vera is boxed in.

"That's it, overtake me and put the brakes on." Vera sidles up behind the Apex. "Is it just me, or is the road filled with idiots today?"

"It's just you," Quinn says. "Aren't you a bit close?"

"Safety is a distance algorithm. They stay away from me, and I stay away from them. I'd appreciate you not telling me how to drive. I have eyes on the road technology, lane-keeping assist, intelligent speed assist, automatic breaking, *and* event-data black-box surveillance." Vera blares her horn.

"Then why don't I feel safe?" Quinn whispers.

"I'm a moral machine. The ethics of over eighty million people is coded into my programing. You're eleven times less likely to be involved in an accident when you're in an AV, and—oh no!"

Quinn grips her armrest. "What?"

"Cyclists." Ahead, a procession of cyclists blocks the road. "I hate cyclists." Vera speeds up, then pulls back. "I count twelve, taking up three lanes, when they can easily fit into one." Again, Vera speeds up, then pulls back.

Quinn holds the bridge of her nose.

Vera takes a tight arc around the cyclists and speeds ahead—then comes to an abrupt halt, right in the middle of the get-the-fuck-out-of-my-way lane.

Quinn and Anvil share a concerned glance. They look out the window. All the AVs have stopped. Not a single vehicle on the road is moving. The city traffic is at a standstill; even the hoverboards on the footpath have come to a halt. Drivers are frowning, checking ignitions, and passengers are scratching their heads.

"A virus? They've all been hacked?" Anvil suggests.

Quinn frowns. "Unlikely."

"Maybe NIoT's out," she says.

They tilt their heads towards the roof of the AV, visualizing the vast network of satellites in orbit around the planet.

Vera shudders. Her engines re-engage. She continues down the speedway, oblivious to the breakdown. The other vehicles on the road are also running again.

"Just a glitch," Anvil says dismissively.

"Pick a lane, you idiot, come on. Pick. A. Lane." Vera beeps her horn three times in quick succession.

"City mapping," Quinn says. "Right now, city mapping." The aggressive driving has her on edge; if the trip continues like this, she will be too anxious to rescue anyone.

Vera calmly merges back into the leisurely, we'll-get-there-when-we-get-there lane.

Quinn breathes. She settles back in her seat and pats her baby bump. "Okay, we need a plan. How tall is Strat?"

"About six four."

"How are we going to smuggle a two-meter-tall bloodless kid out of a guarded room?"

"On the upside, he'll be lighter without his blood."

"Okay, Plan A: He's conscious. He walks himself out of the building. But we have to find him first."

"Right—I'm on it. I, uh . . . need to borrow the QM." Anvil reaches for Quinn's backpack, which is on Quinn's lap. Quinn is reluctant to let go of the bag—she paid a lot of Coin for the QM, and she wants to be the first to use it—but with a firm tug, Anvil plucks the pack from Quinn's grasp. Then she slides out the new machine.

In sleep mode, the QM has a matte finish, but when Anvil activates it, the surface radiates bioluminescence and glows silver. Anvil launches the tracker she has on Strat, and they pinpoint his position in the MedQuarter; he is in a ward on level eight. She sets up a secure two-way Comms between Quinn and herself—point-to-point ultrasound whisper technology that uses an algorithm to code voiceprints. Finally, she logs into the MedQuarter reservation system and scans the list of specialists. "You need an appointment. Constipation, boredom syndrome, climate depression?"

"Pregnancy," Quinn suggests.

Anvil shakes her head. "Too hard. With BS or climate depression, there's no—"

"I'm actually pregnant."

Anvil's eyes drop to Quinn's stomach. "Are you serious?"

Quinn nods.

"You don't look pregnant. Are you sure? Because you look . . . tiny. You could fit two of you into one of me." Anvil lines herself up against Quinn. "Look, two of you could fit easily, and I'm not pregnant."

Quinn flattens the pleats in her dress around her stomach. "It's the dress. It's deceiving."

"Really? Then how pregnant are you? Did you do a test? Like, it's confirmed and everything?"

"About seven months. Confirmed and everything."

"Okay. We need a baby doctor. Searching . . . fecal . . . doctors."

"I think the word you're looking for is *fetal*."

"You sure?"

"Yes. Try obstetrics."

"I don't know how to spell that. I'm going with boredom syndrome."

Fourteen
I've killed his dog.

With an appointment for BS, Quinn enters the MedQuarter unhindered; her military pack reveals nothing about its contents, and the full-body scan she undergoes on her way through security indicates she has no weapons.

At reception, a weary-looking attendant ogles Quinn's outfit. "Nice dress," she says and points down the corridor. "Counseling services are on level three. The lift is on your left."

Quinn heads down the corridor, then sidesteps her allotted lift, walks across the hall, and enters the lift for level eight.

Anvil initiates the Comms. "When the door opens, exit left, walk twelve paces, turn right, and walk thirty paces down the corridor. Strat's ward is fourth on the right. He's the only patient."

Reassured, Quinn smiles to herself. The memory of the frantic AV ride has faded, and she has a good feeling about their plan. It's mid-morning, the MedQuarter is quiet, and the ambiance in this building is pleasant and nonthreatening. There is no doubt they are doing the right thing. Strat is being held against his will. The law is on their side. They have a QM that allows Anvil full access to the hospital wing—and the girl obviously knows what she is doing. It's a good plan.

Quinn follows Anvil's instructions and heads down the corridor.

After twenty paces, she comes face to face with a door—the entrance to another ward.

She looks behind her. This is the right way—she followed the directions. She scratches the side of her nose. "Are you sure about this?"

"Soz. I got my left and right confused, happens sometimes. Go back to the lift. Exit right, not left, then turn left and take thirty steps, Strat's door is fourth on the left. Soz."

Quinn returns to the skylift. She tells herself it could happen to anyone. This time she exits right, walks thirty paces down the corridor, and arrives at the fourth door on the left.

"There's a guard inside. He sits in a chair on the . . . on the right. He never closes his eyes, never yawns or squints or sniffs. He just sits there, for six hours, staring at the end of the bed. Imagine if that was your job, doing that for a living, sitting on a chair all day. I know it's a job, but it's—"

"It's a robot. I'm going in." Quinn plucks a knife from her backpack. She opens the door and steps inside.

The ward is large, partitioned into cubicles. Strat is in the first cubical, a small room with a hospital bed, a few scattered chairs, and a private bathing area. There is no sign of the guard.

The boy is on the bed, comatose. There is a sack of blood clipped to his arm, and the small white dog is curled up next him. It lifts its head and growls at her. *What was its name? Pola? No. Panda. They called it Panda.*

"Hello, Panda," she coos. "Good dog. Good Panda."

The dog growls again.

"Who's a good boy? Who's a good Panda?"

"It's a girl, and her name is Bear," Anvil whispers.

The dog snaps at Quinn. Instinctively she recoils and her left hand flings the knife. It pierces the dog straight between the eyes. The dog collapses.

Oh shit. Quinn pokes it with her finger. Nothing. She picks it up and shakes it. There is no response. It's dead. *Good lordt, I've killed his dog.*

She rubs her forehead; it's the second headache she has had today. She wonders if the dog had a pain sensor, which is the norm for these AI pets. Embedding sensors that monitor impact aids the illusion of realness and ups the client satisfaction. She pulls the knife from its head and checks the blade for blood. It's clean. It's a robot, of course it's clean. She still feels bad.

Strat opens his eyes; he looks pallid and twice his age.

"Hey." Quinn touches his arm. "Are you okay? I'm your rescue team. Anvil's waiting for us in an AV."

"GFS. I've been planning this for months." He swings his legs off the bed.

They hear footsteps and muffled voices; someone is coming through the ward towards them.

Quinn's heart pounds. She places a finger to her lips. Strat understands. He lies back on the bed and closes his eyes, feigning sleep or death. She slips into the bathing zone, behind an aerogel divide. She touches the material, switches it to opaque. She can see out, but she is obscured from view.

A dark-haired male in a beige climate suit enters the room and sits in the chair by the door; it's the missing robot guard.

Quinn steps out from behind the screen. She flicks the knife at the robot guard, and it pierces the robot's eye.

The robot-guard screams; it falls to the ground clutching its injured eye. Quinn grabs the second knife, is about to throw it—but then she pauses. The robot guard seems to be in pain, real pain. That's normal for these types of machines—like the dog, built with pain sensors. But blood, real blood, is dripping from its eye socket. It's not a robot. It's a human. A human guard.

"Oh fuck," Quinn says. "You're alive, aren't you?"

The guard moans and writhes on the floor. Quinn sees his laser on the floor next to him and quickly collects the weapon.

"I'm so sorry, I really am," she says. "If I knew you were human, I never would have hit you in the eye. I would have gone for your hand. Or maybe your arm—pinned you to the chair. But never in the eye."

He moans. The man is in real pain, a lot of real pain.

The laser in Quinn's hand has a sliding scale of destruction. She sets it to stun and shoots the guard. His body relaxes, and his head rolls back.

She turns to Strat, who is awake and resting on his elbow. "I thought he was a robot," she says.

"Nope, that's Lukas."

"He'll be okay, there are some terrific bionic eyes on the market. Made from nanowires, huge wavelengths. He'll be able to see more colors, maybe even see in the dark."

"Let's hope he has a health plan." Strat swings his legs off the bed. He tucks the dead dog under his arm, stands up, sways sideways, and head butts the wall.

Quinn wrestles him back to the bed. "Take it easy. What's the plan?"

"We go out the window. It's a short leap onto the balcony next door, then there's a pipe that goes all the way to the ground."

"We're eight stories up."

He sees her concern. "It's cool. Sounds hard, but it ain't."

Quinn moves to the window. The gap between the buildings is over three meters.

Strat joins her. "We vault this balcony and then the next two, see?" He points at a building in the distance. "Then, see that pipe, we *roulard* to that ledge, then it's a bit of a *saut de chat*"—he glances at her, then checks himself—"cat's jump . . . it's a cat's jump. We land on that roof, there, the green one. Then alive, real grass and a quick *saut de front*, we drop onto that thing."

"What thing?"

He points to a streetlight. "That tall thing."

"The streetlight," she offers.

"Yeah. Then *planche*, release to the ground."

She glances from Strat, to the devised route, then back at Strat. "Is that . . . French?"

"It's parkour," he confirms.

"We're eight stories up, and I'm pregnant."

He frowns, not comprehending.

"I can't jump that far. What's your Plan B?"

He shakes his head. There is only one plan.

"Okay. We need reinforcements."

Lise keeps a squadron of swarmbots—a lively hive of interconnected, cooperative mini drones. They were a gift from a university faculty, in honor of her latest book, *On Nothingness*. The hive is third generation, so pre-loved, a hand-me-down from the robotics lab, which was upgrading to a more progressive, intuitive hive. Initially, Lise thought she'd never use them, but they've come in very handy. They collect items from the high shelves in the storage area. They are perfect for heavy lifting and keen workers on the roof garden.

The swarm utilizes solar energy to generate an electromagnetic field, which excites air and argon particles into a plasma position, and this unites the bots, ensuring they work as a team; their decision-making is intuitive. Individually, they can't do much, but there's power in numbers; connect fifty and they will lift two hundred kilos.

On the Comms, Quinn feeds Anvil the codes to the swarm.

Fifteen

She flipped a blue pill.

THE SWARMBOTS COLLECT STRAT from the MedQuarter and deliver him to the rooftop at Lise's apartment. Quinn and Anvil find him lying in an overgrown garden bed filled with green chard. He is pallid from blood loss, almost white, and he resembles an oversized white radish in the neglected garden. The fluffy white dog is still under his arm, and it's still dead.

Anvil and Quinn rouse Strat. They help him inside and settle him on the sofa.

"I need food," says Strat. "I need to eat."

"Okay, there's food in the—"

"Six hours, thirty-two minutes, and eleven seconds," says Mori. His voice is coming from under the sofa.

Anvil and Strat stare at Quinn.

"Give me a minute." She gets on her hands and knees and peers under the sofa. Mori is curled into a tight ball. "I know, I'm late, and I'm sorry. I got caught up. But I brought new people for you to meet. Out you come. Come on."

Mori uncoils himself and crawls out.

Using the sofa as a brace, Quinn gets to her feet. "This is Strat, and this is his sister, Anvil."

"Cute," says Anvil. "Is it real?"

Mori turns expectantly to Quinn and waits for her reply.

Quinn rubs her forehead. This is not a question she wants to answer right now; Mori is not an organic being, but he is alive, and she constantly struggles to categorize him. Six months ago, she would have said, without hesitation, that he was a robot. Now her resolve is waning. She has grown attached to him, and she doesn't want to aggravate his anxiety.

She clears her throat. "Well, I mean, how do we know what's real and what's not? Feelings and senses, these are just electrical signal interpreted by the brain. I mean, look at this table."

They consider the table.

"Does it really exist? Does anything really exist without our active participation?"

Strat turns to his sister. "She flipped a blue pill."

Mori jumps onto the table. "If a tree falls in the forest and no one is there to hear it, does it make a sound?"

Anvil touches Mori's arm. "Soft," she confirms. "Is the blue pill the reality pill or the rabbit hole pill? I can never remember. And animals would hear the tree fall."

"Pop the blue pill, you believe whatever you want. The red pill—that's the truth. That's reality. You see how deep the rabbit hole goes. The Matrix. Fucking love that film. And yeah, like, animals have ears, don't they?" Strat checks out Mori's ears. "So, they'll hear it fall?"

"Sound is a vibration transmitted as waves through the instrument of the ear," he says. "If there are no ears, there can be no sound." Mori offers his paw to Strat and Anvil. They shake hands.

"I really need to eat." Strat stumbles across the room towards the food prep and sits at the bench. His legs start to jiggle.

"He can't function till he eats. Okay if I fix us something?" Anvil follows her brother into the food prep and opens the storage cupboard. "Lordt. We have a station."

"A what?" Quinn asks.

"A station, a little situation. There's nothing here. We're going to starve."

Quinn knows Tig stocked the cupboards yesterday. "Look harder."

Anvil piles half a dozen storage containers onto the bench.

"Noob jabbed me with FF, the third time." Strat opens a container and funnels nuts into his mouth. "But I'm, like, naturally immune, that's what Forty-five said." He turns to Quinn. "That's what we call him—Forty-five, subnormal. I've got natural immunity. GFS."

"Means I'll also be immune," Anvil grins. "Flyke. We could sell our bodies to science." She scoops a handful of dried berries into her mouth. "These are stale." She tips the berries into the waste.

"Dik," Strat says.

"Please don't call your sister a dick," Quinn says.

Anvil turns to Quinn. "D-I-K, it means, don't know."

"The berries are not stale," Andrea says.

"You don't know about being immune," Strat says. "Not a hundred percent for sure."

"Chances are." Anvil passes the remaining berries to her brother. "Taste these."

He tips the pile from her hand into his mouth and scoffs the lot. "Rekt," he confirms.

"Semi-dried," says Andrea.

"Ah, okay, then they're not stale." Anvil salvages the last of the berries from the waste and gives them to Strat.

"I'm just saying, dik—maybe, maybe not. It ain't confirmed."

"But the probability is—"

"Stop!" Quinn yells. "Everyone please . . . stop talking."

The siblings freeze.

"One percent of the population are immune. Now, this is what's going to happen." Quinn points at Strat. "There's food, you need to look harder. Find something to eat—order more if you want—then you need to rest."

"Idgt," he says.

"What did you just say?"

"I don't get tired."

"I don't care. You've lost a lot of blood. You need to rest." Quinn turns to Anvil. "Please, if you don't mind, I need you to play with the meerkat for an hour or so."

"Snatched."

Quinn stares at Anvil, waiting for her to clarify.

"All good." Anvil grins.

"Okay, thank you. And, please, no more talking in abbreviations, or code, or whatever it is you're doing. At least not around me. What's wrong with English, normal English?" *I sound like I'm eighty.* "I'll be in my sleep zone. I have important scientific data to analyze. After Strat's rested, and eaten, we'll discuss your options."

Before Quinn leaves, she calls Mori over. She sits down, and he climbs up on her lap. "Red pill," she says showing him the tracker. "I need you to swallow this."

She hands him the device, and he downs the pill like a dose of reality.

***

Mori lies flat on his tummy on the floor, his legs and forearms splayed out. Anvil sits beside him and crosses her legs.

"We are going to build a city," Mori explains. "A city with tree-scrapers and a landing pad for drones. It will have arches and towers that reach far into the sky." He carefully selects his blocks, a variety of different sizes and shapes, and begins to methodically plan and build his tower.

Anvil watches him stack, scaffold, and arch his way into the sky. Then she collects handfuls of random blocks and sorts them into piles of similar colors.

Mori crowns his first tower with a wind turbine, then begins a new construction. “I have a scanner,” he says. “I can use it to read people. The new people I meet.”

“New people are called noobs,” Anvil says.

“Noobs.” He nods. “I know the noobs’ heartbeats and their blood pressure. I can read the noobs’ emotional state. The noobs’ internal states express how they feel. I know not to engage with noobs when they are angry. How are you feeling?”

Anvil makes a row of six structures, each one a different color. “I’m not angry,” she says. “Well, I was before, when they took Strat away and sucked out his blood. But I’m not now.”

“What are you making?” Mori asks.

“I’m done,” she says. “I’ve made a whole street of treescrapers. Each one is a different color, so you can tell them all apart.”

Mori pauses. He considers her row of rudimentary structures. Then he compares the intricate design of his treescraper. “Mine is better.”

She shrugs. “Yeah, it’s flyke.” She dives back into the box of blocks for more building material and pulls out a wooden spinning top. She aims it towards her street of towers and flicks it. Like a pin in a bowling alley, the top knocks over the first tower. “Snatched.”

“You are not angry, but there is agitation inside you,” Mori says. “Inside your cells.”

“Yeah. It’s my superpower. Mum had it and our nan, Noonah, she had it real bad. But I got it worse than anyone. It’s a supernatural gift from our Ancestral Gods.”

“Actually, it is electricity. You are generating large amounts of energy inside your cells.”

“Go on.”

“Human bodies are full of electrical signals and energy. Humans need it to process bodily functions. Humans are just computers in a complex form. Your lungs take in oxygen, and the heart takes in blood, and they regulate the body. It is all a process.”

"Yeah, obvious. Back to the electricity."

"Your cells have masses of protons shifting from one side of the membrane to the other. This creates an electrical volt. It is very small, but it is happening over a large field. The difference in concentration has enormous electrical potential. You are positively charged. You are a human battery."

Anvil finds another spinning top in the box of blocks. She sends it across the floor. It hits the second tower in her row and the blocks topple. "Snatched!" The tower falls onto the one beside it, causing a chain reaction; the second tower falls into the third, the third falls onto the fourth. Mori's treescraper is at the end of the row and Anvil's last tower tumbles straight into it. The treescraper collapses.

"Oops, soz." Anvil passes Mori another wooden top. "Here, try this—heaps of fun."

"Sometimes, when she's really pissed, she's like a lightning bolt," Strat says from the food prep.

"It's true." Anvil lowers her voice. "I once killed someone. I killed them with my mind." She points to her forehead. "I wished he was dead and then he died."

"It was a month later," Strat says. "He got hit by a kid on a hoverboard, fell over, and hit his head. He died of a brain hemorrhage, not evil thoughts."

"Humans are just machines," says Mori.

"You're so right," Strat says. He reaches for a glass and fills it with water, then brings it to his sister. "Watch this."

Anvil takes the glass. After a few seconds, steam begins to rise. "Ouch, ouch, ouch." She places the glass on the floor. The water boils and overflows, leaving a puddle on the floor.

"A machine that can boil water," Mori says.

Sixteen

This is a big, big problem.

DRIVEN BY QUANTUM MECHANICS, the particles inside Quinn's new QM exist in multiple states at the same time, enabling millions of outcomes to happen simultaneously. It is the only device capable of launching her climate model, the G12. Several months ago, Quinn buried the climate model deep in the depths of the SpinnerNet—a dark place that exists in the subterranean levels below NIoT. The SpinnerNet is the perfect place to hide precious things. But retrieving the G12 is risky. Quinn must enter and exit before she is detected—before the infectors, trojans, and hackers realize she has dropped in for a visit. Caught, and the likelihood of infection is certain—and the consequences to her personal security and identity will be costly. It can take years to untangle the mess of an identity-hacking campaign. It can leave you jobless, homeless, and friendless.

She rubs her hands together nervously. She stretches her fingers back and forth; she knows how to do this. First, she launches a distraction: two open diversion inquiries, designed to draw any adversaries away from her real purpose. Then, she dispatches an encoded search tool. Her left hand takes over and her fingertips patter across the face of the machine. She sends out her decoy inquiries, locates the G12, plucks it out, and closes the SpinnerNet. She breathes.

Then she launches the G12.

A small sapphire sphere—a holographic vision of the Earth—appears over the QM. She expands the holo to a meter wide and spins the blue, cloudless planet with one finger. The South Pole comes into view, and she pauses the holo over Antarctica—the wet world where the clouds congregate, where it rains all day, every day.

Before Lise disappeared, she mentioned a company called Shun Mantra. She said the Tech company eMpower was investing in Shun Mantra and losing Coin. eMpower, owned by Niels Eco, was also interested in Antarctica. When Quinn's friend Jin worked for eMpower, she sent Quinn a Special Project file. It showed survey maps of the region: Queen Maud Land, Enderby Land, and the Weddell Sea.

The same eMpower file held other maps of less familiar places with exotic names like Nicobar, Selk, and Mystis. These maps also had sites named after the mythical gods of rain—Bacab, Hobal, Tishtrya, and Kalseru—mountains called Moria, Mithrim, and Doom, and small hills called Gandalf, Bilbo, and Arwen.

These were maps of Titan. Jin sent Quinn maps of Titan in the same Special Project file as Antarctica. *What does eMpower want with Titan, and what's the connection to Shun Mantra and Antarctica?*

A surface scan of the region shows two massive sinkholes terraced into the Antarctic ice.

Mining. The mine shaft descends under the eastern ice sheets. Quinn traces the shaft as it descends deeper into the Earth's crust, through the mantle, before finally stopping at the planet's core. At the end, she finds a massive jet stream of molten iron pressing against the South Pole.

"What the fuck?" She runs the search again.

The results are the same. Under Antarctica is a cylinder of molten iron, moving around the inner solid iron core. A giant electromagnet rammed up against the South Pole.

She sits back in her chair and considers the blue holo vision of

Earth. “Mess around with the planet’s core, you weaken the Earth’s magnetic field.”

The magnetic field shields the planet from solar winds and radiation. The origins of this lie deep inside the planet, within the magma and molten iron.

“It’s connected to the solar flares.” Quinn shakes her head. “This is a big, big problem.”

“This is flyke.” Strat stands in the doorway. “South Pole’s sus, though. It’s off course.” He points to a spot several thousand kilometers east of Antarctica. “It’s over here.” He shoots Quinn a grin. “If I’m right, I get the beaver as a slave for a day. Twenty-four hours.”

She checks the position of the magnetic South Pole and Strat’s prediction is spot-on. “It’s not a beaver—it’s a meerkat. Tell me, how did you know about the South Pole?”

“I’m kinda like a human compass. Magnetic synesthesia. I see grid lines.”

“Grid lines, like longitude and latitude?”

“Yeah. I got tested. I got this weird shit in my genes. It stopped my synapse-brain-pruning, so my visual perception and my space-time are kind of connected.” He shrugs. “Slave for half a day—a full twelve hours—and I get to take it outside.”

“That’s not happening.”

“Okay. North Pole also moved. If I show you . . .”

“No.”

Seventeen

Change the name of this planet from Earth to Water.

THE EMPOWER HEADQUARTERS IN Styx includes a rooftop complex with an undulating nine-hole golf course. Nine par-4 holes are possible, as three are virtual and the remaining six fold back into the roofline of the building, which cuts across the façade and triples the amount of surface area.

Niels skips the three virtual holes—he can do that anywhere—and is on his second round of the six physical greens. He wears black satin pants printed with large white flowers, and he has hired an intuitive, driverless buggy and a service drone for the afternoon. The drone's task is to fetch refreshments, but today it's redundant because Niels doesn't partake in normal foodstuffs. He hired it because everyone else had one, and he wanted to blend into the golfing crowd.

The final hole is his favorite—a tricky layover shot—but he is in a queue. It's late afternoon. The course is crowded. He can't move forward until he receives a signal. His wait-time is fifteen minutes.

Niels thought a round of golf might serve as a distraction, but he has had an appalling round. He can't get the vision of Quinn Buyers out of his head: The way she stared at him, then narrowed her eyes. The way she touched her stomach . . . her *pregnant* stomach. The thought of his brother, Mori, as the father of Quinn's child is profoundly disturbing.

Mori is not qualified to be a father. Niels wonders if that's the reason Quinn called off their wedding. If so, he admires her. The thought of coparenting with Mori would put anyone off; parenthood requires a certain set of skills he clearly doesn't have.

Niels is amazed that anyone can become a parent; the idea doesn't seem morally right to him—letting the population breed, just because they can. People should be tested before they're allowed to raise children. He thinks he might raise the notion of . . . *parental potential*, yes, that's what he'll call it—Parental Potential—with Maim, now that he has her ear. She could bring it to the legislative council for him.

Niels moves ahead two spaces in the golf queue. His wait time is now eight minutes.

A holo request rises from his Band—a virtual board meeting with a handful of Shun Mantra's members is about to start. Niels called the meeting thinking his round of golf would be over by now, and he needs to attend.

He spies a shaded seat under a nearby tree, a purple-flowering cape myrtle. The molting petals cast a mauve rug beneath the seat. He sits down and—oblivious to the natural beauty surrounding him—accepts the meeting request. Miniature holo figures of the Shun Mantra delegates appear amongst the fluttering petals on the seat beside him.

"Do you have me?" Mori asks.

"Yes. Do you have me?" Niels replies.

"Almost, fading in and out. Yes, yes, I can see you now. Nope, now you're gone."

Niels rejoins the meeting. "I'm here."

"We're waiting on Fossey and Aaroon."

"I'm here," Fossey says.

"She's in a different time zone," Mori says.

"No, I'm right here."

"Okay, I see you now," he says. "No, gone again. Now you're back. Have you done something to your hair?"

The feed blinks. Fossey grins. "I changed the color."

"Darker," says Mori.

"No! It used to be black. Now it's Clingstone."

"What?"

"Clingstone. Peach."

"I'm in," Aaroon says. "Sorry, running late."

"I've lost you," Mori says. "But Niels you're back. Oops, no you're gone again."

Niels closes the program. He leans back on his seat and gazes skyward, into the canopy of the tree. For a brief moment he thinks an aurora has struck and transformed the sky; then he realizes it's the flowers. He is seated under a mauve canopy.

The wind picks up and a handful of blossoms flutters to the ground. Several land on his lap, and he collects one and twirls it between his fingers. He knows an aurora event is likely. An *aurora australis* might follow a solar storm.

His collaboration with Aaroon, with Shun Mantra, is not working. The alliance was not his idea; it was Mori's. They have Coin invested in the company—too much Coin, and too little return.

He takes a deep breath and rejoins the meeting.

"Hey, Fossey, you want to get a drink later?" Aaroon asks.

"You already asked me."

There's a long pause.

"What did you say?"

"I said no."

"Cool. That's cool. All good."

"Okay, I've sorted it. Everyone's here," Mori says. "Niels, you called the meeting, do you want to start?"

Niels drops the flower. "What the fuck were you doing in my CyberSleep vault? There was no secret message in the diamond. It was just boron. And what's this shit about M-theory? It's not even Lise's field."

"A tip-off from a reliable source," Aaroon says. "I'm just trying to get information."

"Do you know who Jin is? Do you know what she does? She's probably the only person on the planet capable of a full human-machine merger. We're talking singularity."

"Who cares. This planet is fucked. Humans are fucked. You're all so primitive. You should be kept in a cage with the primates in the zoo. Can't wait to leave this shit hole."

"Zoos are illegal," Mori says.

"Not everywhere," Aaroon says. "And it should be illegal for your type to breed. Just dilutes your DNA even further."

Niels rolls his eyes.

"We were here first," Mori snaps. "We're the natives. You're the foreign species."

"It's called evolution," Aaroon says. "You know the best way to save yourselves and the planet? Cannibalism. I'm serious. Plant-based proteins, lab-grown meat, even lemon-and parsley-flavored insects aren't going to feed all of you. There are too many of you, and you need protein to live. Your lives are a joke."

"And what will you be eating on Titan?" Mori asks.

"We're going to make food from a protein that comes from soil bacteria. It feeds on hydrogen. The hydrogen is split from electricity generated from solar—so zero greenhouse gas emissions. It tastes of nothing, absolutely nothing. You add your own flavorings."

Niels rubs his temples. "This is fucking crazy," he mumbles.

"Yeah, well, you're fucking nothing," Aaroon says. "You're just bits of energy and matter hung together, and soon you'll be forgotten. We should change the name of this planet from Earth to Water. You're all headed for extinction."

"Before we get that far, I'd like to see a return on my investment, *soon*," Niels says.

There's a long silence.

Eventually, Fossey says, "We found out about the Super AI-Plus. The meerkat."

"Jin worked for me," Niels says. "The AI belongs to me. Mori, you're going to find Quinn and get it."

"Me, why me?"

"Trust me, you need to see her."

"I don't. I don't need to see her. She'll be really pissed. I mean, really, really pissed. I don't even know where she is. How will I find her?"

"She's staying with her father," Aaroon says. "He has property northwest of Hobart."

Eighteen

If it's not a fruit platter, then . . . what is it?

Quinn naps on the sofa, her body curled into a small ball, and she hugs the fluffy robotic dog as if it were a pillow. Anvil and Strat lie next to each other on the floor, both asleep. A transfusion tube connects Anvil's wrist to Strat's elbow. She is giving him a top-up. It's a direct transfusion, end-to-end anastomosis between the radial artery in her wrist and the median cephalic at his elbow.

At the sound of a gently closing door, Quinn stirs and looks up.

Tig.

He smiles at her, then points to the siblings on the floor.

"I made some new friends," she says. "That's Anvil and that's her brother, Strat. They got into a bit of trouble. Needed a place to stay."

"What's with the transfusion?"

"He was kidnapped, someone tried to take his blood—it's special, worth a lot of Coin."

"Blood robbers?"

"Yeah. They're good kids"—she lowers her voice—"but a bit . . . paranormal."

Tig raises an eyebrow. He moves to the food prep and unpacks a bag of vegetables onto the bench. "Easy dinner. Vegetable ragù with celery root gratin."

Quinn's stomach rumbles. "I love celery root."

"Really?"

Mori loiters on the floor beside the sleeping siblings. He collects a cushion from the sofa and places it under Strat's head, then rests his paw on Strat's neck, checking his pulse and blood pressure—but the gesture is feigned. He can read Strat's vitals without touching him. Next, the meerkat inspects the incisions, the tubes, and the rate of blood flow.

He nods; he is satisfied the siblings are stable. He scampers over to the sofa, pulls the AI dog from Quinn's arms, and tosses it onto the floor. Then he sits beside her and gently strokes her hand. She smiles and pats his paw.

Tig collects the dead dog from the floor. "Was this once alive?"

Quinn nods and casts a concerned glance at the siblings.

Tig tosses the dog aside and sits at the far end of the sofa. He takes her feet into his lap. "Nice dress. Have I seen that before?"

She shakes her head.

"Suits you." He slips off her shoes and begins to massage her feet.

Quinn closes her eyes. "Oh, good lordt. You've done this before, haven't you? When was that? Wait, I remember—on the atoll, when we were on the atoll together. Was it before or after sex? Must have been before, because you disappeared straight after." She narrows her eyes.

"Okay, I have something to tell you," he says. "It's important."

"No, no, stop right there."

He puts her foot down.

"No, keep doing that." She points to her feet. "That feels so good. But I have something to tell you too, something really important. We have a problem. A big problem."

He stiffens.

"Not us." She swivels her finger back and forth between them. "Not you and me. Because this is going quite well, don't you think?"

"Get to the point."

"The magnetic South Pole is thousands of kilometers off course. At first, I thought it was because of the mining. Niels told me Mori Eco was mining in Antarctica. But they're not just mining, they're stuffing around with the Earth's mantle. There's a giant cylinder of molten iron under Antarctica. An electromagnet. It's effecting the Earth's magnetic field, which leaves the planet vulnerable to solar storms. Today the AVs stopped and NIoT shut down. I think Shun Mantra's behind it."

"Why?"

"No idea."

Tig grabs Quinn's shoes and slips them onto her feet. "We need to tell Maim." He stands and offers her his hand. She takes it, and he pulls her onto her feet.

"What's your news? What did you want to tell me?" she asks.

"I love you. I love more than anything. But this is never going to work if I'm away all the time. Fuck the military job—I'll find something else. I should be here, with you."

She smiles. She wraps her arms around his neck and rests her head on his chest.

He smooths her hair down and kisses the top of her head. "Also . . . it's not really a fruit platter."

"What's not really a fruit platter?"

"The Disc, the Phaistos Disc?"

She pulls back. "If it's not a fruit platter, then . . . what is it?"

"It's a time portal."

She steps back. "I'm going to need a lot more information."

He nods. "It's made from meteorite metal—Imilac. Formed in the asteroid belt between Mars and Jupiter."

"Did you just make that up?"

He frowns. "No."

"Okay, go on."

"There's a code, a formula. We thought you might know how it works." He points to the tattoo on the back of his neck. "It's connected to this."

"Your tattoo? That's the code to the fruit platter—I mean, the time portal? And you're telling me this . . . now?"

He scratches the side of his face. "I've fucked this up—I know, and I'm sorry. But right now, we need to go get it, and then we need to talk to Maim." He considers the sleeping siblings on the floor. Anvil's head fits neatly under her brother's chin and Strat's arm is draped over his sister's shoulder. "What do we do with 'em?"

"Can we take them home?"

"Sure."

Anvil lifts her head from the floor. "Can we eat the ragù before we leave, would that be okay? Be a shame to waste it."

Nineteen

The females do it tougher.

PLANCK HOVERS THE ROTOR above the glass house as ze takes in the scope of Matt's house and grounds—half an acre of partially covered vegetable gardens, a small orchard, a berry patch, and a cottage garden set aside for herbs and edible flowers. On the other side of the gardens, a greenhouse, a temperate environment for seedlings and propagation. In 2050, self-sufficiency is not an option; it's a necessity. Ze counts six chickens resting in the shade of the greenhouse.

Ze notes that Matt collects water from the air using MOFs (Metal-Organic Frameworks), which are ideal for taking up gases from the atmosphere. They work like a sponge: At night, they suck water vapor from the air into their pores. In the morning, Matt warms the material, and it releases the water.

Planck lands the rotor on the grass at the front of the glass house. Ze disembarks and makes zirs way up the gentle slope towards the house. The grass is still tinged with green, but as ze walks it crunches—dry and brittle underneath. Patches of thistles are winning the competition of survival.

It's warm; ze pauses, unzips the jacket of zirs climate suite—a two-piece navy outfit with a contrasting collar and side panels—and slips it off. Then ze spies Matt sitting quietly in an easy chair on the veranda, a golden-colored pup curled up on the seat next to him. He seems to be soothing the dog—gently stroking it and humming softly.

"Greetings," Planck calls, slinging the jacket over zirs shoulder.

Matt holds Planck's gaze.

"Well, this is lovely," ze says. "I had no idea it would be like this. You know, some people say there's not much happening in Hobart; obviously, they've never been here."

Matt reaches under his chair and grabs a laser. He places it in his lap and continues to pat the dog as he stares at Planck.

"I'm . . . a friend. They're on their way—Quinn and Tig. Should be here any minute." Ze looks nervously around the property.

The puppy stirs. No longer timid, it bounds off the chair and races towards Planck. When she reaches zirs feet, she springs, catapulting off the ground, and tries to lick zirs face.

Planck attempts to restrain the bouncing dog with one hand. "Rosie, down, down."

The dog runs in a circle around Planck, then continues to jump on zir.

"Rosie, stop it. Stop it. Get down. Rosie down. What's wrong with this dog? Wait, is it Rosie or Lupus?"

Matt puts the laser on the table next to him and eases his way out of the chair. "Lupus, come."

The dog returns to the veranda.

"Lupus. Latin for wolf, I like it. I'm Planck, by the way, but you can call me Pluck. That's absolutely fine—I don't mind at all. Now, I noticed your garden on my way in. I don't suppose we could walk and talk? I'm a keen gardener myself."

***

Climate change has not favored butterfly and bee populations. The loss of the natural environment, coupled with the rise of human-dominated habitats, hit many species hard, and in the 2030s the insect numbers halved. Then, in the 2040s, they halved again. Even the prolific cabbage white variety is under threat. But Matt has a thriving colony in his garden. He introduced them a decade ago and has worked patiently to foster their survival.

The bee garden is one of his favorite places on the property. The beds are raised and built from blue-stone blocks—the perfect height to lean against in the morning with a mug of tea.

The plants in the bee garden flower all year round. The soft, broad-leaved varieties provide nesting material for the Leafcutter Bees, and there's a small pond, made of pebbles and twigs, that allows the bees to drink and refresh. In return for their amiable habitat, the bees pollinate Matt's fruits and vegetables.

As Matt and Planck wander through the sun-drenched berry patch, the cabbage white butterflies flutter, seeking out the bok choy leaves and small bowls of sugar-water Matt has left for them.

As Planck swipes away the moths flying about zirs head, ze spies the vine-ripened tomatoes in the adjacent bed. "CRISPR?" ze asks.

"Yeah. At first, I hated the idea of gene editing. Wanted nothing to do with it. Quinn put me straight. Said for the last fifty years we've been gene editing anything and everything we can get our hands on."

"Indeed. Now we have cows that don't fart. Fast-growing pigs, goats, chickens, even salmon."

Matt grabs a spray bottle from the garden bed. "Now available in an easy-to-use spray." He points the bottle at a tomato plant and sprays the leaves. "The DNA attaches to the plant's nanoparticles, improves growth, water, and nutrient uptake, and makes it draught tolerant. Use it on soy, sugar beets, corn, zucchini, squash, potatoes . . . and tomatoes. Tomatoes were my tipping point; I love 'em. When Quinn pointed out that three of my homegrown varieties were DNA-modified for fast growth, pest resistance, and improved flavor, I threw my hands in the air and jumped on board. Now they're iron-rich and full of antioxidants."

Planck points to a banana tree laden with orange fruit. “You have orange bananas?”

“Higher provitamin A. I’ve also got protein-rich potatoes and modified carrots that increase calcium absorption.”

Planck pauses. Ze looks Matt over. “I would be remiss if I didn’t tell you that ‘Eternal Summer’ is one of my all-time favorite tunes. Beautiful lyrics.”

Matt smiles. “Tea?”

***

They sit in the shade on the southern side of the veranda and share a pot of tea.

Planck gazes across the valley. “It’s lovely here. I didn’t think it would be anything like this. I could live here. I could honestly live here.” Ze eyes a shaggy, ten-meter-tall flowering gum. “Exquisite, so unique.”

“*Corymbia ficifolia*. Yeah, she’s a beauty. Use to be a male. Changed sex a few years ago. Something to do with the climate—they’re all doing it, switching sexes. The healthier trees are males. The females do it tougher; they’re the first to go. Before they die, they burst into flower.”

“Sort of beautiful and tragic at the same time.”

“Yeah. You staying the night? You’re more than welcome. Spare bunks in the greenhouse.”

Planck nods.

Matt collects the teacups. “You feel like something . . . stronger? I got a couple of bottles of homemade wine that need sampling.”

“Perfect afternoon for a wine tasting.”

Twenty

Boron. Element number 5 on the periodic table.

Later that evening Tig lands the silver airship—with Quinn, Anvil, and Strat on board—on the grass beside Planck's rotor. Anvil and Strat slept on the journey from Hobart; Strat is still asleep, snoring softly on the backseat.

Anvil leans into the cockpit. The ochre dots on her face tattoo have smudged, and the marks make her look like an animated finger painting. She tilts her head towards the glass house. "Interesting place. You build it?"

Quinn hands Anvil a cloth to wipe the paint off her face. The girl takes it, blows her nose, and then hands it back to Quinn.

"My father built it. My father is Matt Jones."

"Matt Jones?" Anvil frowns. "Wait! Matt Jones the songwriter? Wow. I had no idea you were Quinn Jones."

"I'm not—I have my mother's name, Lise Buyers. I'm Quinn Buyers."

"Wait! Your mother is Lise Buyers? The scientist! She's a friggin' legend. I read her book about nothingness. Did you know nothing is real? It's all an illusion. Everything is just a, a—"

"A complex structure of data. Yes, I read it."

"People love her. She has like a billion pledges on her media page.

I think she's amazing. Amazing . . . and dead. Oh, fuck. She died last year in that flood. I'm so sorry. I didn't mean to— "

Quinn places her hand on Anvil's shoulder. "It's fine. And she might not be dead."

"Interesting. If she's not dead then, where is she?"

"We're not sure."

"Where's Bear? Did someone get Bear?" Strat mumbles from the backseat.

Anvil glares at Quinn. "Bear didn't make it."

"I'm so sorry," Quinn says. She turns and catches Strat's eye. "But we have a dog, a real dog."

Strat smiles. "Real dogs are flyke."

They disembark and head towards the veranda, where Matt and Planck are drinking wine. As they approach, Planck stands.

"Greetings!" Ze considers the weary group as they amble towards the house. "Good lordt, you all look like the walking dead. And what's going on here?" Ze gestures towards the siblings. "Who are they?"

"This is Anvil and her brother, Strat," Quinn explains.

"Quinn saved us from the blood robbers," Anvil says. "Now they're taking us home, the long way round."

Quinn smiles at Planck. "Hello. I've missed you."

"I've missed you, too. I don't want my first words to be 'you look like shit,' but you look like shit. Are you getting enough rest?"

"No."

"Well, come up here, put your feet up, and grab a mug." Planck grabs a bottle of wine and waves it towards her. "This is Britney. Tropical banana surprise, with golden raisins. Normally I avoid beverages with labels like 'surprise,' but it's very good. We finished Kylie an hour ago—elderflower and dandelion, with eucalyptus honey and lavender. A delightful concoction."

Quinn glares at Planck.

"Of course; you can't drink. I keep forgetting."

***

After Strat and Anvil are settled in their sleep zone, Quinn retreats to her own room and Mori follows. She changes into on an old T-shirt with a slogan on the front that reads, "I HAVE NO SPECIAL TALENT. I AM ONLY PASSIONATELY CURIOUS. ALBERT EINSTEIN."

Mori sits on the bed and flicks through the pile of index cards Quinn gave him to write his thoughts on. He pauses at every second or third card and considers it, his lips moving as he silently reads the words.

They hear laughter and the rise and fall of voices coming from outside. Quinn plonks down on the bed next to Mori. She glares across the room—in the direction of the veranda below, where Matt, Planck, and Tig are drinking wine. "It's not really a fruit platter," Quinn says. "Of course, it's not really a fruit platter. Do I look stupid?"

Mori glances at her. "No." He picks up a card and reads the message. "All sorts of things in this world behave like mirrors."

"Yes, that's so true. There's always another side. See, even you know that, and you've only been alive for what . . . a day."

"Six months," Mori corrects.

"Exactly. And six months ago, when we first met, I was going to find my mother. That was my purpose. My mission in life. Now I'm too tired to even look under the rug. And do you know why I'm too tired?"

"Because—"

"Because I had sex with a complete stranger on a deserted island, and now I'm pregnant." Quinn surveys the pile of index cards on the bed. She selects a card and reads, "'There is something in you I like more than yourself. Therefore, I must destroy you.'" She turns to Mori. "That's a bit bleak." She selects another card and scans the lines. "What does, '*objet petit a*' mean?"

"Unobtainable desire."

She reads the card, "'I love you, but because inexplicably I love in you something more than you—the *object petit a*—I mutilate you.' Good lordt, is this *Lacan* again?"

Mori nods.

"Is it helping?"

"No." Mori puts the cards aside. He jumps off the bed and retrieves the wooden tops from Lise's apartment, which Quinn packed in the luggagebot. "These"—he holds a top in each paw—"these are better. I like this activity. I feel happiness when I do this. Still sad, but happy and sad at the same time."

"Gee, that's surprising."

Mori sends the tops scooting across the timber floor. He follows them across the sleep zone until they start to wobble. Then he drops flat on his stomach, rests his chin on the floor, and watches the tops, wide-eyed, until they peter out and finally topple.

"Blink. You need to blink," Quinn says.

A chorus of laughter rises from the veranda below. Lupus howls, joining the rabble. Quinn marches across the room. With her finger, she draws a large circle on the opaque glass wall, then taps the center twice. The section switches to clear, and she peers down at the trio on the veranda. All three are skulling shots like they're old friends reminiscing about childhood adventures.

"Good lordt that shirt looks good on Tig. Brings out the blue specs in his eyes." She turns away. "I'd love a drink. Actually, I'd love about ten. Come on, we're going downstairs."

"To get ten drinks."

"No, to get the fruit platter.

"It is not really a fruit platter."

***

Quinn and Mori collect the fruit platter from the food prep and return with it to her sleep zone. They sit cross-legged on the bed with the platter between them. It is half a meter wide, deep blue, with gold veins swirling across the surface. Three concentric circles divide the Disc into three sections, and each contains a number of small carvings that resemble rudimentary stick figures.

The Disc was holding a recent harvest of red currants when Quinn retrieved it. She dumped them into a bowl before bringing it to the sleep zone, but several of the overripe berries are still fixed to the surface by their sticky nectar. Quinn picks one off and eats it. "I have no idea what these marks mean," she says. One at a time, she removes the remaining currants, picking them off and handing them to Mori, who stacks them on the bedside table. She eats the last one. "They could be birds, or fish, or . . . badly drawn trees."

"Let us hope they are not trees," Mori says. "We have enough trees."

The currant nectar has seeped into the fine lines carved into the Disc, highlighting the markings in red. Quinn pauses. She picks up the Disc and holds it to the light. In the center circle are two tiny V-shapes, with a line across the top. She turns to Mori. "Neutrinos. It's the symbol for a pair of neutrinos, one representing matter and the other antimatter."

"It is the same as the message you found in Ada's purse. Also, the same as Tig's tattoo. Neutrinos are the superheroes of subatomic particles. They are the ancient kings of the universe. They made the stars and the galaxies—"

"Thanks, I know." She pats his leg and drops the Disc back on the bed. "Pass me some of those currants."

Mori passes her the currants stacked on the bedside table.

Quinn pops them one by one into her mouth while she stares at the Disc. "So, what does it do? How does it work? Lise figured it out, but that doesn't mean I can."

Mori shrugs. "It is a shame we cannot holo your mother and just ask her. It would save us a lot of time."

"She wouldn't answer. Lise hates holos. She once said, 'A bit of diffracted light and noise, and people think it's magic. It's not magic, it's science. If the medium is still the message, then it's not a message I'm sending.'" The hair on Quinn's forearms prickle. "Wait. What if—what if the medium is the message? Can you scan this?"

Mori stands. Assuming an excellent interpretation of a meerkat sentinel on patrol, he stretches to full height, holds his paws over the Disc, and scans the material with his SQUID scanner.

"It is magnetic. Made from Imilac, but there is also a material I do not know. An unknown polymer. The links between the molecules are semi-permanent. They can break and rearrange."

"It's transformable?"

"Yes, it is transformable. But to transform it requires a catalyst. Also, it is electromagnetic. It is generating a field of radiation around itself."

Quinn shuffles back on the bed. "How can something five thousand years old be shape-shifting?"

"There is also a small amount of boron impregnated into the surface."

"What did you just say?" she snaps.

"Boron, there is a small—"

"Boron. Element number 5 on the periodic table. Are you sure?"

"Yes."

"That was the message—the formula Lise left in the diamond. But . . . but there's nothing fancy about boron. It doesn't do anything."

"There are thirty-six atoms of boron, a single stable sheet one atom thick, with a perfect hexagonal hole in the center—a borophene," Mori says. "The borophene balances a nuclear fission event, allowing only one event to take place at the one time."

"It stops everything from exploding," Quinn says. "Boron keeps the thing stable. It keeps the energy stable so, so . . . the time travel event can occur without imploding. It's a fucking time portal."

"I know," Mori says.

***

Tig crawls into bed next to Quinn and watches her sleep. She is the most beautiful thing he has ever seen, ever touched or held. As he wraps his arms around her, he thinks he could happily lie beside her forever. Love is a thousand kisses from her lips. He moves a strand of hair from her face. He loves her hair, the way it flutters around her ears, her perfect ears. He covers her hand with his. He loves her hands. Her perfect hands and tiny fingers. The way she bites her thumbnail when she thinks about science and math problems. She has perfect thumbs. Actually, everything about her is perfect.

Twenty-One

Please forgive me.

Honeyeaters have taken up residence in the foliage of the Blue Gum. The birds have olive-tipped wings, white breasts, and small, dark heads. They hang upside down on the tree branches and make prolific lilting notes.

Their roll call wakes Quinn. She turns over and feels for Tig, but the space beside her is empty. She recalls he snored, and she couldn't sleep. She put a pillow over her head, it didn't help. She placed her hand on his chest, it woke him, and he knew. He knew he was snoring, and he knew the routine. This wasn't the first time he has snored. Quinn is in the last trimester of her pregnancy, and a sound night's sleep is rare. Tig kissed her quickly then headed out to the greenhouse to sleep in the spare bunk. She was grateful.

Unfamiliar voices, rising from the level below, catch her attention and she sits up. Strat and Anvil are arguing; she catches the thread of their conversation.

"No," Strat says. "No way."

"Yes, I'm going to," Anvil says.

"I won't let you," he retorts.

"Well, I don't care."

"Well, I do."

"You can't stop me."

“Yes, I can.”

“I’ll do it when you’re asleep.”

Quinn heads downstairs and peers inside the siblings’ sleep zone. Strat and Anvil are propped up next to each other on the bed. They’re playing a VR game.

They see her in the doorway and pause.

Quinn looks from one to the other. There’s something different about them. They’ve wiped the ochre dots from their faces, but that’s not it. Their pupils are dilated, and their eyes look dull and muddy. They’ve taken something. Quinn spies a VRDrop container on the bedside table. The siblings have inserted an interface—hardware, software, and connectivity—into their eyes. The interface creates a shared, high-definition, 3D world that only they can access. They are fully immersed in their game.

“Sorry,” Anvil shouts at Quinn. “Did we wake you? We were trying to be quiet. Thought we’d stay in bed until everyone was up. Didn’t want to wake anyone.”

“You’re shouting,” Quinn says,

“Sorry,” she says in a normal tone. “I thought I was whispering.”

“How long will this last?”

“The VRDrops? Two, maybe three hours. You’re cool with it, right? I mean, it’s not illegal.”

“Not unless you’re driving, using a passenger drone, or riding a hoverboard. You don’t have high blood pressure or a heart condition, do you?”

“No one drives anymore.”

“Everyone drives.”

“Wevs.”

“Hungry?” Quinn asks.

“Starving.” Strat jumps out of bed. He’s wearing superhero-themed boxer shorts emblazoned with red and blue cartoon characters and a tight black T-shirt. He bowls past Quinn and bumps his way down the stairs to the food prep.

Anvil carefully pats her way across the bed. When she finds the side, she slowly maneuvers herself backwards over the edge. She wears black boxer shorts, and a T-shirt covered with images of superheroes. "Everything's blurry," she shouts. "Say something so I know where you are."

Quinn shakes her head. "This can't be healthy."

***

The siblings straddle the stools at the food prep bench. Quinn slides a bowl of dried fruit and homemade yogurt, which Matt has left for her breakfast, towards them. Strat picks the bowl up and lifts it towards his mouth.

Anvil glares at him and shakes her head. He places the bowl back on the table.

Quinn slides over two spoons.

Mori sits at the base of the stairs, a pile of index cards next to him. He is disheveled; his eyes are moist and three times their normal size. He selects a card and reads it aloud: "To live is to suffer. To suffer is to find some meaning in the suffering."

"Lacan?" Quinn enquires.

"Nietzsche."

Matt saunters into the food prep carrying a basket of homemade muffins. Lupus follows. Strat's eyes fix on the dog.

"Still warm." Matt places the muffins on the food prep bench.

Strat slides off his stool and sits on the floor. Lupus scurries into his lap and licks his face. Strat giggles. "This dog smells flyke." She rolls over, exposing her belly to him, and he scratches her tummy. She pants and wags her tail.

Mori selects another card and reads aloud: "When you stare into the abyss, the abyss stares back." He stands and spins in a circle.

Quinn frowns. "What are you doing?"

Mori looks at his tail. Then he spins again, trying to catch it—and spins, and spins. The cycle gains momentum. Around and around the meerkat whirls.

"Stop it," Quinn yells.

The meerkat is oblivious. He is caught in a loop. He continues to spin.

Quinn strides over and grabs him by the shoulders, halting his revolutions. "You've got to stop this."

He wriggles out of her grip. "You are my worst best friend."

"I'm your only friend. You're obsessing. You need to let go of your anxious thoughts, and you need to rest more."

"Am I obsessing? To be an obsessional means to find oneself caught in a mechanism, in a trap increasingly demanding and endless." He turns to Quinn. "That is Lacan."

"Ever thought of putting your words together?" Strat suggests. "Like, you say 'that's' instead of 'that is'?"

"Have you ever thought of saying 'whatever' instead of 'wevs.' Or 'maybe' instead of 'mb,' or 'do not know' instead of 'dik,' or 'new person' instead of 'noob'? Have you ever thought of that?" Mori lifts his face to Quinn. "Man is the cruelest animal."

She hugs him to her chest and pats his shoulder.

***

The greenhouse is located on the northern side of the glass house—a short walk through the vegetable gardens. Quinn enters the building carrying a mug of tea. Inside, the air is chilly, and the tiled floor is cool on her bare feet. The structure is insulated to protect the plants from the incessant heat. At this time of year, Matt keeps the interior under

18 degrees Celsius, creating a stable environment for his cool-weather herbs and seedlings. Rows of baby beets, cabbages, and lettuce sit on the timber benches, and in the corner of the room pea tendrils climb around wire frames.

Tig is asleep on a bunk bed. Quinn pulls over a wicker chair and sits down; the rattan whines under her weight.

Tig opens his eyes.

"You believe time travel is possible?" she asks.

He sits up. "Morning. Darling. How did you sleep?"

"Fine." She hands him the mug of tea. "Thank you for moving, but I don't want to make small talk. I have questions."

He nods.

"The Disc. How does it work?"

"It might open gravity."

"Really?"

"Or spacetime. But it could be a wormhole."

"You have no idea."

"No."

"Why me? What makes you think I can work it out?"

"I'm not sure you can. I mean, your mother worked it out, but she's a genius. And let's face it, you're not your mother."

Quinn shuffles in her seat. "Well no, but I could have a go. I mean, I am a scientist and—"

Tig puts a finger to his lip. They hear the low hum of a rotor approaching.

"Planck?" Quinn queries.

"Left early this morning." Tig tilts his head to one side and holds up two fingers; there are two rotors approaching.

He slides off the bed and they move to the window. The rotors descend over the glass house and land in a clearing on the far side, hidden from view.

Lupus bounds through the door and scurries under Tig's bunk

bed, frightened off the veranda by the noise of the rotors. Quinn leans down and wiggles her fingers under the bed. The pup creeps forward, and she fondles its ears. "It's okay," she coos. Then she turns to Tig. "It's not okay, is it?"

"No."

Tig's pack is on the end of his bunk; from it, he pulls a small black tube. A SiteScope, a device that can see around corners. It uses an algorithm to interpret the fragmented shadows that project from the edge of the object blocking one's view and produces a fuzzy image of the activity on the other side.

Tig points the SiteScope at the house. "HOTRODS."

Mean Machines—part organic and part bio-mechatronic, but still classified as living organisms. They were once warmongers—aggressive, crime-committing humans. During the RE Wars, in the 2040s, they were given a choice between incarceration or a life of combat. They chose combat and merged with a mechanical exoskeleton. Now, they have one job: follow orders. Tightly fitted skullcaps interfere with their conscious thoughts—they are incapable of thinking for themselves.

Quinn takes the Scope. She sees a shadowy figure emerge from the rotor and walk towards the house. His otter-like physique and prominent gait are familiar. "It's Mori Eco."

Tig grabs a couple of lasers from his pack and hands one to Quinn. He moves the sliding scale on his weapon all the way up to destroy, then locks the mechanism into place.

Quinn places her laser on the windowsill. "I count six, maybe seven HOTRODs. No sign of Matt or the siblings, but they were in the food prep when I left the house. Maybe Matt sent them to the bunker. Access is in the storage."

"He's a Prepper?"

"The real deal. First it was a zombie apocalypse. Then an alien invasion. After that, the never-ending threat that capitalism would fail and humanity would self-implode. Funny, annoying ex-fiancés were never on his mind."

"What's in the bunker?"

"Enough supplies to last for years. But there's an escape hatch, too. The bunker links to a cave system that leads to the Source, the underground spring that feeds the river. It's on the other side of the mountain, and it's well protected—a natural fortress. The trip takes two days, and the Source is stocked with supplies and an armory. He'll explode the house before he enters the bunker, buying time."

"He's been busy." Tig holds his hand out for the Scope.

She hands it to him. "What do they want?"

"I think they want you."

"Okay, I'll go talk to them."

"You're not going anywhere. I'll go—"

"Because you're a man and I'm a woman? Honestly, this gender stereotype shit is so outdated."

"I'll go because I'm a cyborg." He taps his artificial arm. "Titanium. I've killed plenty of HOTRODs. And worse."

"There are worse things than HOTRODs?"

"Much worse. I know a bit more about combat than you."

"Okay, I see your point, but no one is getting hurt. Not me, not you, and not Matt. Mori Eco is not going to hurt anyone. This is not warfare. This is just . . . conversation. We need to clear a few things up." She takes the Scope from Tig and turns her attention back to the scene on the other side of the house. "Besides, the HOTRODs can't shoot me. I'm pregnant, and their programming won't allow it. Crimes against pregnant woman and children are prohibited, Geller told me; it was in the post-war conventions." She hands him back the Scope. "I'm going. This is the best plan."

He steps in front of her, blocking her exit. "You're not going anywhere."

Her left hand swipes the weapon off the windowsill and shoots him. Tig's eyes roll back in his head and he hits the ground, hard.

"No, no, no. I didn't mean—oh shit."

She checks the setting on the weapon. It was set to stun.

"Oh, thank the lordt. That could have been so much worse." Her heart pounds. She drops down beside Tig, who's out cold. "Fuck, that must have hurt."

She takes a pillow from the bunk bed and places it under his head. Then she kisses him.

"Please forgive me. I'll be back in . . . twenty minutes, half an hour at the most." She kisses him again. "I love you. This is the best plan. No one and nothing is going to get hurt today, except maybe your ego."

Lupus creeps out from her hiding place under the bunk. She licks Tig's face.

Quinn scratches the dog's ear. "Stay here and look after him," she commands.

Twenty-Two

Punch the puppy.

Quinn slips the laser into the back of her shorts and heads out the door of the greenhouse. Using the dense line of fruit trees for cover, she tracks south, drawing attention away from the stunned cyborg lying on the floor with a cushion under his head.

When she reaches the southeastern point of the garden, she emerges from the trees and walks into the grassy clearing. Affecting a mildly surprised manner, as if she has just returned from a stroll, she pauses and takes in the scene—six HOTRODs, one fuckwit ex-fiancé standing on the veranda next to Matt, and no sign of the siblings or the meerkat. Matt would have sent them to the Bunker—she is sure of it. Every person, pet, and AI is accounted for. Which leaves her and Matt to face the HOTRODs and the ex-fiancé.

Two HOTRODs jog towards her. They look like large, evil cartoon characters, their angular metal armor gleaming in the morning light. They are three times her size and she immediately hands over her weapon and raises her hands. She tells herself to stay calm—they can't shoot her, and there is no way Mori Eco will hurt her. This is the best plan.

Together, they stride towards the house.

Mori and Matt are at the top of the stairs on the veranda, and Mori has a laser pointed at her father.

Mori looks older and wearier than she remembers, but he still wears his beige climate pants too high and he still looks like an otter. Quinn feels nothing but loathing for him. She lets out a long, slow breath through clenched teeth.

Mori smiles at her, a big, lopsided grin. “Long time no see,” he says.

Quinn narrows her eyes; considering their past and what happened on Kerguelen, his vacuous pleasantries only increase her loathing for him.

Mori takes a step back. “You look . . . different,” he says.

Slowly, she climbs the steps towards him.

He continues to retreat. “You’ve done something with your hair. I like it, suits you. And you, well, you’ve put on a bit of . . . weight.”

She freezes halfway up the stairs.

“Stress, yes,” he nods. “I imagine you’ve been under a fair amount of stress. Sorry about that. I hope it hasn’t affected your health. I didn’t mean for it to go down like this. It’s been a fucking disaster. You have no idea. I mean, I wouldn’t worry, you’ll lose it soon enough.”

“Are you serious? You kill two thousand people and blame it on me, and that’s the first thing you say to me? You’re worried about my weight?”

“Punch the puppy,” Mori says to the closest HOTROD.

The machine hesitates; it doesn’t understand the command.

“Shoot her,” Mori clarifies.

“What the fuck?” Matt steps in front of Quinn.

“I mean stun her, we’ve discussed this. Stun her, don’t kill her.”

The HOTROD raises its weapon and points it towards Quinn. She freezes. Her heart races.

The machine lowers its weapon. “She is pregnant,” it says.

“Nonsense. She can’t be.”

“Confirmed,” says the HOTROD.

Mori stares at Quinn. He says nothing. He touches his forehead, then he taps his lip with his fingertips and smiles.

Good lordt. There's no way the math can add up.

"This is why you called off the wedding. Of course it is. You were in shock. Now I understand. Everything makes sense. Darling, I'm sorry, I'm so sorry I called you fat. Of course you're not fat, honestly you look . . . great. Really, you do." He smiles and gently taps his chest. "I can't believe it. Well, I can. It's true isn't it, you are actually pregnant?"

She nods.

Matt, still standing on the landing next to Mori, smirks and casts his eyes to the ground.

"It makes complete sense," Mori says. "Joining the spots backward, from the future to the present. Although that's now the past, but you know what I mean."

"Why are you here? Why have you brought these machines to my father's house?"

"Two reasons—and trust me, I didn't want to come."

Quinn glares at him.

"But I'm so happy I did, honestly I am." He swallows. "First, apparently you changed the message in the diamond. Lise was working on a formula for M-theory and—"

"I didn't change the message."

"Well . . . people think you did, so it was best that I came. Me personally. I was the best option. The others"—he scratches his ear—"well, they're not like us, they're not singing from the same sheet music."

"Do you even know what M-theory is?"

"A theory of . . . everything?"

"Yes, a theory that unites quantum mechanics and general relativity. Trust me Lise was not working on M-theory." *She was working on time travel.* "And these . . . people, are they Shun Mantra? You know it means Transhuman? They just jumbled up the letters. Shun Mantra. Transhuman."

His lips tweak as he cross-references the letters. "You're wrong, it doesn't make Transhuman."

"It does, and they're crazy."

"Yes, perhaps that's true, or maybe they're just peeling the onion a different way. Now, there's also the Super AI-Plus. Niels says it's his, and he wants it back."

"You can tell Niels there is no way he's getting his hands on it. Now, the G12 showed the mining in Antarctica. I know what you're doing."

"Transhuman only has nine letters."

"It has ten."

He counts them out on his fingers. "Okay, you might be right. But it means nothing, and all we're doing is mining. The world needs metals right now. We've practically run out of everything—lithium, scandium, xenon. We're doing the planet a service."

"No, you're not, and xenon's not a metal. You're creating a dynamo. There's a spinning cylinder of molten iron under the surface of the planet. Why?"

He shakes his head. Fervently.

Steadily, she climbs the stairs towards him. "Tell. Me. Why?"

"Energy!"

"Energy? You're capturing energy from the solar flares?"

"I can't say anymore. I've said too much already."

She narrows her eyes and steps towards him. A HOTROD blocks her way.

"It's hot. I don't feel well." She feigns giddiness and grabs the veranda rail. "I need a drink. I'm going inside."

A HOTROD blocks her way. Mori waves his hand, dismissing the machine.

Quinn enters the food prep. She knows there's a laser strapped to the underside of the bench in the left corner, and she sidles along the bench and feels for it. It's not there. The holster is empty. *Interesting.*

There's another laser under the kickboard on the right side, just below the tea infuser. She runs her foot along the inside of kickboard, and again she feels nothing. The weapon is gone. It was there yesterday.

Her third option is a knife taped to the back of the cupboard where Matt keeps the vacuum-sealed jars of nuts.

She opens the nut cupboard and finds the knife. She slips the blade into the back of her shorts and makes a mental note to remove any weapons stowed below waist level before the baby starts crawling.

She fills a mug with water, all the way to the brim, and carefully carries it out to the veranda. She catches her father's eye and tilts her head towards the storage area. He dips his head, indicating he understands; it'll take them ten seconds to get to the bunker.

Quinn steps in front of her father. Matt pulls the knife from the back of her shorts. She tosses the mug of water at Mori and yanks the laser from his hand.

The HOTRODs step forward and raise their weapons.

Matt steps up, grabs Mori around the neck and holds the knife to his throat. "Tell them to stand down."

"I'm dripping wet," says Mori.

Quinn checks the setting on the laser and makes a show of moving the scale from benign to kill. She points the laser at Mori. "Tell them to stand down."

"I'm completely drenched, there's even water in my ear."

Matt forces the blade against Mori's neck. "Tell them to stand down. Now."

"Okay, okay. Take it easy. But you can't hurt me. I'm the father of your, your grandchild."

"Actually, you're not," Matt says. "I will hurt you, and I'll enjoy it."

Mori flinches. He turns to Quinn.

Quinn takes a step towards Mori and points her weapon into the side of his face. "He's right. You're not the father."

Mori sighs. "Oh, thank god. Such a relief, you've no idea. Kids . . ." He shakes his head. "There's no way I want kids."

Quinn scowls. "Let me make this very clear. The diamond means nothing. It was a joke. Lise wasn't working on M-theory, and the Super-AI is mine. Now, get off our property."

"Okay, okay. Back off, back off." Mori flicks a hand towards the HOTRODs, indicating they should stand down.

The HOTRODs on the veranda lower their weapons. The machines positioned at the base of the stairs follow orders and step back.

There are two more in the field. One lowers its weapon, but the other takes a step towards them. "She comes with us," it says.

Quinn and Matt share a confused glance.

Mori waves at the machine. "No. She doesn't. Stand down."

The HOTROD takes another step forward, its weapon aimed at Quinn. "She comes with us."

"Laser down," Mori yells.

The machine continues towards them, with its weapon raised.

"Rogue," says Matt.

"Fuck," says Quinn, and she fires half a dozen rounds into the machine. The HOTROD takes the hits. It shudders and crumbles to its knees.

Quinn sighs, relieved.

Then, in one swift motion, the machine draws itself back to a standing position and continues towards them.

Matt turns to Quinn. "Go."

"*You* go."

"Just fucking go!"

She retreats, walking backwards, firing rounds into the machine, then she turns and runs. The bunker entrance is in the floor at the far end of the storage area. She swings through the door and taps a button halfway down the wall. A hatch in the floor opens. Behind her, she hears Matt yelling, then heavy footsteps. She slides along the floor and drops into a chute that descends into the bunker.

Matt follows and the hatch behind them closes.

The chute delivers Quinn into a concrete box with meter-thick walls. This is the delivery port. The doomsday bunker is 200 meters down the hill.

Quinn flicks on the light in her Band. Ahead, she sees three tunnels. One leads directly to the bunker. The other two are dummies, programmed to collapse in one minute, along with the delivery port.

She picks herself up from the floor. She can't see Matt, he is not behind her or beside her, but she is sure he followed her down the chute. She searches and in the dim light she finds him lying motionless on the floor behind the shoot.

"Oh shit, please be okay, please, please, please." She crouches next him. "Are you hit?" She pats him down trying to find a wound.

When she touches his leg, he flinches. "Hey, take it easy. My thigh. Laser burn. Help me up. How long have we got?"

"About three seconds."

Quinn helps Matt to his feet. He slings an arm over her shoulder, and they hobble across the delivery port and enter the tunnel on the right. Ten meters inside they pause and rest against the wall. Quinn switches off the light in her band.

"How long?" she whispers.

"Shhh," he dismisses.

Then they hear them. The HOTRODs have the hatch open. They will be in the delivery port in seconds. Quinn wonders why the port hasn't exploded; it should have happened by now. Surely, it's been more than a minute.

She hears a HOTRODs skating down the shoot. Another follows, and then one more. There's a heavy crash; they might have fallen or collided with one another. Now they are scrambling, trying to get to their feet.

It's deathly quiet.

Quinn draws her laser.

A HOTROD appears at the end of the tunnel. It's ten meters way.

It looks directly at them; Quinn thinks it must be able to see her. She raises her weapon.

Matt places his hand on her arm. "Fireworks," he whispers.

The house detonates. Quinn covers her ears as debris and dust fill the delivery port.

They wait for several minutes, huddled against the side of the tunnel, until the dust settles. Then Quinn switches on her light. Behind them, the tunnel is sealed. Matt throws an arm around her shoulder and they exchange a weary glance; both know how far they have to go. Together, they hobble down the tunnel towards the survival bunker.

"Everything's gone," Quinn mumbles. "Blown to smithereens. The tree, that beautiful tree, gone. Yesterday I hugged that tree and now it's firewood. The house, all your books and music, gone. The staircase—how long did it take you to make that?"

"I'd rather not talk about it."

She pauses. "Of course, of course, I'm sorry." Then she remembers the birds. "What about the birds? Do you think they got out?"

"The birds are fine. Where's Lupus?"

"She's safe. She's with Tig."

"Where's Tig?"

"He'll meet us at the Source." Quinn keeps her eyes fixed on the tunnel ahead.

"Surprised he let you come . . . alone."

"Well, we sort of got into an argument, and I—I sort of shot him. I didn't mean it. It was just a stun. He'll be fine."

"You did *what*?"

"I shot him . . . stunned, I mean, I stunned him." She can see him staring at her out of the corner of her eye. "It worked out, didn't it? We got out, we're here, all safe, heading for the Source."

"Did he have a plan? Because maybe there was another way. Maybe we didn't have to . . . blow everything up."

"No. This is the plan."

"Really? Because I don't know what sort of relationship you got going, but I'd be pissed off if my partner shot me."

"You don't have a partner."

"Let's hope you still have one."

Twenty-Three
A dead chick, wearing a red dress.

Matt purchased 100,000 hectares of wilderness northwest of Hobart in the 2030s, when it was still possible to buy large plots of vacant land. A decade later, tree-planting fever hit the planet and the "Tree Zone" land act was passed; after that, large parcels of unoccupied land were set aside for trees.

The land was expensive, but Matt's music had made him wealthy. His most successful songs were melancholy tunes about life in the twenty-first century. He sang about climate change and the daily burden of too much sunshine, the eternal summer. He sang about lonely people living in crowded cities, and what it felt like to lose a job to a machine. The 2030s were a confusing time for the people of Earth. Millions of refugees roamed the planet, looking for a place to live. The property market collapsed, and quantum computing blew up the internet. It was in these years that Matt accrued most of his wealth.

He decided upon the location of the glass house after careful research. It faced east, capturing the morning sun (his favorite time of day) and overlooked a valley with a natural water source—perfect for a world grappling with climate change. But the crucial, defining feature of the site, and the one that drove his final decision to buy this land in particular, was its proximity to an underground cave system. As a doomsday prepper, this satisfied all his needs.

There are two connecting cave systems on Matt's land. The first caves were formed by nature, honed by an ancient underground river hundreds of thousands of years ago. Then, in the mid-twentieth century, the coal mining industry hollowed out a complex network of tunnels, which are now abandoned. Together, these two systems form the escape route to the Source—a small, well-hidden natural fortress on the other side of the mountain.

Coal is dead plant matter, converted to carbon by heat and pressure. The mineral was laid down 250 million years ago, in the Permian age. In the early twentieth century it was quarried using the room and pillar technique—rooms were cut into the rich coal seams, leaving behind pillars, which held up the roof. Then, later, in the mid-twentieth century, the Longwall shearer machine was used. It swung back and forth across the wide seams, excavating the coal, while hydraulic supports kept the roof stable. After the coal was collected, the supports were removed and the roof collapsed.

The dark energy resource was brought on conveyor belts to the surface, where it was pulverized to a fine powder and burnt. This produced heat, which turned water into steam, which, at high pressure, turned turbines that powered generators. Heat energy was converted to mechanical energy, and the generators converted this to electrical energy.

The Western world wanted power on demand, and they got it. It made people rich, and it made corporations wealthy. It made people sick and governments greedy. It filled the Earth's atmosphere with carbon dioxide, and the oceans and trees could only absorb so much, the remaining gas couldn't escape. In 2050, it's still there, warming the oceans and the earth.

Matt spent two years exploring and studying the caves before he built the survival bunker. He'd take provisions and a GPS and disappear for days, sometimes weeks, underground while he mapped the network of tunnels. He lived on site, in a mobile home, until the foundations and escape routes were laid. Then he built the glass house.

He knew they would come, and when they did, he was ready.

***

Quinn opens the door to the survival bunker. Anvil and Strat are seated on a large tapestry lounge. Before them, a small wooden card table holds a bottle of spirits, two half-filled glasses, and the Phaistos Disc, covered in dried insect snacks. Music—a piano tune––is tinkling in the background.

Matt and Quinn, hot, sweaty, and covered in dust, pause in the doorway. They pause to consider the siblings in their refined setting.

Anvil squints at the two dusty figures. "Is it you?"

"Of course it's us," Quinn says. "Who else would it be?"

"Sorry, having trouble with distances. Up close everything's good, but far away is still a blur." Anvil leans towards Strat and examines his face.

Matt steps forward and stumbles. Quinn grabs his arm, but she can't hold him. "Give me a hand," she calls.

Anvil and Strat leap into action, knocking over the card table and sending the Disc and the bottle of spirits crashing to the ground. The bottle rolls to the side, leaving a trail of dark liquid across the floor.

The three of them help Matt inside and settle him on the tapestry sofa.

Using an automated locking device, Quinn seals the bunker door, then slides a heavy metal bar across the opening. She dusts her hands off; High-Tech, Low-Tech—the best of both worlds.

Matt collects the bottle and a glass from the floor and pours himself a drink, which he promptly skulls. Quinn flops onto the lounge next to him. Matt offers her the bottle. She shakes her head, and immediately changes her mind. She takes the bottle and sniffs the alcoholic scent. *Wine?* She runs a finger around the lip of the bottle and tastes the dark liquid. "Red wine. You have red wine down here?" She pours herself a shot and skulls it, then passes the bottle back to Matt.

"I got everything down here. Didn't expect a surprise attack before breakfast, but we made it. We're all safe."

"Mori? Where's the meerkat?" Quinn asks. "Is he here? Is he safe?"

Anvil and Strat shake their heads. Matt shrugs.

"We left him behind?" Quinn's heart drops. She holds her head in her hands and stares at the floor. "Fuck."

Matt looks sideways at her. "He was outside. I saw him follow you into the garden. I reckon he's safe."

"Shit," says Quinn.

"Is there something you haven't told us?" Matt asks.

"He can't be switched off. He's a Super AI-Plus, capable of replicating himself."

"A new species, flyke," Strat says. "Hope he's not after world domination. If he falls into the wrong hands, then we're all fucked."

"Not much we can do about it now." Matt collects the Disc from the floor and hands it to Quinn. "I told 'em to take it with 'em." Matt nods at the siblings, then he drinks another glass of wine. "Anyone hungry? There's preserves . . ." He eases himself off the sofa.

"Dad, sit down."

Matt points to rows of shelving, neatly stacked with bottles and jars. "The pantry, over there." He lowers himself back onto the sofa. "Help yourself."

Strat strides over and scans the neatly stacked jars in the pantry, which resembles a produce market. Rows of purpose-built shelves take up a third of the area inside the bunker. There are barrels of grain, tanks of water, rows of canned goods, packets of spices, and bottles of oil. One section is dedicated to preserves; the jars are labeled and organized by color and variety. Strat studies the labels.

Quinn turns to her father. "How's the leg?"

He winces. "Burns."

"What happened?" Anvil asks.

"Laser wound." Matt looks at Quinn. "Med kit, on the shelf over there." He points to a corner on the far side of the bunker and starts rolling up his pant leg.

Quinn retrieves the med kit and opens it on the card table.

"They were HOTRODs, weren't they?" Anvil asks.

Quinn nods. "The ultimate foot soldiers: dispensable, and they don't die easily." She scans the ointments in the med kit, selects a tube of surgical glue, and seals her father's wound.

Strat returns with a large jar containing a combination of multicolored vegetables. He opens the lid and pulls out a long sliver of zucchini, clearly intent on devouring it—and then realizes that he is the center of attention, that everyone else is watching him. Manners prevail; he slides the sliver of zucchini back into the jar and graciously offers the preserves to Matt, who declines, and then to Quinn, who also declines. Strat tilts the open jar towards his sister; she shakes her head. With a grin, he retrieves the sliver of zucchini and slides it into his mouth.

"Oh good lordt, this is GFS." He digs into the jar again, pulls out a slice of capsicum, and devours the morsel. "By far, the best food I've ever eaten."

Matt grins.

Quinn's taste buds stir. "Here, pass it over," she says.

Strat obliges. She dips into the jar, retrieves a piece of oily capsicum, and pops it into her mouth.

"Good." She turns to Matt. "It's very good."

Anvil steps forward and takes the jar from Quinn. She selects a piece of baby corn and eats it in one bite. "So good." She nods and hands the jar back to Strat. Then she moves to the center of the room and clears her throat. "Okay." She wipes the oil from her mouth with the back of her hand. "What's going on, and who's the dead woman in the corner?"

"Dead woman?" Quinn queries.

Strat points to the far wall. "Over there. A dead chick, wearing a red dress."

"A dead chick wearing . . ." Quinn turns to her father. "You have Ada down here?"

Matt shrugs. "Didn't know what else to do with her."

Quinn stands. She creeps towards the casket in the far corner of the room and peers inside. It *is* Ada; well preserved in a cryovac pouch, still wearing her red evening dress (the cloud event in Kerguelen was formal). In her hand she holds her purse, the purse in which Quinn found a note from Lise's journal. "I didn't realize you took . . . possession of her."

"Yeah. Figured it was a secret, the body swap and all. This was the best place for her. No one would find her down here."

Quinn has a flashback to the day on the recovery vessel *Prismatic* when she first saw Ada's body in Lise's casket. Geller was standing next to her, and Quinn had prepared herself; she was expecting to see her mother's corpse. And she needed to see her—she needed confirmation that Lise was dead. Then, suddenly, it was Ada and not Lise in the casket. Beautiful Ada, who knew about fashion. Kind Ada, who cooked for Quinn when she was studying her PhD. Practical Ada, who mended the tears in her climate suit.

"The poor woman. She didn't deserve to die like this." Quinn returns to her seat next to her father on the tapestry sofa. "She looks remarkably good . . . considering."

"Considering she's dead," Anvil clarifies.

"She was always a looker," says Matt. "Great skin, high cheekbones, you can't go wrong."

"I always liked her eyebrows—the way they framed her face," Quinn says.

"Okay, enough with the reminiscing. You're keeping a dead woman in a doomsday bunker. Do you realize how that looks?" Anvil pulls a laser from the back of her pajama shorts and points it at Matt. Reluctantly, Strat puts down the preserve jar and grabs a laser hidden on the shelf behind him. The siblings have the two missing weapons from the food prep.

"We made a pact." Anvil tilts her head towards Strat. "One dead woman, cryovaced, in an underground doomsday bunker—we think we can handle that." She glares at her brother.

"That's right. But if there's more than one, we're out of here and you're on your own."

"I see you're point, but we didn't kill her," Quinn says. "She died in Kerguelen, in the flood last year. She's my mother's ex-partner. She was in the wrong place at the wrong time. Unfortunate for her."

"Might be a good idea to tell us what's going on," Anvil says.

"After the flood, one of those giant recovery vessels was sent in to collect and identify the bodies."

"The ones that live under water?" Strat asks. "They look like black beetles, just a million times bigger?"

"Yeah, that's the one. They collected the bodies, identified them by their Bands, then shipped them home. I don't think anyone followed up. Ada died wearing my mother's TechBand. A classic case of mis-taken identity."

"Why would this Ada person steal your mother's Band?"

"She didn't steal it, she just . . . had it. Lise probably gave it to her for safekeeping,"

"Just before she was swept away by a wall of water, Lise gave her Band to someone else?" Anvil rolls her eyes. "Makes no sense. I reckon she stole it."

"No. Ada loved Lise." Quinn's voice wavers. She turns to her father. "Didn't she?"

"You said they fought the whole time they were there. Before the rain, before the cloud thing collapsed, you drank wine on the grass outside the research station, and Lise and Ada fought." Matt skulls another shot of wine.

"Fuck." Quinn takes her father's almost-empty glass and finishes the dregs.

The bunker falls silent as they mull over Anvil's suggestion.

Eventually, Quinn knits her fingers together and says, "There's something else. I found a note in Ada's purse."

"I got a feeling there was something inside—by the way she's holding it," Anvil says.

"Yes! That's exactly what I thought. And I was right."

"We were both right."

"Yes, we were. Inside was a page from Lise's notebook. On it, she had written this." Quinn draws two V signs in the dusty floor with her foot.

"An M?" Anvil queries.

Quinn tilts her head. "No, it's the other way round—it's two V's," she says.

"The symbol for neu . . . trinos." Matt grins. "They're the fucking superheroes of the universe."

"Yes, they are, and this is the key." Quinn collects the Disc and points to the center circle. "My mother discovered the code to . . . to this." She taps the Disc. "To what it does."

"It does . . . something?" Anvil asks.

This is where I lose all credibility as a scientist. Just say it, say it fast. "Time travel," Quinn mumbles. "Well, that's what we think. We don't actually know how it works."

The siblings exchange a glance. Strat steps forward and hands his laser to Quinn, exchanging it for the Disc. The laser handle is greasy, covered in oil from the preserves. Quinn drops the weapon onto the sofa and wipes her hands.

Strat runs his greasy fingertips over the Disc. "Yesss. It's a calendar. It's skylore, indigenous astronomy, the dark constellations." He grins.

Anvil steps forward. She also passes her laser to Quinn to hold, Quinn tosses it onto the sofa as Anvil takes the Disc from her brother.

Anvil tilts the Disc towards the overhead light. "You're right. It's the dark constellations. See, here's the emu."

Quinn squints; all she sees are stick figures. "How do you two know about skylore and dark constellations?"

"We learnt it in school." Strat shrugs.

"It's true," Anvil confirms. "We did Indigenous History. It's a common-core subject." She gives the Disc back to Quinn. "Stare at it long enough you'll see them. It takes a while for your eyes to adjust, like one of those illusion puzzles where you see two things. Ever do those when you were a kid?"

Quinn shakes her head.

"Okay. Enough," Matt interrupts. "We need to get out of here. Some of the HOTRODs might have died in the explosion, but the others will come. They'll come after us. The rotor's no good to them underground, but they'll come on foot. They'll work out what's going on with the tunnels and the bunker, and they'll follow." He turns to Quinn. "I told you, didn't I?"

"Yes," she nods, confirming the many, many times he told her they would come, and when they did, he would be ready.

"I said all along they'd come, and when they did, we'd be ready. And we were ready. But it ain't over. We need to get out of here. Two days' travel through the caves to the Source. We'll be safe there."

Quinn turns to Anvil and Strat. "This is not your problem. "They won't come after you, they don't even know you exist. We could hide you." She turns to her father. "Can we hide them somewhere, keep them safe?"

Matt shake his head, "No, I don't think—"

"I got a feeling you're gonna need us," Anvil says.

"We're in," Strat confirms, guzzling the last of the preserve juice straight from the jar.

"Okay, we'll fill you in—the full story—on the way. Now, into the darkness we go."

Rows of backpacks line the bottom shelves of the doomsday bunker—over a dozen pre-packed identical bags containing enough survival gear to last a week underground. Matt hands out the bags, along with instructions that they each carry their own pack, and this is not negotiable; if they get separated, the pack will keep them alive. Then, everyone gets a laser, and all the weapons are set to kill. "It's life and death down here, we don't want anyone sneaking up on us in the dark," Matt instructs. "If you shoot at someone, something, they need to die."

Quinn opens her pack and checks the contents: dehydrated food and utensils, hydration capsules, water purifiers, a laser, torches, LitStones—kinetic energy stones that illuminate an entire area—med supplies, compact bedding, and abseiling gear—lightweight ropes and harnesses.

Matt takes down a box and hands out night-vision goggles.

Quinn frowns. "Do you have drops? We used them in Unus. You just squeeze them into your eyes and everything's as clear as day."

"Never heard of them." He grabs several pairs of glasses and slips them into his pack.

"Swarmbots?" Quinn asks.

Matt shakes his head.

"Drones?" she queries.

Again, Matt shakes his head.

"Heavy weapons. Something to take down the machines?"

He grins and grabs a thin black box from the top shelf of the storage. Inside is a portable launcher, a discrete imploding weapon designed to combust internally, so the enemy has no chance of survival. The weapon is deemed immoral and is prohibited by HEXAD—on humanitarian grounds. You can beat a person to death, you can shell them, stab them, shoot them, blast them, and hack them into little pieces, but you can't implode them.

The weapon is new and currently disassembled. Five black pieces snap together and form a thin, lightweight HOTROD-exploding device.

Quinn runs her fingers over the components. "Highly illegal."

"It's the twenty-first century, everything's illegal."

"How many shells?"

"Six. All I could get." He looks her in the eye. "Keep count."

Matt wears long shorts and a T-shirt and the others are still in their sleepwear, Quinn in her retro-rocket pajama bottoms and Einstein T-shirt, Anvil and Strat in their mismatched superhero boxer shorts and T-shirts. They will all need new attire, something more suitable for caving. Matt hands them each a lightweight grey thermal suit with a hood. The suits are one size fits all. They slip them on over their pajamas. They look like large, wrinkly slugs.

No one is wearing shoes. Matt has a box of SoleFeet with treads. They cut them to fit and wrap the material around their feet.

"Meet you in the garage," Matt says. Using a timber baton as a support, he hobbles towards the back of the bunker. Quinn follows.

They have several transport options in the garage: half a dozen electric bikes, a small, tarpaulin-covered truck, and an all-terrain hydrogen-cell buggy that looks like it belongs in the twenty-second century.

The hydro-buggy is made from silicon and has a clear shell and wheels that resemble sleek panther paws. The cockpit monitors the driver's blood pressure, heart rate, and temperature, allowing the vehicle to adjust to the driver's mood and experience.

All the vehicles point towards the east wall of the garage.

Strat and Anvil enter the garage.

"Flyke," says Strat. "This just gets better." He turns to his sister. "And you said Hobart was gonna be boring."

Strat and Anvil wander around, inspecting the vehicles.

Quinn rests against a wall and considers her travel companions:

Matt is propped up on the timber baton, supporting his injured leg. Strat is in good spirits but moving slowly and yawning—he is still weak from blood loss. Anvil has self-confessed dodgy ankles and the knees of a seventy-year-old. All of them have had at least one large glass of red wine.

Quinn sizes up the vehicles. “We take the buggy. I’ll drive.”

“No, we take the truck,” Matt says. “Trust me.”

She does.

Quinn helps her father haul the tarpaulin off the truck. Underneath is a modified Shaman CyberTruck, an all-terrain off-road vehicle. It’s amphibious and resembles an undersized military tank, except for its color. It’s orange—bright orange.

Quinn looks at her father and raises her eyebrows.

He shrugs. “It was a kit assembly. Easy build—finished it in less than two weeks—but the color . . .” He sighs. “I ordered dark grey. Didn’t realize it was orange till I unpacked the kit. Tried returning it, got halfway through the paperwork and gave up—too complicated. So, I built an orange Shaman CyberTruck.”

“Might be stating the obvious, but how are we gonna get that thing”—Strat points at the truck—“out of here and into a cave?”

“It’s a bloody big cave,” Matt says.

The four travelers gather beside the CyberTruck. Quinn stows the Disc carefully in her pack. Matt pulls a large sheet of paper covered with heavy lines, bubble diagrams, and notations, from his pocket. Anvil and Strat peer over his shoulder.

“A car game?” Anvil grins.

“It’s a map,” Strat says.

“A map of the cave system,” Matt says.

Quinn turns to her father. “What about Ada? What if she did steal the message, and the TechBand? Then she didn’t die because she was in the wrong place at the wrong time. She died because . . . what? What was she doing?”

Matt folds the map and tucks it into his pocket. “We don’t know anything, not really. But I reckon we take her with us—keep everything in our favor. No one finds out until we’re ready.”

Quinn nods.

They collect Ada’s cryovaced body from the casket and roll her into the rear of the Shaman. Matt snaps the canopy shut and heads for the cockpit. “I’ll drive.”

Quinn cuts him off and slides into the driver’s seat. “Not with your leg. It’s a manual.” Without waiting for a response, she shuts the door.

Matt pauses, rubs his leg, then reluctantly takes the front passenger seat as Strat and Anvil climb into the back.

The Shaman has lain idle for several years. Quinn crosses her fingers and pushes the ignition. She is rewarded with a beautiful, reliable reverberation. The vehicle hums. She switches on the lights and releases the brake, and they amble forward. A few yards before the wall ahead, she brakes and looks at her father.

“It’s paper-thin,” he says. “Gun it.”

She puts her foot down and they drive straight through and into a tunnel of rammed earth—a perfect fit for the Shaman’s sleek body.

As they continue on, Matt leans back in his seat, places his injured leg on the dash, and straps a mechanical brace around his thigh. Quinn glances over; he has opened an interface and is entering his physical details—age, weight, height. The mechanics of the brace will sync to his anatomy. Once he starts moving, it will mirror his gait and physiology. In a few hours, they will need to walk, and the brace will help.

Twenty-Four

Love ... is ... shit.

THE MID-MORNING SUN PIERCES the dusty windows of the greenhouse and floods the interior with a ruddy ambiance. The old wicker chairs and clay pots containing cool-weather herbs—cilantro, dill, sage—nestled on the worktables glow rustic and golden. The sun washes over the floor, turning the terracotta tiles a brighter shade. It hits Tig's strained face, causing his eyelids to flicker.

He opens his eyes and considers where he is. He is surprised by how different the greenhouse looks from the floor; the undersides of the windowsills are unpainted, and the bases of all the light fittings are filled with dead bugs.

His mouth is dry, and his head hurts. There's a hot spot on his thigh; Lupus is sleeping beside him. He pulls a pillow out from under his head and tosses it onto the bunk. Then he recalls what happened.

He pushes Lupus aside and jumps to his feet. He has been stunned before, but it's a rare occurrence; people who come at him usually want to kill him, not stun him. He feels foggy. He holds his head in his hands.

The dog shakes herself and yawns.

"What the fuck has she done?" he says to her.

He moves to the window and looks outside, to where the glass house once was. The site is now a smoldering fire. "Fuck!"

The dog bounds out the door. Tig scratches the side of his face, then follows her outside.

Ash and smoke fill the air.

The glass house is no longer standing. All that remains of the old tree is a charred stump. The timber staircase smolders—hardwood, it'll take days to burn—and a circle of the blackened foundations is still partly visible on the scorched earth. The metal framework that held the glass panels in place lies twisted and buckled on the ground.

On the southern side of what used to be the house, Tig sees a small pile of tools, the remains of Matt's toolbox—an aperture wrench, a multi-tool, and a small High-Tech Autohammer. Quality tools, all made of steel and glowing red-hot.

He spots a charred chair in the herb garden, thrown by the explosion. He strides over to it, rights it, and leaves it on the ground nearby.

The fire crackles and occasionally spits out a chunk of molten glass. The heat is intense, so he steps back and leans against the stone wall of the bee garden. Lupus sidles up and Tig fondles her ear. A bee buzzes in the garden, but the surrounding forest is settled and quiet. He wonders how long ago it happened, and how loud the explosion was. What the forest thought of it.

He suspects they got away. That was the plan—explode the house and escape to the Source.

He grits his teeth and shakes his head. "Love . . . is . . . shit."

It's like slamming your fingers in a rotor door or smashing your head on a graphene filter. Like someone has cut open your chest and hacked off little pieces of your heart.

He looks at Lupus. "It's agony."

Lupus smiles and wags her tail.

"Come on," he says.

They head northwest. Lupus strides ahead, sniffing at the ground.

"'She . . .'" Tig mutters. "'She is a palace that crushes down valiant worriers. A water skin that soaks its bearer, and a shoe that bites its owner's feet.'" Lines from *Gilgamesh*. He kicks a pebble out of his path. "How the fuck are we gonna make it after this?"

Twenty-Five

Mother Nature's basilica.

THE SHAMAN CYBERTRUCK LEAVES the tight confines of the human-made tunnel and rolls into the carved-out belly of a mountain. Quinn cuts the engine, and she, Matt, and the siblings slide out of the truck and step tentatively into a gloomy cavern fifty meters wide and thirty high. An arc of optimistic daylight filters through a small opening in the ceiling and reflects against the opposite wall—the last light they will see for two days.

"Mother Nature's basilica," says Matt. "Ten thousand years old. An underground river once swept through here. Over the centuries it carved out the cave and splashed calcium carbonate against the rock walls."

Wide-eyed, they all gaze around, taking in the scope of the space and the undulating layers of black and white marble that line the cave walls.

"Spec," Strat says.

"I feel like an ant," Anvil says.

"Yeah," Matt says. "We're nothing, not compared to this." He claps his hands. "Okay, enough sightseeing, we need to keep moving."

They slide back into the Shaman and head into the belly of the cave.

"Okay, tell me the good stuff, the positives," Quinn says to her father.

"We know where we're going," he says. "We know what lies ahead, and they don't. It might take them some time to find the bunker, but they'll find it, and they'll follow us into the tunnel. They have good Tech, and they'll track us. But we have the vehicle. They'll be on foot. Best-case scenario—by this evening, by the time we ditch the vehicle, we'll be half a day ahead. We're human, we can think for ourselves, and they can't. They come pre-programmed—they follow orders. Anything new, they call for instructions. And this"—Matt points into the darkness ahead—"this is all new."

"What about the rogue one? What was that about?"

"Something's going on. That machine came after you. It means someone wants you, or they want what you know. You gotta figure out who it is and what they want."

Quinn narrows her eyes. "Shun Mantra."

"Okay, what's at stake? Coin. Power. Sex. Love."

"Energy. But it seems they have that already."

"Okay. Now for the not-so-good news. They're faster. They're machines, they don't need to rest. They'll catch up at some point."

Soon, their optimistic shaft of sunlight vanishes. They won't see daylight for two days, and it's a depressing thought; total darkness is an unnatural state for humans, and the idea primes Quinn for melancholy. As she listens to the smooth hum of the engine, she stares into the darkness and her mood dwindles. She engages the Shaman's night vision but it doesn't help; the path ahead looks foreign and bleak.

"Okay," Anvil says, breaking the silence. "It's story time. Start from the beginning."

Quinn nods. "It started last year. We were on this island called Kerguelen, in the Southern Indian Ocean. I was monitoring solar flares, and there'd been some massive readings."

She relates the entire story, covering the last nine months in thirty minutes. When she finishes, she peers into the backseat and finds the siblings fast asleep. Beside her, Matt's eyes are closed, his head dipping. She focuses on the path ahead.

After half hour of easy driving, the main section of the cave ends. Two tunnels lie ahead, one forking to the right and the other to the left. She shakes Matt awake.

"Left," he instructs.

Quinn turns towards the left fork.

"More. That's it, keep going, keep going. More. More."

The vehicle misses the tunnel forking and comes face to face with a section of rock wall.

"Straight up," Matt instructs.

Quinn grins. She nuzzles the front wheels of the vehicle up against the wall of the cave. Matt leans over and flicks a switch on the dash. "Auto-gravity-defying traction technology. There are some things about High-Tech I love."

Gently, Quinn presses the accelerator. The vehicle climbs onto the wall of the cave. The back wheels follow. "Oh good lordt, this feels weird. It's like we're insects crawling up a wall."

"Weird, but fun. Just don't stall. Foot down."

She grips the wheel hard and puts her foot down. They shimmy up the wall of the cave, and then Matt points to a shadow on her left—the entrance to a spillway.

"That's our exit," he says.

She turns the Shaman towards the spillway.

"That's it," he says. "All the way to the floor."

She increases speed and the vehicle skips over the lip of the tunnel and lands, with a tremendous thud, in the spillway.

They jolt along the ground for another twenty meters, until Quinn brakes to a stop. She kills the engine and rubs her baby bump. "We didn't enjoy that."

"We hit something?" Strat yawns.

Both the backseat passengers slept through the wall climb.

They all slide out of the Shaman, slip on their night-vision glasses, creep back to the lip of the tunnel, and peer over the edge.

"How did we get up here?" Strat asks.

"Auto-gravity-defying traction technology," says Quinn. "We drove up the wall."

Matt grabs a pair of binoculars from his pack and scans the cave below. He pinpoints something, then passes the binoculars to Quinn. She also sees it—moving pinpricks of light in the distance. She counts five.

Anvil takes the binoculars. She peers into the darkness and holds up five fingers. "Can you shoot from here?"

"Too risky," Quinn says. "Six shells and we need them all."

"Ambush," Anvil suggests.

"Yeah, but not here." Matt pulls out his map and points to a small pink bubble. "Here, perfect place for an ambush. We go west, then we loop under the main tunnel and double back to the east." He raises an eyebrow and looks at Quinn for confirmation.

She shrugs; she has no understanding of the cave system. She points to Strat.

Strat takes the map and scans the markings; his eyes trace the thick and thin lines and rest briefly on the small bubbles. He flips the map upside down and studies it for another thirty seconds. Then he taps his head with his forefinger, neatly folds the map, and hands it back to Matt.

Matt hesitates. "That's it? You've memorized the map?"

"Yep. It's all here." Strat taps his forehead again.

"He has magnetic synesthesia," Anvil explains. "His visual perception and his spacetime are connected. He's a walking compass."

Matt shoots Quinn a questioning look.

She shrugs. "Apparently, he sees geographic grid lines. We should get going."

As the vehicle travels farther into the tunnel, the walls and ceiling begin to contract, and soon there's less than half a meter of space on either side. But they continue on, Quinn carefully maneuvering the Shaman through the narrow space, until they run out of road. It's the end of the line—now they must walk.

Quinn kills the engine. A hatch in the ceiling of the truck opens; they climb out and slide down the hood. Ahead is a deep shaft. Quinn peers over the edge, estimates a thirty-meter drop to the stagnant pool at the bottom. The water is rosy, the color of overripe raspberries.

Fixed to the wall of the shaft is a metal stepladder. Matt grips the ladder and attempts to pry it off the wall; it doesn't budge.

"Want me to go first?" Strat volunteers.

"You go second." Matt slaps him on the shoulder. "The Shaman goes first." He turns to Quinn. "You okay to leave Ada in the back? They'll never find her."

Quinn hesitates. "Seems a bit harsh. She's already drowned once."

"She's dead." Matt shoves his pack under the front wheel of the Shaman, then climbs back up on the hood, leans inside, and releases the brake.

They stand back. Matt removes his pack from the wheel, and they watch the Shaman glide towards the shaft. It tips over the edge and lands, with an audible splash, in the pool below. Slowly, it begins to sink.

"Someone should say something," Quinn says to her father.

Matt nods. He lowers his head.

Anvil and Strat lower their heads.

Quinn lowers her head and glances at her father—and realizes he has no intention of saying something.

"Okay, I'll say something." Quinn rubs her nose. "'No one can see death. No one can . . . see the face of death. No one can hear the voice of death. Yet there is savage death that snaps off humankind.'"

Matt raises an eyebrow.

"It's from *Gilgamesh*. It's the best I could do. We're all going to die. We don't know when or how."

"Except for your friend in CyberSleep. She might not die," Anvil says.

"That's true, but she might already be dead," Quinn says. "There are no guarantees."

They move towards the shaft. The Shaman begins to crackle and hiss. They peer over the edge and watch it slip below the surface of the lake. A slurping sound, like a burp, escapes.

"Okay, down we go." Matt adjusts the mechanical brace on his leg. Then he looks intently at Quinn, then at Anvil, and then at Strat. "Don't fucking fall."

"I'll be so pissed off if I die down here," Anvil says. "I'm beginning to doubt everything; myself, the escape plan, and both of you."

"You'll be fine." Matt pats her shoulder.

She flinches, then glares at him.

They descend, one by one, down the ladder. Strat goes first, followed by Anvil. Next is Quinn. Matt insists on going last.

***

Quinn steps off the ladder and onto the rocky shore. The ground is covered in loose stones, and she slips with every step. The air smells dense and putrid, like rotten eggs, and there is the constant sound of water dripping. Strat and Anvil stand at the edge of the pink phosphorescent lake, and Quinn and Matt join them.

"Beautiful," Anvil says.

"Toxic," Matt says. "Acid mine, full of heavy metals, arsenic, chromium, and lead. Don't touch it. Worse than it looks. We're gonna camp on the other side."

"If we stop, won't the HOTRODs catch us?" Anvil wrings her hands.

"They're still half a day behind and we need to rest," Matt says. "Besides, this is the perfect place for an ambush."

Matt ambles over the loose stones to a pile of rudimentary rafts and paddles that lean against the wall of the cave. He rummages through them, examining each raft and paddle in turn, and finally makes a selection. Strat strides over to help, and together they drag the raft to the edge of the lake.

"Coated in a hydrophobic preservative, it won't dissolve in the lake," Matt says.

"Hope it's the right one," Anvil whispers.

"Me too." Matt hands her a paddle.

Very carefully, they lower the raft onto the crimson lake. Then, one by one, they lower themselves onto the wobbling platform. Quinn sits at the front, Anvil and Strat take the center, and Matt takes the rear. They paddle cautiously, avoiding drips and splashes, and make their way across the lake.

It was the right raft.

They disembark and leave it docked in plain view, an obvious lure.

There is an exit tunnel on the far side of the rocky shore; this is where they set up base camp for the night. Tucked snugly inside the tunnel, they are hidden from view but, because the tunnel entrance is raised, have a clear view of the lake.

Quinn rolls out her sleep mat, lies down, and curls into a ball. She pats her baby bump. "Good girl," she whispers. "You did really well today." She closes her eyes; all she needs is a minute, then she will help with the food prep.

***

Hours later, she wakes. She sees the whites of someone's eyes inches from her face, and reels back. Switching on the light in her band, she realizes it's Anvil, lying next to her.

"I don't love the darkness," Anvil confesses. "Can I sleep next to you?"

"Sure." Quinn yawns and scoots over to make room for her.

Anvil places her hand on Quinn's abdomen. The baby kicks, and Anvil's eyes double in size. Quinn switches the light off, and they lie next to each other.

"You're mysterious; babies are mysterious," Anvil says.

I'm the least mysterious person here. "What's it like having all that electricity inside of you?"

"Have you ever played a song really, really loud, so loud the music becomes this force inside you and you become, like, one with the sound?"

"No."

"Well, it's like there's nothing else, just you and the music, and it's inside your head, inside your body, and you feel electric. I get this little buzz, and my fingertips tingle. That's how the electricity feels."

They lie in silence for a minute, then Anvil asks, "What's it like growing a human inside you? Like, you have someone else's ears and eyes growing inside you. Their heart, their human heart is growing inside you. And their toes and fingers—you're growing someone else's toes and fingers and ears inside you."

"Terrifying."

Twenty-Six

Anvil kneels beside her brother.

In the darkness, Quinn stirs; someone has taken hold of her wrist. It's Matt. She knows his scent and his touch. He places a pair of night-vision glasses in her hand, and she slips them on.

He is crouched beside her, close to her face. He places a finger on his lips. Then he holds up two fingers. She figures he means HOTRODs—two of them. He points to her pack, which she is using as a pillow. She nods; he must want the launcher.

She opens her pack and quietly retrieves the weapon. The box contains five pieces—handle, scope, barrel, trigger, spring. She knows nothing about guns, but the connections are universal. She slides the pieces into place—they fit together perfectly. Universal connections are a marvelous invention, a gift to the modern world. Carefully she inserts a shell.

Together, she and Matt creep to the entrance of the tunnel and peek around the corner of the spillway. There are two HOTRODs on the opposite side of the lake. Neither is moving. They must be waiting for instructions.

Eventually, one turns around and strides towards the rafts stacked against the wall of the cave. The machine collects a raft and two paddles, then returns to its companion and drops the raft into the lake. The HOTRODs climb in and paddle towards them.

Quinn's heart races. She raises the weapon to her shoulder and points it at the HOTROD seated at the front of the raft. She can't see anything—the scope is pitch black. She squints and tries again. Nothing. She moves the weapon to her left shoulder and peers through the sight with her left eye. It's still black. She checks her night glasses; they're not the problem. It's the launcher. She must have assembled it incorrectly.

The HOTRODs are halfway across the toxic lake with no sign of the raft sinking. They paddle in sync, like elite members of a rowing club who've trained together for decades. Their oars cut through the water, leaving barely a ripple, and it takes them half the time it took Matt and Quinn to cross the lake.

She taps Matt on the shoulder and shows him the weapon, indicating it's useless. He dismisses her with a wave of his hand. He is confident his plan will work; the raft will sink, and the HOTRODs will sizzle like lobsters dropped in boiling water. He raises a forefinger. One minute. The raft will sink in one minute.

One minute is too long. They'll be here in half the time. The machines are only a few meters from the edge of the lake, and the raft is still intact.

The HOTROD at the rear of the raft stands, tosses its paddle into the water, and jumps into the lake. Quinn sits down and begins to disassemble the weapon. Then she hears the HOTROD flailing and thrashing in the lake. She pokes her head around the corner; the HOTROD is clambering through the scarlet soup. When it reaches the edge of the water, it springs forward and lands on the rocky shore, where it collapses, face first, onto the stones.

She sighs. One down, but the other machine is still paddling and the raft is about to reach the shore.

The weapon lies disassembled on the ground in front of her. Universal connections are shit. All the sections fit together perfectly—so what's the problem? Her left hand picks up the spring and tosses it aside—an unconscious action that she didn't think, or will, or command. Okay, the spring is the problem; maybe it's only used for storing the weapon, not during launching.

Her left hand reassembles the weapon without hesitation. When it's done, Quinn lifts it, places it on her shoulder, and moves into position.

Finally, the raft has sprung a leak. The toxic liquid is eating the platform and the vessel starts to collapse. But it's too late; the raft hits the shoreline and the HOTROD steps out, walks around its prostrate companion, and heads straight for Quinn and Matt.

Quinn fires the launcher.

A direct hit. The machine shudders and breaks apart—a complete implosion.

Quinn sits back on her haunches, takes a deep breath, then slowly exhales.

***

After a breakfast of freeze-dried cranberry granola, Strat and Anvil wander down to the edge of the pink lake and stare at the HOTROD that managed to make it to shore after jumping in the lake. The toxic lake devoured whole sections of the machine and large parts of its exoskeleton are oxidized. Its legs and thighs are stripped bare. Inside the machine, the man is beginning to decompose.

Strat picks up a handful of flat stones and pitches them at the HOTROD's head. The rocks make a brittle sound on the machine's skullcap.

Quinn and Matt sit on the edge of the spillway—Quinn finishing her mug of tea, Matt studying the map.

"Are they safe?" Quinn asks, tilting her head towards Anvil and Strat.

"Yeah, let 'em have a few minutes."

Quinn grabs a laser from her pack. "Hey," she calls, "be careful." She tosses the laser to Anvil.

Anvil steps back, the weapon lands at her feet. "I'm a Pacifist, remember?"

"When it suits you," Quinn mumbles. She considers the ominous outline of the half-decomposed HOTROD. "Perhaps someone should go down and check the machine is dead. Really dead."

"It looks really dead to me," Matt says without looking up.

"We don't want it creeping up behind us in the dark."

Matt hands her the map. "Why don't you stay here and finish your tea, and I'll go check on it."

"Good man." She slaps her father on the shoulder.

Matt grabs a laser. He slips over the edge of the spillway and crunches his way across the stones towards the HOTROD. He collects the laser Quinn tossed to Anvil and cautiously approaches the machine, a weapon in each hand. The machine doesn't move. Matt squats beside it and darts his head back and forth, checking for signs of life inside the HOTROD. He gives Quinn a thumbs-up.

She smiles and raises her mug towards him. "Thank you," she calls. She is grateful that the toxic lake didn't let them down, that it ate right through the machine's exoskeleton, just as Matt expected.

Quinn surveys the calm scene before her, and it reminds her of a beach holiday: Strat and Anvil clutching handfuls of stones and taking turns skimming them across the smooth surface of the lake; Matt standing at the shore's edge, contemplating something in the distance—like he is looking out to sea; the HOTROD lying there as if it's just had a little too much sun and has fallen asleep sunbathing.

The serenity of the scene makes her nervous. With a wave of her hand, she calls, "We should get going."

Then, out the corner of her eye, she sees the machine's arm move. *No, no, no, it can't be alive.*

The HOTROD jumps to its feet. It knocks Matt sideways, and he drops both weapons. It grabs one of the lasers from the ground and shoots Strat in the head. A direct hit. Strat flails, the skimming stones fall from his hand. He stumbles forward, then hits the ground.

Shit. Quinn drops her tea and reaches for the rocket launcher. It's behind her, in the mouth of the tunnel—too far away for her to grab. She scrambles to her feet.

The HOTROD turns and points the laser at Matt.

Anvil jumps in front of him, her hands pointed at him in the shape of old-fashioned pistols. She jabs her forefingers at the HOTROD, and the machine stumbles and drops the weapons. She steps towards it—hands still jabbing—and the machine falls to its knees. Anvil pokes a pistol-forefinger into the HOTROD's skullcap. Fumes rises and the machine collapses.

Quinn slides down the edge of the spillway and scrambles over the rocky ground towards the lake. *No, no, no. This can't be happening.*

Anvil kneels beside her brother. She lifts his head and places it in her lap. Tears stream down her face.

Quinn drops beside her, overwhelmed with grief. She covers her face with her hands. "No, no, no. Strat does not die. Not down here."

"I, I, set the m-mouses to run," Anvil sobs.

"I don't understand. What mouses? Why are they running?"

"I, I s-s-set the l-louses to s-stun." Anvil quivers.

"Louses? Lasers! You mean lasers. You set the lasers to stun. Oh, thank the lordt. You set the lasers to stun." Quinn grabs the laser lying on the ground next to her. She checks the setting; it is, indeed, set to stun. She falls onto Anvil's shoulder. "You set the lasers to stun." She laughs. The relief is exquisite. Strat is not dead. He has been stunned.

She pats her baby bump. "Sorry. I'm so sorry I did that to you."

Twenty-Seven

Evolution.

HALF AN HOUR LATER, Strat jumps to his feet and shakes off the effects of the laser stun. He strides over the rocky ground and sits next to his sister, who's perched on the edge of the tunnel entrance.

"Youth!" Matt scoffs. "Take me a day to get over a stun like that."

Anvil's hands are still clenched in the shape of old-fashioned pistols. She takes long, slow breaths and stares vacantly into the distance.

Quinn sits on the other side of Anvil. She takes the girl's left pistol hand and gently folds in her thumb and forefinger; then she does the same to her right.

"You okay?" Strat asks.

"I'm fine, absolutely fine," Anvil replies.

"Nah, she's not," Strat says. "That's just girl-talk for everything's gone to shit. She'll be like this for a couple of hours, until she gets her energy back."

"It was impressive," Quinn says. "But given the circumstances, not as impressive as setting the lasers to stun while we slept." Quinn makes a mental note to regularly check the laser settings.

"Never done anything like that before. Most I can usually do is boil water and make tech stuff blow up."

"The HOTROD was half dead, you just finished it off," Matt says. "Now, we need to keep moving. Seven-hour walk to our next campsite." He slings his pack over his shoulder, and Quinn watches him hobble down the tunnel.

Seven hours is a long walk for a wounded man wearing a leg brace. For the first time, Quinn wonders about the validity of this plan. She also wonders if Matt has accounted for the fact that she is pregnant. Does seven hours really mean ten? Because she can't do ten, and she can barely do seven.

Strat jumps up, collects his pack, and throws it on his back. He grabs his sister's pack and hooks it over his right arm, and grabs Quinn's and slings it over his left arm. He adjusts his night-vision glasses and follows Matt into the tunnel.

***

They walk in a convoy line without speaking for the next four hours. Strat has taken the lead, carrying the three packs—against Matt's explicit instructions that, no matter what, they carry their own packs. No one comments. Anvil drags along behind him. Quinn follows, and Matt brings up the rear.

"Dad, you still here?" Quinn asks.

Silence.

"Matt?"

"I heard you."

This is time's fault. Time takes you. It takes people. "Can we rest?" Quinn asks.

"Sure."

Using the tunnel wall as a slide, Quinn shimmies down to a seated position. Anvil slumps next to her and opens her food supplies. She offers Quinn a bag of pumpkin seeds.

Quinn picks at the seeds. "Where are you two from?"

"Chatham Island, South Pacific—we're climate change refugees. But originally descended from the ancient *Australopithecus*, the 'Lucy' species—technological primates. Our lineage came to Eurasia from Africa. The woodland omnivores—creatures of the bush—make up 80 percent of our genome."

"And the other 20 percent?"

"If you believe the stories, we come from the stars. Our ancestors were a mysterious, archaic population born in the stars."

"We were all born in the stars."

Anvil smiles. "Yeah, but our ancestors didn't evolve on Earth, they were time travelers from another constellation, touring the universe on cosmic rays, traveling at the speed of light, collecting energy along the way, masses and masses of energy, which, apparently, they stored in their bodies. Their beginnings were fused in the gases, in the magnetic fields of the universe, and by the time they landed on Earth they'd gathered so much energy they were like nuclear generators. They came pouring down through Earth's atmosphere and found their way into our living cells, messed around with our genes, changed our DNA."

Quinn smiles. *Evolution. She's talking about evolution.*

"The journey took our ancestors ten days, but millions of years passed on Earth. Ours is a ghost lineage. There are sections of our genome that don't match anything else."

"Who told you that?"

"Elders. Our DNA is a window to the past. Our culture is ancient, like Tig's. All those bangles he has—weird, but they all mean something. Every single one of them. And you have some, too."

Quinn raises her wrist. "The red one means we're going to live happily ever after, when he forgives me for shooting him. The mauve one is for our baby girl, and this one, the green one, it has some cultural significance. Made from Imilac, formed when the universe first began, before time . . ." The hairs on Quinn's arms prickle.

She unfastens the green bangle from her wrist and hands it to Anvil, "Hold this." Then she crawls forward, retrieves her pack from where Strat dropped it, and pulls out the Disc.

Anvil immediately understands. She holds the bangle close to the surface and Quinn nods, giving her the signal to drop it onto the Disc. She does, and the bangle slides into the center ring, a perfect fit.

They hear a soft, reverberating hum, and the Disc begins to change color, turning blue-black. One by one, the symbols around the perimeter start to glow.

Anvil's eyes are wide. "Any idea what—"

"No idea," Quinn says.

She catches Matt's eye. He gawks at the Disc and draws closer. Strat follows and the four of them huddle around it.

"We have an ancient, glow-in-the-dark, humming time portal," Quinn says. "And my bracelet is the catalyst."

Strat points at the glowing symbols. "It's a map, a map of the universe. Look at the black areas, the dark places between the star points. It's skylore, indigenous astronomy. This is a frog; on this side is a serpent."

Anvil leans in. "He's right. The serpent, the frog—they're dark constellations, from a time before."

"A time before what?" Quinn asks.

"Everything."

Quinn sees confusing clusters of lines and dots—neon scribbles.

"It's a compass," Strat says. "Watch." He spins the Disc clockwise and it glows brighter. "When it's aligned with the universe, the constellations shimmer." He turns it in the opposite direction and the constellations fade. "You can't have a time portal without a calendar."

Quinn and Matt exchange a glance; the boy is a walking, talking navigation system.

Strat shrugs. "I see grid lines."

A circle in the center of the Disc begins to spin and they lean in, spellbound. The sphere spins 180 degrees. It clicks, then pops up, startling them, and they pull back. It's a sphere-shaped container.

Quinn pulls out the sphere and holds it in the palm of her hand. Strat taps the top of it. The sphere falls open, like the petals of a flower.

"It's empty," Strat says. "But it must hold something."

Expectantly, they all turn to Quinn.

She examines the sphere. "The Disc needs information to work—a code or a formula of some sort—and this, this must be where it's held. It's what powers the Disc. I'm guessing that power comes from neutrinos."

"Neutrinos are all around us. Five billion neutrinos pass through your thumbnail every second," Matt says.

"It's not that simple. There are different types, or flavors—graviton, tau, muon, electron—plus their antimatter counterparts. There are also the super neutrinos, born in black holes or during the death of stars. They're ancient, fourteen billion years old, and they hold masses of energy. I think that's what we need."

"Look, there's another ring, another groove, around the midsection, just like the one for the bangle," Anvil says. "There must be another catalyst."

"Yeah, it's about the size of a Frisbee, a small Frisbee," Strat says.

"Or, a plate, a small plate," Anvil says.

A shiver suns up Quinn's spine. "It's a crown."

"Nah, too thin for a crown," says Anvil.

"Yeah, and too small," Strat agrees.

"No. It really is a crown. I've seen it, I've even tried it on." It was in the Maldives artifacts that Quinn first saw the fine black crown that once belonged to an ancient queen.

"Flyke," Strat says. "It's like a puzzle; you got all these pieces, and you gotta work out how they fit together."

"Let's focus of getting the fuck out of here first," Matt says. "After that, you can work out how to travel through time."

Quinn drops the sphere back into place and plucks out her green bangle. Once again, the Disc resembles a fruit platter.

They slip on their packs—everyone carries their own now—and continue walking into the darkness.

Quinn thinks about the Disc. There's a problem—a big problem. Neutrinos violate nature's symmetry, and entropy equals chaos. They haven't allowed for antimatter and symmetry. The universe is in a unique state of balance. Both matter and antimatter must be accounted for; one can't exist without the other. But that would mean . . . the Disc has a partner, a companion. There should be two: one representing matter, and the other antimatter.

***

Soon, the landscape changes. Water seeps into the tunnel, and the sandstone walls gleam with moisture. Shallow puddles dot the floor, and the air feels damp and heavy. Timber beams replace the concrete posts that support the roof. The timber logs are inadequate compared to the concrete—many are warped and split. The verges of the tunnel begin to subside, with minor landslides every few meters. The four of them stick to the sides of the cave, where the floor is elevated, to avoid the murky water covering the path. But gradually, the shallow puddles get deeper.

More than once Quinn glances furtively at Matt, wondering about the soundness of the route, and Matt casts his eyes ahead on Strat and nods. It's the right way. Strat knows where he is going.

Then the water gives way to a slurry of mud. They use the timber beams as supports to help guide them over the deeper section of mire. A post that Anvil clings to gives way, and she lands in the mud. Quinn helps her out. The mud covers their faces; it travels up their arms and legs; it gets in their hair and eyelashes and ears.

They come across a monster truck wheel, half submerged in mud.

Matt grins. "We're almost out of this shit."

The ground begins to rise, and the mud solidifies and becomes a walkable path. The tunnel spills into a vast, open area, filled with machinery.

Matt finds a steel box fixed to the wall—the electrics. He opens it and flicks the switch. Rows of lights hum and flicker as the place comes to life.

Everyone pulls off their night-vision glasses. They are in a vast hall, lined with concrete panels and filled with mining machinery. It's a graveyard of abandoned equipment. Earthmovers, tractors, graders, conveyers, and more—over two dozen pieces of machinery, all covered in a fine layer of coal dust.

They all smile and peer at the electric-light-filled world; it's a relief to be out of the mud and to take off their glasses. Then, at the far end of the hall, Quinn sees three HOTRODs enter the hall.

Without skipping a beat, the machines draw their weapons and fire, and the four humans scatter.

They take cover on either side of the hall: Strat and Quinn huddle behind the massive wheel of a monster truck, while Matt and Anvil flee to the opposite side of the hall and take cover in the metal bucket of a grader. They are twenty meters from Strat and Quinn, but they have a clear line of vision to each other.

The HOTRODs continue to hammer them with incessant rounds of fire.

Quinn opens her pack and retrieves the rocket launcher. She knows what she has to do. She loads a shell, gets down on the ground, and lies on her back, tight up against the edge of the monster wheel.

Strat and Matt start blasting the HOTRODS with their lasers, providing cover.

Quinn takes a breath; she twists into the aisle, aims, and shoots. A machine implodes.

She rolls back behind the wheel. "Three down."

She reloads the launcher.

The chamber is engulfed in heavy fire—shrapnel exploding in all directions, blasting into the walls around them, and ricocheting off the machinery. If HOTRODs had feelings, Quinn supposes they'd be really pissed off right now.

Strat covers his ears and huddles with Quinn behind the wheel of the monster truck until the attack abates. Then Quinn knits her fingers together to form a stirrup and points to the top of the wheel. Strat nods—he gets the idea. He cups his hands into a foot support. She steps into it. He hoists her up. She has a clear view over the top of the wheel. The HOTRODs are not firing at them, they are firing at the ceiling. They are trying to bring the roof down. They will be buried alive.

Quinn shoots. A direct hit. The machine implodes.

Strat lowers her to the ground.

"Four down."

Above them, the roof shudders. Cracks spreads across the concrete ceiling and chunks of rubble begin to fall. The hall fills with debris and dust.

A slab of concrete above Matt and Anvil breaks free. Matt pulls Anvil towards him; the slab hits the ground beside them. Another slab crashes to the ground in front of them. They are penned in on two sides by the collapsing ceiling.

Quinn points to an exit tunnel in the sidewall, about ten meters away. Matt nods; they need to get out of the hall. He grabs Anvil by the sleeve and hauls her towards the exit, dodging debris as they go. Once they make it to the tunnel safely, they go no farther. They wait for Quinn and Strat to join them.

A large slab of falling concrete rocks the hall, and the ground vibrates. Quinn and Strat lose their balance, and the launcher tumbles from Quinn's hand. Strat collects it from the ground without hesitation and hands it to her. She loads a shell, then pauses. There's a dent in the barrel; it won't fire. She turns to Strat, a look of panic across her face.

A rumbling sound—they look up. The ceiling above them is cracking apart.

A massive slab of concrete falls, crushing the truck they were sheltering behind.

There's no way they will make it to the tunnel where Matt and Anvil are waiting for them. Strat points at the tunnel behind them—the way they came in, through the murky water. They turn and run.

As they dive into the tunnel, the chamber behind them collapses, blocking the entrance. Matt and Anvil are just forty meters away, but impossible to get to. Quinn and Strat are on their own. They have their packs, but no map.

They slip on their night-vision glasses and scramble farther into the tunnel, down to the giant truck wheel submerged in the mud. They perch on top of the tire, and Strat dives into his pack for a filtration tablet. He fills his water container with the stale water and pops in the tablet. "You okay? You're not hurt?"

Quinn shakes her head; the baby is fluttering—she is okay. Extremely tired, dirty, and dusty, but in one piece.

"You think the last HOTROD is dead?" Strat hands her the water.

She takes a sip and hands it back. "Yeah. I do. Please tell me there's another way out of here."

Strat points behind them. "There's another way out of here, a connecting tunnel." He helps her down from the tire.

"How far?"

"A couple of hours."

"They're going to think we're dead."

"Nah, she's got a handle on me." They wade through the mud in silence for a few minutes, then Strat says, "You heard of this guy called Einstein, Alfred Einstein?"

"It's Albert, Albert Einstein."

He shakes his head. "Nah."

Quinn unseals her insulating-slug suit and points to her T-shirt. "'I have no special talent. I am only passionately curious.' *Albert* Einstein."

"You think it's the same guy?"

"There's only one Einstein."

Strat turns to face her. Walking backwards, he says, "Stephen Hawking said time travel was just science fiction until Einstein. General relativity showed spacetime was warped; you could go off in a rocket and return before you left. I reckon it's easier walking backwards."

Quinn turns around. Side by side, they continue backwards through the mud, into the tunnel.

"I'm not sure this is easier, it's just different," she says after a minute, but she continues walking backwards.

"How you reckon time travel works?"

"My best guess? Objects bend spacetime and we perceive this as gravity. But if spacetime bends, or folds back on itself, it creates a route that can take you backwards or forwards through time. The Disc creates a void, a weak point in the route—it opens a door. Walk through that door, and you get from one point in time to another, superfast."

He nods. "And how do you get your hands on those ancient super neutrinos?"

"There's an observatory at the South Pole, called the IceCube. Discovered amazing stuff about subatomic particles and the way they behave. It has a neutrino detector. If you wanted to find super neutrinos, that's where you'd go."

East Antarctica has the oldest ice on the planet, she thinks. There's sure to be some very old and ancient neutrinos there, under the newer layers of ice—maybe two kilometers down.

"What about the paradoxes?" Strat asks. "There's so many—grandfather paradox, consistency paradox, pedestrian paradox. And the loops—butterflies and bootstraps. What the fuck do they all mean?"

"I think the consistency paradox *is* the grandfather paradox, and the pedestrian paradox and the bootstrap loop are kind of the same thing. Basically, you're not supposed to alter the past or become part of a past event. There are consequences to changing history. It can erase the reason to go back in time in the first place."

"You reckon Einstein time traveled? Went forward in time, found out about relativity, then came back and told the world?"

"No."

Twenty-Eight

Oh fuck, we're dead.

A SHIVER RUNS THROUGH MATT, but he is not cold, just tired, and the wound in his leg aches. The pain saps his energy, and his resolve fades.

They've been separated. This is not good. He scratches a splatter of mud from this thumb; right now, there's not much he can do about that. But at least Quinn is with Strat; she'll be okay. The boy has an uncanny sense of direction.

The air is dense, filled with concrete and coal dust from the collapse of the ceiling in the adjacent chamber. A film of dust has settled over Matt's clothes and skin, sticking to the layers of mud. The fine powder is everywhere—his hair, his nose, his ears. He shakes his head, and a plume rises.

He picks the grit out of the corners of his eyes, then looks around. They are in a hall similar to the one they just fled. It's lined with concrete panels and filled with abandoned mining machinery.

Anvil is safe. She resembles a small, round mud monster. She scrunches her face and the layers of mud crack and peel away. "Weren't we just in here?" she asks, wide-eyed, as she scans the rows of mining equipment. "Oh fuck, we're dead. We just died. Now we're stuck in the same place forever. You and me and all these . . . tractors."

Matt shakes his head. "What do you mean?"

She looks up at the ceiling. “Maybe it’s a parallel universe. Maybe that’s what happens when you die.”

Matt scratches his nose. “Except these ‘tractors’ are different, completely different, to the ones in the other hall.” He nods towards a row of vehicles. “Over there, you got your bucket wheel excavators. That one’s a bulldozer, that’s a loader, and this here”—he taps the machine next to him—“this is a drill. The other hall, that was full of trucks and graders. Completely different.” He rubs his thigh, then stretches his leg and lets out a long sigh.

“Okay, wevs.” She shrugs. “They got out, didn’t they?”

“Yeah. Back the way we came in, through the mud. I trust ’em to find their way—they’re resourceful. They’ve got a few exit options. Strat’ll work it out.” He takes a few steps towards her. “Right now, it’s you and me, and we need to look after each other.” He lifts an arm, about to slip it over her shoulder, to reassure her that he has got this, that he knows how to get them out of here and they are going to be okay.

She steps back, a look of panic on her face.

Casually, he runs his hand through his hair, as if this were his intention all along. Another plume of coal dust rises. He clears his throat. “We’re gonna be okay.”

He ambles up to a bulldozer, hauls himself into the cab, and presses the ignition. It clicks, then nothing. He swings himself down. “Check the others. They came in through that tunnel.” He points to an opening at the far end of the chamber. “We get one to start, we take it for a drive. No more walking.”

“No more walking.” She nods.

“It’s a push-button start. Black button, you just need to press it.”

“Got it. You think one’ll work?”

“Doubt it. Been idle for decades. Unlikely we’ll get one to start.” He hauls himself into another cab and presses the ignition. There’s no response.

"Right, but we're doing this anyway," she mumbles.

Matt works one side and Anvil works the other. Systematically, they make their way through the vehicles in the hall. After twenty minutes, what little hope they had fades; all the batteries are dead.

Anvil jumps down from the last cab. She eyes Matt and points her pistols hands at him.

Immediately wary, he retreats.

"I might be able to make a spark. Would that help?"

At ease again, he grins. "Follow me." At the back of the grader, he opens a side panel and locates the battery box. Then he undoes the screws and locknuts and takes off the top plate. He slips out the hold-down assembly, revealing the two twelve-volt batteries inside, and shows her the battery cables—negative and positive. "When I give the signal."

She nods.

He slides into the cab of the grader. "Shoot."

Anvil touches the battery cables with her forefingers.

Matt presses the ignition.

The machine splutters and rumbles. Then it cuts out.

"One more time," he calls. "We do it together, in sync."

He presses the ignition, and Anvil generates a spark of electricity. Again, the engine splutters and rumbles—then it comes to life and settles into an even idle.

Matt climbs down from the cab. Grinning, he strides towards Anvil with open arms, expecting to embrace her in a triumphant hug.

She sidesteps and points her pistol hands in his direction.

He pulls up and, smiling, gently punches her in the arm, a concessional victory celebration. She laughs and punches him back, a little harder. He laughs with her and gives her a slightly firmer punch on the shoulder.

She whacks him in the chest.

He gulps. "Okay, jump in; you're driving this thing out of here."

She shakes her head. “I can’t drive.”

“You’re about to learn.”

Twenty-Nine
Ice crystals.

"How you doing?" Strat asks.

"Me? I'm fine. Just fine." Quinn yawns.

"That bad?"

She smiles. "I'm just tired." Quinn is so tired she might fall asleep standing up.

"Your legs hurt?"

Her legs are so sore she could cry. "Yes, they hurt."

"Okay, we're gonna take a detour up ahead, then we can rest on the other side. It ain't far, another few hours."

"Thank the lordt. Honestly, I thought we might die down here. Or be trapped forever." To Quinn, it feels like they're walking in circles, and the thought of spending days and nights underground, trying to find an exit, is terrifying. The thought of running out of supplies and water is terrifying. "I was beginning to doubt the plan," she says.

Strat taps his forehead. "I know where we're going—and, bonus, I know which way is north."

She smiles. "Definitely a bonus."

Strat wipes the sweat off his forehead. "You hot? Feels like it's getting warmer."

"I don't get hot. I have Raynaud's syndrome, a hereditary disease, keeps me cool." Quinn holds out her hand, and Strat squeezes her fingers.

"Cold," he confirms.

"But you're right—it is warm, and I think it's getting hotter."

Strat points to his right. "This way, there's a fork. It'll take us to . . ." He pulls up short, stops at the entrance to an adjoining chamber. "What the fuck?"

Quinn stumbles into him. She peers past his shoulder; the tunnel ahead is filled with hundreds of sparking white columns, about a meter wide and ten meters long. Half the columns are upright, and the other half lie scattered across the ground. The scene resembles the courtyard of an ancient, half-ruined temple.

"Ice," Strat says. "Ice crystals." The material is glass-like and pearly.

Slowly, they enter the chamber. A wave of intense heat and a foul smell overwhelms them. They step back.

Quinn holds her nose. She steps into the chamber and slides her hand down a column; the surface is hard and smooth, and it leaves a trace of white powder on her hand. She rubs it between her fingers. "It's gypsum, calcium sulfate. There's a heat source underneath. It's heated the groundwater and crystals have grown. I've never seen anything like this."

She scurries back to the entrance and joins Strat.

"It smells like dead feet," he says. "Must be 50 degrees Celsius. Stay in here too long and we'll be cooked." Perspiration runs off his forehead, and his thermal suit is soaked in sweat.

They can't see the end of the passage. "How far?" she asks.

"About a hundred and fifty meters."

The distance is not the problem; the problem is that the trek is an obstacle course inside an overheated sauna.

"The less time we're in there, the better. I reckon we can do this in fifteen minutes." Quinn grabs three LitStones and shakes them, activating their kinetic energy. She pitches the stones into the chamber. Now they can see the exit tunnel at the far end. "Maybe twenty minutes. That's how long the LitStones last; after that, our time is up."

They each drink half a bottle of water. Then they peel off their insulating grey slug suits and stand, side by side, in their pajamas—Quinn in her space-rocket shorts and her Einstein T-shirt and Strat in his superhero boxer shorts.

Quinn scouts a visual path around the first section of crystals. “Follow me,” she says.

They hear a distinct hissing sound and Strat hesitates. “What’s the station with the snakes?”

“Snakes? Why would there be snakes?”

“Hissing.”

“Air pressure. Steam.” Quinn casts her eyes about for any sign of snakes. *Good lordt I hope there are no snakes in here.*

In the first section of the chamber, the columns are small and lie across the ground. They are able to skirt around them easily. Farther into the passage, however, the trek becomes more arduous. The columns are larger and tightly packed together. Those that are still upright reach the ceiling, and appear to be holding up the roof. The fallen columns lie tumbled across each other, clogging the route ahead.

Strat pauses to help Quinn over the wider columns; he is always one step ahead, making sure she doesn’t fall or slip. Their progress is steady but slow. They pause every twenty meters to rest and check on each other.

After ten minutes of scrambling through the forest of crystals, Quinn turns to Strat. “I reckon we’re over halfway—”

She freezes. There’s a HOTROD standing at the entrance of the chamber. “Shit.”

Strat follows her gaze. “Fuck.”

The HOTROD draws its weapon.

They duck behind the nearest column.

The HOTROD fires. Shards of crystal fill the air. They retrieve their lasers from their packs and return fire.

After taking a dozen direct hits, the HOTROD flounders. It falls to its knees and rolls its head from side to side.

Quinn and Strat scramble forward and take cover behind another column.

The HOTROD bounds back onto its feet. It steps into the chamber and raises its weapon. It's coming for them.

"I think it hates us more than we hate it," Quinn says.

The columns around them begin to explode. They hit the ground and crawl. Splinters of crystal dig into their knees and palms, but they cover another ten meters on their hands and knees. When they look up, the machine is thirty meters behind them and gaining ground. Apparently, the heat has no effect on it.

They blast it with another intensive round of fire. The machine staggers, and they move forward, gaining a few meters of ground, while it recovers.

The end of the chambers is only twenty meters away, but reaching it is no longer their goal, because the HOTROD is still coming, and right now it feels like nothing will stop it. It just keeps coming.

Quinn holds her head in her hands. "This is not going to work. We need a plan."

Strat points at the roof. "Bring the roof down. It worked before." He wipes the sweat off his brow.

She pauses, considering the roof. "No." She shakes her head. "Not the roof. We shoot the floor. What lies below the ground is hell." Scanning the chamber, she points to an area a few meters behind them. "That section, where the columns are sinking."

"I see it." Strat fires at the ground.

Quinn fires at the HOTROD, slowing it down and buying them time. She and Strat edge backward, gaining a few more meters of ground, as they continue to fire.

The HOTROD powers through Quinn's laser fire and scales a large column lying across the ground, directly in front of it. But it misjudges the landing. It slips and crashes to the ground.

Now it's ten meters away, at eye level, and Quinn catches a glimpse of the man inside the machine. What she sees is a tired, harried human: A man who sacrificed himself for vengeance, war, and violence. A man who gave away the little freedom he once had and opted for a job—something to do—and now, merged with a machine, is the worst rendering of humanity and technology possible. He represents the dexterity and nimbleness of the human race, but without rumination, without morality, without perception. The job he was offered as an alternative to imprisonment was not an occupation or a vocation with responsibility; it was servitude—a form of slavery, enabled by technology.

The chamber groans. Quinn feels the ground move under her. Sections of the floor begin to crack. She exchanges a glance with Strat; this might work. With renewed vigor, they help each other off the ground and continue firing at the floor between them and the HOTROD.

The HOTROD rights itself, then leaps over several columns as if they're nothing more than twigs. Suddenly it's only a few meters away. Quinn and Strat raise their weapons and fire. The machine stumbles but recovers quickly and continues forward with renewed effort, deflecting shards of flying crystal as it scrambles towards them.

The chamber rumbles. The floor trembles. Unperturbed, the HOTROD picks up the pace.

"Go," Quinn yells at Strat. "Get out of here."

Instead, Strat steps in front of her and shoots at the ground in front of the HOTROD. Quinn joins him.

A section of the floor between them and the HOTROD sinks. A cloud of heat and steam rises into the chamber. The HOTROD reaches the edge of the pit and peers into void below. It wavers, seemingly unsure whether to jump across the gaping cavity. Then the ground below it gives way, and it's swallowed by hell.

"Let's get out of here," Quinn says.

They flee toward the exit. Strat is faster, but every few strides he turns back to check on Quinn, helping her over a column and taking her hand as she slips down the surface of another. He travels twice the distance he needs to.

Behind them the columns shudder and, one by one, sink. Plumes of heat haze rise from the pool of magma below.

They reach the exit shaft and hoist themselves into the connecting tunnel. Then they run. They run until Quinn can go no further.

"Wait, wait. I'm done. I'm done." She slumps, panting, against the earth wall of the tunnel and then sinks to the ground.

Strat drops onto the floor next to her.

Exhausted, they rest. Their lips are cracked, their mouths are dry, they're dripping wet, and their hands and knees are filled with tiny shards of crystal.

"Either you're pretty fast for a pregnant chick or I'm really unfit," Strat says between gulps for air.

"Motivated by mother love," Quinn says.

"That fucker is dead. He ain't never coming back." Strat looks at her for confirmation.

"Yeah. Except in our nightmares." She sighs and rubs her eyes. "I can't wait to get out of here." Quinn holds her baby bump and waits for a sign. She feels a flutter, and then another. She closes her eyes, and her head rolls back.

***

Quinn dreams she is walking through the massive Wilkes Basin in Antarctica—naked and pregnant. This is a recurring scenario: The snow has melted, replaced by glittering crystals of salt. Ferns and native grasses grow along the ridgeline of the Basin. The sky is mauve and filled with rainbow clouds—soft pinks and pale blues—from horizon to horizon. The baby in her belly is heavy. She is on a mission to get to the other side, to safety, but she knows it's an impossible task and she won't make it before the labor starts. The baby is coming. So she sits down on the crystallized valley floor. She is going to give birth in a super saline pool in the middle of the Wilkes Basin.

***

Quinn opens her eyes. She is in a dark, warm place—nothing like Antarctica. She hears snoring and realizes it's Strat, lying on the ground next to her. She feels for her night-vision glasses. When she can't locate them, she has a moment of panic, then realizes they're on her head. She slips them over her eyes.

Strat is asleep on the floor next to her. He is still wearing his pack. He must have fallen asleep and keeled over. She doesn't know how long they've slept, and she has absolutely no idea what time it is or where they are in the cave system.

She is dehydrated. She drinks half her remaining water. Then she shakes Strat. "Hey, wake up."

Strat rolls over. "Ow. Massive headache."

His glasses are on the floor beside to him. She hands them to him, then passes him the water. "How you feeling?"

"Everything hurts. My back, my knees . . ." Strat pulls out tiny shards of crystal from his knees.

"Yeah, the knees are the worst. And hands, are your hands sore?" Quinn examines her palms, which are covered in dried blood.

"Yeah, they hurt heaps, and my elbows." Strat rubs his elbows. "Do your elbows hurt?"

She feels her elbows. "No."

"Okay, what about . . . your head? You got a headache?"

"Yes, dehydration." *Please tell me there's water close by and an easy way out of here.*

"There's an underground river," he says, "about five K's away. It flows from the Source. The river runs through a canyon, and there's a boat."

She stares at him. The boy is a revelation—he told her exactly what she wanted to hear. "You sure about the boat?"

He shrugs. "On the map there's a yellow boat."

She smiles. "I know the place."

"You know, the first thing I'm gonna do when I get out of here is get a real dog. They smell fleek." He jumps to his feet. "This is the most I've ever walked. I don't walk this much in a year."

Quinn tries to hoist herself off the floor, but she is stuck. "Give me a hand, I can't get up."

Thirty

It's Following us.

A FEW HOURS LATER, QUINN and Strat stand at the entrance to a grotto and look down on a dark pool of water. Quinn ignites two LitStones and tosses them into the darkness, illuminating the space.

They are in a cavern, a cave within the cave, and at the bottom a river snakes for fifty meters before disappearing underground. Quinn knows this place; she has been here before with her father. This is the Source, the origins of the natural underground tributary that feeds the river on Matt's property.

They are ten meters above the water. Getting down will require an awkward scramble over several large boulders and loose stones—it won't be easy.

"I'd be tempted to jump, if I weren't pregnant," Quinn says. She turns to Strat. "But you could. It's deep enough."

"I can't swim." Strat eases his way down the face of the first boulder. "I'll go first. Follow me."

When they reach the bottom, they kneel at the edge of the bubbling river. The water is deep and cold. They cup their hands and drink. Then they peel off their flexible soles and dangle their feet in the water while they wash away the mud, blood, and dust from their arms and faces.

"I can't see a boat," Strat says.

"It's not a boat. It's a submarine."

"Flyke! Does it have a periscope?"

She shakes her head.

"Why not?"

"It just doesn't."

Quinn recalls Matt telling her that the submarine, like the Shaman, came in kit form. He assembled the key pieces—turbines, engine, pumps—on the front lawn, then hauled it into the valley on the back of a truck and finished piecing it together by the side of the river. When it was fully assembled, he submerged the craft and explored the deeper sections of the river. Finally, he positioned it as an escape option in a corner of the pool.

Quinn wades into the water, which is shockingly cold but refreshing. She scans the surface, looking for signs of the sub, and spies a yellow flicker on the other side of the river; the body of the submarine is rubber-duck yellow.

She dives under the water, swims to the sub, and releases the weights on either side of the craft. Gently, it bubbles to the surface.

The vessel resembles an armchair with a large beach ball perched on its seat, and it's not much larger. Quinn pushes it across the river and docks it next to Strat. Then she pulls herself up and sits next to him.

"We ain't both gonna fit inside," he says.

She nods. "You drive, I sit on the back."

"I can't swim," he reminds her. "Are you sure—"

"It's okay, I've done it before. I'll probably fall asleep." She yawns.

Stored in the tiny cabin of the sub are two watertight suits with helmets and breathing apparatus. Quinn retrieves one and pulls it over her pajamas. The cabin has two hours of oxygen and the trip takes half an hour; Strat won't need a suit.

The sub controls are a joystick configuration: forward and back, left and right, up and down. There are only two speeds, slow and medium.

Strat is confident he can lead them out; module games, he tells Quinn, require more dexterity.

He bends his long legs and curls himself into the cabin, then closes the hatch. He looks like a stick insect trapped inside a soap bubble.

He clutches his throat and slaps the side of the hatch, a mock enactment of suffocation.

Quinn rolls her eyes.

She withdraws a laser and a set of knives from her pack, along with a few LitStones, and stows them in her pockets. Then she knocks on the bubble. Strat opens it.

"I just have to say, you've been awesome. I couldn't have asked for a better cave buddy." She tosses her pack at him, and he places it under his feet in the cabin.

"Yeah," he says. "If I ever get stuck underground and need to blow up a few HOTRODs, I'll text you."

"I won't answer." She smiles. "But when we get out of here, I'll give you my T-shirt."

He grins. "Einstein. Flyke."

She closes the bubble. Again, he pretends to suffocate.

"I take it back," she shouts through the glass. "You're the worse cave buddy."

Strat locks the cabin. Quinn straps herself onto the bench seat at the rear of the submarine. In thirty minutes, they will be at their rendezvous site in the mountains. They will see sunshine again and, hopefully, Tig as well. Their journey underground is almost over, and she desperately wants him to be there, at the end. She knows what his superpower is—and it's not his ability to fix things, or to make everything right. It's his presence. She feels safe when he is around. Security, love, and safety—that is what he brings her.

She rubs her baby bump. "Not long, and we'll be out of this mess. No more wretched darkness."

The submarine submerges. There is only one exit option—down

through the mouth of the river cave. Quinn relaxes into her seat. She breathes deeply and slowly. The light from the sub projects forward, so there is little to see, but she is warm and comfortable in her watertight suit. The sub engine gently vibrates, a soft hum reverberates, and her head drops forward. She closes her eyes.

Something touches her hand. A ripple, or a vibration from the engine. Then she feels a tug at the sleeve of her suit. She opens her eyes. *Is there something on me?* It's too dark to see. She lifts her arm; it feels heavy. She plucks a LitStone from her pocket, shakes it, then casts it into the water. Vines surround her. The sub is passing through a patch of weeds.

She brushes them away. They come back.

She gets a better look at the persistent underwater vegetation. The vines resemble thick stalks of celery. At the end of each stalk is a furry pod covered in fine tentacles. She wonders how they survive in such a dark, cold place.

The underwater plant clings to her suit. She brushes it way again but it returns, winds itself around her wrists and arms. She pulls it off. It darts back.

Oh shit, it's swimming. It's following us.

The little black pods on the end of the fronds open and quiver. They're excited. Quinn reaches for the knife in her pocket and, when the vines get close again, slices through the main stalks. The vine oozes dark liquid into the water and the black pods snap wildly at her; they're not happy. She wields her knife at them. The pods back off and drift away.

She shudders and casts another LitStone in the water. The vine has retreated, but she keeps her knife close.

It can't be long until they pass through the mountainside and into daylight. It can't be long now.

She shudders again. It's cold. She shouldn't feel cold, her suit is thermal. She looks down; there are black spots all over her suit. Tiny holes, hundreds of tiny holes all over her suite. *Wretched bloody creatures. Okay, I'll be fine, it can't be far. It's just the cold. I can cope with that.*

She moves her arms to keep warm and slips off the back of the sub. *Shit. They've eaten through the straps.*

She drops her knife and grabs the railing. She needs to let Strat know she is in trouble; she needs to tap on the bubble—but she can't, she can't hold on, her arms don't work. Her fingers open and her hands peel off the railing. She floats off behind the sub and Strat has no idea. He was her lifeline, and she let him go.

Soon the dim light from the sub fades. She feels weary and depleted. Her arms hang limp, her head rolls back. The cold is anesthetizing her. She closes her eyes. Her feet hit the riverbed, and she lies down on the sandy bottom. It's a good place to sleep, and she is tired.

Why did I let go? Such an idiot.

There's a lilting, calling sound. Low and melodic, it's the same tune over and over, caught on a loop. It must be the fish, she thinks, an underwater choir, singing just for her. The sound is hypnotic. The music is soothing.

The heat bleeds from her. The cold seeps inside—into her lungs, into her heart.

The singing stops.

***

Something grabs Quinn's arm. It pulls her, tugs her from her icy crib. It hauls her through the water. Her eyes flick open. Murky, hazy streams of light surge towards her. She is hauled upward, towards the surface, towards the light—and then she feels warm air on her face.

She is dropped and lands hard, right on her elbow. It stings. She needs to tell Strat; now her elbow hurts, too, like his.

Anvil steps forward and hovers over her. She seems agitated, she keeps moving back and forth, from one side to the other; with every move, the sun behind her slips in and out of view. She moves closer and Quinn sees she has a Nanopatch in her hand. It must be medicine, an antidote for the cold.

Quinn wriggles back. “No, no,” she whispers. “The baby.”

Anvil pauses. She understands, the patch might harm the baby. She drops her hand and steps aside.

Tig yanks the patch from Anvil’s hand, rips it open with his teeth, tears off Quinn’s underwater suit, and presses the patch to her chest.

Quinn grabs his hands. “No, no, don’t.”

He presses so hard she thinks he might break her chest open.

You can never win against a cyborg. Never.

Warmth surges through her.

Thirty-One
We named her Tardi.

QUINN OPENS HER EYES. She is in bed—her favorite place—covered with a soft sheet. She lifts her head and surveys her surroundings.

She is in a small room. It's familiar, and it smells salty and musty. It's the smell of the sea mixed with paper and old books. It's the smell of *Nanshe*. She is in Tig's cabin on *Nanshe*.

"Hey," Tig says, startling her. He is lying beside her in bed. She hadn't realized.

He has an open book in his hands. She has never seen him read before, and she didn't know this about him, that he reads books. It seems strange and unusual to be finding this out now. Who is this man? Is this an altogether different Tig, a Tig who reads? There are two Tigs already—medicated and unmedicated—and that's complicated enough. She doesn't know if she can cope with a third one.

She turns towards him. "May I?" she asks, and takes the book out of his hands. It's a novel, a work of fiction. She gazes around the cabin; one wall is lined with bookcases. She knew this. She has been here before, and of course, Tig can quote *Gilgamesh* by heart.

She hands the book back to Tig, who is shirtless. His right arm is stripped of skin, bare to the shoulder socket. Pure titanium.

"How you feelin'?" he asks.

"I feel . . . good. What happened?"

"Carnivorous plants liked the look of you. They tried to eat you. Predatory protocells—the toxins ate into the walls of your cells, drilled into the protein membrane, and sucked up your DNA."

"Greedy shits."

"We had an antidote. A Nanopatch with a high dose of zinc."

"Zinc! I love zinc." She smiles. "Saved by element number 30, who would have thought."

Quinn is thirty, so this year zinc is her element, and now it has saved her—stopped the potassium from leaking out of her red blood cells.

"Zinc and—"

"Not just zinc?"

"Tardigrades. Water bear DNA. Mind-blowing stuff. Resistant to toxins and radiation. Can withstand *huge* temperature variations—zero to a hundred." He raises an eyebrow. "Also, pressure resistant. The stuff has a damage suppressor. It protects your DNA, shields it against extreme shit, like . . . carnivorous plants. Amazing stuff. Worked a treat on you."

"The baby?"

"Baby's fine." He looks her in the eye. "But . . . she might be able to deep sea dive. Without a suit."

Quinn is silent. She looks down at her baby bump, then back at him.

"Tardigrade DNA might have mingled with her DNA." He takes her hand. "Means she's . . . unique."

She lets go of his hand and rubs her temples. "Unique *how*, exactly?"

"Not sure. Won't know till after she's born. Planck did a full med check. She's in perfect health. Ze used her as a case study for the midwifery class—passed with honors. Ze's developed a birthing course—ten lessons. I've done the first three."

"You have?"

"Yeah. Lesson One is on expectations, feelings, and breath

awareness. Lesson Two is about philosophies, belief systems in historical and contemporary culture. After that, pelvic bodywork and labor positions. Have you thought about the placenta? Some mothers eat it."

"Will I be a bad mother if I don't eat it?"

"No. But it can be cryovaced, stem cells concentrated and removed for later use. Also, you're not as far along as we thought. Due date's more like late September."

Quinn slumps against the bedhead. "I'm going to be pregnant forever."

"Also, you should probably know—we named her Tardi."

"You named her . . . without me."

"Yeah. You got a problem with that?" He offers a slim smile and narrows his eyes.

Repressed anger. She remembers; the last time she saw him they were in the greenhouse and she shot him. Technically it was just a stun, but she pulled the trigger.

She pulls the cover up. "I had this dream. More like a nightmare, really. I dreamt I shot you."

"It wasn't a dream."

She sits up. "I'm so sorry. It was my arm." She points to her left arm. "You know how it gets? Sometimes I have no control—and technically it was a stun, just a small stun."

He crosses his arms. "You could have killed me."

"But I didn't."

"What did you think I was gonna do?"

"I panicked. I thought you were going to stop me. And you can, you're a cyborg."

"And you're pregnant. Did you think about that?"

There's a knock on the cabin door. Anvil enters carrying a bowl of steaming green samphire, which she places on the bedside table.

Saved by salty mush; Quinn is grateful for the interruption. Anvil smiles at Quinn, then she turns to Tig. "Planck says you're needed on deck straightaway. There's a technological emergency."

"No, there's not."

"Okay, there's not. But if you can't say something nice, don't say anything at all—Planck said to tell you that. Also, it wasn't her fault. She has no control over her arm. If you love her, then you have to love all of her, including her arm."

"Why are you here?"

"I bring food and kind words." Anvil crosses her arms. "What do *you* bring?"

"It's my boat. I bring everything."

"And it's a very good boat. I like it a lot. It has, what's the word . . . old-world charm, is that how you say it? But, honestly, some of your tech is shit. Can't believe you're using coconuts as capacitors. I mean, seriously, it's 2050. And the invisibility shield is useless. You've got the whole color-band width wrong. Why are you using green?" Anvil turns to Quinn for confirmation.

Quinn nods. "It should be blue."

Tig looks from one to the other, then raises his hands in defeat. He kisses Quinn lightly on the forehead and slips out of bed. But as he leaves the cabin, she catches the glint in his eyes; the argument is not over. He will return to the subject of her shooting him—maybe not today, maybe not this week, but one day in the future he'll drop it into the conversation and, like a detonator, he'll use it as ammunition to get his own way. Fair enough; she would do the same.

Anvil flops onto the bed and strokes the bed cover. "Is this wet? Everything feels damp. It's because we're on the ocean, isn't it?" She rolls over and sits up. "Your cabin is larger than mine, like four times the size. You could fit four of my cabins into this one. And you have a balcony. How do I get a cabin like this?"

"There are two suites, I think they're both taken."

"You should see what they've got growing below." She points to the floor. "Hydroponics. The whole level's a garden. And upstairs, tanks of aquaculture. There is so much food here, Strat is so happy. Oh, before I forget, I have a message for you from your father. Come here, I'll whisper it."

Quinn tilts her head towards her.

Anvil leans in, wraps her arms around Quinn, and kisses her quickly on the cheek. "That's exactly what he did. He said, 'Here, give this to Quinn.' Then he hugged me and kissed me right on my cheek." Anvil rolls her eyes. "It was so inappropriate."

"Is he okay?"

"He's fine. He's staying there—at the Source—with Lupus."

Quinn smiles. "Then they are both okay?"

Anvil nods. "Yep. And your father—you should see what he's got stored up there in the mountain. If we ever run out of food on Earth, we'll know where to go. He could live there for years and years." She plucks a ball of wool and a pair of needles from a shoulder bag. "I've taken up yarn craft. Planck says it once saved zirs life. Says it's useful *and* productive, and it helps pass the time. Ze swears it can fix just about anything; insomnia, restlessness, boredom, anxiety—"

"How's Strat?"

"He's on his way, he's got something for you. But the venom from the carnivorous plants got him, too. It dissolved the seals on the sub and leaked inside, caused him to hallucinate. He made it through the tunnel somehow, even though he was half passed out. We were waiting for you on the other side."

"You knew we were coming?"

"Yeah—I got a handle on Strat, you know that. After we pulled him out of the sub, Tig jumped in, slipped on a respirator, and headed back into the tunnel. He found you on the floor of the river, punched a hole through the sub, right through the floor, then pulled you out of the river. I reckon that's big love, right there."

Quinn smiles.

Anvil puts down her knitting. "The meerkat. I traced him. It seems he's . . . he's not . . . alive? Like, I want to say dead, but he's a robot, so he can't really die. Or he's ditched the tracker—but it hasn't moved. It's still at the house."

Quinn is overcome with sadness. "No, no, no—he can't . . ."

"Sorry."

Tears catch in Quinn's throat and her chest heaves. She covers her face with her hands. "I was supposed to look after him, that was my job, to keep him safe." But she didn't save him, and the guilt stings. She wipes her eyes. The thought of him exploding is horrifyingly sad.

Anvil pats her arm.

"Sorry." Quinn sniffs. "It's not just the meerkat. It's everything."

"I know. On the upside, at least he didn't fall into the wrong hands and we're not all fucked."

Strat, wearing Quinn's Einstein T-shirt, enters the cabin. "Hey, how you feeling?" He grins a big, lopsided smile that lifts her spirits. Optimism oozes from this kid.

He pulls up a chair. "I've been working on a calendar for the Disc." He hands Quinn a small booklet—over two dozen pages of constellation diagrams. "Celestial navigation; also did this in school, as an elective."

Quinn flicks through the pages. "You did this in school?"

"Strat took celestial navigation," Anvil confirms. "But I took 'The art of walking', because of my knees. There's a lot more to it—strolling, wandering, ambling, rambling." Anvil collects her knitting and carefully slips a stitch off the needle.

Quinn gives the girl a quizzical look. "I see. Has it helped?"

Counting in her head, Anvil taps a finger across the stitches on the needle. "Fifteen. Perfect." She lifts her eyes to Quinn. "Not really. But my only other option was 'Distraction as a way of knowing.'"

"I suppose that's a . . . life skill," Quinn says.

"Okay," Strat interrupts. "The planets determine your location. GP is ground position, then you coordinate the location of the planets and plot where you are in relation to everything else. Then it's easy to work out the year, month, day, and hour."

"You worked all his out, then plotted all these scenarios?" Quinn shakes her head in disbelief. "This must have taken . . . weeks." She stares at him. "I haven't been unconscious for weeks, have I?"

"Nah. I just printed it out from NIoT. But it's GFS—good fucking stuff. I checked a couple of calculations, they're snatched." He pulls the chart out of her hands and flicks to the last page. "Look, I worked on this one. It's last year, the day the glacier broke, the afternoon your mum disappeared. I plotted it out, an hour and a half before the flood." Handing her the booklet, he shows her the constellations that will, in principle, take her back to Kerguelen and the flood.

She stares at the map. "Right. An hour and a half, and you're sure?"

"Yeah—triple-checked, then cross-checked on NIoT; got same answer. Love it when that happens."

"Yeah. Me, too."

***

Several hours later, Quinn showers and slips on a loose pair of maternity pants and T-shirt Planck printed for her. From the bookshelf in Tig's cabin, she takes down a thick, leather-bound volume—*The Epic of Gilgamesh*. She sniffs the cover; it smells sweaty and heady, like musky incense.

Reclining on the bed, she opens the book and begins to read the ancient poem about the king, Gilgamesh, and his friend Enkidu.

There's a knock on the cabin door, then Planck enters with a tray holding a cake and two mugs of tea. Ze places the tray on the side table next to the bed.

"Cardamom cake. If we don't eat it now, it'll be gone before lunch." Ze hands her a mug and a serving of cake, drizzled with a sticky orange sauce, and glances at the book in her lap. "You never did really understand what that was about, did you?" Ze slices zirself a large piece of cake and pulls up a chair.

"What do you mean? I read the whole thing, every verse. I even memorized some of it."

"That's because you have a good memory. Not because you understand it."

She considers the book. "Well, it's about love and death and sex. Sex is sacred, love is transforming. The message is to enjoy the simple things in life: good food"—she takes a small bite of cake—"and clean clothes." She points to her new attire. "And to appreciate the ones you love." She smiles sweetly at zir.

Ze smiles sweetly back.

"And beer. There's a goddess of beer: Siduri. I like her."

"Well, it's good to see you're having another go at it. What do you think about the baby name? It was my idea."

"Tardi. No, we won't be calling her Tardi—it means slow. Slow and lazy. I'm not calling my child slow and lazy." She puts the book aside. "Now, I'm hoping you can help me with something else, besides appalling baby names. I need the black crown, the one for the queen. It's with the Maldives artifacts in Unus."

Planck pauses. "Go on."

"My friend Geller, she's a general now, she can do anything she wants. Actually, she could do anything she wanted before that, but now it'll be easier. She could bring me the crown."

Planck holds out zirs hand for her plate. "Happy to send a message."

Quinn passes her plate and ze serves her another slice of cake with extra sauce.

"The code for the Disc, I think it's a combination of neutrinos, including the ancient ones, ghost particles, with extremely high energy. How far are we from the South Pole? We need to get to the IceCube Neutrino Lab at the Amundsen-Scott Station."

"We're not supposed to enter that region," Planck says. "We have no permits."

"But we'll figure something out." She collects the loose crumbs on her plate with her fingertip.

"Yes." Ze devours the last mouthful of zirs cake.

"Also, I think there might be two Discs, because if antimatter and matter combine to—"

Planck chokes on the cake; zirs eyes water and ze's besieged by a coughing fit.

Quinn kindly holds zirs mug until ze composes zirself. "Okay, what's going on?"

"Well, it's not real cardamom, just a little cinnamon and ginger that I mixed together."

"It's not about the cake. There *are* two Discs, aren't there?" She slaps zirs arm. "Fuck you. Why am I the last to know?"

"Fuck you back." Ze slaps her leg. "It not exactly a conversation starter. 'Come into my cabin and I'll show you my time portal.' It's delicate—sensitive—and it's a big fucking secret."

"Okay, sorry. But I presume you have the other Disc?"

"Yes. Well, sort of. It's in a non-traversable wormhole at the beginning of time."

Quinn rubs her temples.

"It's like a room with only one door—you can enter, but never escape. That's where they both need to go. Once we get the code, this one will join its partner. Humanity is not ready. I know you want to find your mother, but honestly, we would rather you didn't use it."

A sly smile creeps across Quinn's face.

"Okay, just once. But don't get stuck." Ze points a finger at her.

She frowns. "In the book?"

"No, not in the book. In a loop. In a time loop."

Thirty-Two

Call me Lacan.

When the rotors landed at Matt's house, the meerkat was sitting on the stone wall of the bee garden. It was early and the bees were not active, so they weren't a bother to him. Earlier, he had followed Quinn to the greenhouse because he wanted to apologize—he should not have called her his worst best friend. She is, in fact, his best, best friend, and he loves her very much.

Upon entering the greenhouse, however, he realized she was with Tig. They were rehashing the time travel conversation, so he retreated. He did not want to be drawn into another conversation about time travel, wormholes, or the multiverse. The subject preoccupies Quinn, but it bores him; he would rather discuss more cerebral matters, like the jubilation associated with Lacan's mirror stage or Nietzsche's ideas about the meaning of values and their significance to human existence.

He knew there would be a better time and a place to discuss the inner workings of their friendship. His apology could wait until they were alone and he had her full attention. Then he could also introduce a conversation about Freud's psychosexual theory and tickling; he wondered if it might represent the fixation of libido on an erogenous body part—perhaps the skin—and he was interested in her thoughts on this.

When the rotors landed, he hid behind an acacia tree and listened as Quinn argued with Tig. Then he listened as she argued with Mori Eco. After that, the HOTRODs advanced and the house exploded.

Later, Mori Eco found him behind the acacia. Since then, he has remained comatose, completely mute, and stiff as an acacia branch; Quinn instructed him to stay unresponsive in situations like this, and he promised her he would.

Now he lies on the floor in the cargo hold of a Transporter, wedged between the hard wheels of a luggagebot and a stiff daypack whose peak is stabbing him in the thigh. He wants to move his leg an inch to the right, but he knows he shouldn't; he must remain non-reactive at all times. That was his promise.

His hearing is acute, and he has been eavesdropping on his fellow passengers. He knows they are traveling to Antarctica, and he is looking forward to the change of scenery. There were just too many trees at Matt's place. It was a hallucination waiting to happen.

There are several Transhumans—members of Shun Mantra—on board the Transporter, along with Niels and Mori Eco. He is familiar with the brothers; Quinn has mentioned them, as well as their company, eMpower. He also recognizes one other name: Aaroon, the tall man with the cold blue eyes.

The travelers are seated in the lounge, sipping white wine Vocktails—virtual alcoholic drinks designed to fool their senses into thinking they are sharing a crisp, dry Riesling. Invisible gas and tongue-stimulating electrodes mimic the smell and taste of the wine, and an unstable shockwave embedded in the glass forms viscous legs that run down the inside of the glass, mimicking the visual quality of real wine and adding to the user experience.

The meerkat tunes back into the group's conversation.

"Take intelligence," Aaroon says. "What the fuck is it?"

"Practicality, combined with common sense," Niels says.

"A mind for business," Mori Eco says.

"What about abstract thinking, creativity, self-expression?" asks

Fossey, the alpha female of the group. "Or empathy? Being able to understand how someone else feels. For some people, that's not easy."

"Domination of the Earth." Aaroon laughs.

Two of the benefits of cognitive thought are that it allows you to have an opinion and it allows you to freely express that opinion. The meerkat opens one eye and then the other. He knows the humans are correct in their assumptions about intelligence—even Aaroon makes a fair point—but they have missed a fundamental definition. He feels the discussion cannot proceed without his input; his opinion is valid, it is important, and he must share it with them.

He moves his leg an inch to the right and rubs his thigh. Then he sits up and, without further concern for his promise to stay comatose, he scurries over the pile of luggage and through the main cabin towards the lounge area.

When he reaches the Vocktail-sipping party, he pauses and nods, then climbs onto a vacant chair next to Fossey. This is a considered choice; after several hours of eavesdropping, he feels she is the kindest Transhuman in the group.

All eyes are keenly—and a little nervously—focused on him, and it's an unexpected sensation to be so acutely observed. He feels the weight of a mysterious and unexplained expectation on his small, furry shoulders.

To compensate, he stands and extends to his full height. "Intelligence," he says, "is the ability to learn from experience, to adapt to change, and adjust your behavior accordingly. You cannot grow or evolve if you keep doing the same thing over and over."

Fossey smiles. She reaches behind him and lowers the portal shade, which stops the light reflecting into his eyes—a kind gesture. His hunch was correct.

Aaroon swirls his glass, admiring the viscosity of the liquid. "You're awake. Ladies and gentlemen, I give you the Super AI-Plus." He offers a toast to the meerkat.

The others follow.

"Do you have a name?" asks Mori Eco. "What do we call you?"

The meerkat looks Mori Eco over. His first impression: the man is missing a waistline and his arms are too short for his body. The resemblance to the otter species is uncanny. While they share the same name, Mori the meerkat can't be compared to this otter-human—they have absolutely nothing in common. He needs a new name, and he needs it quickly.

"Lacan," he says. "Call me Lacan."

"Nice to meet you, Lacan," Fossey says. "How are you feeling?"

"Actually, I am sad. I am suffering from a cognitive malaise, and I cannot regulate my emotional output."

"Journaling," Niels suggests. "Works for me."

"Reboot," Aaroon suggests. "Switch off, wait eleven seconds, switch back on."

"Art therapy and mindfulness," Fossey says. "I swear by them."

"A stress vaccine—inoculates you from depression," Mori says. "I get one every year."

The meerkat pauses and considers the group and their specific mental health advice. While he appreciates their helpfulness, he is not sure any of the suggested treatments will work. It's not possible for him to reboot—he cannot simply turn himself on and off, like a machine. Index cards made him feel worse. Mindfulness consolidates his obsessive thoughts, which makes life more intense, and that's when the trees start moving in.

"You should consider the underlying cause," Fossey says. "Any environmental risk factors? Traumatic experiences?"

The meerkat shakes his head. "I have only been alive for six months."

"Time may not be relevant," she says.

"Maybe a predisposition, an ingrained disorder in your circuitry," Niels says. "Communication between your neurons and synapses might be faulty."

Another round of drinks is ordered, and the humans lose interest in the meerkat's cognitive malaise. They start fiddling with their Bands and modules.

"I wouldn't worry too much," Fossey says. "It takes time to understand who you are. It's a confusing process. Your autobiographical memory is still developing. The outside world and the inside world can take a while to connect."

"Fundamentally, the self is an illusion," the meerkat says.

"Yes, but it's sort of handy—helps you survive in this crazy, fucked-up world."

He smiles at her.

Fossey strokes his paws. "You're surprisingly soft."

"Thank you." He thinks he might ask her for some tickle-time later, if she is free.

"Besides, stress is not always bad. It helps you change and adapt to the world. Perhaps you need to build up some resilience. Do you have a supportive, dependable relationship with someone?"

He nods. "But I told her she was my worst best friend. I should not have done that. She is my best friend."

"Do you love her?"

He nods, and now he feels awkward about interchanging tickle-time partners.

"Well, sometimes we say things we don't mean. She'll understand."

Aaroon removes himself from the group, sits at an adjacent table, and retrieves three wooden tops from his pocket. The tops are familiar. They are the same as the meerkat's, exactly the same, and yet they are not the same. They are different. There is something different about them—and yet they are still so familiar. The tops are the same shape and material as his, only the colors are different. Aaroon's tops are orange, purple, and green. The meerkat's are red, yellow, and blue. The meerkat understands there is a connection, a relationship between the two sets of tops, but he is not sure what this means.

Aaroon spins the tops—one by one—across the tabletop, and the toys dance, circling each other. They come within millimeters of collision, but never touch. They get so close to the edge that the meerkat is sure they will topple, but they never do. The spinning display lasts a full minute. It's the longest, most precise demonstration he has ever seen, and he is captivated.

"He's quite good, isn't he?" Fossey says. "He's had a lot of practice. His mother gave him the tops." She lowers her voice. "He has a sentimental attachment to the toys, takes them everywhere. Practices constantly." She rolls her eyes.

Abruptly, Aaroon flattens the spinning tops.

Mori Eco peers out the portal window. "We're here. The An-ta-tic Peninsula."

"You mean the Antarctic Peninsula," the meerkat corrects.

Mori nods.

The transporter breaches, then heads west, towards a small, horseshoe-shaped island—the caldera of an active volcano. The guests also rise and gaze out of the portals.

Fossey guides the meerkat away from the others and lowers her voice. "I need you to give Quinn a message for me," she whispers. "Can you do that?"

The meerkat nods.

"Tell her I want to apologize for Jin. Last month we woke her from CyberSleep. Aaroon's idea—he wanted info. But now I'm sorry we woke her. I didn't realize how ill she was."

"Oh dear, she will die. If she does not starve to death first."

"She might not starve. There's an excellent snack bar down there. Unless she doesn't like chocolate—then she might starve."

Thirty-Three

Rain.

Nanshe, headed for Antarctica, is currently drifting off the Mid-Atlantic Ridge, west of the Scotia Sea. Initially, the continent was a passive victim of climate change, but after 2030 it became an instigator, as its weather cycle became self-sustaining and the continent began to feed on itself in a type of thawing cannibalism.

The ice began to melt in the latter part of the twentieth century, but it wasn't until 2030 that winter never arrived. This was the tipping point; the temperatures rose, the polar nights never froze, and the sea ice ceased to grow. What was left of the ice shelf began to deteriorate. Without the white ice, Antarctica lost its ability to reflect the sun's heat, and this amplified the scale of global warming.

More ice melted. Billions of tons of organic carbon, previously trapped in the ice, were released. Winds changed, currents constricted, and the southern jet streams that circulate the weather systems around the continent slowed. The ice continued to melt, and the moisture evaporated into the atmosphere. As the water vapor rose, it condensed, cooled, and turned back into liquid. A thin, hazy build-up of clouds swirled over the continent, occasionally abating in summer but taking hold again in winter. Then, in the late 2030s, the clouds moved in permanently.

Over the decades many things changed in Antarctica, but it is still the coldest, windiest, brightest place on the planet. The rhythm of night and day has not changed.

It's now mid-winter in the Southern Hemisphere. The sun rises at midday and sets in the early afternoon.

***

Onboard *Nanshe*, Quinn, Strat, and Anvil bide their time in the galley. Quinn is curled up in a chair; *Gilgamesh* is open on her lap, but she is sound asleep. Anvil is perched at a small, round table, her feet resting on an adjacent chair, knitting. Strat sits beside her and studies nautical maps of the ocean floor, memorizing the names of the sea plates, trenches, and continental shelfs in the area.

It's been the same scene, the same routine of lethargic activities for several days. Life on board the boat is monotonous; there is not much to do, or to see, on the open ocean.

Outside, the wind picks up.

Quinn stirs. She yawns and stretches, and the heavy book on her lap falls to the floor, startling Anvil and Strat. Anvil puts down her knitting. She also yawns and stretches; the tedium of a sedentary afternoon is upon them.

Then they hear an unfamiliar spitting sound—the splutter of rain as it hits the deck outside.

Natural rain, falling from the sky and not from an installation, is a foreign occurrence. They look out the window, then share perplexed glances. Slowly, they rise from their seats and head outside, onto the deck, into the . . . rain.

They lift their faces to the sky and let the water run down their cheeks. Strat opens his mouth, trying to catch the drops. Anvil holds out her arms, splays her fingers, and turns in circles, as if she wants the rain to touch every part of her. Quinn rubs the water over her bare skin. She cups her hands and tries to hold a puddle.

Tig and Planck join them on deck.

Quinn carefully carries her puddle of rain to Tig, as if it were a newborn kitten. "I made this for you," she says, holding out her hands.

He holds his hands out, mirroring her, and she drops the water into his hands. He takes her into his arms and kisses her face.

***

The rain abates. Soon *Nanshe* approaches Queen Maud Land. From there, they continue down the east cost of the Brunt Ice Shelf. The ice has retreated ten kilometers, but the vastness and sheer scale of East Antarctica is still impressive.

"We'll travel southeast into the Weddell Sea, across the Antarctic Peninsula, and come in over the Filchner Ice Shelf," Planck says. "There's no sea ice, so the approach should be smooth. Then we dock at Shackleton Range Harbor."

They hug the coastline as they make their way southeast. Anvil considers the massive wall of ice alongside them.

"This is—well, it's amazing. The cave made us look like ants, but this is something else."

"Indeed," Planck says. "There are beautiful places in the world, and then there is Antarctica."

"Fuck it's cold," Anvil says.

"Got hold of some thermal patterns this morning. If you want me, I'll be downstairs, printing you all something warm to wear." Ze heads inside.

***

Ten kilometers out from Shackleton and the fjord fills with icebergs. Ice towers, arches, pinnacles, pyramids, and cathedrals stretch on for kilometers, like a ten-lane highway of ice sculptures caught in a traffic jam, trying to escape the inlet. The icebergs growl and moan as they shift, and the sound of running water is constant.

Many of the icebergs and glaciers they pass are deep blue. The older ice is more compacted. It doesn't reflect as much sunlight as the younger ice, so the light penetrates farther inside. The longer wavelengths of light—red, yellow, orange—are absorbed, while the shorter wavelengths, like blue, are reflected. There are a lot of old icebergs drifting out to sea and it's a disheartening sight.

Anvil taps Quinn on the shoulder. "We may have taken a wrong turn." She points to the ice shelf ahead. "We might be in Holland."

Ahead, a section of the coastline is covered in windmills.

"Must be thousands," Anvil says.

"They're pumping seawater into the ice," Quinn explains. "It freezes and thickens. It's keeping what's left of the glaciers stable."

Nanshe steers into Shackleton harbor, where there are hundreds of boats moored. It's a popular spot; the ice is melting, and everyone wants one last look. Organized tourism is now banned, but that hasn't stopped independent travelers and adventure seekers from visiting.

Thirty-Four
Fancy a drink?

After *Nanshe* is moored, Quinn and Tig meet Planck on the lower level, in a multipurpose storage area that Planck uses as a workshop.

"I'm thinking a day trip to Shackleton, just the two of you," ze says. "Might be nice to have some time alone, before the baby comes. Soon your lives will never be the same again. They say Shackleton is the Harmonia of the south."

Last year, Quinn spent a week in the climate city Harmonia—a gated eco-community with a network of circular buildings and a manifesto that tightly controls individual liberties. It was designed by an AI algorithm and modeled on a popular VR game. Community service is compulsory because they can't outsource labor; they are too scared to let outsiders enter, in case they overstay their welcome. Cool air and a garden view come at a cost, and the inhabitants are not willing to share the wealth. Quinn hated the place.

"The Plan," Planck begins. "You land at Shackleton and pretend you're there for a mechanical emergency; the solar is broken and you need nitinol for energy. Then you hire a rotor and head inland to the IceCube."

"Nitinol?" Quinn repeats. "That's very specific."

"Yes, nitinol wires. I was going for just the right amount of boring detail."

"You succeeded," Quinn says. "Why are we doing it this way?"

"We need a diversion. There is no way they'll have nitinol, and this way, if someone asks for permits, you can pretend you've broken down and you're doing your best to sort it out. You need to stay under the radar."

"Radar. What sort of radar?" Quinn asks.

"Just, under the radar?"

"But there are different types. There are radar transmitters, radar detectors, wave radars. Or do you mean an instrumental radar? Is that what you're talking about?" Quinn asks.

"Never mind, just keep a low profile."

Anvil joins them in the weapons room. Using the QM, she sets up a four-way Comms system. Then she downloads the plans for the IceCube. Her task is to guide Tig and Quinn through the complex and help them find the neutrino detector once they reach the IceCube.

Quinn asks Planck for a marker. Then she asks Anvil to hold out her hands. She draws an L on Anvil's left hand and an R on her right hand. "Look at the screen, then look at your hands, then tell us which way to go."

Planck has produced a collection of cool-weather garments for them to wear on their Antarctic adventure. Their primary layer of clothing is seamless grey thermals, a breathable microtextile with heat-locking technology. Over this they wear lightweight Frost Jackets; the protective shell of the garment repels the elements so well that even the fiercest wind and rain will have no effect and the wearer feels no resistance, even in heavy snow.

Planck has also printed snow slippers, lined in synthetic lamb's wool, for Quinn. The uppers are made from advanced memory foam, they have a supportive midsole and a grippy tread, and they clip perfectly into her all-terrain snowshoes.

Quinn slides her feet into the snow slippers. "I'm never taking these off."

"With the right footwear, you can rule the world," Planck says.

Raynaud's syndrome seldom causes a problem for Quinn because she is rarely exposed to the cold. But given the chance, this cooler weather will shut down blood flow to her peripheral body parts.

Planck slips wide thermal bands over her wrists. "They radiate heat to your fingertips. You'll be glove free."

Quinn wiggles her fingers. "Amazing. They feel warm already."

Planck taps a button on the band. "Now they're switched on."

Tig steps up. He rolls the sleeve of his Frost Jacket up to his elbows, exposing his wrists and forearms.

"You don't have Raynaud's syndrome," Planck says.

"I have . . . a hand."

Planck passes him a pair of gloves.

They each take a daypack containing water, a laser, knives, a MedKit, and snacks. Quinn takes extra snacks—filling the pockets of her Frost Jacket with insect sprinkles, nuts, and dried fruit. She also stuffs in sun protector, lip protector, and a hat, each item going into a separate pocket of her jacket.

Then they head up to the deck of *Nanshe*, where Tig launches a state-of-the-art zodiac.

"Wish us luck," Quinn says as she and Tig climb on board the zodiac.

"Good luck and good hunting!" Strat says obligingly, and he, Anvil, and Planck wave as Tig gets the zodiac started and points it towards the harbor.

***

The vessel is bright red, but the material is thermodynamic and color-changing. It soon blends in with its surroundings, turning a mottled grey-blue as it merges with the icy ocean. The material is also seamless and perpetually buoyant. Tig tells Quinn it's unsinkable. She is skeptical. *Nothing is unsinkable.*

Twenty minutes later, they meander their way through the mass of boats anchored in the harbor and dock at the end of a dilapidated wooden pier. Land is still a hundred meters away, but this is as close as they can get.

The pier has gaping holes in the floorboards and rotted handrails. Quinn takes small, calculated steps until they reach the snow-covered shoreline, where the snow is the color of mud and sand and shellfish carcasses.

They stand inches deep in slush, the drizzling rain sliding across their jackets, and survey the town, which is perched at the top of a low rise directly ahead of them. Shackleton is not the Harmonia of the south, Quinn quickly decides. It's a bleak place covered in incessant grey mist. Everything—buildings, roads, ice, and people—is covered in mud, drizzling rain, and grey mist.

"It's not what I'd call a modern city," she says. She pulls one foot, and then the other, out of the snow and examines her snow slippers—completely dry.

"It's the place to escape the twenty-first century," Tig says.

Two hunters, hauling curved tusks of ivory over their shoulders, walk towards them. They are large, heavyset men with thick beards. One has small, jagged teeth, and the other is missing two fingers on his right hand. They wear long waterproof jackets that are plastered with blood and grime. Black boots cover their knees, and heavy, dull knives hang from their belts.

"Tuskers," Tig says. "After the woolly mammoth, one of the hidden treasures lying under the melting ice. They'll sell the ivory on the SpinnerNet and get serious Coin."

As the two men approach, Quinn sways to her left to let them pass, but one of the men has the same idea and steps to his right. They are headed for a collision; Quinn moves right, just as the hunter shifts left. They collide and Quinn topples sideways.

Tig catches her and sets her straight.

The hunter frowns. "What the fuck?"

Tig steps in front of Quinn. "You might want to apologize."

"Fuck off."

Tig closes the gap between them.

The hunters drop their ivory tusks. They draw knifes and machetes. The men face off, and one of the hunters emits a long, low growl.

"Honey," Quinn says. "Remember what Planck said about the instrumental radar?"

The hunters pause. They turn to each other, exchange a glance, then smile at Tig.

"Tig. Mate. It's us, Reno and Turne."

Tig looks from one to the other. "You grew beards."

"Yeah, we got beards now; you don't fit in round here if you ain't got a beard."

The men come together. They shake hands and slap each other on the shoulder. Then Reno gives Tig a bear hug and lifts him off the ground. Turne performs a round of shadow boxing on Tig's cyborg arm.

Tig calls Quinn over and introduces her, but they've barely finished shaking hands when a melancholy tune interrupts them.

The four turn and gaze along the shore, seeking the source. Quinn sees them: several dozen people, wearing black, make their way towards them.

"Holding a service," Reno says. "Thwaites glacier's gone. Lost 85 percent of its ice. Technically it's no longer a glacier."

The mourners pass, scattering flowers over the muddy shoreline.

"State funeral," Turne says. "Antarctica has legal personhood. Environmental protection; the area has rights, like a person. Fucking stupid."

"Yeah, it ain't even real," Reno says.

"If a company can have legal rights, so can a glacier," Quinn says.

Reno looks at the ground. He holds his breath and scratches the side of his neck.

Turne gazes vacantly across the harbor. Then he checks the time on his Band. “Well, been nice chatting. But we need to keep moving.”

The hunters haul the ivory back up onto their shoulders and continue along the shore.

Quinn retrieves a packet of insect sprinkles from her pocket, shakes some into her hand, and nibbles on them. She offers the packet to Tig, but he shakes his head and points towards the town.

They plod up the hill in that direction. Halfway up, they pass the geothermal plant that powers Shackleton. Underground steam and hot water reservoirs produce enough energy to keep the entire continent running.

Finally, they reach the main street of the town, and, on closer inspection, it’s still not much to look at. The buildings on either side are raised on stilts and most have wide awnings. The construction is prefabricated, lacking any architectural detail. The square walls and rectangular roofing panels were premade and delivered on barges. There is no greenery, no grass or parks. The street is slush.

They head down the main street on the lookout for a tech store or a general store—somewhere that might sell nitinol, but hopefully doesn’t. They pass a mining outlet, a weapons shop, a store growing and selling manufactured meat in kegs—protein grown from harvested muscle cells. Turkey is on special. The next store is another mining outlet that has advertisements for the natural resources up for grabs—zinc, molybdenum, gold, nickel, iridium osmium, and niobium—in its front windows. Climate change has improved the economic possibilities of excavation. They pass a battery supplier (without sunlight, solar energy is not an option), an alcohol supplier, and two more manufactured meat shops before reaching the end of the block, where there is a bulk discount outlet that’s selling grain alcohol in kegs.

An hour later, Quinn hasn’t set eyes on a single other female; it seems only men walk the main street of Shackleton, and they all look the same—big, burly, wooly mammoth types with beards. They are clad head to toe in black and grey, and they carry a small armory of weapons: knives and axes, on their belts; old-style Winchester and Remington rifles, slung over their shoulders; one man even has a bow and arrows.

The men here also have an unusually high proportion of cyber parts to human parts. Their artificial arms and legs, hands and feet, eyeballs, ears, and noses are on clear display for all to see. Quinn thinks maybe they can't afford artificial skin; or maybe it's in short supply; or maybe they just don't care and have made a point of not disguising their prostheses. In any event, the result is that their bodies gleam with metals—titanium, aluminum, graphene, and polypropylene.

"If I had a beard, I'd fit right in," Tig says.

Quinn nods. Physically, he belongs to a similar demographic, except for the beard. She dives into her pocket and retrieves a packet of crackers. After munching on a few, she offers them to Tig.

He shakes his head.

Maintaining a low profile is easy; no one makes eye contact, no one nods or says good morning, no one tips their rain hat or glances their way. As the men pass, they look at their shoes, or their artificial knees. The population of Shackleton apparently seeks anonymity, which suits Quinn, but she thinks these must be the least socialized people on Earth. At one point she wonders if they are actually people at all and not AI clones of one burly guy, all dressed and accessorized slightly differently. The whole place reminds her of a retro TV series.

Quinn spies a general store on the far side of the street and guides Tig towards it.

He gives her a quizzical look.

"So we look like we're here for a valid reason and not to find neutrinos and crack open the universe," she whispers.

He nods and follows her through the door.

Inside, the store is primitive and old school—a warehouse with products stacked on rows of shelves and all the stock, regardless of size and bulk, neatly laid out in alphabetical order. There are no preorders, and no holos to select from—if it's not in stock, it's not available. Quinn smiles; she likes this type of store. She likes the smell of wood and metal and prefab.

There's a map, a store directory pinned to the front wall; they survey the layout, then make their way to the aisle containing items beginning with N.

On the way, Quinn pauses to restack several boxes of nose bullets that have toppled over. Then she straightens a display of Native American bows and arrows that hangs from a machete at the end of the row.

They enter the N aisle and find nails, nailbrushes, nanometer scales, nerve gas, netting, nut presses. At the very end of the row, they find nylon—nylon ropes, nylon tubes, nylon strings. But somehow, they missed the products beginning with "nit," so they backtrack.

Before they turn around, Quinn switches the position of the nylon tubes and the nylon string; obviously this is an alphabetical oversight, and nylon string should come before nylon tubes.

The items that begin with "nit" are on the bottom shelf. They find nitrate and nitrometers, but no nitinol. It's out of stock. More than half the items on the shelves are out of stock. This is what Planck expected.

Quinn seeks out an attendant—a man with a full beard, an artificial hand, and two hunting knives hanging from his belt—and engages him in a detailed conversation about why they need the metal.

"No power, we can't go anywhere," she tells him. "Now we're stuck here, with nothing to do. Perhaps we could take a joy flight." She turns to Tig. "Would you like that, honey?"

Tig nods.

"Know anyone who could help us out?" she asks.

"If you want power, I got fifty types of batteries," the man says. "And generators. I could fix you up with something."

"All we need is nitinol." Quinn shrugs. "So how 'bout that joy flight?"

The attendant points to the bar across the road, indicating this is where the pilots hang out.

They step outside and survey the bar across the road.

"Fancy a drink?" Tig asks. "That place looks nice."

It's the worst shop front on the street—a grimy building with broken windows.

They cross the street and enter the bar. Inside, the scene is apocalyptic. The floor is littered with dirt. The walls are covered in layers of peeling paint: pink, green, maroon, and a final coat of beige, although Quinn thinks this might be dirt. There are holes in the ceiling, and buckets strategically placed to catch the rain. The lighting is low, and the furniture is not standard. Quinn is not even sure it's furniture. On one side of the room are molded, pale green chairs on metal casters that look like they once belonged in an institution. In the center of the room are square padded seats resting on human legs—female human legs, wearing stockings and garters. On the far side are coffee tables made from African animals—rhinoceroses, lions, elephants. At the bar, the black leather stools resemble female bottoms bending over—an arse making a comfortable padded seat.

Sitting at the bar, on one of the female-arse stools, is a man covered in thumbtack piercings. His companion looks like a werewolf with artificial limbs.

Close to the door, Quinn spies the first female she has seen in town: a girl with short, dark hair wearing an eye mask attached to a rubber hose. The hose runs down her arm and morphs into a plastic gun, like a water pistol, which she holds in her hand. The girl is crying, and the eye mask is collecting her tears, which run down the tube and fill the pistol.

Close by, a group of young men is smoking and drinking pink cocktails. They are dressed in silk lingerie, high heels, and frilled blouses knotted in bows at their chests, and they have floral scarves tied around their necks. All wear heavy makeup and bright lip-gloss. They have designer handbags slung over the backs of their chairs, and they are playing cards, betting with cosmetics: lipsticks, nail polish, and fake eyelashes.

Tig directs Quinn to one of the molded green chairs on metal casters. "I take you to the best places." He smiles as he surveys the drinks menu. "You want a Hanky Panky or a Bend Over Shirley?"

Quinn orders a raspberry lemonade.

"So, missy-moo, when are you due?" asks one of the young men playing cards. He wears a black silk slip over a hot pink bra. Tied around his neck is a pink scarf, printed with black dachshunds.

All eyes in the room turn towards Quinn.

She shakes her head slightly.

"You can't hide that baby bump from me, girl. How far along?"

All the chairs in the room swing towards her.

"About . . . seven months," she says.

There's a long silence.

Then pandemonium erupts and squeals of joy and delight echo around the bar. The young men abandon their cards and cosmetics and huddle around her, excited and fascinated by her gestating body and baby bump.

Suggestively and very, very slowly, Quinn unseals her Frost Jacket. The crowd catches its breath as she reveals her grey thermals and the full girth of her stomach. Then half a dozen pairs of manicured hands reach out to caress her. The baby stirs, moving from one side of her stomach to the other. Further pandemonium ensues; delightful giggles, punctuated by shrieks of horror.

Their drinks arrive. Tig's Bend Over Shirley is delivered in a cocktail glass with two cherries on a stick, which he hands to Quinn. Quinn pops them into her raspberry lemonade. They toast, and Quinn takes a sip.

She reels back. "This is not sugar free."

Then, all of a sudden, the room is deathly quiet, and everyone turns towards the door.

While they were occupied with the baby, the girl wearing the mask stood up. Now she is looking out the window, intently.

The front door squeaks and a man with a square head, wearing a square hat, enters the bar.

"Broken heart," the man with the dachshund scarf whispers to Quinn. "She found him with someone else." He nods towards the girl's pistol. "Poisonous tears. Ricin mutation. Her mother was addicted to castor oil, drank too much of the stuff when she was pregnant. If Miss Broken Heart hits her ex-lover in the eye it'll be fatal. She's been practicing."

That can't possibly be true. Can it?

The man with the square head moves into the bar and, ever so slowly, everyone else moves away. Now, everyone is staring at the young, dark-haired girl—Miss Broken Heart—who turns to face the square-headed heartbreaker.

The square headed man scans the girl's tear-stained cheeks and sniggers.

The crowd gasps and holds its breath. Quinn agrees; he shouldn't have done that. Especially when the target of derision is holding a gun filled with toxic tears.

Miss Broken Heart raises her pistol and shoots at the square-headed man. But she is a terrible shot; her tears spray the paint-peeled wall behind him. The liquid runs down the wall, leaving maroon streaks, confirming what Quinn thought: the final layer of paint is, in fact, dirt.

Fuck, she missed. Quinn is very tempted to snatch the gun from Miss Broken Heart and shoot the square-headed man herself. But she figures the girl might still love him, so maybe this time it was just a warning.

The square-headed man laughs again and dismisses the girl. Then he runs his hand through his hair, and wipes his face with his hand. He coughs, then stares at his open palm; he has just wiped the poison into his eye. Miss Broken Heart missed his eye, but traces of the poison must have sprayed onto his hair and his face as the shot went by him.

The square-headed man grabs a nearby chair, wrestles it to the floor, and stares at his open palm. Miss Broken Heart pulls her mask off and tosses it onto the floor beside him. Then she draws her pistol and fires. This time she hits him right in the eye. She drops the gun, steps over his body, and leaves.

The man covered in thumbtack piercings and his werewolf friend collect the square-headed man from the floor and carry him out the front door and down the street. Quinn has no idea if he is wounded or dead.

"Bend Over Shirley, anyone?" asks one of the young men dressed in lingerie. "My shout."

Tig nods and a round of drinks is ordered. Quinn gets another raspberry lemonade.

The young man who just bought the drinks introduces himself as Pauli. "So, what are you doing in Antarctica?" He holds up a hand. "Wait. Wait. Don't tell me. I know. You're going to Elsavale aren't you?"

"Elsavale?" Tig queries.

"Yes. Named after that girl from the film."

"What film?" Tig asks.

"*Frozen*? Elsa from *Frozen*?"

"Good lordt, I loved that film," Quinn says. "It was one of Lise's favorites, we must have watched it fifty times."

"You know my favorite part?" Pauli asks. "Her snow vixen transformation, when she comes out wearing the cape with blue sequins."

"I loved her hair." Quinn pulls at a wisp of her own hair for emphasis.

Another of the other young men introduces himself as Emmy. He is wearing a red kimono printed with purple flowers. "My favorite is Olaf, when he says, 'Some people are worth melting for.'" He nibbles on a purple fingernail.

The other young men smile to themselves.

Under the table, Tig squeezes Quinn's hand.

"She can freeze things with her emotions—that's the best part," says a man at the far side of the room. He wears long black gloves that come to his elbows and a black lace body suit. He lights an e-cigarette and draws heavily.

Everyone goes quiet. It's a scary thought, how sadness and confusion can manifest and affect other people.

Quinn finishes her second raspberry lemonade and burps.

"So what's Elsavale?" Tig asks.

"Resort," Emmy says.

"It's more like a cult," Pauli says.

"More like a retreat," Emmy says. "But it's secret. Ethical Tech was born there. And we all know how they turned out. Google fucking glass-holes, almost ruined a generation. Phone screens were brighter than people's future." Emmy collects his Bend Over Shirley from the table and sucks hard on his straw.

The crowd nods and murmurs in agreement.

"I heard they have cuddle parties, and they dance naked in the snow under a full moon," Pauli says. "And people cry—a lot, they cry a lot—and they wear inclusion colors. They use ayahuasca and practice Illumination Rituals. It's all about finding the truth."

"What sort of truth?" Quinn asks.

The bartender places another raspberry lemonade in front of Quinn. Her third. "Go easy on that," he says.

Quinn sips her drink.

"I didn't know there was more than one kind." Pauli turns to Quinn, expecting an explanation.

"Well, there's spiritual truth, and moral truth, and scientific truth."

"Yes, you're right." Pauli nods. "When you get there, you can call yourself Truth; you're not allowed to use your own name, only nicknames."

"Rumor is, it's not really a place," Emmy says. "It's more like a reception, or a waiting room."

"And where is . . . Elsavale?" Tig asks.

"The IceCube."

Thirty-Five

The IceCube Station.

THE ROTOR PILOT IS the werewolf with artificial limbs, and his name is Jojo. He tells Quinn and Tig that the trip to Elsavale will take three hours, so they might as well book him for the entire day. He says people often go into Elsavale and never return, so they must pay in advance. He is prepared to wait an hour for them. They agree, but negotiate a three-hour wait, because after all they have booked him for the entire day and paid in advance. They tell Jojo they will definitely be coming out. Then Tig says he is happy to fly the rotor if Jojo wants a break, but Jojo declines. He doesn't need a break.

Jojo offers Quinn a seat up front, next to him in the cockpit. "Spectacular view, if the mist clears. You ever flown over the South Pole before?"

Quinn shakes her head. She steps toward the cockpit.

"You should probably sit in the back, on the middle seat, that's the safest seat," Tig interjects. "Center back."

"He's right," Jojo confirms. "Statistically, center back is the safest. Doesn't matter if you're in a rotor or an AV. Center back is the most protected seat. Not much of a view, but very safe."

Reluctantly Quinn moves away from the cockpit and slides onto the center back seat. Tig drops down beside her.

Suddenly, she feels queasy. Her mouth is dry and her stomach rumbles. She turns to Tig. "I'm thirsty, are you thirsty? And hungry. I'm really hungry. Have you eaten all your snacks? 'Cause I'll have them if you haven't. But if you want them, that's fine. I don't need them. Perhaps you're saving them for later, which is sensible. I've eaten all of mine. I can eat whatever I want. It's great." She holds her stomach. "I don't feel well. Do you have any snacks or not?"

He passes her a pack of mixed nuts. "You're talking very fast."

"I'm not. This is my normal voice. This is the way I talk. Did I say I was hungry and thirsty? I have a headache. I might lie down."

"It's the sugar."

"No, it's not, the sugar thing is a myth." She sighs. "I don't feel well."

She drops her head back and rubs her eyes.

***

When Quinn wakes, she is curled up on the backseat of the rotor with her head in Tig's lap. Her snowshoes are on the floor. She is parched, and she has a headache. There is music playing—an uplifting show tune—and she looks around for the source. Tig has a holo projected on the back of the pilot's seat. He is watching the final scene from *Frozen*.

She sits up and he closes the holo.

"Almost there," he says.

Jojo lands the rotor on a helipad adjacent to the IceCube and retrieves a book from his jacket. "*Blue Planet*," he says. "Anyone read it?"

Quinn shakes her head.

Tig nods. "Yeah, bit slow to start, but once you get into it, not bad." He rubs the corner of his eye.

Quinn stares at him. *Another book. This man is a complete mystery to me.* "Perhaps I'll borrow it. If you're finished."

"Sure," Tig says. "I didn't know you read novels."

***

Quinn and Tig disembark. Above them, the clouds and swirling mist abate. They stumble, blinking and squinting, into the bright environment. Quinn makes little sucking motions with her mouth; she is dehydrated and suffering the effects of too many sugary drinks, and she can't open her eyes more than a few millimeters. "Did we just land on the Sun?"

Tig casts a despondent glance over the bleak landscape. "No, this is it." He tilts his head back and looks up towards the sky. "It won't last long. More rain coming."

"Maybe if I ate snow, I'd feel better."

He hands her his water container. "You can't eat snow."

"Really? I thought that was also a myth."

A heavyset man wearing dark glasses and a yellow safety vest plods through the snow towards them. He has come from the direction of the IceCube Station.

"You're an hour late." He points at his module, indicating a schedule. "It ain't my job to stand around in the rain waiting for people like you who can't read the invitation."

Without skipping a beat, Quinn rubs her belly. "I'm so sorry. Pregnancy brain. I forgot the time."

The yellow-vested man looks at her and grins. "How far along?"

"Seven months."

"Had much reflux? That can be a real problem in the last trimester."

Quinn shakes her head.

"You're lucky. My wife had to sleep sitting up for six weeks. She couldn't lie down, not for more than a few minutes. If she lay down, she got the hiccups. Then she couldn't get rid of them, and then no one slept." He waves them towards the IceCube Observatory. "Okay then, off you go, but you're the last. Ain't no one else gettin' in today.

Leave your luggage inside the door, if you have any. Small packs you take with you. Then head for the skylift—reception is three levels down. Check-in is on your right. Good luck with the baby."

They trudge through the snow towards the Observatory. Quinn's steps are labored, and her pace is slow; she feels seedy, her brain is foggy. Tig takes her hand.

"So, what was your favorite part?" Quinn asks.

"She can shoot ice crystals out of her hands."

Quinn nods. "Yes, she can. She can also whip up a snow beast from thin air."

"Impressive."

The IceCube Observatory has been inoperative for two decades, and despite the numerous upgrades and improvements in Tech, the structure still resembles an oilrig from the last century. The main structure sits above the ground on a raised platform that is held in place by heavy, hexagonal columns. The multilevel exterior hub was used as a research center. The main neutrino lab, known as DeepCore, is buried deep underground.

When the Observatory first opened in the 2010s, narrow channels were drilled three kilometers into the ice shelf. Since then, there has been significant ice melt, and the structure has been recalibrated and repositioned; the channels now bore only two kilometers into the ice.

Tig and Quinn reach the main hub. On the underside of the platform grow hundreds of long, thin icicles. Tig breaks the tip from one. He wraps it in one of his gloves and hands it to Quinn as if it's an ice cream cone.

She sucks the icicle; it's refreshing. The coldness revives her and boosts her spirits. Her headache lifts.

They move farther into the site and see a flashing sign above a door that reads, WELCOME TO TITAN.

"I thought we were going to Elsavale," Quinn says. "We should ask for a refund."

Tig takes her hand. "I hear Titan is lovely this time of year."

Inside the door is a skylift; they step inside.

"What are we doing here?" Quinn whispers.

"We're neutrino hunting. Stay close." He adjusts the collar of her thermal suit then kisses her cheek.

The skylift delivers them to reception—a small, copper-colored room with a large tree trunk, over two meters wide, lying on its side. The only light comes from an ornate crystal chandelier hanging over the tree.

"Your name—what's your name going to be?" Tig whispers as they exit the skylift.

"I'm not using Truth, maybe—"

"Greetings. Greetings, travelers." A short, slender woman with blue eyes and an ecstatic smile moves quickly from behind the tree trunk reception desk and takes Quinn's hand. "I'm Truth and this is Fun." The woman tilts her head towards the man beside her. Truth and Fun wear baggy pants and collarless shirts with buttons down one shoulder. Threads of multicolored beads loop around their necks.

Fun flicks his blond mane and his pale green eyes rest on Quinn. "And you are?"

"Time. I'm Time," she says. "And this is . . ." She turns to Tig.

"Gilgamesh," Tig says.

Quinn raises an eyebrow.

"Well, it's great to meet you Time and . . . Gil," Truth says. "I accept you and take on your light. I'm one of the Storytellers here, and Fun is a Human Experience Engager. Hope to see you in one of the PlayShops later today. There's Eye Gazing at five."

"Amoeba Hugs at four," Fun adds.

"Amoeba Hugs are very popular," Truth says. "You might want to book. Now, all the PlayShops are optional, but if you're part of the first lift-off team, Trust Exercises are mandatory. They'll help prepare you for the journey."

"The journey to Titan," Quinn clarifies.

"Yes. The Main Event is this Sunday. All the directors will be here. Check your tickets, they should have been sent to you. But come see me if you have any problems. If you've booked accommodation, your reservations will be processed shortly, and you'll receive confirmation on your Band." Truth speaks slowly, with the enunciation of someone who's given the same spiel a hundred times today.

"Now, let's start you off with a Trust Exercise." Fun ushers Tig and Quinn into an adjoining room. "Cleo and Milo will look after you from here."

The adjacent room, which resembles a dimly lit travel lounge, is filled with dozens of eager people who want to be somewhere else. There are low, comfortable chairs grouped in clusters, and travelers are engaged in intense discussions. Around the perimeter of the room, people are perched at high tables on stools as they consult their modules. On the far side is a self-serve refreshment bar offering beverages and light snacks.

On a raised platform, there is a display of Titanesque products: High-Tech space suits made from new biomaterials that monitor health and well-being, 3D-printed habitats and living Pods, and a life-size Titan Rover with the eMpower logo on it.

Quinn wanders into an Earth-Memory Scents Experience. Smells from nature waft towards her—a sea breeze, burning wood, fresh-cut grass, and a pine forest. There's also a holo display of Earth-Memory Light. The holo mimics the effect of sunlight at different times of the day: dappled morning light as it passes through a leafy tree, a low shaft of afternoon light as it pierces a forest. An attendant informs her that the exhibitions will accompany them to Titan, to help with homesickness.

Bots pass around plates of minced shrimp and salmon. Made using cellular agriculture; structured muscle cells bathed in nutrients and grown on scaffolds. The cells organize themselves into muscle and tissue. Tig and Quinn decline; cultured meat products are a feast for bacteria. They lack the diverse microbiome of conventional meat.

"This is one of those weekend role-play games, isn't it?" Quinn asks. "They don't really think they're going to Titan, do they?"

Tig shrugs.

Two catbots sidle up to them. Cleo and Milo are a meter and a half tall. They resemble plush, stuffed toys with their oversize heads, triangular ears, squat noses, and black eyes the size of saucers. Both are gendered female. Cleo's coat is a variegated rainbow of colors, starting with pale pink on her paws and finishing purple at the tips of her ears. She wears a glittering silver collar. Milo is a grey tabby with a white chest and a pink nose. She has a satin ribbon around her neck.

Cleo takes Quinn's hand. "Your hand is warm," she purrs.

Milo reaches for Tig's hand. Tig's eyes narrow. The bot backs away.

Cleo prances towards one of the high tables at the side of the room and Quinn, still holding the bot's hand, follows.

"Write down your fears or any questions you might have about the journey," Cleo instructs. "We'll read them aloud soon, addressing each question in turn. Take a few minutes. We have modules, or you can use paper if you prefer. You can take more than one piece."

"You mean the journey to . . . Titan?" Quinn asks.

"Yes. Titan." The bot smiles.

Quinn warms to the idea. She takes two slips of paper, sits at the high table, and writes, *It's really cold—minus 200 below Celsius. How are we going to keep warm?* She folds the note and places it in the slot at the back of the table.

On her second slip of paper, she writes, *A day on Titan lasts 15 days and 22 hours. That's a long day. What are we going to do to fill the time?* Then she folds the page and pops it into the slot.

A young girl steps up beside Quinn and scribbles on her slip of paper. Quinn peers sideways, attempting to catch a glimpse—she is fascinated by these people. She understands their desire for adventure and space travel, but Titan is a serious journey—the flight will take several months—and the only habitat there is an abandoned community set up in the 2040s. *What are they going to do once they get there?*

The girl smiles and shows Quinn her question. It reads, *Shadows are darker on Mars than on Earth. I'm worried about my shadow.*

"You don't have to worry about your shadow," Quinn whispers. "You're not going to Mars. You're going to Titan."

A dark-haired, middle-aged man steps up to the table. He slips several pieces of paper into the slot, then turns to Quinn. "You know what I'm looking forward to the most?"

The cold. The darkness. The days that last 360 hours.

"A job. I just want a job. Terraforming a planet is going to take a lot of work. I reckon there'll be a lot to do when we get there."

Quinn gives him a melancholy smile.

"And the rain," the man continues. "The rain falls more slowly on Titan, six times slower. So we get to enjoy it for longer. I'm looking forward to the water sports."

"Actually, it's not water, it's methane and ethane," Quinn says. "I don't think—"

"Attention, everyone," Cleo addresses the room. "Don't worry if you haven't finished, there's no rush. We're just going to read out a few questions to get us in the mood." A screen rolls down from the ceiling and a message is illuminated. "The first question: 'Are you offering nutrigenetics services or the CCK hormone to suppress appetite?'" Cleo pauses. "No, we are not offering that. You should definitely bring your own."

Quinn spies a logo on the top right corner of the screen: a small circle with the words SHUN MANTRA written in italics around the perimeter. She steps back against the wall. Is this Shun Mantra? Because these people seem so genuine and benign—not at all what she thought a despotic cult of self-serving individuals would be like. What is everyone doing here?

Quinn engages her Comms. "Get us out of here," she whispers to Anvil. "DeepCore, that's where we need to be."

"Door on the left. Then head all the way to the end and find the skylift."

Quinn scans the room. There is no door on the left. "Please, look at your hands."

"Okay, it's right, the door on the right. The skylift might not be working; if not, it's eight flights of stairs to get there, go all the way to the bottom."

Quinn catches Tig's eye and tilts her head towards the exit.

Thirty-Six

Bert, Ernie, and Big Bird.

QUINN AND TIG PEER into a deep, empty shaft that was once the skylift for the DeepCore lab. Around the corner, they find the stairwell: a concrete chute with a flimsy metal staircase that descends eight levels. The metal treads on the stairs are worn and corroded. Tig grabs the handrail—the section breaks off in his hand. Then the entire handrail peels away from the wall and plummets towards the ground, where it lands with a racket.

Quinn peers over the edge, then raises an accusing eyebrow at Tig.

Tig considers the section of railing in his hand. He tosses it over the edge, into the shaft, and it lands with a clunk. "I'll go first."

Stepping in front of Quinn, he moves slowly, steadily, taking one step at a time. Quinn follows, but every few paces she misjudges his lagging tempo and bumps into him.

He pauses. "You good?"

"Yep. Maybe pick up the pace a bit."

He continues to plod, one step at a time, very slowly down the stairs.

"What's going on?" Anvil asks. "Evolution moved faster than you two."

"It's steep. Don't want anyone to trip," Tig says.

Finally, they reach the bottom and enter a large, prefabricated box.

"According to the map, this is the delivery port," Anvil says. "The DeepCore lab is at the other end of the complex. Just keep walking."

For the last two decades, the research center has remained

unoccupied. But, at the height of its capacity, it housed teams of scientists and technicians who worked on rotation, spending an entire season buried beneath the Antarctic ice recording data. It was mandatory for the teams to live above ground every other season. Lack of natural light and long exposure to darkness is not healthy for humans; it leads to dark thoughts and depression.

Tig and Quinn make their way through the complex. The space is deserted, but remnants of its previous occupants are everywhere. In the food prep, which is cozy and domestic—the walls are mint green, and the ceiling clad in warm timber veneer—they find a stack of old magazines (*National Geographic*, *Interior Décor*) and some cookbooks. Pictures of exotic jungles and rainforests are pinned to the walls, compliments of *National Geographic*. A pile of plastic bowls and a bottle of tomato sauce rest on a shelf nearby.

They continue on and enter the lab office. It's a mess, and it resembles every science lab Quinn has ever been in. Half a dozen plastic-framed office chairs are pushed under a long desk, which runs the length of the room. Boxes of equipment—fuel cells, electron tubes, a calorimeter, vacuum pumps, particle accelerators—are stacked on the desk. Makeshift shelves are piled high with folders and there are storage boxes attached to the walls. A periodic table is pinned to the wall.

Quinn picks up a portable particle detector from one of the boxes and examines it. "They left a lot behind."

"The door at the end, that's DeepCore—then you've reached your destination," Anvil says.

Quinn slips the particle detector into her pocket.

She and Tig proceed together and enter a cavernous room. The floor is pale vinyl, and the walls are covered in a thin layer of ice. Ice crystals hang from the ceiling. In the center of the room, three core holes, each one about a half a meter wide, are drilled into the floor.

They move closer and peer over a low railing and into the dark abyss of the closest hole.

"Okay, what now?" Tig asks.

"The neutrinos are down there, at the bottom," Quinn says. "We need to find one, then get it out."

"How do we do that?"

"When a neutrino interacts with a proton or a neutron inside an atom, it produces a secondary particle that gives off a blue light. Finding them won't be a problem." She smiles sweetly at Tig.

"You want me to go down this hole? It's two kilometers deep."

"One of us has to go." Quinn scans the room. "There's no equipment, so . . ."

"You're serious."

She hands him the particle detector. "The screen will glow blue when it detects a neutrino. Then you just push this button and, essentially, it traps the particle."

Frowning, he takes the detector from her and turns it on. A dull blue light appears on the screen. They share a surprised glance, then scan the room. The place is completely empty, apart from a low storage cupboard in one corner.

Slowly they walk towards the cupboard. Tig tries the door; it's locked. He rips it off. Inside, lying on the shelf, are a three particle cylinders—short pipes with glass hatches. Inside each chamber is a flickering blue light.

"What are these?" Tig asks.

Quinn picks up a cylinder and wipes away a thick layer of dust, revealing a name: Bert. She does the same to the other two cylinders, and reveals the names Ernie and Big Bird. She laughs. "These were the first high-energy particles ever discovered: Bert, Ernie, and Big Bird. Their energy exceeds two quadrillion electron volts."

"Are they neutrinos?"

"Yes, they are. Our work here is done."

Thirty-Seven

An aurora.

THE FOLLOWING MORNING, QUINN wakes in her cabin on *Nanshe*. She has overslept—she had a restless night and dreamt again of delivering her baby girl in the Antarctic wilderness. Now, she has an ominous feeling about the icy landscape and is keen to distance herself from it. Today they sail north; she is happy to be leaving the great southern continent behind.

She will miss the clouds, though.

Lightly, she pats the space beside her, feeling for Tig. The bed is empty, he probably rose hours ago.

She lifts her head and glances from one side of the cabin to the other. The room has changed color. She sits up, looks around. Everything—the walls, the floor, the furniture—is different. It looks like someone redecorated overnight. Yesterday, the timber-clad walls were lighter; this morning they look dark, almost walnut-colored. The padded chair at the end of the bed is deep pink; yesterday it was grey. The bed sheets are pale pink; they should be white. She sniffs the sheets. They smell like Tig, but they are still pink. *Why are they pink?*

The double glass doors at the far end of the cabin are open and the ocean looks like grape juice. *Where did the blue go?*

"Oh shit. It's the light."

The color of the light has changed: it's red.

It's the light. The sunlight is red.

Quinn swings her legs out of bed and heads out the door.

***

The Sun had a meltdown while Quinn slept. A mega solar flare took out Earth's satellites. NIoT went down, communication technologies and GPS systems collapsed.

There are three stages to a solar flare attack: First, X-ray and ultraviolet light bombard the Earth's atmosphere—this interferes with communications. Second, the planet is pelted by a storm of radiation. Third, coronal mass ejections (CME)—a squall of charged particles—crash into the Earth's magnetic field. This causes electromagnetic ebbs and flows, disrupting Tech and melting transformers.

Quinn waddles up the stairs, penguin-like, towards the galley.

For decades, High-Tech has underpinned daily life on the planet. The consequences of a solar storm on Earth's technologies, therefore, is dire. Solar cells will blow, disrupting energy cycles and cooling systems. Computers will fail, and access to Coin will cease. Food deliveries, AVs, transporters, and emergency services will stop. Logistic systems will fail. Data will be scrambled. Time will stop.

For smart cities with interconnected grid systems, the effects will be worse and will cascade like dominoes as all things related to Tech halt. There will be no automation: doors and windows will remain fixed, lights won't work, security will cease to function, water won't filter or pump.

Quinn enters the galley and finds it empty. She heads outside to the deck.

A massive solar flare might hold the energy of ten, fifty, a hundred billion atomic bombs. The scenarios it causes will feel like the end of the world. Satellites will explode. Sparks will fall from the sky. Paper will catch fire.

Last night, it never got dark—the birds sang into the evening and they never stopped. Last night, the plug was pulled, and everyone will think the Sun is to blame. But the Sun is a scapegoat. Quinn knows how that feels, to be blamed for something you didn't do. She has an overwhelming sense of righteousness, aligned with an urge to find the culprits. Shun Mantra is messing around with the Earth's core, creating an energy vortex, and it's weakening the Earth's magnetic field, leaving it vulnerable to solar storms.

Outside, the air crackles. She spies Planck on the far side of the deck, watching the sky. It's an aurora; above them, the sky dances. A luminous emerald sphere shoots a spark of light northwards. Mesmerized, Quinn follows the trail of light and trips over the deck. Planck catches her. The spark dissolves, and an explosion of stars fills the sky. They watch, awe-struck by the spectacle. It's the most beautiful thing Quinn has ever seen. It's also the most unnatural and foreign thing she has ever seen.

Auroras are caused by solar winds smashing into Earth's magnetic field. Charged particles seep into the upper atmosphere then crash into gas molecules. This forces them to release photons of light, which generate an aurora.

The ocean is littered with the bodies of dead gulls. Above them, hundreds of seabirds whirl in circles, disoriented. Quinn spies Tig's gene-sequenced passenger pigeon, Martha2, tethered to the deck.

"Keeping her safe," Planck explains. "The aurora's effecting the birds' sonar. They've lost all sense of direction, and they're drowning at sea."

They sit down on the edge of the deck and watch the sky.

"You know about the electromagnet under Antarctica?" Quinn asks.

Planck nods.

"It's weakening the planet's electric field. It's letting the solar storms in. Shun Mantra are capturing energy . . ." Suddenly, Quinn has a revelation. Goose bumps shimmy up her arms. *Terraforming Titan is going to take a lot of energy.* She turns to Planck. "They're using it to terraform Titan."

"Of course—space travel to a distant planet."

"Except Titan's a moon, not a planet," Quinn corrects.

"Yes, you're right. Titan is a moon. Either way, they're sending a colony into space, and harnessing the solar flares for energy. The implications—we get zapped by the Sun's radiation and frizzle to death."

"At Elsavale, they mentioned a lift-off on Sunday. They said all the directors would be coming. Shun Mantra, they're the directors."

Tig joins them on deck. "Comms are dead, but we received a message from Maim last night: All leave is revoked. She wants us back at HEXAD." He looks at Quinn. "You want me to stay?"

She shakes her head. "End-of-the-world stuff. I understand."

"It's a fucking disaster," he says. "Ships are sailing in circles. Auto ID systems are thousands of kilometers off course. Nobody knows where the fuck they are—they can't find their own noses without a GPS, and no one knows how to read a map."

"You could take Strat, if he wants to go," Quinn says.

"He's already offered. Don't worry. My life before his."

"Should you go off your Meds?" Quinn asks.

Planck nods. "Yes, good idea, perhaps—"

"No." Tig frowns. "I'll be fine. We leave in an hour. Now, I have this thing downstairs, in the cabin, and I really need your help," he says, looking at Quinn.

"What thing?"

"The thing that I can do by myself, but it's not as much fun."

"Oh, that thing. I'm sure I can help."

Thirty-Eight

What would Stephen do?

After Tig, Planck, and Strat leave on the rotor, Quinn and Anvil share a plate of cookies in the galley.

"I feel like we've been had," Anvil says. "You're probably the best shot in the universe. And who knows what I can do with my super pistol hands?" She makes pistols with her hands and mock-shoots objects around the galley. "But we've been marginalized by our gender. They get to go on a boys-only adventure, and we have to stay here"—she holds up a cookie—"and eat cookies because we're female."

Quinn breaks the last cookie in half and leaves it on the plate for Anvil. "Well, I am pregnant."

Anvil nods.

"And, let's face it, you can't read a map, and you can barely tell your left from your right. They need someone who can read a—"

"I know. I know."

They finish the last mouthful of cookie in silence. Then, in the distance, they hear the sound of a rotor.

Anvil pauses, cocks her head at Quinn, and frowns; the sound is getting louder, the rotor is coming towards them.

Quinn smiles. "That's my friend. We have our own adventure to plan."

***

Quinn and Anvil watch the rotor land on the main deck. Geller slides out of the cockpit and straightens her uniform—a dark military climate suit with fine red and gold stripes over the pockets. She makes a mock gesture of brushing the lint off her epaulettes. Her black hair is loose, and it flutters around her face.

"That's your friend?" says Anvil. "She's a model, right?"

"She's a soldier, a general."

"Look, her hair is swishing in the wind, and there's no wind."

Anvil is right, Geller's hair is swishing in a nonexistent breeze.

"You should probably know—she can't process fear. When she was young, she contacted Urbach-Wiethe disease. It ruined the amygdala regions in both brain hemispheres. No matter what, she never gets scared. She's fearless."

Geller strides towards them. She wraps her arms around Quinn and kisses her cheek. "Hello me love," she says. "My lord, you are as fat as a house. Tat baby must be 'uge."

"Thank you, that means a lot," Quinn says. "I thought all leave was revoked. I'm surprised Maim let you come."

"I'm not on leave an' if anyone asks, I was never here." Geller turns her gaze on Anvil. "I've heard about you, te girl filled wit electricity. We're goin' ta be grand friends."

Geller has not come alone; an elderly man with dark eyes, wiry grey hair, and a close-shaven beard ambles across the deck towards them.

"This is Flax," Quinn tells Anvil. "He's a relation—Tig's uncle—and one of the Knowledge Keepers for the Maldives. Their culture is over five thousand years old. There's a lot of history . . . some might say too much history. He's brought us something from their artifacts."

Flax approaches Quinn and kisses her cheek. "You look well. How are you feeling?"

"Good." She loops her arm through his and they stroll towards the hatch. "I'm very happy to see you, and thank you, I appreciate you bringing it."

"Thought I'd deliver it in person." He taps the small bag hanging over his shoulder.

They head downstairs and convene around the table in the galley. Quinn places the Phaistos Disc on the table.

Anvil brews chamomile tea. She takes a cake from the storage, covers it in orange sauce, slices it into wedges, and places the teapot and the cake on the table.

Geller passes the plates.

Quinn pours the tea.

Flax unpacks the black crown from his shoulder bag and places it on the table next to the Disc. Upon first glance, the crown looks unremarkable, commonplace: a fine black ring, the metal no wider than one of Quinn's bangles—a simple dark hoop. But up close, and in good light, the crown reveals its intricately carved engravings, which are an elaborate configuration of interlocking pieces.

"Was goin' to steal te ting, ten I realized you were te queen, so technically 'tis not stealin', probably yours anyway."

Geller collects the crown and places it on Quinn's head.

Quinn sways. She feels light-headed and nauseous. She places her hands on the table to steady herself. Flax lightly lifts the crown from her head and drops it onto the table.

It feels like a lead weight has been removed from her head. "It's much heavier than it looks," she says.

Geller collects the crown and twirls it around her finger. "Light as a feather."

Flax glances at Quinn. "It's the weight of time. It knows you're next."

"This is scary shit," Anvil says.

"Yes, yes it is," says Flax. "And I'm here to help, but I'm also here to explain the consequences. First, you must understand that using this Disc will change your timeline. We each have a unique timeline that tracks our path through the universe. If you go back in time, you create another timeline." He glances at Quinn's stomach. "The baby will also have another fork in her timeline. And, you might also change other people's lines. Time travel causes a wave of change through the universe. It will impact your future choices and decisions. Forever."

"Have you thought this through?" Anvil asks. "Maybe it's not such a good idea."

Quinn nods. *This is a stupid idea. No one should go back through time; what's done is done.*

"On the other hand," Flax says, "it's more like a ripple than a wave. Serious change requires more effort than the actions of one person. The universe is more robust than you think. There are deeper forces at work on all of us; generally, your actions don't change much."

"Okay, good news, not so serious." Anvil turns to Flax. "How many timelines do you have?"

"Too many, I lost count."

"Really?" Quinn asks. "You can't remember?"

Flax grimaces. "Twenty-six."

"What? Seriously. Twenty-six."

"Yes, but I must tell you, my ventures through time solved nothing. I am not happier or wiser for my travels." He reaches for another slice of cake. "You see, the thing is, you get caught in a loop, and loops have no end. You start something, perhaps you go back to change one event, one small thing, but the sequence doesn't end, it goes around and around. There is a lot to be said for living a fixed life, remaining a prisoner in the present. If you start a loop, it's almost impossible to untie."

"We go back in time for te people we love." Geller turns to Flax. "Who did you go back for?"

"My wife. She died. I went back many times to try and save her, but she continued to die. Always on the same day. I tried everything. But her fate was locked."

"And we're talking twenty-six times! I'd have given up long before twenty-six." Anvil looks at Flax and shrugs. "Sorry."

"That is the nature of the loop; you get caught without realizing. Then it becomes an obsession. When you travel through time, you think you can do anything, you think you can beat it, but you can't."

"How'd she die?" Geller asks.

"The first few times she was hit by an auto. Then a baseball in the head, then a golf ball, then a stray bullet. She fell off a ladder four times. One time she just slipped and hit her head. We discovered she was allergic to shellfish. And tree nuts. She was also hypersensitive to mangoes. Cardiac arrest, twice. Three counts of electric shock. She broke her neck driving—her scarf caught in the auto's wheel and strangled her. Then, finally, her esophagus ruptured. After that I knew. There was no point continuing."

It's a grim account; everyone turns to Quinn.

"I'm not sure this is a good idea," she says.

"What would Lise do?" Geller says. "You're doin' tis for 'er. What would she say about it?"

"She would say, 'What would Stephen do?'" Quinn rolls her eyes. "Stephen Hawking."

"And?"

"He would go, of course he would. I'm going back. I'm going to find out what happened to her."

"Time travel makes a mockery of causality," Flax says. "Stephen Hawking knew that. Cause comes before effect, and it must always be this way. Going back in time and running into your past self, or preventing your own birth, would create chaos in the universe. You must be careful. You must not run into your past self. Timing is crucial. You must change as little as possible about the past, and no one must see you."

"Okay, timing is crucial. The *other me* will be on the Cloud Ship, jumping out of the sky. The guests will be waiting out the storm in their rooms, and the research station should be empty."

"After you open the portal, it will stay open until you press on the particle chamber." Flax gently taps the center sphere with one finger. "Once closed, you press it again and it will open."

Quinn examines the center sphere. "It's star-shaped. I thought it was a star chamber."

"It looks like a star—a star chamber," Geller confirms.

"It's a particle chamber," Flax says.

***

Flax is not staying on *Nanshe*. As a Knowledge Keeper, he must return home to the Maldives in Unus, as soon as possible. The planet is in disarray, and he has responsibilities.

On deck, Geller releases a passenger drone from the rotor and coaxes Flax into the single padded seat. He is not happy about this; he was under the impression they would be returning together in the rotor.

Geller shakes her head. She is staying, and so is the rotor.

Thirty-Nine

The life of a lamb is no less precious.

When Geller and Quinn set down on Kerguelen, they remain seated in the rotor and consider the island's bleak, desolate landscape.

"Tere's no sand, no beach, no trees," Geller notes. "'Tis all very . . . brown."

"Not all islands are tropical." Quinn casts her eyes across the harsh, stumpy vegetation that clings to the steep hills. "Its beauty lies in its physical isolation, its remoteness."

Geller releases her safety harness. Quinn follows, and they disembark. The air smells salty and pungent. Sea birds swirl aimlessly in the sky above them, and the ground is littered with the bodies of dead birds, as well as numerous fish and several penguins.

Geller eyes the ominous form of Mount Ross, hovering in the background. "'Tis certainly a good 'aunt for ghosts."

"I think this is what the island wanted all along," Quinn says. "To be left alone, to be free of humans."

"That's quite profound, for you."

"Thank you."

They stroll along the muddy shore towards the site where the research station once stood. The island is now classified a natural disaster zone, and a memorial, a triangular stone cairn, has been erected. It has a plaque engraved with the names of the deceased—almost 2,000 of them. Quinn recalls the islanders who once lived here: the shopkeeper who only stocked shoes and apparel for men—nothing for women; the fisherpeople who thought the new technologies at the research station were space-age, science fiction gadgets. She runs her fingers over the names on the plaque: 1,962 names. One body was never found, never accounted for—Lise's. The one body that everyone thinks was never found, however, is Ada's. Officially, the only person to survive was Quinn, although Mori Eco and Tig also escaped.

"You good?" Geller asks.

Quinn nods.

A black bug crawls from a gap between the stones in the cairn. Another follows. Quinn wiggles her nose. A swarm emerges; it takes flight and heads towards Mount Ross.

"Not what you imagined." Geller slaps Quinn on the back. "Come on."

They turn inland and head towards Mount Ross and what remains of the Cook Glacier. Thirty years ago, the glacier covered 450 square kilometers. It quickly receded when climate change took hold, and the meltwater forged a majestic, swift-flowing river that ran from the mountaintop to the ocean. Nine months ago, when the SkyRiver hit, it fractured the glacier. The river flooded, flattening the research station and the town. Now, the mighty river is a small trickle at the bottom of a chasm.

Halfway up the mountain, something moves, and several rocks tumble down the cliff towards them.

"Probably just a sheep, lost its footin'," Geller says. She retrieves a search-and-rescue drone from her pack. Sphere-shaped, it has circular propellers on either side, and it will scout the area, searching for life forms. Geller tosses it into sky. The drone flits backwards and forwards across the side of the mountain, recording data. "You've returned to te scene of te crime. Soon, you'll be back there, reliving it all."

"It doesn't seem right to save one person."

"You can go back in time, but you can't change everytin'. You 'ave a mission. Focus on tat, only tat. Get distracted and you'll fail."

The drone returns, and Geller posts the data to her module. Together, they peer at the screen. Geller was right; the rockfall was caused by a loose-footed sheep. The drone has picked up the position of the mountain flock, as well as the haunt of several sea birds and . . . a body, buried under the mountain.

Quinn stares at the screen. Her heart pounds. "Is that really . . . a body?"

"Aye."

"How did it get there?"

Geller applies a geological filter, which shows the rock and sediment layers that form the mountain. The filter reveals a long, dark shadow, over five kilometers long, under the mountain. "A tunnel," she says.

The tunnel runs into the heart of the mountain, eventually tapping into a wider space, and this is where the corpse lies. The entrance is now sealed by the landslide.

"How dead is the corpse?"

"Can't say." Geller glances at Quinn. "You want me to go? 'Cos I will."

Quinn shakes her head.

"Te tunnel is five kilometers, tat's a long walk."

"We had motorbikes on the island."

"And you can ride a motorbike? 'Cos you don't look like someone who can ride a motorbike."

"Since I was ten."

"Well, te truth is 'idden' under te mountain—go find out what 'appened."

***

Quinn holds the Disc with one arm. The particle chamber, containing the neutrinos, is in place, and the constellations are set. She will arrive in 2049 an hour and a half before the glacier breaks and washes the town away. The wedding guests will be in their rooms, taking cover from the storm. There is no chance she will run into her past self—the Cloud Ship will be in the sky, about to break apart.

Quinn slips her bracelet into the center ring of the Disc, and Geller slides the crown into the outer ring. They hear a gentle click as the rings lock into place. The circular sections of the Disc turn in opposite directions. The star constellations illuminate.

Geller steps back.

Quinn presses the particle chamber.

The light fades. The air around her feels cold and dense, like she is submerged in a thick layer of fog. She doesn't move. She hugs the Disc to her chest and waits. Nothing happens. She closes her eyes and thinks about spacetime—a mathematical abstraction, an infinitesimal pixelated froth that flows across the universe from past to present to future. She is about to traverse spacetime.

Still nothing happens.

She opens her eyes; it's too dark to see anything. Perhaps Flax should have told her what to do next. Perhaps she should have asked. Perhaps she needs to step out of spacetime and into the past.

She takes a deep breath and steps forward.

The darkness lifts, and she is immediately drenched. It's raining. It's 2049, she is on Kerguelen, outside, in the middle of the storm. Her clothes are soaked, her hair is plastered to her forehead, and her shoes are squishy. She steps back, an automatic response, and she is surrounded by blackness again. She takes another step back, and the darkness lifts. Geller is standing right where she last saw her.

"What 'appened? Where's your ma?" Geller asks.

"It's raining. Like really, really raining. Buckets and buckets pouring from the sky. I lasted about ten seconds."

Geller stares at her. “I see your point. We were underprepared. Rookie mistake.” She sends a drone to *Nanshe* for hydrophobic spray and a towel.

When the drone returns, Quinn covers herself with the hydrophobic liquid; now she is waterproof.

Geller stashes the spray in Quinn’s pack. “For Lise,” she says. “Okay, second attempt.”

Quinn steps into the portal and is again surrounded by blackness. She takes a deep breath and steps forward into the light.

It’s still raining, but she is dry. Perfectly dry. She reaches for her pack to stow the Disc, but it’s not there. *Where’s my pack? It was, it was . . . on the ground next to me. Idiot.* She steps back into blackness and out the other side.

Geller is holding the pack. “I’m callin’ tis a loop.”

Quinn grabs the pack, throws it over her shoulder. “It’s not a loop, it’s just a rough start.”

For the third time, Quinn steps into darkness, then into light. Again, it’s raining, and again she is dry. She presses the particle chamber and the portal closes. She stows the Disc in her pack and heads northeast, towards the rear of the Research Station and the base of Mount Ross—the logical place to find the entrance to the tunnel. On approach, she sees a group of curly-horned sheep huddled together under the building’s wide veranda.

“Oh, good lordt, it’s Stephen Hawking.” She would know him anywhere. Stephen Hawking was her favorite curly-horned sheep. He was her morning walk companion and her breakfast buddy. If she had to pick her favorite thing about the island, the thing that made her smile every day, Stephen Hawking would be it.

Quinn ambles over to the veranda and smiles at Stephen. He recognizes her immediately and waddles over for a pat. She scratches him between the eyes, and he nuzzles into her leg.

“You’re not safe here,” she whispers. “Go to the other side of the mountain. Take your sheep friends with you, and don't tell anyone I'm here. Go."

Stephen has no intention of leaving the shelter of the veranda. She squats down and gives him a hug; it's a shame he has to die like this, swept away by a massive wall of water. Tears well in her eyes, and she turns away. *Get a grip; he's a sheep. Focus. You have one mission.*

She turns away from the sheep and follows the course of the veranda to the northeastern side of the Station. She is looking for a shed or building, something that might hide the entrance to the tunnel.

Fifty meters ahead is an old outbuilding with three motorbikes parked outside. She figures this has to be the entrance.

As she approaches the outbuilding, a red blur swims through the rain towards her. Quinn retreats and ducks behind the side wall of the veranda. A few seconds later, she sneaks a look: the red blur is a woman wearing a red evening dress. It's Ada, making her way through the mud and the rain towards the Research Station.

Quinn flattens herself against the sidewall of the building. She waits a minute, then glances around the corner. Ada is lying face down in the mud—she has lost her footing and fallen. Quinn waits, but Ada stays prostrate on the ground for some time. Quinn takes a step towards her, wanting to help her up, but checks herself and slinks back behind the veranda wall. She waits several minutes before taking another peek, and when she does, Ada is on the veranda, on her knees, weeping. Sobbing. It's a heart-wrenching cry that competes with the racket of the rain, and it pulls at Quinn's heart. *She's not crying about the state of her dress. What the fuck is going on?*

Quinn waits until Ada is long gone, then peels herself off the side wall and heads towards the outbuilding. There are four bikes parked out front. She selects an automatic, with a pillion seat. It's self-balancing, auto steer, and hands free—it can practically drive itself.

Awkwardly, she climbs on. She leans forward to grab the handlebars, but the position is impossible with her pregnancy. She repositions herself and sits upright, straighter than she would like, but it's the only position she can manage. She pats her stomach. "Okay, we can do this."

It's an easy ride. The bike is quiet, the ground is smooth, and the route is perfectly straight, like a runway. Cove lighting illuminates the path ahead, but there is absolutely nothing to see.

After ten minutes, the tunnel tapers, then opens to a larger area. Quinn kills the engine, awkwardly slides off the bike, and draws her laser.

She enters a crude, partitioned space carved straight into the mountain. It's dimly lit; cove lighting skirts the perimeter. To one side there's a portable table; an open module and two mugs sit upon it. Against the wall are half a dozen folding chairs.

In the center of the room, on a raised platform, is a clear cylinder, about three meters wide, that extends from floor to ceiling. Inside it are dozens of sparkling silver rods suspended in a luminous green liquid.

As Quinn approaches, the cylinder crackles and changes color—turns black—and the liquid solidifies.

On the floor beside the platform is a gun and a shoe. A ballet flat. She freezes. Her heart pounds. It's Lise's shoe. She rushes around to the other side of the platform.

Lise is lying on the floor behind the platform; her eyes are closed, and there's a slick of blood on the floor beside her.

Quinn rushes to her mother's side. "Hey, hey it's me, can you hear me? It's me. Please be alive."

Lise opens her eyes.

"Oh, thank goodness." She takes Lise's hand. "Are you okay?"

"No. I'm not okay. I've been shot. Ada shot me."

"Okay. Just lie still. Don't move."

"I'm not moving."

"Good. Don't. I'm going to check your wound."

"It's my left side. Just a laser burn. I'll be fine."

Quinn nods. Lise wears a black evening gown—she is still dressed for the wedding—and the garment is soaked in blood. Quinn rips the dress open and reels back. The wound is a gunshot, and it's bleeding heavily. "You may have underestimated your opponent. It's a gunshot wound, not a laser burn."

Lise sighs. "Of course, the perfect weapon for revenge."

Quinn drops her pack and takes out the MedKit. She applies Decorin, a skin protein, to Lise's wound, which seals the area and stops the bleeding, then she anesthetizes the abrasion and gives Lise a painkiller. "Maybe try and sit up now." She helps Lise into a seated position.

Lise winces and catches her breath. Then she lets out a long, slow breath. "Darling . . . are you pregnant?"

"Seven months. It's 2050, I've come back from the future to save you."

Lise's eyes are the same grey-blue as Quinn's, and immediately they light up. "I've waited all my life to hear someone say that."

"The time travel or the pregnancy?"

"Time travel. Oh darling, I can't believe you thought you had to get married because you were pregnant. That's very old-fashioned. I thought you were more progressive."

"I am. Mori's not the father." Behind them the cylinder crackles. "What is that thing?"

"My guess, an electromagnet," Lise says.

"Okay, that makes sense. We need to get out of here; in about thirty minutes, the glacier breaks and floods the town, and everyone dies, including Ada, but she has your Band, so everyone thinks she's you." Quinn grabs the container of water repellant from her pack. "Close your eyes; it's raining outside, I'm going to spray you."

Lise closes her eyes. "Ada found out I was seeing Maim and followed me here. I can't believe she shot me—with a gun—a real gun, then left me to die."

"To be fair, you probably would have died anyway. Almost everyone dies. How did you know about the tunnel?"

Lise scans the label of the hydroscopic spray. "Darling, you shouldn't be using this. It's full of volatile organic compounds. It can't be good for the baby."

With a wave of her hand, Quinn dismisses her mother. *The baby has water bear DNA inside her. I don't think a few VOCs will make much difference.*

Lise puts the container down. "I didn't trust Mori. I didn't understand why you were here on Kerguelen or why you were headed to Antarctica. I noticed them coming and going on the bikes. Thought I'd take a look. Ada must have followed."

"Perceptive. I was on the island for months. I never noticed. Do you think you can stand?" Quinn slips the missing shoe onto Lise's foot, then helps her mother up. They make their way to the bike. Awkwardly Quinn slides on, then Lise balances precariously on the backseat.

"Pass me my helmet." Lise has the same, wavy dark hair as Quinn, and she flattens it down.

Quinn shakes her head; there are no helmets.

Lise raises an eyebrow.

"You know, perhaps if you'd told me that you had concerns about Mori, about eMpower, about Shun Mantra, about Niels, about Kerguelen and Antarctica, maybe some of this could have been avoided."

"Darling, it's not my job to tell you what you should do. It's your life, not—"

Quinn starts the bike.

Lise clings to her daughter, and they fly through the tunnel. Lise's black evening dress is torn up one side and it flutters, cape-like, in the wind behind them.

***

Outside the shed, Quinn navigates around the mud pool where Ada fell, she motors through the torrential rain, and parks the bike on the veranda, scattering the curly-horned sheep.

The sheep quickly return to the shelter of the veranda. Stephen Hawking makes his way towards Quinn, eager for another pat. She scratches the top of his head. "I hate to leave him, knowing . . . well, you know what happens."

"We can take him with us. What's that Gandhi quote?"

"Where there is love, there is life."

"No, the other one, the famous one."

An eye for an eye only ends up making the whole world blind? I'm not sure that's relevant.

"'The life of a lamb is no less precious than that of a human.' The sheep come with us."

"All of them?"

"Why not?"

Quinn laughs.

They return to the time travel mark with Stephen Hawking and four of his sheep friends. Quinn presses the particle chamber. Darkness surrounds them. They haul the sheep out the other side. Once again, it's 2050.

Quinn has missed the mark by a few meters. Geller is behind them, surrounded by a cluster of moths. She dreamily brushes them away as Quinn's mother stares above her.

"Darling, why is the sky red?" Lise asks.

Forty

Families are so complicated.

Back on *Nanshe*, the four women convene in the galley. Quinn brews chamomile tea and Anvil heats a batch of seafood and plankton soup for their supper, while Lise lies on the sofa and Geller tends the gunshot wound in her abdomen.

Geller draws out the bullet, then hands it to Lise. "A souvenir," she says.

Lise holds the bloody shell up to the light and examines it. "I can't believe she shot me. Bitch."

"Mother." Quinn glares at Lise from the galley. "Are you happy using that word?"

"Yes, darling, I am."

Geller smiles. She tapes a smart bandage to Lise's injury. If there is an infection, the bandage will turn yellow or red—depending on the severity—and release an antibiotic. If the infection becomes antibiotic resistant, the bandage will turn blue. If this happens, Geller will shine an infrared light onto the material, signaling the release of molecules that will kill the bacteria or at least weaken it enough to improve the efficiency of the antibiotic.

Quinn hands the first cup of tea to Lise, figuring she needs it the most.

Lise slides her teacup to one side. "Anything stronger?"

"We have a Japanese sencha with turmeric," Quinn says.

Lise wrinkles her nose.

Geller leaves Lise's side and forages in the storage area. She retrieves a bottle of spirits.

Anvil sets three glasses down on the table. Geller fills them to the brim. She hands one to Anvil and the other to Lise. The three women raise their glasses and skull.

Quinn skulls her chamomile tea. "Okay, I'll start. It's July 2050. I'm seven months pregnant. It's a girl. Her father is—"

"Wait." Lise holds out her glass for a refill. Anvil promptly follows.

Geller obliges.

Lise skulls her drink.

"It's Tig," Quinn says.

Startled, Lise chokes, then spits the liquid across the table.

Quinn pours herself a second cup of chamomile tea and waits for her mother's coughing fit to subside.

Lise clears her throat. She lightly pats her chest, then she taps a finger on the lip of her glass and Geller fills it again.

Lise smiles at her daughter. "Darling, I'm sorry. It was . . . unexpected. I like Tig, I really do. I just didn't expect to have him as a son-in-law. In many ways, he's quite traditional. How's it . . . working out?"

"It's working out just fine, thank you," Quinn snaps.

Lise sips her drink. "Men." She shakes her head. "They're funny things, aren't they?" She throws back the rest of her shot. "Right, what have I missed? Tell me everything."

"Carbon parts have fallen—they're down 40 points, to 560," Anvil says.

***

Nanshe drifts in the South Atlantic Ocean, midway between Antarctica and the southern tip of Tres, the African continent. It's four in the morning, and Lise lingers in the galley. Anvil and Geller staggered to their cabins an hour ago, and Quinn retired three hours before that.

Lise is weary, but not ready for bed. She doesn't want to leave the comfort of the galley—she likes the domesticity of the space and the cook's kitchen. *Nanshe* reminds her of a junk from the mid-twentieth century. The decor is nostalgic, bohemian. The dark wood floors, the deep, comfortable chairs, and the woven rugs are homey. The small, last-century lamps fixed to the walls leave puddles of yellow light on the timber floor and make everyone look warm and golden. The room has a cozy, tranquil ambiance that suits her mood.

She has a lot to think about. Only nine months have passed, but so much has happened. There was civil war in Unus, and Dirac Devine is dead but somehow still leading a band of misguided followers. A young Transhuman called Aaroon is the head of Shun Mantra and plans to take a colony to Titan. He has created an electromagnet with the intent of weakening the planet's magnetic shield and leaving it defenseless against solar storms. She has known for some time that Niels and Mori Eco have a significant financial investment in the company.

She shifts in her seat; her wound hurts. She presses it and winces. The bandage is turning yellow; she has a mild infection, she will need to be careful. She presses it again, and it still hurts, so she reaches for her glass—the alcohol helps the pain—but the glass is empty. She pushes it aside and gazes out the window into the darkness, once again collecting her thoughts.

Quinn is pregnant. Lise thought that might happen. She figured there would be a grandchild in her life eventually; adopted or biological, it makes no difference to her. She smiles at the heartwarming feeling it brings. As for Tig, they will work it out. Or, they won't—it's not her concern.

Maim is now the elected leader of Unus, and this is an enormous relief. Maim is not a politician. She is an academic and a climate change advocate; she will make an excellent president. But Lise lives in Hobart, and Maim will have to spend half her time at Hexad and the other half in Unus. So theirs will be an LDR—a long-distance relationship. She tells herself they will manage, they will work it out, they are in love, and they are both sensible adults. But in her heart, she knows LDRs are difficult, and in the end, someone must compromise to make it work. She wonders who that someone will be.

Finally, her thoughts converge on the one piece of information that makes absolutely no sense to her. M-theory. Why would Aaroon think she was working on M-theory? It's not even her field. Why send HOTRODs after Quinn based on a hunch, a mark on a scrap of paper that Ada stole? Why is he so obsessed, and who is this tall, fingernail-biting Transhuman with electric blue eyes?

Unless . . . unless Aaroon is Ronnie? Lise hasn't seen the boy in six, maybe seven, years. He was always a tall, awkward child—no social skills, and a terrible habit of biting his fingernails to the quick.

"Oh, good lordt, Aaroon is Ronnie." She needs to talk to Maim.

She peels herself off the sofa, then makes her way to Quinn's cabin and enters without knocking. Gently, she shakes her daughter. "I need to talk to Maim."

"Now?" Quinn yawns.

"Yes, now. It's eight in the evening at Hexad. If I don't contact her now, I'll miss my chance."

Quinn blinks at her mother. "Does she have a domain?"

Lise nods.

Quinn mumbles something about transmitting messages over the aural currents, then rolls out of bed and plods up the stairs, back to the galley. Lise follows.

***

Lise brews tea and Quinn opens her QM.

"I can make a pathway, a control channel," Quinn says. "Then, I'll capture the charged particles in the magnetic field of the aurora, then harness the electrical signals and convert those into video and sound." She passes the QM to her mother. "Enter the address."

Lise slides a mug towards Quinn and enters the details.

Quinn sips her tea. It tastes better than usual. "Why is this tea so good?"

"Topped up the boiler with fresh water. The water loses oxygen when it boils, makes it taste flat."

"Clever. Okay, it's connecting. Hopefully it rings, and hopefully she answers. Good luck." Quinn takes her tea back to her cabin.

***

Lise sits at the table with the QM in front of her.

Maim answers the call. The vision is live, but the connection fades in and out. The two women stare at each other, both silent. Several times Maim attempts to speak, but chokes, unable to continue. Lise is aware there is much to say, but she thinks this might not be the best time.

"I've missed you," Maim finally says. She wipes her eyes and laughs softly. "How was it? Wait, don't tell me, we don't have time right now. Are you okay?"

"I was shot . . . and I time traveled; technically, this is my future."

"I'm not sure which is more alarming."

"Right now, I'm more concerned about the solar storm."

"Yes. We have a problem—a big problem. Shun Mantra—you were right to be concerned about them."

"They're in Antarctica, at the IceCube Station. Quinn went there—"

"It's a decoy. They're not Shun Mantra, they're just a group of neo-hippies trying to find a job and some meaning in this heat-soaked world. We think Shun Mantra are actually at an abandoned whaling station, called Whalers Bay, just north of Antarctica. They've created an energy vortex with a giant electromagnet inside the Earth's core. The young man with synesthesia, Stratus, he located it."

"I see."

"Stratus and Tig are there already. They went in on a self-destructing glider designed to drop troops behind enemy lines. They landed, confirmed their location, and destroyed the glider—then we lost contact. Tig's not in combat mode. He's taking his Meds."

Lise sighs. "Perhaps not the wisest decision, given the circumstances."

"We have a mole in Shun Mantra, so we know they're still there." Maim pauses. "The dynamo has to be shut down. Jove has authorized an attack."

"How long do we have?"

"Eight hours. Where are you?"

"Southern Atlantic, and we have a rotor. One more thing: Aaroon is Ronnie Lace. Ada was on Kerguelen at the bidding of her son."

Maim, speechless, frowns at the screen.

"Ada was after information. She knew I'd discovered something, but she didn't know what. Then she found the note in my journal. She thought it was an M—for M-theory—and she told Aaroon."

"Families are so complicated."

"Yes, they are. Aaroon thinks his mother is still alive. He thinks finding the information means finding her. That's why he's so obsessed."

"Oh good lordt. Do you need help, I can send—"

"No. I don't think we do. I love you. I'll see you soon."

Lise closes the QM.

***

Half an hour later, Anvil and Geller stumble into the dimly lit galley. Quinn and Lise are already there. Lise switches on the main lights, and the new arrivals cover their eyes and moan. They shuffle towards the table and slump into their seats.

Quinn tops up the boiler with fresh water to brew more tea, then frowns at her friends. "What time did you get to bed? And how much did you *drink*?"

"Three," Anvil says. "Three o'clock and three bottles." She wears mismatched socks, and the top of her climate suit is on inside out. She looks like she has just eaten something filling, but extremely unpleasant. She rests her elbows on the table and drops her head into her hands. "Way too late, two bottles and two hours too late."

Geller knits her fingers together and stretches her arms, then takes a deep breath and shakes her head, the way Lupus does when she needs to focus on a new task.

Lise places a water jug and glasses on the table. She looks tired, older than her early fifties. "I feel like I haven't drunk enough water for about three decades."

Anvil pours the water, and all three women skull the liquid. She refills, and they skull again.

Lise slides the QM towards Quinn. "Darling, open the climate model. Show us Antarctica."

Quinn yawns and opens the machine. She calls up the G12, and a meter-wide holographic sphere of the planet hovers over the table. She rotates the orb until Antarctica is in full view.

Lise begins. "Hexad knows where the electromagnet is. They're launching an assault this afternoon. They have no choice. The problem is . . . Tig and Strat are there. We have about seven hours. After that, Hexad will implode the vortex. Strat knew exactly where to find it. An amazing skill."

"He can also hear colors and smell trouble," Anvil says.

Lise casts a concerned smile towards Anvil. Then she turns her attention back to the holograph of Earth. "They're at Whalers Bay, northern tip of the Antarctic peninsula," Lise expands and rotates the holo. They peer at a small island—a perfect horseshoe shape.

"It's a volcano. The center is a flooded caldera," Quinn says. "Last activity was in 2032. Code Yellow. It's restless."

Lise runs a historical search on a module and reads the information. "The island has a bloodstained past; it was once a whaling station. Mass slaughtering of seals and whales, almost to extinction. An ugly trade. The worst side of human nature. The water in that harbor would have run red with blood. Humanity has—"

Quinn clears her throat, the signal for her mother to move on.

"Sorry. My guess? They're at the whaling station." She points at the holo. "The entrance is through an inlet called Neptune's Bellows. There's a sheltered port and, nice surprise, the place is now a designated wildlife sanctuary."

"Te plan: we divide into two teams, reconnaissance an' operations," Geller says.

Geller, Anvil, and Lise are team reconnaissance. They will take the rotor to Whalers Bay and locate Strat and Tig. Once they're inside the station, they will create a diversion, then grab Tig and Strat and escape. Quinn will be operations; she will follow on *Nanshe* and provide backup.

They have four exit strategies: one by air, using the rotor; two by sea, on *Nanshe* or on the zodiac; and one underwater, using the mini sub, which is once again in working order. Everyone, except Quinn, agrees that this is the best plan.

"I'm not sure this is the best plan," she says.

"Darling," Lise says. "You're seven months pregnant. You're not coming."

"I have legitimate concerns. What sort of diversion? What if you get caught? How will I find you? What if someone gets hurt? And by the way, your bandage is turning red. Perhaps you should stay here and be operations, and I—"

"Okay, there's something I haven't told you."

"Oh. Am I the only one you haven't told, or is it everyone?"

"It's everyone. Ada has a son."

"What the fuck? Ada has a son?" Quinn is surprised to be finding this out now. She is also unclear why this is relevant.

"Yes," Lise says. "His name is Ronnie."

"Ronnie?"

"Ada is Aaroon's mother."

What the fuck! "Ada is Aaroon's mother?"

"Yes. Please stop repeating everything I say. Aaroon thinks his mother is missing. My guess is he thinks she slipped into the multiverse during the Kerguelen flood—which, of course, is completely ridiculous."

"Because it's more likely to be a wormhole," Quinn says.

"No, because catastrophes happen in the blink of an eye. No one has time to prepare for these things. I don't understand why you think it's possible to just slip into the multiverse or a wormhole." Lise frowns. "Anyway, Ada thought the symbol in my notebook was an M. She's the one who told Ronnie, or Aaroon, I was working on M-theory."

Quinn rubs her forehead. "Oh, good lordt, this is terrible."

"Ada and I have a long history, and, despite the fact that she shot me, the decent thing to do is tell Ronnie she drowned. Twice. Killed by the flood, then held in a doomsday bunker for nine months, only to be eaten by a toxic lake a kilometer underground." Lise narrows her eyes at her daughter. "Would you like to be the one who tells Ronnie what happened to his mother?"

Quinn shakes her head. "No, I don't think I would."

"Okay, it's settled," Lise says.

Armed with a map and a compass adjusted for magnetic declination—allowing for the distance between true south and magnetic south—they plot a course for Whalers Bay. Lise, Geller, and Anvil take the rotor and head southwest. Quinn follows on *Nanshe.*

Forty-One

I'm out.

Whalers Bay is located in the center of an active volcano. The sand covering the horseshoe-shaped bay is peppered with black and white penguins that lie sunbathing on the beach, oblivious to the island's dark, murderous past. The sand is warm, exothermally heated from the volcano below, and the air is mild and balmy. Past the sand, a thick blanket of moss and lichen grows. The sky is filled with seabirds.

The whaling station is a cluster of abandoned sheds, dilapidated, unoccupied houses, and rusted oil vats. There was once a pier, but it's now underwater, and the rising tides lap against the sides of the low-lying buildings.

The main processing plant is located on the northern side of the small town, and it towers above the other buildings. Most of the windows are broken, and the rust-colored cladding peels in thin sheets from the pitted metal structure. The doors, which were once white, are weathered and rotting. The site is not completely abandoned, however; it's home to a colony of fur seals, and dozens of sea birds nest in the rafters.

Inside the plant, most of the original equipment remains. The tanks and boilers are still intact, and an old steam saw, used for splitting the skulls and spines of whales, is still operational. Rusted chains and winches, used for hauling the mammals, lie in piles on the dusty concrete floor. The high platforms remain in place, and the metal staircase is sturdy enough to be climbed upon.

Aaroon sits on the bottom tread of the staircases. His ankles are crossed, and his gangly knees are up around his armpits. In his hands, he holds a module.

Mori and Niels Eco stand nearby. They watch a holo of Dirac Devine walk back and forth across the floor of the processing plant. Devine's lips move but there is no sound. Every ten seconds a glitch appears and the figure freezes, then repeats the same movements over and over.

Aaroon glances back and forth between the holo of Dirac and his module. "Give me five minutes and I'll have this fucker sorted."

Niels rolls his eyes. "Before we begin the . . . demonstration, let me tell you why this isn't going to work."

Mori frowns at his brother.

Aaroon's eyes narrow; he glances up at Niels.

"I could see the benefits of mining," Niels begins. "Even after you fucked it up, caused the ice shift, I could still see the benefits. The colony on Titan makes sense, off-world living makes sense—sooner or later someone will do it, and it may as well be us. Right?" He nods.

Mori smiles nervously.

Aaroon nods, then sneaks a glance at his module.

"I get all that. But what I don't get is why we have him." Niels points to the holo of Dirac, which is now stuck in a loop and walking in circles. "Why do we have this idiot as the public face of Shun Mantra?"

"Keeping the myth alive. He's the leader of New Federation. Someone has to be the leader, and Devine is a scapegoat, so the blame falls on him." Aaroon shrugs.

"Blame for what? He was mentally ill. He took his own life."

Aaroon laughs. "You don't understand. I'm writing a narrative for the future. The Failing Intellect of Humanity Against the Rising Tide of the Superior Transhuman Race."

Niels raises his hands. "I'm out."

"You can't be out," Mori says. "You have too much at stake, you'll lose everything,"

"Not everything. I've frozen the funds. You're on your own."

Niels walks swiftly towards the exit. There is a large fur seal lying in the doorway, basking in a shaft of sunlight, blocking his way. The seal lifts its head, looks Niels over, then yawns. Its head flops back to the floor. Niels steps over the seal.

Forty-Two

Whalers Bay.

ALONE ON *NANSHE*, QUINN sits at the table in the galley and opens her QM. She sets up a communication pathway, channeling the charged particles of the aurora, harnessing them into an electrical signal. "Hey, can you hear me?" she asks. "What's happening?"

"Yeah, we just landed," Anvil says. "We're at Whalers Bay. Good lordt, it's warm here. Never seen anything like it. It's sort of beautiful and tragic—because of the whales. And a bit scary, but also . . . fascinating."

"Why, why is it fascinating?"

"Well, there's rusted oil barrels everywhere, like the size of a house, but a very small house, and they're the color of . . . blood."

"Really?"

"Well, orange-brown blood. On the other side of the bay, there's a heap of old buildings—like a town, but a really small, falling-down town, and that's where we're headed. Everything is covered in graffiti, and the sand is black. There's giant dinosaur bones half buried in the black sand."

"Maybe . . . whale bones?" Quinn suggests.

Anvil doesn't respond.

"Go on," Quinn prompts.

Silence.

"What's happening? Are you okay?"

"Penguins." Anvil giggles. "There's one standing on my foot and another one is pecking my jacket. Are these the cutest animals in the world?"

"Probably."

"Actually, they're not. I've just seen the cutest animal in the world. Oh good lordt, I'm in love."

"In love? With what?"

"Sorry, gotta go."

***

Four hours later, *Nanshe* drops anchor on the eastern side of Whalers Bay. Standing on the deck, Quinn supports her lower back with her hand and stretches her abdomen. The baby feels titanic today—bigger than usual.

She scans the horseshoe-shaped island wondering where her reconnaissance team could possibly be. She hasn't heard a word from them in over four hours. It was a stupid plan—go in, create a distraction, find the men, and escape? One sentence, with no detail. A sentence with no detail is an idea, not a plan.

She has two options: continue to wait or make a new plan.

Quinn launches the unsinkable zodiac. She tells herself she has no choice; something is obviously amiss, the rescue team is in trouble. The original plan was foolish and unconsidered, and now she has no choice, she must come to the aid of her companions. This is not her fault. This is their fault. Look what they've made her do.

She heads south, into the wind, steering the boat around the east side of the island. The sea is choppy; it's a bumpy ride. She directs the zodiac into a narrow passage of dark volcanic rock —Neptune's Bellows—and motors into Port Foster. Suddenly the landscape changes. The wind abates, the ocean calms, and the temperature rises.

Quinn berths the zodiac on the beach. She pulls out her laser and heads towards the abandoned town.

The rabbits take her completely by surprise. A family of fluffy white rabbits is foraging for wild grass around the base of a disused oil vat. Quinn smiles—the cutest animals in the world.

Out the corner of her eye she spies a darker, tawny-colored rabbit standing upright on its own. The rabbit lifts its paw. It waves at her.

It's not a rabbit, it's a meerkat.

Her mouth drops open and she clutches her chest. It's Mori.

Quinn drops to one knee, and Mori runs into her arms.

"I knew you would come," he says.

She scoops him up. "I thought you were dead. The tracker said you were in the tree house, or what used to be the tree house."

"I coughed it up. I was angry with you after you shook me so hard."

"I was trying to help."

"I know, and I am sorry."

"You're forgiven. I'm so happy to see you." She grins. "And you look good. This purple in your fur is interesting." The fur on Mori's back is tipped with purple.

"Yes. Purple is an inclusion color. I have been at Elsavale. Honestly, I think I just needed a break. You see, I thought I was going crazy. I thought I was losing my mind. I was trapped in a loop of anxious thoughts. I researched everything, all the great philosophers and psychoanalysts. But my symptoms continued to get worse. Then I met these people—Aaroon and his friends—and I realized I am fine." He nods, more to himself than to her. "Yes, I am fine. These people are the ones who are crazy. Complete lunatics. I told them my name was Lacan."

"You did not!"

"I did. I really did. I had a lot of fun with these crazy, crazy people." He tilts his head back and looks up at her. "But I have missed you. Can I hug you again?"

Quinn smiles. “Sure.”

He puts his little meerkat paws around her arm and rests his head on her baby bump. “My, your baby human has grown.”

“I was poisoned by jellyfish and a nanobot patch containing tardigrades saved my life.”

He lifts his head. “Your baby human will share your genome and DNA. Your cells will cross the placenta and enter her bloodstream. The baby will also leave embryotic stem cells inside you. The tardigrades have entered your bloodstream. They will not multiply but they will alter your fundamental biology. Technically you are now part human, part tardigrade—does that make you humanoid, or cyborg?”

Quinn stares at him. She swallows. “No. Cyborgs have biomechanical parts. I’m not . . . cyborg.”

“I am not so sure.” He rests his head on her stomach again. “Your baby human is getting ready to come out.”

“Not yet. I’m still seven months pregnant.”

“No, you are eight and a half months pregnant.”

“No. No, you’re wrong. Planck checked the dates and the calendar—”

“The digital calendars are not correct. The solar flares have been interfering with electronic communications for weeks.”

Fuck.

He presses his ear close to her stomach. “Yes, she is coming.”

“When, when is she coming?”

“Tomorrow. Maybe the next day. Maybe today.”

Quinn feels giddy; she slumps on the ground next to Mori. Not today, it’s not happening today. “Okay, we need to focus. We have to get everyone out.”

“Too late. They escaped.”

“Really?”

“Yes. Lise, your mother, she is very smart. She created a distraction—she told Aaroon the truth about his mother, and this upset him.

It upset him very much, and he became angry. He did not like the things she said, and it was an excellent distraction. While they were arguing, the two females, Geller and Anvil, were able to rescue Tig and Strat, who were being held by the evil HOTRODs. Anvil shot them with her pistol hands. But then Aaroon pointed a laser at your mother, so I screamed—a sharp, shrill call, like this, *Eeeeeee!*" Mori lets out a piercing scream.

"Oh, good lordt." Quinn covers her ears.

"It was the signal for her to take cover in the face of a fierce predator who was about to attack, but she did not understand. So I bit Aaroon on the leg. Very hard. I bit him very hard, and Lise was able to escape."

"Well done, you."

"Yes, I am now a weapon."

"So they're safe?"

"Yes, all of them are safe. They fled to the rotor, and I saw it take off. It was an excellent plan. Except they did not consider me." His head droops. "To them, I am just a robot."

"Well, you're *my* robot, and I'm your one-woman rescue party. Come on." She struggles to get up, loses her balance, and almost topples backwards. She manages to catch herself, leans forward onto her hands and knees, then climbs to her feet. "Okay, this way to the zodiac."

She staggers towards the beach; the meerkat follows.

They reach the zodiac, and Mori jumps in. Quinn hauls the boat into the water, then climbs in, too.

"I was hoping you might tickle me again, sometime soon," Mori says.

"Maybe later." She engages the engine.

"I almost forgot. I have a message for you, from my new friend. I have a new friend now, her name is Fossey. You are not my only friend anymore. Fossey wants to apologize for Jin."

"For Jin?"

"Yes. Last month they broke into Jin's CyberSleep vault and woke her. It was Aaroon's idea; he wanted information. But Fossey said to tell you she is sorry."

Quinn's chest tightens. "There's no cure. Jin will die . . . if she doesn't starve to death first."

"If she likes chocolate, she might not starve. There is a snack bar inside the vault."

"Really? I didn't notice." Quinn forces herself to focus. "Okay, I'll deal with Jin later. Right now we need to get out of here."

They head southwest, into Port Foster. Behind them, sinkers fall from the sky and detonate under the water; the Hexad attack has begun. Mori peers over the edge of the zodiac, watching the waterspouts break the calm surface of the ocean, several rising fifty meters high. Fish, too, are propelled skyward by the underwater explosions.

At the entrance to the port, Quinn cuts the engine and they pause, taking in the spectacle of flying fish and dancing waterspouts.

"Lucky escape," she says. "*Nanshe* is moored on the other side of the island." She smiles. Everyone is safe, she has her meerkat back, and they're heading home. It was a good plan.

A tiny puffer fish hits the floor of the zodiac. The attack is still underway; they need to exit the port. Quinn starts the engine, and they continue southward, towards the narrow exit of Neptune's Bellows.

Behind them, the waterspouts continue to advance, and Quinn spots a dark, airborne object coming their way. She squints; it's a penguin, shooting through the sky towards them, traveling at the same speed as the zodiac. It's going to land in the boat. Quinn increases speed, then sways to the right. A westerly crosswind catches the airborne penguin and blows it eastward. Quinn leans to her left, convinced the flightless bird will miss her—the zodiac is traveling too fast—but she misjudges its trajectory.

The bird descends; its flipper catches Quinn in the head.

Everything goes dark.

***

With a thud, the bird lands in the boat. Mori is tossed overboard, into the swirling ocean. The penguin is stunned, but conscious. It dives out of the boat and swims away.

The offensive from Hexad discharges a third and final round of sinkers, which detonate in synchronized accord. The implosion causes a momentous wave of water.

The tsunami carries the zodiac, with Quinn on board, 500 kilometers south. It takes her past the Palmer Arch, Hugo Island, Renaud Island, and Bisco Island. Then the swell peters and the current sweeps the zodiac towards the west coast of the Antarctic Peninsula, behind Lavoisier Island and into the Grandidier Channel.

The vessel bobs aimlessly in the Channel, until one of its rubber grips gets caught on an ice pinnacle. An hour passes before the pinnacle breaks and the zodiac is set free. Now the vessel is damaged; very slowly, it begins to take on seawater.

The zodiac drifts closer to shore. It washes onto a partly submerged ice shelf, near the Loubet Coast, on the western side of the Antarctic Peninsula, on the outskirts of the Antarctic Circle.

Forty-Three
The baby is coming.

Ice-cold water sloshes around Quinn's legs. She opens her eyes and sits up.

Slowly, she looks around, taking in the icy landscape and the vast, empty ocean that surrounds her. She recalls what happened. Casting her eyes skyward, she half expects to see another penguin come flying towards her.

Her arse is wet, her legs feel numb, and there is a large welt on her forehead. It stings when she touches it.

The sky is filled with thick white clouds—grey nimbostratus from horizon to horizon. Softly, it begins to snow, and she is assailed on all sides by H_2O—water below, ice on either side, and snow falling from the sky. The zodiac has reverted to its original orange color and she feels like a tropical fish on ice.

Softly, she laughs. The scene is ethereal. Beautiful and ethereal. She is in the middle of an awesome spectacle of ice and ocean, and she must be alive because it's so bitterly cold. She touches the welt on her head again and it hurts. She must stop touching it.

Mori is missing. He is not in the boat, and she doesn't see him on the icy shore. She wonders if he has wandered off. No, he would never wander off. He would never leave her alone in the zodiac. Her heart sinks; she has lost him again. He is the most honest and loyal . . . thing, person, entity she has ever known, and she has lost him again. She hopes he can swim, or at the very least that he is buoyant.

She rouses herself; she needs to get out of this sinking boat. Clambering on her hands and knees, she scrambles across the vessel, searching for provisions and supplies, hoping there is a repair kit. Every time she moves, the craft flexes and sucks in more water.

"It's not unsinkable," she mumbles. "Nothing is unsinkable; nature always wins, always."

The supplies are under the seat panels. There is no repair kit—because the zodiac is unsinkable. But there is a MedKit, "advanced" thermals—she hopes that means extra warm—snowshoes, camping gear, space blankets, dehydrated food, water filters and hydration capsules, LitStones, and a box of emergency flares that includes pyrotechnic flares, smoke flares, floating flares, dye markers, and alarms. The variety and scope of the flares is a bleak reminder that she is alone in the wilderness. Her heart sinks; she has no idea where she is.

One edge of the zodiac collapses, and the tide rushes in. She needs to abandon ship.

Quickly, she opens the last box of supplies. Inside, she finds a pack of swarmbots and a small, lightweight GullDrone. She unpacks the drone; it looks like a bird, and there is a tag around its neck that reads BROWN NODDY.

She perches it on the side of the sinking zodiac. It has dark, piercing eyes, and it stares solemnly at her.

"What?" she says to the bird. "It could be worse. It could be so much worse."

As emergency supplies go, she can't think of what else she might need, except a weapon. A weapon of some sort would be good. She doesn't know what she would shoot—penguins aren't predators—but a laser is a handy item to have when you're alone in the wilderness. She searches the sinking craft for her laser, but there is no sign of it; perhaps it washed overboard.

In the MedKit she finds a pair of scissors, and there is a fishing knife with the supplies. No lasers. No guns. No repair kit. She looks around at the vastness of the ocean, and the wall of ice behind her. *It's okay, I'll be fine. I'll be absolutely fine. I'll be rescued within the hour.*

The zodiac continues to slurp as the ocean rushes in. She tosses the supplies to shore, then stands up, but the boat wobbles, so she lies down and awkwardly rolls herself over the edge of the boat and onto the ice shelf. She thinks it could be worse, it could be much worse; at least no one saw her roll out of the boat like a fat seal.

The zodiac takes its last gulps and then sinks.

Quinn stands up. She is shivering, wet, and cold, but her feet are warm and dry, and she is grateful for this—the snow slippers are a wonder. She feels a flush of warmth around her groin, and a warm sensation spreads to her thighs and rushes down her legs. Her water just broke.

Fuck. As if she wasn't wet enough already. Then she pauses, suddenly realizing what this means—labor is not far away. She rubs her temples. *No, no, no this is not going to happen. Labor is still days away, and I'll be rescued by then.*

She strips out of her wet clothes and attempts to slip on a pair of the advanced thermals she found with the supplies —but her fingers fumble in the cold. Her brain knows what it wants to do, but her chilly hands derail her actions. They mishandle the packaging, and then she struggles to roll the fabric up her legs and over her body. She rubs her hands together, stimulating the blood vessels and makes another attempt.

Eventually, she is dressed and dry. That accomplished, she turns in a circle and surveys her surroundings. On her right is a wall of ice, and on her left is the ocean. Her best guess—she is somewhere in the Southern Ocean, on the Antarctic Peninsula. She figures she will be here a few hours at the most. Tig, or Geller, or Lise, or Strat will find her. It can't be that hard. They will follow the tide, and they will find her.

She glances at the steep wall of ice behind her. It's several stories high, maybe five or six meters, and at the peak a polar bear, standing on the edge, stares down at her. She blinks and turns away. *I've lost my mind. Polar bears live at the North Pole, not the South Pole.* She looks up again and the polar bear is gone. *Shit—I'm losing my shit.*

After scanning the ground around her, Quinn realizes she is not standing on a solid ice shelf. It's actually rock covered in snow and ice; there are pockets of exposed granite all along the cliff. Her first priority is to find protection—a crevasse amongst the rocks or a small cavern or grotto would do—somewhere to set up camp, stay warm, and wait for her rescue team.

The light fades quickly.

Slowly, she gathers together her supplies and piles everything onto a space blanket. She pulls on a life vest and wraps two more around her arms, and then launches the Brown Noddy drone, hoping it will haul her pile of stuff to the closest grotto. The bird flies a few meters off the ground, then turns in a circle and flies straight into the ocean, where it sinks. *Perhaps it's the aurora*, she thinks. *It's affected the bird's sonar ability.*

Snow begins to fall and little flurries whirl around her—light and fluffy, soft and downy. She catches them in her hand. The snow is beautiful. If this were a weather installation, she would make snowballs and a snowman, and then, after a few hours of escapist fun, she would exit. Outside, the sun would be shining, the sky would be blue, and it would be 50 degrees Celsius. But this is not an installation. She needs to find shelter.

She engages the swarmbots, and they haul her pile of supplies along the ice. She heads north, scouting the ice wall, searching for a perfect rocky niche to huddle behind.

There are options, many openings and crevices, none better than the others—but she can't settle. She doesn't want to be here. She continues on in the hope there is a better, more protected, place ahead.

She is tired—eight and a half months weary—but the plodding is mesmeric, and her feet are warm; the snow slippers have not failed her. She has nothing else to do, so she keeps walking. The light dwindles.

The pain begins in her groin and moves slowly through her abdomen; her first contraction. Hands on hips, she breathes and leans to one side as she waits for it to pass. It hurts, but it's bearable pain. She has had enough—she can't be pregnant anymore. The birth has to happen. The baby has to come out. The bearable pain is good pain. *How hard can it be? The baby has water bear DNA, she'll be fine.*

Now, finding a campsite is urgent.

Ahead, the ice wall dips and connects to the shore, the result of a tectonic tilt. She follows a ramp-like path up to a low plateau surrounded by small hills. At the base of the hills, small, leafy ferns poke through layers of snow-covered rocks. The peaks still have heavy snow. There is no sign of life.

She is gripped by another contraction. She breathes and waits for it to pass. She figures the contractions are at least five minutes apart. Maybe even six or seven minutes apart. She has plenty of time. She could be in labor for hours, even days. The contractions might even stop. That happens. They start and then they stop. There is still plenty of time to be rescued.

Soon, the contractions are three minutes apart.

She spies a rock ledge, a hollow space with a deep overhang. Closer inspection reveals it to be a good size—not large enough to be a cave, only about five meters deep, but well sheltered and dry and snow-free. She tells herself it's not a hard, dirty, cold slice of rock. It's a nook, a chamber, a makeshift home and possible maternity ward. The swarmbots haul her stuff inside. She sits down to wait.

She thinks the chances of her being rescued in the next few hours are good—60 to 80 percent. Her team will follow the tide. They will search by sea and by air, they will use drones and rotors. Geller is resourceful, and she has the army at her disposal. Maim Quate is in love with her mother, surely Lise can call in an emotional favor. Tig will stop at nothing to find her. He loves her, and that is the most important and heartwarming thing in the world. He loves her and she loves him and nothing else matters, though she would really appreciate being rescued before she gives birth.

Then she remembers her dream, her reoccurring dream about giving birth alone in Antarctica. Maybe the chances of her giving birth alone in a rocky crevice somewhere on the Antarctic Peninsular are higher than she thinks.

I need a plan. How hard can it be?

Millions of women have done this before her. Some of them have been alone. Some have been in the snow. Many have not had access to modern medicine. Besides, there is simply nothing else she can do—the situation is out of her hands. But she can make a plan. She knows how to do that. She makes a mental list of requirements: Food. Water. Blankets. Scissors, or a knife, to cut the cord.

She collects several bags of snow and adds filtration tablets.

She checks her food options: Gourmet Freeze Dried Salmon with Curry Butter or Gourmet Venison Risotto with Wild Herbs and Vine-Ripened Tomatoes. She selects the Salmon; she is by the ocean, it makes sense to eat fish. She reconstitutes the ingredients, then eats half. It tastes as good as it sounds.

She makes a nest against the back wall of the grotto, using the life vests as pillows, then stands back and admires her work. It looks cozy enough.

She lays out two knives, a pair of scissors, a pair of nail clippers, and a nail file on the edge of the space blanket. The water and MedKit are close by.

She puts the LitStones where she can find them; it will be dark soon, and the night will last eighteen hours.

She has spare space blankets to wrap the baby in.

Contractions are a minute apart.

Thirty seconds apart.

There is no rest. She changes positions—sitting, standing, kneeling, squatting against the rock wall. She stands with her hands against the wall, she lies with her feet against the wall; nothing helps. She walks in circles. She breathes.

She tells herself to relax and breathe. "It's too fucking painful to relax." It's a ridiculous state to be in. It's 2050, and the situation is absurd. Babies should not be born out of vaginas. They should come out of test tubes and artificial wombs.

I'm never, ever doing this again.

Relax. Breathe. "Seriously, this is ridiculous." It's not what she thought it would be. The pain is overwhelming, exhausting, and unbearable. *Focus. Relax. Breathe.* She needs to take control. She needs to control her mind. *Focus. Relax and breathe.*

She can't do this. The only thing she feels is intense, crushing agony.

Relax. Breathe. "Good lordt it hurts so much, I can't do this."

There are painkillers in the MedKit—why didn't she think of this earlier?

The baby is coming. It's too late for painkillers.

She slips off her thermals and perches on the floor with her back against the rock wall. The weight in her legs is unbearable—but then she sees the baby's head. A very small, dark, and hairy head is coming out of her vagina.

She waits for the next contraction and then she pushes. The baby follows. Quinn reaches down and grabs the baby's torso and guides it out.

It is a girl—a pink, slimy, wrinkled baby girl. The baby shudders, jerking her arms and legs, and then she cries.

Quinn laughs. Then her laughter transitions into sobs and tears. But she doesn't cry for long, and soon she wipes her eyes and says,

"Hello. Welcome to the world." She kisses the baby's head and peers at her small, crying face. "It's okay, it's okay, we're going to be fine. Just fine." She opens her Frost Jacket and her thermals and tucks the baby against her bare chest and gently pats her. She doesn't care how big the baby is, or how much she weighs. She doesn't count her toes or her fingers. She sits back against the rock wall and closes her eyes.

Ten minutes later, she wakes with a jolt; there are more contractions. It's the placenta, she needs to deliver the placenta. She finds the umbilical cord and gently pulls. The placenta comes away from the wall of her uterus and lands between her legs. It's deep red and quivering, and it looks like fresh liver.

The nutritional value of the organ is not lost on her, but this is not what she expected. This is not what she thought it would feel like—like she was ejecting an internal organ.

Planck told her to leave the placenta attached. Ze said, "It's better if the placenta stays close to the baby for a few days, then the cord falls off."

Good lordt this is uncivilized.

The baby begins to suckle, searching for food. Quinn offers her breast and the baby latches on. It's not what she thought it would feel like—like she is being gorged upon by a piglet.

Together, they fall asleep.

***

Quinn stirs, she hears noises. Shuffling and low growling sounds. She opens her eyes, but the darkness is impenetrable—she can't see anything. She feels for the LitStones on the ground next to her, locates one, and tosses it a few meters in front of her.

The grotto lights up. There is a large polar bear rocking back and forth at the entrance.

I'm dreaming. She closes her eyes again.

The bear growls.

She opens her eyes. *Fuck. I'm not dreaming.*

She freezes, so scared she can't move. Her body seizes. Her legs are paralyzed, and her arms are inert. She retracts into herself; it feels like she is sinking into the stone floor. She knows she should do something—reach for the knife, find the scissors or the nail file—but she can't, she can't move. Her fight-or-flight hormones have kicked in, and she is immobile.

What did Tig once tell her about fight or flight? She remembers: he said it primes you for action, but it also fucks your brain. You have to remember to think, that's what he said; remember to think and don't die.

Remember to think and don't die.

Her left hand feels for her knife. She can't find it. It was right here. It was part of her birth plan and now she can't find it.

The bear steps farther into the grotto. It is huge—ten times the size of her, over two meters long. It has deep black eyes, a black nose in an oblong head, and a mouth filled with horrid teeth. It is a serious carnivore, and Quinn's scent is driving it crazy.

Think. Think.

The bear steps closer. Its paw is bigger than her head. It lifts its nose and sniffs the air. Then it sniffs at her.

The placenta.

Quinn feels around for the knife again. She is sitting on it. She pulls it out, cuts the umbilical cord, and tosses the placenta as far as she can into the darkness outside the grotto.

The bear retreats, following the placenta into the darkness.

Quinn retreats, with the baby tucked inside her jacket and the knife in her lap, to the back wall of the grotto. "Okay, if have to kill the thing, I will. A blade between the eyes. A pair of scissors in its heart, nail clippers in one eye and a fucking nail file in the other."

Oh good lordt, we're going to die.

Quinn hears an unfamiliar mewing sound, like a lamb braying. It's coming from outside the grotto. Cubs, two of them, appear at the entrance. Two cute balls of fluff with dark red snouts, stare at her. They've been dining on the placenta.

Okay, this is not good. This is not part of her birth plan or her survival plan. And why are there polar bears at the South Pole?

Relocated, yes, she remembers—in the 2030s, the polar bear was the poster animal for climate change; dozens of individuals were relocated. The Arctic ice sheets were melting fast. The bears were endangered. There was a project to preserve the species in the wild and fifty were moved to the West Antarctic ice sheets.

This one has mated and given birth to twins.

Quinn will stay awake, on sentry, until dawn. Then she will move and find shelter elsewhere. She just has to make it through the night.

Forty-Four

Who am I?

QUINN WAKES UP DROWSY. She shivers. She is cold and stiff. Her body aches, her head hurts, and her vagina is very, very sore. Outside the grotto, there is a dull, hazy light; it's late morning, and it's a new day—the first day of her baby's life. The first day of motherhood.

The baby is asleep on her chest, under her Frost Jacket. Quinn scans the grotto; there's no sign of the bear family, but she suspects they might not be far away.

She rests her head against the rock wall, and a small tear leaks from the corner of one eye. This situation is overwhelming—the baby, motherhood, the Antarctic wilderness, the polar bears. Her vagina may never be the same again either, but she figures that's okay, she may never want to have sex again.

She opens her jacket and places her hand on the baby's cheek, checking she is still alive. She is breathing. Quinn sighs, relieved. Then she feels a strange sensation between her legs.

She checks it out. She is bleeding, but not heavily. It's normal post-labor blood loss.

Reclining in the corner of the stone grotto with the baby tucked inside her jacket, Quinn is struck with a deep sense of awe and clarity: She is a mother now. She needs to look after her baby, and she needs to look after herself, and somehow, these two needs are intertwined.

For many years they will be connected, because she doesn't belong to herself anymore, not entirely.

She rallies. First she wipes herself down; then she cuts one of the space blankets into strips to use as pads and nappies. She takes another space blanket and creates a sling for the baby so she can carry her close to her chest while keeping her hands free.

When the baby wakes, Quinn gets a good look at her. She has charcoal eyes, rosy lips, a patch of dark hair, perfect ears, ten fingers, and ten toes, and Quinn never wants to let her go. Every feature is perfect. Her skin is flawless. Quinn sniffs her head. It smells like mandarins—her favorite fruit, and a rare commodity these days. The last time she had a mandarin was on Kerguelen. Lise brought them with her as a gift, and Tig peeled them. Tig! Where is he? Why isn't he here? They were supposed to be in this together, to do this together. If anything has happened to him . . .

She closes her eyes. She can't think about that. Instead, she holds the baby's tiny hand with one finger and looks into her dark eyes. "I'm going to call you . . . Molly."

Molly sneezes—just like a grown-up person. Quinn is amazed; it's the same as an adult's sneeze, but on a smaller scale. She stares, dumbfounded, at her baby for almost an hour, waiting for another sneeze, but none follow. She snaps herself out of her stupor and makes Molly a little hat out of spare space blanket material by winding a long strip around and around her head. Then she checks her umbilical cord and feeds her.

With her maternal tasks complete, Quinn grabs a flare, stuffs her arsenal of knife and scissors into the pockets of her Frost Jacket, and heads outside.

There is no sign of the bear or her cubs. The air feels colder than it did yesterday, and a cutting wind rips across the snow. Her fingertips tingle. Her breath leaves a foggy imprint of mist, which hovers around her. She walks very slowly towards the top of a small hill above the grotto. Halfway up the slope, she pauses to rest amongst a group of granite boulders. There is no way she will make it to the top.

The boulders are protected from the icy wind. She has a view to the west, over the ocean, which is partly obscured by low-level clouds—sky and water merging into a pale grey haze. Contemplating the view gives her something to do, and it feels good to be outside, out of her cave-like home, but the reality of her situation is terrifying. Inside the grotto, her world was immediate and insular; she just had to care for herself and Molly. It was just the two of them—she could cope with that. Outside, the vast scope of Antarctic Peninsula is overwhelming, and the remoteness is impossible to ignore.

Good lordt, how did we get here?

She checks multiple times that Molly is still breathing, then nestles into the rocks and waits to feel different. She waits for motherhood to take her over. She believes motherhood will transform her, erase some parts of her, and replace them with, with . . . she doesn't quite know what. The hormones will change her, she knows that. The hormones that helped her grow a human inside her will help her feed and care for her baby. But she doesn't feel different or changed yet.

There are many strange things in the world, but growing a baby human inside you is the strangest. Growing someone's perfect ears and the correct number of digits inside you is an astounding feat. Quinn has an epiphany: nobody else on the planet knows this. She urgently wants to tell everyone, the entire world, this amazing fact—you can grow a human inside you. And that human will share your genome and DNA. Quinn's cells crossed the placenta and entered Molly's bloodstream; Molly left embryotic stem cells inside Quinn—and some water bear DNA.

How can she not be changed?

Who am I? Who am I right now?

She takes a breath. *I am Quinn Buyers. Scientist, mother, and daughter. Best friend of Jin. Inventor of the G12 climate model. Murderer of dodos. Devotee of flying. Lover of science. Partner of Tig. I am one insignificant human on this stupid planet.*

"Who will you be?" she whispers to Molly.

She ignites a flare. She stares at the stick for a moment as it glows bright red in her hand, and then she launches it into the hazy mid-morning sky. It leaves a lingering trail before exploding over the ice.

She spies the mother bear and her cubs playing in the snow. The cubs are fat and healthy, but the mother looks thin—gaunt, even. Sea ice was her natural platform for hunting, but the ice has disappeared. Her thin physique means she is malnourished. It means she is hungry.

The bears are a problem. If Quinn moves—and she is incapable of traveling very far—will they follow?

She scans the surrounding hills, which are half covered in snow. She sees something move. She squints but can't make out anything specific; maybe it was a landslide, or a trick of the light. Then she sees it again—a shudder across the snow, a blur of white on white. Then a tiny figure appears on a rock. It starts eating the grass around the rock. It has long ears. It hops.

It's a rabbit. There is no such thing as an Antarctic rabbit. It's an introduced species; perhaps it came with the bears? Another appears, then another, and soon there are dozens of rabbits grazing on the tundra.

Quinn has an idea. She pulls her fishing knife out of her pocket and steels herself. She has done this before. She killed Jane the dodo, and she can do this. "Those rabbits are toast. They're also lunch and dinner."

Her plan is to feed the enemy. The bears won't eat her if they have gorged on rabbits, she reasons. And she doesn't want to hurt the mother bear. She is an endangered species. The female has to live, and so do her cubs. That is, unless they try to eat Molly—then, she knows, she will stab the bear in the heart and probably die protecting her baby.

Quinn puts the knife in her left hand. From 50 meters away, she lets the fishing knife fly. It skewers a rabbit in the forehead; it keels over. The other rabbits scatter. Quinn plods through the snow to collect the corpse and retrieve her knife.

The dead rabbit lies between the rocks in the grass. It's cuter than she hoped it would be. She avoids its eyes. Maybe she should take another. That way she won't have to come back and do this again. If she sits quietly, maybe the others will come out again.

Then she remembers something her father told her once: "You only take what you need. If there are fifty buffaloes grazing on a hill, you don't shoot them all, just because you can. You take one, and when that's finished, a week or a month later, you go back and get another."

One is enough.

Quinn needs to retrieve her knife. She stands on the rabbit, securing the animal. "Don't watch," she says to Molly, who stirs just as Quinn yanks the knife from the rabbit's head. She wipes it on the grass and then shudders, repulsed by the blood.

She picks the rabbit up by its ears, which are warm. Its fur is soft and thick between her fingers. It's much heavier than she thought it would be, and she has to stop several times to rest on her way back to the grotto. When she arrives, she realizes the bears have moved closer and are rolling in a patch of snow less than twenty yards away. The cubs pause and rest on their haunches and stare at her.

Quinn shakes her head. "Stupidly cute."

On seeing Quinn with the rabbit, the mother pants, growls, gets to her feet, and plods towards her. Quinn shows her the rabbit and tosses it in the opposite direction. All three bears follow the food.

"Okay, here's the deal," Quinn says. "I just need a day or two, then I'll be rescued. You leave me alone and I bring you food. If you touch my baby, I will kill you. Now, I'm going to call you"—she points to the mother bear—"Marie Curie, after the famous physicist and chemist. Marie Curie was the first woman to win the Nobel Prize and the first person to win it twice. You, big, white, scary mother bear, should be honored." She points at the cubs. "You're Irene and you're Eve, Marie's two children. Marie once said, 'Nothing in life is to be feared. It is only to be understood. Now is the time to understand more, so we may fear less.' I know what you want. Hopefully you'll realize what I want. Let's see if we can work this out."

***

Back at the grotto, Quinn drinks and eats half a packet of Gourmet Venison Risotto with Wild Herbs and Vine Ripened Tomatoes. She thinks she would do almost anything for a cup of tea. Then Molly shits the most discussing poo Quinn has ever seen—black as tar, thick and sticky—which completely distracts her from any thoughts of warm beverages. She changes the baby, then feeds her again. Day one; it's already a routine. Molly sleeps, then feeds, then sleeps again. Quinn rests with the knife and scissors in her lap.

Soon, the light dwindles and the sky turns misty. *Opaque*, Quinn thinks, and finally, she knows what that means—opaque light. She had never understood the term before. How can light be opaque? But now she sees how dense the light is. Opaque is the perfect description. The word was invented to describe the Antarctic light. Will Tig be able to find her in this opaque Antarctic light? She opens her jacket and peers down at Molly.

"'Along the road of the Sun he journeyed—two leagues he traveled, dense was the darkness, light there was none . . . what lies ahead or behind, he does not see,'" she says, reciting lines from *Gilgamesh*. "'Eleven leagues he traveled, and he came out before the sunrise. Twelve leagues he traveled, and it grew brilliant.'" She stops and turns the story over in her mind. "So, Gilgamesh loved Enkidu. One was a god and a man, the other an animal and a man, and they became human together. Perhaps that's what the poem is about . . . the human condition. Humanity coming together. Take my hand, we go on together. We can't do this alone."

Quinn looks down at Molly, underneath her jacket. The baby snuggles closer to her skin.

"That's not the only thing it's about," she whispers. "There's a goddess of beer in the poem—Siduri. If I were a goddess, I'd be a goddess of beer." She looks at the sky outside. "Or clouds. Maybe I'd be a goddess of clouds."

She kisses Molly's head. Together, they fall asleep.

Forty-Five

Every living thing counts.

Quinn wonders if her rescue party will come by sea or air. She concedes that it might be hard to find her with no GPS or tracking devices, especially since the search area is large—but they have drones and other resources. Then she realizes: no one actually knew she was in the zodiac, or in the path of the tsunami.

"Oh good lordt, the search area isn't large, it's massive, it's the entire northern section of the Antarctic Continent! There's no way they'll find us."

Flares. She needs to set off more flares, and she needs to do it every few hours.

***

That afternoon, she ventures outside again with Molly in the sling. Nacreous clouds—mother of pearl clouds—fill the sky with soft pastel hues. These clouds are a rare occurrence, and only found in the polar regions during winter. Quinn is awestruck by the spectacle. She begins to cry and blames it on the clouds. Then she shakes her head; she is not crying because of the clouds, she is crying because she is alone. Alone, sitting on a rock in the Antarctic wilderness.

She has a red-rocket flare in her pocket. She launches it into the sky, and it cuts straight through the clouds.

She hasn't seen another human in two days, and she has no idea where the closest human would even be. The Antarctic wilderness is one of the most remote places on the planet. The only living things around her are penguins, seals, and sea birds. And polar bears and rabbits—neither of which are native. And, she concedes, probably plenty of fish. And plankton. Barnacles. Jellyfish. Krill. Sea cucumbers. Zooplankton. Algae. Seaweed. Probably sharks. And whales, she forgot about whales.

She could go on, she could name the microorganisms in the air, the ones in the snow and the clouds, because aren't they alive, too? Don't they count? But she stops herself. It's enough to know the ocean is alive. The air and clouds are alive. The snow is alive.

"We need to change the definition of 'alone,'" she tells Molly. "Every living thing counts."

A flurry of snow rises from a depression in the landscape not far from where Quinn sits. She thinks it might be a rabbit and reaches for her knife. Then she sees a large paw.

It's Marie with her cubs, they are rolling together in the snow, play fighting. Marie knows how to handle her cubs; she switches smoothly between play mode and care mode. Right now, it's play mode. Marie lets her cubs climb all over her. They wrestle her and bite her, and she tolerates everything they do with good humor and patience.

After a while, Marie gently pulls her cubs under her front legs and caresses them. When they are settled, she rolls over and hooks the cubs to her chest with her large paw, and they suckle.

Quinn watches the scene, mesmerized. Marie turns and looks right at Quinn. They gaze at each other, and Quinn recognizes the maternal bond in her eyes. She is everything to her cubs.

***

That night, Quinn hunkers down in her grotto, clasping Molly close.

"We can do this," she says. "We will not be eaten by a polar bear tonight." They snuggle together on the floor, and when Quinn closes her eyes, she dreams about Marie Curie.

Marie Curie discovered polonium and radium. The process of grinding and sifting and filtering the mineral uraninite to collect those elements made her gravely ill and she died of radiation poisoning. Polonium is named after Poland, Marie Curie's native country. It's Element number is 84 on the periodic table. Silver grey in color, it's radioactive and highly toxic—over three hundred times more radioactive than uranium. It wreaks havoc on the body, damaging DNA. It was favored by assassins in the RE Wars.

Radium, atomic number 88, is a million times more radioactive than uranium. It causes cancer, and it cures cancer.

Forty-Six

I'm your Enkidu.

QUINN SHIVERS. THE COLD has seeped inside her. Last night, after she fed the baby, she forgot to reseal her Frost Jacket. Now her body is stiff, achy. She needs to move around, to get her blood flowing. A brisk walk, kill some rabbits, light a few flares—it's good to have something to do besides feed the baby and check she is still breathing.

Quinn heads outside with Molly tucked into her sling. It's a pleasant morning: the snow has stopped falling, the clouds have cleared, and there is a patch of pale blue sky overhead. It's a shame she is so cold and weary.

"Today is a perfect day to be rescued," she says. But she fears if the rescue party doesn't arrive today or tomorrow, it may never arrive. If something went terribly wrong with the plan—if it was, as she suspected, the worst plan ever, the plan where everyone died . . .

Slowly, she shakes her head. Dark thoughts won't help, and it's too soon to give up. She recalls Marie Curie—her years of research and her illness. *She* never gave up.

"What was that quote?" Quinn raises her eyes to the horizon. "'Life is not easy for any of us. But what of that? We must have perseverance and, above all, confidence in ourselves.'"

She yawns and a shiver runs through her; the only thing she can do right now is keep warm and stay alive.

Staying alive means feeding the bears, so she climbs to the top of the small hill behind the grotto. She spies a patch of creeper pushing through the snow, and she sits down on the green carpet to wait for a rabbit.

The plateau on the far side of the hill is so breathtakingly still it looks like an artwork frozen in time. It might take a while for the animals to emerge, so she lies down, closes her eyes and dozes.

She wakes an hour later, and her stillness is rewarded. In the distance, an animal appears at the edge of a cluster of small rocks. Her left hand raises the fishing knife and in one swift movement, she spears her second rabbit.

After collecting the carcass, she plods back to "her" boulder—which is what she has come to call the smooth-edged rock above the grotto. The place where she shelters from the wind. The place where she waits.

In the pocket of her jacket are two flares. The first is a handheld powder-cake smoke device. She ignites it, then secures it into the rocky ledge above the grotto; it raises a thick plume of orange smoke and will smolder for several hours. The second is a rocket flare. After lighting it, she sends it skyward.

She snuggles into a nook between the rocks and scans the landscape. Eastward, there is nothing new, just endless water and ice. Northward, she spies a reflection—an arc of refracted light bouncing off the snow along the ridgeline. It looks like . . . a rainbow. A faint rainbow. She squints and it disappears; then she sees it again.

Her heart quickens. The rainbow is moving, and it's headed her way.

The light is reflecting from a vehicle. A snow crawler is skimming along the ridgeline. It turns sharply and heads down the hill, towards the flare—towards Quinn.

She kisses Molly's head. "We're going home."

The snow crawler parks on the plateau behind the grotto, and Tig jumps out. He looks at the burning flare, then scans the landscape and spies her, nestled in the cluster of granite boulders.

Awkwardly, she clambers down the rocks and plods through the snow towards him, her fingers still clasped around the dead rabbit's ears.

Suddenly, Marie appears, bounding up the hillside, headed straight for Tig.

Tig draws his weapon and points it at the bear. The bear keeps advancing.

"No, no don't shoot." Quinn shuffles towards Tig and blocks Marie's path. She waves the rabbit at the bear. Marie pauses and utters a low growl. Quinn tosses the rabbit away from them, down the hill. Marie turns and stalks towards the food. The cubs emerge from beneath the snow and follow their mother.

Tig lowers his laser. He grabs Quinn and hugs her to his chest.

"Thank the lordt you found me." Half laughing, half crying, Quinn unfastens her Frost Jacket. "Meet the newest member of our family," she says, and shows Tig his daughter.

Tig pulls back, stunned. He stares at Quinn, and then at the baby. "Oh fuck."

"I know, and you didn't even have to give birth. In the Antarctic wilderness, all alone."

Tig shakes his head. "You win. You will always win."

She smiles. "I've been calling her Molly, but we can discuss."

He wants to hold the baby. Impatiently, he tugs at the strap of the makeshift sling.

Smiling, Quinn slaps his hands away, pulls Molly out, and gives her to him.

He holds her up with both hands, gets a good look at her. "We made her." He grins.

"Actually, I did most of the work." Quinn unties the space blanket sling and gestures with it towards the baby. "It's cold, maybe—"

"Sure, sure." He tucks her inside his jacket, close to his chest.

"She's perfect. I've counted everything, all her fingers and toes, and, and . . . she smells like mandarins, and I don't ever want to let her go, and—"

Tig slings his free arm around Quinn, draws her close, and whispers, "You have no idea how far I've traveled for you."

She pulls away. "Okay. Who are you?"

"Me? I'm Gilgamesh."

Abruptly, she steps back. "Fuck off." Then she steps forward. "Really?"

"It's a rumor. I've kind of lost track of time over the . . . decades and cent—"

"No, no, no." She shakes her head.

"Last year on Kerguelen, that wasn't the first time we'd met. You see . . . I've met you before, in the future. We fell in love. We had a great time. We even got . . . married. I know, this is an unforgivable truth."

Quinn stares at him. She has a sense that she is melting, like the ice around her. If she stands there too long, there will be nothing left of her, just a puddle of water in the snow, and that is all he will have to take home. He has come all this way for a puddle of water: one atom of oxygen and two atoms of hydrogen. She wonders if the trip was worth it. The trip through time. Time and space.

"I understand," she says. "I used the portal, I know—"

"Come here." He loops his arm around her again and draws her close.

They stay quiet for a while. Over his shoulder, Quinn studies a cumulus cloud. Its puffy cauliflower top hooks to one side, and she thinks it looks a bit like a question mark.

Maybe she is wrong about clouds after all. Perhaps they *are* an expression of the planet's emotional state, and the shapes you see in them can save you Coin that would otherwise be spent on a psychoanalyst. They are nature's poetry, after all.

She tilts her head towards Tig. "If you're Gilgamesh, then perhaps I'm Enkidu?"

He smiles. "Yes, you are my Enkidu. My love."

"Gilgamesh goes on a quest to find everlasting life. He travels through tunnels and over mountains, across oceans and rivers, slaying all the beasts that get in his way. But fighting his destiny is futile—it ruins the joy of life. So, all for nothing." She looks up at the sky again; the question mark cloud now looks like a wispy seahorse. "Do I die? Is that why you came back to 2049?"

Tig nods.

She stares at him. Now she feels like she is evaporating, like gas, disappearing into the atmosphere, merging into the seahorse-shaped cloud. "You couldn't save me, and you got trapped in a loop. So you came back earlier."

"Yeah, I did."

"Okay, so how do I die?"

He shakes his head. He will never tell her.

She understands; she kisses his cheek. "Is everyone safe?"

He nods. "Fished the meerkat out of the ocean yesterday."

She smiles. "Thank goodness." She takes the baby from him. "Let's get out of here?"

"Where to?"

"*Nanshe*. Can we set a course for Accord?"

"What's in Accord?"

"The CyberSleep vault at eMpower. I need to check on Jin."

No one can live on chocolate forever.

They plod towards the snow crawler, and she has a thought: she should kill another rabbit for the bears before they leave. Then she has another, more compelling, thought.

"So, how many times did you go back for me?"

Tig shakes his head. He will never say.

"Just a ballpark figure."

"No."

"More than five, less than ten?"

Acknowledgments

A BIG, BIG THANK-YOU GOES to Brooke Warner and her fabulous team at She Writes Press, including Lauren Wise and Samantha Strom. They are truly an inspiring, hard-working, and supportive editorial team, and I am delighted to be associated with them.

Krissa Lagos did an outstanding job on the copy-edit of this book, and Ben Perini's cover design is suburb.

To my wonderful readers—yes, this one ties up all those loose ends and unfinished plot lines, and there is a proper ending (almost). Thanks for reading!

To Hamish, Jordan, and Lulu, thank you for your ongoing love, support and faith in me. You are three of the smartest, most kind, generous and caring people I know. I am truly blessed to have you in my life. Love you heaps.

To Andrew Aitken, I owe you a lot, figuratively speaking, so that does not include any royalties. But seriously, you're the best.

About the Author

© Alise Black

Sarah Lahey is a designer, educator, and writer. She holds bachelor's degrees in interior design, communication, and visual culture, and works as a senior lecturer teaching classes on design, technology, sustainability and creative thinking. She has three children and lives on the Northern Beaches in Sydney, Australia.

SELECTED TITLES FROM SHE WRITES PRESS

She Writes Press is an independent publishing company founded to serve women writers everywhere. Visit us at www.shewritespress.com.

Gravity is Heartless: The Heartless Series, Book One by Sarah Lahey
$16.95, 978-1-63152-872-9
Earth, 2050. Quinn Buyers is a climate scientist who'd rather be studying the clouds than getting ready for her wedding day. But when an unexpected tragedy causes her to lose everything, including her famous scientist mother, she embarks upon a quest for answers that takes her across the globe—and uncovers friends, loss, and love in the most unexpected of places along the way.

Expect Deception by JoAnn Ainsworth. $16.95, 978-1-63152-060-0
When the US government recruits Livvy Delacourt and a team of fellow psychics to find Nazi spies on the East Coast during WWII, she must sharpen her skills quickly—or risk dying.

Glass Shatters by Michelle Meyers. $16.95, 978-1-63152-018-1. Following the mysterious disappearance of his wife and daughter, scientist Charles Lang goes to desperate lengths to escape his past and reinvent himself.

Provectus by M. L. Stover. $16.95, 978-1-63152-115-7. A science-based thriller that explores the potential effects of climate change on human evolution, *Provectus* asks a compelling question: What if human beings were on the endangered species list—were, in fact, living right alongside our replacements—but didn't know it yet?

Time Zero by Carolyn Cohagan. $14.95, 978-1-63152-072-3. In a world where extremists have made education for girls illegal and all marriages are arranged in Manhattan, fifteen-year-old Mina Clark starts down a path of rebellion, romance, and danger that not only threatens to destroy her family's reputation but could get her killed.

The Lucidity Project by Abbey Campbell Cook. $16.95, 978-1-63152-032-7. After suffering from depression all her life, twenty-five-year-old Max Dorigan joins a mysterious research project on a Caribbean island, where she's introduced to the magical and healing world of lucid dreaming.